Kind of Kin

ALSO BY RILLA ASKEW

Harpsong
Fire in Beulah
The Mercy Seat
Strange Business

Kind of Kin

RILLA ASKEW

Atlantic Books
London

First published in the United States in 2013 by HarperCollins Publishers.

First published in Great Britain in 2013 by Atlantic Books, an imprint of Atlantic Books Ltd.

10 9 8 7 6 5 4 3 2 1

A CIP catalogue record for this book is available from the British Library.

Trade Paperback ISBN: 9781782390107
Hardback ISBN: 9781782390114
E-book ISBN: 9781782390121

Printed in Great Britain by the MPG books Group

Atlantic Books
An Imprint of Atlantic Books Ltd
Ormond House
26–27 Boswell Street
London
WC1N 3JZ

www.atlantic-books.co.uk

For the two Carmelitas in my family
y para las familias separadas en todo el mundo

A little more than kin,
and less than kind.

HAMLET, ACT I, SCENE II

Kind of Kin

Part One

A Felon and a Christian

"Your grandpa is a felon," Aunt Sweet said. "A felon and a Christian. He says he's a felon *because* he's a Christian. Now, what kind of baloney is that?" She jerked the bib strings tight around Mr. Bledsoe's neck. The old man coughed. "Sorry, Dad." Aunt Sweet loosened the ties and snatched a baby food jar off the table. She pointed the spoon in her left hand at me like I might be fixing to argue. "Tell him I'll be up there tomorrow. You tell him I said he's got a serious amount of explaining to do." She scooped up a dab of prunes. "Open your mouth, Dad. Carl Albert, hurry up."

My cousin kept licking the Cheez Whiz out the sides of his sandwich like we had all the time in the world, which we didn't. Visiting hours start at one, the preacher said, and it was already twelve thirty. I heard a car motor outside and I ran to the front room to look, but it was only old Claudie Ott driving her Chrysler home from church. I squinted across the railroad tracks and the highway toward First Baptist at the far end of the street, but I couldn't see Brother Oren's car coming.

"Dustin Lee! Get back in here and wash your hands!"

I did like she said. My aunt's kind of high-strung at all times, but for sure I didn't want to cross her right then because Uncle Terry got called in to work the night before and he hadn't got home yet. Aunt Sweet wanted to go with us to see Grandpa but she can't leave Mr. Bledsoe by himself on account of one time he rolled his wheelchair out the door and straight across the highway to the E-Z Mart and everybody's afraid he'll get hit by a BP truck or something. I thought to ask her how come she didn't make Carl Albert stay home so she could go, but I was afraid she might take the notion for me to be the one to babysit the old man instead. He's all right but I can't stand to watch him eat, and anyhow I wasn't about to take a chance on missing out on seeing my grandpa. When I came back in the kitchen, Aunt Sweet was still trying to get Mr. Bledsoe to open his mouth.

"Aw, hell," she said, and jammed the spoon back in the prunes. I don't know where she got the name Sweet. It don't exactly fit her. Anyhow, her real name is Georgia. She reached up over the sink and got down a different jar. "Look here, Dad. Peach cobbler, your favorite." Mr. Bledsoe isn't her real dad—my grandpa is. Mr. Bledsoe belongs to Uncle Terry, and he's not even his dad, either. He's his stepgrandfather. "Carl Albert," Aunt Sweet said, "if you don't hurry up with that mess, I'm going to take it away from you."

My cousin licked faster. I don't know how come he can't eat a sandwich like a normal person but he can't. I popped him in the back of the head on my way to the sink. He swiped at me and missed, but he didn't say nothing. He didn't want to get any more of his mom's attention. He gave me the look, though, like *Don't worry, Dustbucket, I'll get you back.* We been fighting more since Grandpa and Brother Jesus wound up in jail. That's Brother Jesus Garcia, from over around Heavener. They locked him up with Grandpa, but they took all the other Mexicans someplace else. Aunt Sweet don't like us calling him Brother Jesus. She says it's a sacrilege to call somebody after Our Lord and Savior. She don't even like to hear us call him Brother Hey-soos, and that's his real name. Carl Albert says Grandpa's going to get sent to the state pen and there won't be no place for me to live except in town with them, and if he's got to share his bedroom with a dweeb, he's going to make the dweeb pay. He says they aim to throw the book at Grandpa for transporting illegals and our only hope now is the Supreme Court of America on appeal, and that could take years. I said having Mexicans in your barn don't mean you're transporting them—this was in the bedroom that first night when we were getting ready for bed—and Carl Albert said, "Use your brain, Dustface, they had to get there some way." I punched him then, and he jumped me and got me down with my arm twisted till I hollered, "Okay, okay, I give!" But really I didn't. I aimed to get him back. That pop on the head at the table was just a reminder.

In the kitchen I dried my hands on the dishtowel and told Aunt Sweet I was going to go watch for the preacher. "Holler when he gets here," she said, pressing the spoon against Mr. Bledsoe's shut mouth. "Come on, Dad," she said. "Open up." I hurried to the front room and squinted along Main Street past the closed video store and the boarded-up bank building with its caved-in roof from the straight-line winds last April until I seen Brother Oren's car backing out of his driveway. I yelled toward the kitchen, "He's here!"

When the preacher's rattly old Toyota pulled in, Aunt Sweet was waiting with me on the porch in her pink rodeo boots and her bluest jeans, which goes to show how much she still thought she'd be going to the jail with us when she got dressed that morning. She was shivering because she didn't have on a jacket. I had on my black hoodie with the hood pulled up, not because I was cold. I just like my hood up. Carl Albert came racing out the front door in just a T-shirt and still zipping his britches. He squeezed past the preacher coming up the steps and ran out to the car so he could grab the shotgun seat. I tried to lag back, but Aunt Sweet told me to go on. She had her arms crossed and her mouth set, so I did like she said. I took the long way around, though, by Mr. Bledsoe's ramp. Carl Albert leaned up for me to flip the seat forward, and when I climbed past him, he knuckled me a good one, but I didn't do nothing, just settled into the backseat. I was still biding my time.

I felt kind of bad that none of us had made it to church that morning, especially with Brother Oren giving us a ride to Wilburton and all. I was kind of hoping Aunt Sweet might be explaining about Uncle Tee getting called in to work, but it appeared more like she was bossing him by how Brother Oren just stood on the porch in his brown suit, looking down at the concrete and nodding and frowning. He kept reaching up with his fingers to rake his skinny hair across the top of his head. Come on! I was saying in my mind, come on, come on, come on. When the preacher got in the car, he gave us a big grin. "Tell you what, boys, we'll stop at Sonic on the way home and pick up a sack of burgers." He said it like that was what Aunt Sweet had been telling him, though I was pretty sure it wasn't. The preacher laid his arm across the top of Carl Albert's seat and twisted half around so he could see how to back out of the driveway. I looked at my Iron Man watch. It said 12:42. Wilburton's thirteen miles from Cedar, so traveling sixty miles an hour I figured we'd actually be three minutes early. But then east of Panola we got slowed down behind a semi hauling a giant piece of drilling equipment that took up half the road. We were practically crawling. I was about to go out of my skull. "Can't you go around him?" I said.

Brother Oren glanced back at me. "We don't want to be breaking any more laws, do we, boys? It's illegal to pass on a yellow line."

"Yeah, Dustball," Carl Albert said. "Don't you know nothing? Quit bouncing. You're making my seat rock."

"We're going to be late!" I said. "They might not let us in."

"They're not going to keep you from seeing your grandpa, Dustin. Just relax."

But I couldn't. I counted every gas rig and dead armadillo and roadside grave marker from Panola to Lutie until finally, *finally*, we got to Wilburton, and the preacher turned off Main Street and drove to the courthouse and stopped next to the little cinder-block building with the chain-link fence out back. There's no sign saying it's the Latimer County Jail, but you could maybe guess by the barbed wire strung crossways along the fence top. I leaned around Carl Albert for the door handle, but the preacher said, "Hold on, Dusty. We'll wait here till they bring your grandpa out."

"Bring him out?" I said. "He's coming home?"

"Not exactly."

Right then the back door of the jail opened and out into the fenced yard came five ladies in orange coveralls like the guys at the Poteau Jiffy Lube wear. They were blinking a little, looking around, but they all went pretty fast over to one side of the fence and lined up.

"Shoot," the preacher said. "I was afraid of that."

"What?" I said.

"What?" Carl Albert said.

"Oh, it's women's visitation first. I get the times mixed up. It's been a while since I've been up here."

People were getting out of their vehicles all around us, and that was the first I noticed other cars and pickups parked in the alley and next door in the VFW lot. Mostly it was guys getting out of their trucks, but there were also a few little kids and one gray-headed couple in church clothes climbing out of a Mercury Grand

Marquis. They must have all been from Wilburton or someplace,
I didn't know any of them. Inside the fence a deputy sat in a tall
chair next to the building keeping an eye on everything while the
families came and stood in front of whichever prisoner was theirs.
Well, that part was kind of sad, how the lady prisoners would
reach through the fence to touch their little kids' hands.

"We're not going in?" I said.

"There's no room inside for all the visitors they get now."

"What about when it's raining?" Carl Albert said.

"Everybody gets wet."

"Man," Carl Albert said.

"When women's hour is over, they'll bring out the men. Then
you can see your grandpa."

"You mean we got to sit here an *hour*?" Carl Albert said.

"Half hour," the preacher said. "Y'all want to go to Sonic now
and come back?"

"No," I said.

"*I* do," Carl Albert said.

"You just ate," I said.

"Well, I don't want to just sit here. It's boring."

"Y'all could go take a walk. You could walk around Main
Street."

"Nothing's open," Carl Albert said. "It's too cold."

"I'm sorry, boys. I should've called to check which was which.
But it'll be time before you know it. Here, I'll turn on the radio."

But the station he put on had church music, which didn't really
help anything. Carl Albert kept messing with the glove box, opening and shutting it and twisting the lock. I guess the preacher felt
bad about getting the times mixed up because he didn't tell Carl
Albert to quit, so I had to do it. Not that he paid me any mind.
Carl Albert's only a year older than me but he acts like he's the

boss of everything. He found a Swiss Army knife buried under all the papers in the glove box and that kept him busy a while, pulling out the little scissors and nail file and stuff. I watched the people by the fence. It wasn't that cold out, just sort of chilly, and the sun was shining, but the lady prisoners looked cold anyway in their orange outfits with their arms wrapped around themselves. Everybody was smoking except the little kids and the old couple. Carl Albert was right though, it was boring, because you couldn't hear what anybody was saying, and plus it was weird how the lady prisoners kept smiling with their bad teeth and you knew they didn't mean it. I mean, how could you be really smiling if the only way you could touch your little kid's hand was through a chain-link fence?

After a while Brother Oren turned the radio off and started saying things that made me nervous, like for me not to worry, they'd had the prayer chain going since they got the news about Grandpa being arrested Friday night. He was talking to me, not Carl Albert, because I'm the one that lives with Grandpa. I've lived with him practically my whole life, or anyway as far back as I can remember, and if he gets sent to prison like Carl Albert says, that'll be the second time everything has gone from bad to worse. Brother Oren said he was going to speak to the deacons about whether the church might want to take up a special offering. I was scared to ask what for.

"They're going to throw the book at him," Carl Albert said. "You watch."

"Quit saying that!" I punched my cousin in the neck. He turned around and went to whacking at me across the seatback, but I scrambled over behind the preacher.

"Boys! Boys! All right, let's get out, it'll be time here in just a minute."

So we got out and stood by the car. Carl Albert started complaining about how he was cold, and I said, "You should've wore a coat, Clodhead," and he said, "You should've changed your ugly face, Dusthole," and the preacher said, "Boys, please." Finally the deputy signaled to the lady prisoners that they had to go in. They took their time putting out their cigarettes and touching their kids through the fence again and then they all filed inside the building and the families went back to their vehicles and left while other cars and pickups were pulling in to take their place. The yard behind the jail was quiet and empty-looking with just yellow grass and bare brown spots along the fence where the grass was worn off and the dirt showed. Then the jail door opened and the men prisoners started coming out. There was more of them than the ladies so they had two deputies to guard them instead of one. Man, I never knew we had so many criminals in Latimer County. You only hear about people getting robbed or murdered every once in a while here, so probably the crimes these men did weren't so bad. Or maybe like my grandpa they weren't even criminals but just Christians and felons, the way Aunt Sweet said. Brother Jesus came out the door combing his hair with his fingers, and then way at the back of the line here came my grandpa, and I took out running.

Carl Albert tried to outrace me. He's bigger than me but I'm the fastest, and I ran to the fence way ahead of him, but when I got close, I stopped. I didn't want to be like one of those little kids sticking their hand through the holes, plus my grandpa didn't look right. He looked smaller than he was supposed to be. The orange coveralls were too big and his hair went every which way. My grandpa don't go anywhere without his hair combed, not even to the breakfast table. Carl Albert came chugging up beside me.

"Hello, boys," Grandpa said, but he wasn't looking at us.

He had his eyes on Brother Oren still standing back by the car. "Where's your mom?" He was asking that to Carl Albert because my mom is dead.

"She had to stay home with Mr. Bledsoe," Carl said. "Are they fixing to throw the book at you?"

"Shut your mouth," I told him.

"Cody Johnson says they are."

"Cody Johnson don't know squat," I said.

"Where's Tee?" Grandpa said.

"He got called in to work."

Brother Jesus came over and stood at the fence with Grandpa. I guess he didn't have any family to come see him. Maybe they couldn't drive all the way up from Texas just to stand around for a half hour outside in the cold. "Hello, young fellows," he said, squinting the way he does so his eyes go nearly shut.

"Hey," Carl Albert answered.

"Hola," I said.

"Cómo estás, Dustin?"

"Bien," I said. "Y usted?"

"Así, así." Brother Jesus sort of blinked and smiled at me. He's been teaching me Spanish. He's definitely one of the ones that's a Christian not a criminal, because for one thing he's a preacher, same as Brother Oren, except his church isn't Baptist, it's Pentecostal, and he preaches in Spanish because most of the folks that go there don't speak English anyway. It's over in Heavener where they raise all the chickens. It used to be a schoolhouse and then it was a hay barn and then Brother Jesus fixed it up and turned it into a church. I've went there a bunch of times with Grandpa. Aunt Sweet says we're grazers when it comes to churchgoing, and what she means is, the way me and Grandpa go to church is not right. We go to the United Methodist in Poteau, the Assembly of God at Dog Creek, Wilburton Presbyterian, Living Word Church in McAlester, just wherever the spirit moves us to drive any given Sunday. Sometimes Grandpa picks and sometimes he lets me. Aunt Sweet says we ought to quit that and go to just one church because I need a church home. She says it's not good for me to be getting all different doctrines like no piano playing at the Church of Christ and sprinkling instead of baptizing at the Methodists and talking in tongues at the Holiness and all that Spanish preaching in Brother Jesus's church. Aunt Sweet's got a lot of opinions about everything but especially about churchgoing. She's plain Southern Baptist like me and Grandpa used to be.

"Hello, Mr. Brown. Pastor Garcia." I felt Brother Oren's hand on my shoulder. "How y'all doing this afternoon?"

"How do you expect we'd be doing?" Grandpa said.

"Well, not so good, I guess."

"Not so good is right. I appreciate you bringing the boys."

"Glad to do it. We've got the prayer chain going, got both your names in this morning's bulletin."

"Well, that's good. Reckon you could add in the names of some of them people they hauled out of my barn Friday night?"

Brother Oren's hand got a little tight on my shoulder. In a minute he said, "If you can get me their names, Mr. Brown, I'll put them in the bulletin next Sunday."

"They can't wait for Sunday," Grandpa said. "Those people need prayers this minute, all they can get of 'em, plus they need a bucket of luck and some good lawyering, too."

"Yes, sir. Sweet wanted me to talk to you about that. She said for me to tell you she's got a lawyer coming from Stipe's McAlester office tomorrow. He'll get y'all bailed out."

"Tell Sweet never mind," Grandpa said. "I don't need a lawyer."

"If it's about money, I believe the church—"

"It ain't about money."

"We decided to let the Lord work in this," Brother Jesus said.

"The Lord can work through Gene Stipe's law office same as any way else," Brother Oren said.

"You're a good man, Oren," Grandpa said, "and I appreciate you. But you don't know a thing in the world about this."

Carl Albert said, "You gotta get a lawyer, Grandpa! They're going to throw the book at you!"

Grandpa looked down at Carl Albert. "Which book is that, Carl?"

"I don't know. That's just what they're saying."

"Who's saying?"

"Cody Johnson, Zane McKissick. My mom." Carl Albert looked miserable. I was afraid he might start crying. I started saying in my mind, Don't you dare. Don't you dare. I stared hard at Grandpa's work boots under his pant legs. They looked sort of normal. I've seen those same tan boots practically every day of my life, only now the leather bootlaces were gone. I heard Carl Albert say, "Zane McKissick says you're a beaner smuggler."

I hissed under my breath, "Shut up, Carl."

"He says you got caught dead to rights and they're going to put you in the McAlester state pen."

"Listen, boys," Grandpa said. He squatted down on his heels, grabbed hold of the fence loops to steady himself. There was a white line on the back of one of his fingers where his Masonic ring was supposed to be. "This isn't going to be easy on you all," he said. "I know that. People are liable to say no telling what. You'll just have to be thick hided, you know it? Don't pay them any mind." Crouched down like that, he was actually shorter than me and Carl Albert. I could see the freckles in his bald spot, and also a little red-looking gash like he'd whacked his

head on something. "Dustin," he said, "look at me." So then I
had to. Either because of the sun or the orange jumpsuit, his eyes
behind his glasses were really blue. "I'm going to need you to take
care of things for a little while, okay? Be a good boy. Mind your
Aunt Sweet." He cut a glance at Carl Albert stubbing his sneaker
in the worn spot on our side of the fence. "Something bothering
you, son?"

"No," Carl Albert said.

"Well, that's a fib."

"How come, is all. Why'd you have to go and do that?"

"What is it you think I did?"

"Smuggled Mexicans."

I kicked Carl Albert in the leg then, and he turned and jumped
me so fast I didn't have time to run. Then we were wallering in the
grass, rolling over and over, till I could feel the asphalt under me,
and I could hear all the men yelling and Brother Oren shouting,
"Boys! Boys!" I tried to get up, but Carl Albert kept punching me
in the side of my face till I grabbed the fat part of his arm and
bit the ess-aitch-eye-tee out of him. He screamed like you never
heard nobody scream in your life, but I held on. I aimed to be like
a dadgum snapping turtle, I wasn't going to unhook my jaw till the
thunder cracked. Somebody bopped me in the back of the head,
though, and I accidentally let go. Next thing I knew Brother Oren
had me by the belt, dragging me off, and one of the deputies was
swatting Carl Albert on the butt with his hand. Carl Albert was
still screaming and the prisoner men in the yard were all whooping
and laughing. My grandpa wasn't whooping, he was holding on to
the fence loops with his fingers. I could see his face though, and I
just felt sick.

Brother Oren hauled us back to the car. He made me get in the
backseat on the driver's side and motioned Carl Albert to the front

seat on the other side. He told us to keep our hands to ourselves and he'd better not hear another peep out of us. I'd never seen Brother Oren mad, ever, so I figured we'd better cool it, but Carl Albert had to pop off. "You're not my dad!"

"I'm standing in for your dad," Brother Oren said. "I'm his eyes and ears here in this situation, and your mom's, too. You want me to tell them how you been acting?"

Carl Albert got in the car and the preacher walked back. I was so mad I could spit. "What'd you go and do that for!"

"*Me?* You started it!"

"You jumped on me."

"You kicked me!"

"You wouldn't shut up."

"*You* shut up!"

"Keep your voice down. You want the preacher to come back?"

"You bit me! Look at that!" He showed me the mark.

"So what." I could see Brother Oren by the fence now, doing the same with my grandpa like he did with Aunt Sweet, listening and frowning and staring at the ground. I pushed the button to roll down the window, but it wouldn't work without the key on.

"That hurt!"

"All right," I said. "I'm sorry."

"Like hell you are."

I didn't say nothing, I just wanted him to shut up. I needed to hear what my grandpa was saying. I felt like it was probably something to do with the rest of my life.

"You're *going* to be sorry, though." He shoved his arm over the seat again to show me. "Look!" His face was smeared red from crying. I turned back to see what Grandpa was doing. I couldn't hear anything, and it was too far to tell what anybody's face said. The deputy that swatted Carl Albert was inside the fence again,

tipped back on his high stool with his sunglasses on. I started
thinking I could just get out and walk over there, what was that
old deputy going to do? Or the preacher, either one. I leaned over
the seat for the door handle, and my cousin whipped across and
smashed his fist in my nose, *pow!*, like I'd walked smack into a
tree. I didn't yell, or cry, either. I just sat back with the blood gush-
ing down all over the front of my hoodie and onto Brother Oren's
backseat. I didn't know what to do. I heard Carl Albert shouting,
"I'm sorry! Don't tell them! I'm sorry! I'm sorry!" I got out of the
car and stood by the back bumper. I was trying to catch the blood
in my hands but it just poured through. Somebody in the yard seen
me and hollered. I looked up, and here came Brother Oren across
the lot at a dead run.

Monday | *February 18, 2008* | *4:30 A.M.*

Sweet's house | *Cedar*

Sweet set her coffee cup on the low table in the dark, took the can of Endust and sprayed the top of the TV cabinet, flicked the feather duster around vaguely, using spillover light from the hall to see by. It was 4:30 A.M. She hadn't slept a drop. Shoot the gerbil, she said to herself. Shoot the gerbil, shoot the gerbil, shoot the dadgum gerbil. But the gerbil kept scrabbling around on its stupid chattering wheel like it had been doing all night: her daddy in jail, her niece's husband deported, the boys fighting like heathens, and her own husband gone since this time yesterday with no way to tell if he was alive or dead, gone working half the time, gone too much of the time, while their son turned into a coward and bully—no. Hush. Don't say that. Shut up. But, oh, she could wring Terry's neck for not calling. The pipeline break was likely so far down in the mountains there wasn't a cell tower for miles, she knew that, but he could have sent somebody out to call. Or somebody from Arkoma Gas could let the families know their men were all right. Surely. You'd think.

She stumbled against the coffee table, sloshed coffee from the cup onto the doily beneath the Bible. Despite her recent rededication and determination to do better, Sweet cussed. She snatched up the book and hurried to the kitchen for the dishrag. There in the lit hallway stood Dustin, his hair tousled, his nostrils blood crusted, both eyes bruised and swollen, way worse than when she'd sent him and Carl Albert to bed yesterday evening. "What are you doing up?" she said. "Get back in the bed, it's not even five o'clock." She swept past him.

"I thought I heard Grandpa."

Sweet stopped in her rush to the sink. For an instant she half believed that her father was calling out for help in that Wilburton jail cell where he was locked up with thieves and dope dealers and one useless Mexican pastor. "You heard Mr. Bledsoe moaning, is all," she said. "Go back to bed."

But the boy stood blinking at the huge family Bible in her arms. "Here." She thrust the book at him, grabbed the dishrag off the sink faucet, and hurried to the front room, flipped on the overhead light. She dabbed at the doily, heard the boy's sticking barefoot step on the hall tiles. "Put it on the mantle," she said, bobbing her head at the false mantle above the gas stove. Dustin carried the Bible over and set it sideways on the ledge. "Are you hungry?"

He shook his head.

"Go back to bed then. It won't be daylight for hours."

"Did Uncle Terry get back?"

"He'll be here in a little bit."

"Is he going to the arraignment?'

She was startled. "Where'd you learn that word?"

"What word?"

"Arraignment."

"I don't know. Brother Oren maybe." The boy went to the window and twisted the shade wand to look out.

"Nothing to see this early." Sweet studied his thin frame, slim shoulders, his too-long brown hair curling down over his collar. Those pajamas had fit Carl Albert when he was eight. Dusty was ten going on eleven, and the pajamas swallowed him. "I'll scramble you an egg."

"I'm not hungry."

"Come over here and talk to me a minute." She sat on the divan and patted the seat cushion. Dustin came obediently and sat next to her with his head down, his hands folded quietly, unboylike, in his lap. "You want to tell me what happened?" she said. Dustin shrugged. He kept his gaze on the stained doily on the table in front of him. There'd always been something troubling about the kid, Sweet thought. Not *trouble*, like his mother and sister, but troubling. Wrenching somehow. "You know the rules about fighting." The boy nodded.

She and Terry had set the rules when Dusty stayed with them last Christmas and the two cousins had argued and jabbed and poked at each other day and night. First offense, no video games for one week. Second offense, no video games and no TV for two weeks. For the third infraction it would be no video games, no television, no movies, no McDonald's or Sonic for one entire year. This was Tee's version of Three Strikes and You're Out, which wouldn't have much effect on Dustin since he lived with his grandpa, but it would devastate Carl Albert. Sweet had never expected to have to deliver the ultimate punishment, but yesterday afternoon was the third fistfight the boys had had since the sheriff dropped Dustin off on his way to Wilburton after the raid Friday night. There was no way she could simply let it slide, act like she didn't know—not with Dustin's bruised face and the bloody bite mark on Carl Albert's arm. Lord, what were their teachers at school going to think? "Who started it?" she said.

The boy's only response was to shift his gaze from the doily to the coffee mug. "Well, it don't matter who started it," Sweet said. "The consequences are the same."

"I know."

"Plus, I'm going to add one other little note to it. When Carl gets up, I want to see you two hug each other's necks and say you're sorry."

Dustin cut her a sidelong glance but said nothing.

"Well?"

Again the boy shrugged. His swollen nose made him look different, older, ethnic, not quite so fragile. Like his father, probably. Had Gaylene known how the boy's looks would turn out when she named him? The same dusty brown color all over, skin, eyes, eyebrows, hair. This whole mess could be traced back to Gaylene, Sweet thought. One more bunch of trouble to lay at her dead sister's feet. "If you're not going back to bed," she said, "come help me get Mr. Bledsoe up."

"Aw."

"Your choice. Back to bed or make yourself useful."

The boy stood and followed her down the hall. Sweet clicked on the bedside lamp. The old man was snoring, his toothless mouth open, the top sheet all knotted and twisted. Dustin hung back by the door. She knew how Mr. Bledsoe's old-manness bothered him, the sickly sour smell, gaping mouth, whitish gums, the purple marks all over his neck and arms because his skin was so fragile. Well, it bothered her, too, but there was nothing she could do about it. "Get me a diaper out of that sack in the closet."

The boy rummaged in the plastic bag, brought her a Depends, then edged backward toward the hall, fake yawning, patting his mouth. The old man blinked, staring around the room with confused, rheumy eyes.

"Hand me them wipes."

Dustin handed her the blue plastic tub, yawning broader.

"All right," she said. "Don't wake your cousin when you go in." The boy slipped quickly out the door toward Carl Albert's bedroom. "No playing that Gameboy under the covers!" Sweet called after him before turning to clean the old man. She'd learned all the tricks from her three-month stint at the Latimer County Nursing Home two years ago—how to roll him, how to plant her feet good to hoist him. The nursing home was exactly where Mr. Bledsoe ought to be, but her husband wouldn't hear of it. Well, it wasn't Tee washing the old man's privates and hauling him up out of the bed and into the chair every morning, now, was it? Sweet had quit that nursing home job because she hated the work, and now here she was. That was sure life, wasn't it? Whatever you most didn't want to have to deal with, that's precisely what came your way. Your own daddy in jail, for instance.

When she got Mr. Bledsoe diapered and dressed and sitting on the side of the bed, she clamped his two arms around her neck, put both her arms around him, braced her shoulders, set her legs. "Come on, Dad," she said. "Work with me." The old man grunted as she levered him up from the mattress and over to the wheelchair. Mr. Bledsoe was thin as sticks but he weighed like a log when she had to lift him. She unflipped the chair locks and maneuvered toward the door, but then she heard Terry's truck rumbling out front, the diesel engine unmistakable; she flipped the locks back down and left Mr. Bledsoe sitting as she hurried toward the front of the house.

Her husband didn't look at her when he came into the kitchen from the carport. He went to the fridge and stood with the door open drinking 7UP straight from the two-liter bottle, which he knew she hated, but Sweet didn't comment. Terry's thick curly

chest to keep him from falling forward, went to check on the boys. In the light from the hall she could see her son snoring on his back with his arms flung over his head and his breathing coarse as a turbine. On the inflatable mattress on the floor Dusty lay curled up with the covers pulled over his head. She couldn't see any light leaking around the quilt to show he was under there playing Carl Albert's Gameboy, which was a relief. She wasn't even sure she'd call him out if she did see it. Sometimes a person just got tired of trying to make them grow up right. Sweet returned to the front room and stretched out on the divan. Terry was home now, it wasn't yet daylight, she had time to rest her eyes a minute, she told herself, before she had to start getting the boys ready for school.

Grayish light was seeping in the front windows, dull and murky looking, when Carl Albert woke her. "You'll never guess what Dustin did."

"What!" Sweet sat up like a shot. "What time is it?" The mantle clock said almost eight thirty. "Oh my word. Terry, honey, wake up and go to bed." She rubbed her face. "Carl, get your backpack. Y'all hurry up and get ready, you're going to be late."

"Come look."

The quilt was thrown back on the air mattress to show where he'd rolled up a bunch of her son's T-shirts and briefs and old pajamas in the shape of a sleeping boy.

"He's gonna get it now, ain't he?" Carl's voice was gleeful.

What do I do? Sweet thought. She was still half asleep, rum-dum, she couldn't think. "Go wake your daddy. Tell him to come here a minute."

"Dustin's in big trouble this time, right?"

"Don't sound so proud. Go on."

She found the note on the floor where it had fallen when Carl

Albert pulled off the quilt. The boy's hand was small, extraordinarily neat, laid out in tiny block penciled letters on ruled notebook paper:

I'LL BE BACK FOR SUPPER, PLEASE DON'T WORRY.
PLEASE. YOURS TRULY DUSTIN LEE ROBERT BROWN

Monday | *February 18, 2008* | *8:45 A.M.*

State Capitol Building | *Oklahoma City*

State Representative Monica Moorehouse was feeling very good about things this cloudy blue Monday, the third week of the new legislative session. True, she wasn't properly prepped for her committee meeting in fifteen minutes, a huge stack of unread House bills clogged her To Read tray, and Kevin had lightened her hair way too platinum on Saturday—she'd have to stay out of sight of the cameras until he could fix it—but the national press had picked up on the raid story, and that was worth everything. She sifted again through the clippings, sorting them according to prominence. Only two-inch AP articles on the inside pages in the *New York Times* and the Dallas papers, but they'd made the front page above the fold in the *Tulsa World,* page three in the *Houston Chronicle,* and they were the lead screaming headline in the *Sunday Oklahoman.* She buzzed the front office, told Beverly to hold her calls—"except for my husband, you can put him right through, and also please call Kevin back, tell him he has *got* to see me this afternoon, I don't care what's wrong with his Chihuahua!"—closed the inside door, and unlocked her desk.

From the top drawer she pulled out her Personal Press File. She trusted no one with this, not even Beverly, who'd proven herself to be as loyal a legislative assistant as any lawmaker could hope for, but the press file was Monica's private domain. One by one she slipped the laminated articles from the folder, laid them out in chronological order across the mahogany desktop. Her favorite was the one of her giving the speech at the Family Values Voters Conference in Denver last summer. The photographer had caught her smiling her most bemused smile, her hands raised in a graceful gesture of bafflement. Her hair was perfect. The caption read: "Oklahoma State Representative Monica Moorehouse wants to know, 'What's wrong with those people?'" The article below failed to make clear that she had *not* been referring to illegal aliens per se but to the federal government and its failure to act, forcing lowly state legislators, such as herself, to take matters in their own hands. Well, it was the *Denver Post,* what could you expect? There'd been several resultant nasty e-mails from out-of-state idiots accusing her of being a racist, et cetera, but the story had played well inside the state, and it was a fabulous picture.

The intercom buzzed. Beverly's voice was pitched low. "I know you wanted me to hold your calls, but Senator Langley is here. Personally. In the office. He says it's urgent."

Monica groaned. Dennis Langley was the opposition state senator whose district overlapped her own, a lanky good ole boy with hound dog eyes, a Will Rogers drawl, and the cunning of a backwoods lawyer. She did not like him, did not trust him, dared not turn him away. "All right, give me a minute." Quickly she cleared the desk, locked it, grabbed a stack of House bills and scattered them across the leather blotter before buzzing Beverly to send him in. She stood up, stretched forth a languid hand with perfectly lacquered French nails, invited the senator to have a seat. He nodded his thanks but remained standing, so Monica did, too, realizing a half beat too late how it put her at a disadvantage. Far better to lean back in her chair delicately arching her neck to peer up at him until he had the good manners to sit down than to stand behind her desk, merely short. She smiled.

"What can I do for you, Senator?"

"My, my, look at this here." Langley lifted a framed photograph from her desk. "I don't believe I ever saw this." He glanced from the photograph to her and back again. Comparing, she felt sure, the soft mocha of her hair in the picture with the shrieking platinum it was right now. Oh, Kevin was going to fix this, *today*, if she had to camp out in his veterinarian's office. Langley cocked his shaggy head at the picture. "You're sittin' in some mighty high cotton here."

"Yes," she said through her gritted smile. She was not sitting in that photograph, she was standing, flanked by both Oklahoma U.S. senators in the middle of the congressional rotunda. She'd been invited on that Washington trip hardly two weeks into her first term, a sign of just how much the powers that be believed in her future. The frame was sterling silver, an elegant cowboy-hat-and-horseshoe motif; it was one of her most prized possessions, and she had to grip herself to keep from reaching across the desk and snatching it out of Langley's hands. "So what's this urgent business of yours, Senator?"

"Urgent? Well, now, I don't know as I'd call it urgent. Very handsome." Langley set the frame back on the desk. "Just thought I'd drop by and visit with you a minute this morning."

"Oh, I'm sorry. My assistant must have misunderstood. Anyway, I've got an Agriculture and Rural Development meeting to get to, but maybe we could arrange something for next week?" She thumbed her desk calendar. "How's Thursday? Say three thirty?" She reached to buzz Beverly to tell her to put it on the schedule, but Dennis Langley's lazy drawl stopped her.

"That'd be fine, ma'am, but what I wanted to visit with you about, well, it's sort of relevant here this morning."

Ugh. She hated being called *ma'am*. They all talked like that, like they'd just dropped off the potato truck; it was the sort of thing she'd moaned to Charlie about when he moved her down here from Indianapolis eight years ago. Charlie would just wave her off, tell her she had to get used to a few things. Plenty of things she had gotten used to. Being called *ma'am* was not one of them.

"I expect you know all about that little raid they had in Latimer County Friday evening. Where they nabbed all those Mexicans?" She nodded. Of course. "And you also know they scooped up a couple local men along with them."

She kept smiling as if to say, *I know, isn't it perfect?* Now the whole world was going to see that her law had teeth! Well, not *her* law, of course; she'd merely coauthored the House version— but her name was on it, wasn't it? A first-term state representative pushing through a bill of that magnitude, well, she could be forgiven the teensiest bit of pride. From the minute the law had gone into effect last November her office had been flooded with calls, citizens groups, state legislators, town mayors, from Iowa, Utah, Colorado, Arizona, all over the country, all hoping to get similar legislation moving in their own states.

"I heard from the Latimer D.A.'s office this morning." Langley plucked his creased slacks at the knee, perched himself on a corner of her desk. "Tom Waters is an old friend, me and him go way back. He's got a few concerns. They're not real keen on all this publicity, for one thing, and then—"

"Senator Langley, if people are going to hire and harbor illegal aliens, they are no less criminal than the aliens themselves. That's the whole point of the legislation. Naturally there's going to be publicity. Taxpayers are tired of their money going to support lawbreakers!"

"Yes, ma'am."

Oh for God's sake, shut up with the *ma'am*s. Irritably she watched Langley trace a finger along the humped back of the Kokopelli paper-clip holder on her desk.

"Latimer's a small county," he went on, his voice all lackadaisical. "Naturally they haven't got a real big budget to cover security and all."

"Security."

"Well, this stuff provokes a lot of anger. There's already been a few threats. And then, too, there'd be reporters to deal with, camera crews, news vans, all that. They're just not set up for that sort of thing down there."

"If space is a problem," she said, "I'm sure we can have the proceedings moved, like they did for the Terry Nichols trial." Yes, why hadn't she thought of that before? Move the trial to her home base in McAlester—so much the better! Ah, Terry Nichols, the second Oklahoma City bomber, what an exciting time that had been. The streets blocked off for security. CNN, Fox News, the networks, they'd all been there! At least at the beginning, although the trial had dragged on for months, and they'd drifted away, lost interest, until it was time for the verdict—but then they'd all come swarming back. She'd been on the McAlester City Council then, a great platform, actually—as her husband so endlessly liked to point out.

"Yes, ma'am," Langley drawled, "we talked about a venue change. He's not sure that'd exactly satisfy the situation."

"What situation?"

"Well, apparently, according to Tom Waters, there might have been a few . . . irregularities."

"Please speak plainly, Senator Langley." This was another part of the good ole boy act that just irritated the snot out of her—how they'd pussyfoot around a subject and never come right out and *say* anything. Charlie told her she needed to learn to read metaphor and subtext. But Charlie could kiss her derriere. He wasn't the one who had to deal with these people. The senator crooked his head, studied the portraits of the governor and the president smiling down from her office wall. Oh, would he never get on with it? She felt like her cheeks were ready to crack.

"One of these fellows they arrested," the senator mused, "Bob Brown his name is, well, he's something of a fixture in the county. I know him a little bit myself, actually. He's a white fellow, you know, and a Christian. A real religious man. Naturally some folks are going to feel sympathy toward him. And then, of course, I know it, some won't. The other man's a Mexican, but he's a citizen—they already checked that out—and he's a Pentecostal preacher, so that's a problem, and his name is Jesús, and that's another problem, because you know in the newspapers that's going to look like Jesus, and some folks won't like that. Well, and then that terrible thing happened in Texas, that's a real sad story. I know it's nobody's fault, but still, it's not good."

"What happened in Texas?"

"That girl that died?" He turned to look at her. "No, I guess you don't know yet. One of the girls they took out of Bob Brown's barn and bused down to Houston, well, she went into labor somewhere along the line, and I guess she was having trouble and either nobody saw it or nobody understood. Or maybe they thought she was faking. Anyway, both her and the baby died. Now, that didn't happen here, but she was part of that bunch they rounded up in Latimer County, so, well, it's a situation."

"Why are you telling me this? What do you think I can do about it?"

"Just wanted to give you a little friendly heads-up, is all. Waters is thinking he might have to drop the charges against the two Americans."

"No!" she nearly shouted, but then she caught herself. "I mean, he can't do that. It's not his call. Those men were caught red-handed harboring fourteen illegal aliens, not one proper document or word of English among them—that's a felony in this state. We made it a felony!"

"Yes, ma'am. But, then, like I said, there might've been some irregularities."

"What does that mean?

"How the sheriff went about things, well, let me just say, Sheriff Holloway's a fellow who doesn't necessarily hold real tight to regulation." Langley unfolded his lanky frame and stood up, towering over her. "Welp, just thought I'd let you know. We may be on opposite sides of the aisle, but we both serve the same constituency down there."

"The D.A.'s got to uphold the law!" she burst out.

"Oh, well," the senator drawled, "probably not if he thinks he hadn't got a case. Might've helped if the sheriff had got himself a proper search warrant. Anyhow, I didn't say he's definitely going to drop them, just said he's thinking about it. That's all he told me." Langley started for the door, paused and turned back. "One thing about it, ma'am, Tom Waters, the county judge, county sheriff, they're all in the same boat you and me are."

"I beg your pardon?"

He cocked his shaggy head, gazed down at her. "Why, we all got to get elected if we intend to serve."

Monica remained standing for a long time after the senator left. What did he mean by that last remark? House Bill 1830 was a win-win, that's what Leadership kept saying. A win-win. Dear

God, she couldn't go into committee like this, her mind a whirling mess thinking about how her fabulously high-profile achievement was on the verge of being ripped away! And yet there was no way for her *not* to think about it. She lifted the receiver to call Charlie, slammed it down again. No! She would figure this out herself. Oh, damn that Langley for coming in here and filling her mind with such crap—that was just exactly what he'd intended, wasn't it? That sly old lawyerly aw-shucks-ma'am act. He wanted to strip her of her confidence, make her fumble, make her second-guess herself. She was *not* going to let that happen. All right then, what to do . . . what to do . . .

A press conference. Of course. She would fix the cowardly D.A., and that old fox Langley, too, and she knew just how to do it: she would put in a call to every friendly contact she had at the local networks, the newspapers. Standing in the rotunda downstairs, she would praise Latimer County law enforcement to the hilt. In particular she'd want to thank District Attorney Tom Waters for having the *courage* to uphold the state's laws, no matter *who* transgressed them, because no one is above the law, and Tom Waters is a man of *principle*, she'd say, a man willing to prosecute transgressors no matter how *personally difficult* the circumstance might be for him. Then just let him try and slither out of pressing charges!

She had to get on it today, though, right now, this minute, in time for the clips to make the evening newscasts. No, God no— her hair. She couldn't do it today. She'd have to arrange things for tomorrow morning. Surely that would be soon enough. Just so long as she held her press conference before the D.A. gave one or, heaven forbid, quietly dropped the charges. Monica jabbed her knuckle on the intercom button so as not to chip a nail. "Beverly, bring your Rolodex and come here a minute. And *please* tell me you've managed to get Kevin on the phone!"

The whole time I was walking out to the farm I kept wishing I had on my hoodie, but it was in Aunt Sweet's dirty clothes hamper with blood on it so I'd just put on two shirts. All yesterday's sun was gone, the sky was dark cloudy, turning cold. I've walked home from town a bunch of times, it's only like three miles, and then the gravel turnoff, but seemed to me like right then it was taking forever. I had to jump down in the bar ditch to hide every time I seen a car coming, and then I'd climb out and walk fast to try to keep warm. I reminded myself to get my feeding coat out of the hall closet before I go. Me and Grandpa don't feed anymore but we used to, or I used to. That used to be part of my chores, slop the pigs, feed the goats, throw scratch to the chickens, till Tipper and Anna killed the rooster last November, coming at it from both sides inside the chicken pen, with me yelling and running from the barn to stop them, which I couldn't. I wanted to hide that old bloody rooster but I knew that wouldn't do any good. My grandpa would just ask me what went with it, and I'd have to tell. Sure enough, when he got home and seen what the dogs done, he went right to the house for his .22. Once that starts, he said, they won't never quit, they're no use to anybody, and I said they're use to *me*, Tipper is. Grandpa looked at Tipper wagging her tail with her tongue out and Anna skulking in a wide half circle about as far away from Grandpa as she could get—she knew she did a bad thing, but I don't think Tipper ever knew it—and then he looked at me real still a minute, turned, and carried the rifle back to the house.

He never once blessed me out for not shutting the gate properly, but the next Saturday morning he got me up early, told me to come help him, and we loaded the goats and the two brood sows in the trailer, lashed the chickens in their crates in the truck bed, and Grandpa called Anna and she jumped into the cab between us, and we took them all to the sale barn at Wister. We had to give Anna away to a kid from Summerfield because wouldn't nobody buy her—she was too old—but we sold all the rest. Since then we been out of the farming business, but we still call our place the farm. That happened in November, a little before Thanksgiving, right around the time my grandpa started to change. Or *change* maybe isn't the right word. He was still like himself, only fierce.

Then, over Christmas is when Tipper disappeared. I was staying in town for Christmas break so I didn't know, but when Uncle Terry took me back to the farm, she wasn't in the yard to meet me. I whistled and called for her. I knew something was wrong by how Grandpa and Uncle Tee looked at each other. She'd went hunting on her own one night, Grandpa said, and never came home. We drove around the country roads and checked down in the creek bottoms, we even took a flashlight and went into the old coal mine back in the ridge behind our place, calling and calling, but we never found her.

Man, I was freezing. I tried walking faster. I ticked off the chores I needed to do before heading out to the cemetery: get the mail, check the propane tank gauge, fill the wood box, light the stove in the bathroom and leave the tap dripping in case it gets really cold. Haul off the trash. When I reached the gravel turnoff to our place, I looked in the mailbox. Nothing but an Alco flyer and this week's specials from Roy's Cardinal Food Store. I took out running, covered the half mile to the house in no time, but when I got to our yard, I stopped.

My aunt's house in town is kind of regular-looking and brick, but ours is real old. It sits where the first son of the original Robert John Brown built his own house after the Browns came here from Mississippi as illegal immigrants—that's what Grandpa says, or that's what he's been saying since November—and it's got a peaked roof like a pyramid hat and a big porch and two front doors. There was yellow plastic tape crisscrossing both doors and the porch posts and windows. I could see black writing on the yellow plastic, POLICE LINE, DO NOT CROSS. I didn't know they did that. They must've did it after the sheriff put me in a headlock and wrestled me into his backseat for the ride to Aunt Sweet's house. I looked yonder at the barn. It was the same, yellow strips across the wide open barn door. Where's the truck? I thought. Grandpa always parks in front of the barn. I went around behind the house, but I didn't see the truck back there, either. Now how was I going to get to the cemetery? I'd never drove on actual roads yet, but I've been hauling trash to the gulley and driving to the mailbox since last year when I got tall enough to reach the pedals with only two cushions behind me. I figured that old dirt road to Brown's Prairie Cemetery wouldn't be any problem, but I couldn't get there without the truck—at least not quick enough to be to Aunt Sweet's house in time for supper. It's almost ten miles. I started feeling mad.

I stomped onto the porch and grabbed one of the yellow tapes covering the back door and tried to jerk it down but it just stretched, so I took out the Swiss Army knife I'd snuck away from my cousin who stole it from the preacher and cut the tape. I cut down every yellow tape at the back of the house, and then I went to the front and got all that and wadded it in a ball and took it to the burn barrel. Then I went to the barn. Our barn's pretty old, too, maybe even older than the house. Nobody uses that kind of barn around here anymore. They all got pole barns and steel sheds delivered on trucks and set up by the company. I had to reach up high where the tape was nailed to the outside wall, and I wadded that bunch, got the kerosene off the porch and poured it over the whole mess in the burn barrel, and then I went to the house for some matches.

I was standing at the kitchen window thinking how that yellow plastic might make a terrible smoke and some neighbor might see and drive over to check, and then they'd be wanting to know how come I wasn't in school and where was my grandpa and who smashed up my face and all kinds of questions I didn't feel like talking about, so I was thinking maybe I wouldn't light it but just haul it out to the trash ditch, when I seen something move inside the open square of the barn door. I eased over behind the kitchen door for the .22, and that's when I found out my grandpa's rifle was gone. Well, that made me even madder. They got no right to just take a person's gun, I thought, it's in the Constitution! I went to the window and looked at the barn door again. I didn't see anything now. Probably it was just the wind blowing an old feed sack, I told myself. I stepped real quiet onto the back porch.

Out past the smokehouse I could see Sugar in Mr. Herrington's pasture, grazing with her head down. That's when I got my next idea. I went down the steps and stopped at the woodpile and got me a stick of wood and walked on out to the barn, stood at the door and called, "Anybody here?" A stirred-up pigeon flapped across from one of the rafters. I waited awhile. I didn't hear nothing, so I ran in fast and jumped up on the stall and reached high on the wall for the old bridle. It was stuck or something, I had to use both hands and I jerked it a bunch of times and got it down finally and raced out the door. I didn't stop till I was back up on the porch. I had to drop the bridle to get my breath, it made a loud chink on the porch planks, and I stood doubled over with my hands on my knees. My heart was pounding like crazy. I'd lost my stick of wood. I watched the barn door some more. Nothing. All right, I said. Okay.

I went back inside the house for an apple. My grandpa buys 'em by the bagful at Roy's Cardinal Food Store in Wilburton on account of they're cheaper that way, but when I looked in the bottom drawer of the icebox, the bag of apples was gone. So were the potatoes and carrots. And then, when I got to looking, so was pretty much everything else, the milk and orange juice and cheese and baloney, even the jar of pickles. Alls that was left was the Arm & Hammer box and the tub of butter and the stuff in the door, pepper sauce and mustard and ketchup and jelly. Well, that made me maddest of all. They'd took my grandpa's gun and stole all our food and taped up our house! It wasn't right. I could see why my grandpa was getting so fierce about everything. Plus, it looked like they'd got his truck, too, because it wasn't here, it wasn't at Sweet's house, and Grandpa sure wasn't out someplace driving it around. And now with no apples, what was I going to use to catch Sugar? And then I thought, Well, how about sugar? She'd probably like that. So I grabbed the sugar bowl off the table and went out to the back fence.

When I whistled, she raised her head, and pretty soon here she came, trotting across the field. I climbed through the barbed wire and stood with the sugar bowl behind me because I didn't want her to know I didn't have any apples for her today. The reason I call her Sugar is on account of the white spots on her rump that look like sugar sprinkled on top of the rusty roan color because she's part Appaloosa, or that's what Grandpa says. I don't know what Mr. Herrington calls her. Him and my grandpa don't talk anymore. They had a fight about something Mr. Herrington said in church, and right after that's when me and Grandpa took our membership and started going around. That was like about three years ago, and now Mr. Herrington and Grandpa act like they don't see each other when they see each other, so I never heard what he named her. But I don't want you to think I had it in my mind to steal the neighbor's horse. I just wanted to borrow her to get to the cemetery to visit my mother, then I aimed to bring her right back.

Monday | February 18, 2008 | 9:55 A.M.

Latimer County Courthouse | Wilburton, Oklahoma

Sweet Kirkendall was not a person who ran late but here she was pulling up to the courthouse at almost ten o'clock. Dadgum Terry's hide, he was so dadgummed stubborn. She grabbed her purse from the floorboard and hurried in through the side door and up the stairs, her boots thunking on the tile steps; she slipped into the courtroom and sat on the nearest bench before she realized that nothing had started yet. The judge wasn't even here, or the D.A. or anybody, only a few family members scattered around the room. Sweet sat tapping her boots, digging in her purse for her Tums, glancing up at the wall clock—she'd been hurrying so fast it was hard to stop. She considered going back out to the hall to see if the lawyer from Stipe's office was there.

Somehow, communicating through the not-real-smart girl at the answering service over the weekend, Sweet hadn't quite got it straight if the lawyer would meet her here today or if she was supposed to go to McAlester and give them a check first. Sweet's chest tightened with the familiar money dread. They were going to have to cash in Terry's retirement CD, she'd already figured that out. He was going to have a fit when she told him—but it couldn't be helped! Where else were they going to get the money? She wasn't about to leave her daddy's fate in the hands of some

Legal Aid lawyer! People in this state got sent to prison for decades on just the least little old drug charges, and the majority of them were represented by Legal Aid. Sweet had no idea how much worse her daddy's case was going to be, but she thought probably a lot. She bit her lip, started to stand up, but then several young men in orange coveralls started coming up the stairs, crowding her view through the glass doors, so she sat back down.

They filed in like a work gang, five skinny white boys in handcuffs and one Indian and Pastor Garcia, and her father at the end, trailed by a big deputy with a dark crew cut. In spite of how upset she was, Sweet felt a rush of pride. Sixty-four years old but he moved like a man half that age: small, tough-boned, his thinning hair combed back neatly over his bald spot. The light from the big windows reflected off his glasses. He didn't look at her, even though he had to know she was there—he walked by not six feet away—but followed the others into the row of seats to her right. The big deputy sat in the row behind them. Oh, it killed her to see her daddy in handcuffs. It just cut her to the quick. The assistant district attorney, a skinny guy with a huge Adam's apple who'd moved here from Arkansas, came in and sat at his table with his suit coat open, and in a moment the pretty ponytailed court reporter slipped in from the back, took her place next to the judge's bench—Sweet had served on jury duty before, this part was familiar—and Mr. Cramer the court clerk called out, "All rise," and Judge Yates entered. "You may be seated." Everybody sat down.

The clerk started calling the cases. Turned out that the ones she'd thought were family members were here for court, too—scraggly guys and their overweight girlfriends, a sullen-looking teenager with black chopped-off hair and black eyeliner and black tattoos on her neck, sitting with her grandparents. Each one came forward as the names were called: you are hereby charged with . . .

public intoxication, driving without a seat belt, open container . . . Sweet barely listened. She was staring hard at her father, trying to will him to turn and look at her, but he kept his gaze straight ahead. She needed to talk to him. She needed to tell him about Dustin running off, and also tell him to quit talking crazy in public—he most assuredly *was* getting a lawyer—and also ask him what the blue blazes did he think he was doing. They'd barely spoken since Friday, just those short couple of minutes when he was allowed to make a phone call—well, that hadn't turned out so good. Since then Sweet had phoned the jail a dozen times, but they wouldn't let her speak to him. "Visitation's on Sunday," whoever answered always said. Probably they wouldn't let her talk to him today, either. Probably she shouldn't worry him about Dustin, at least no more than he was already worried—except he didn't look all that worried. She didn't know what he looked like, actually, sitting there with his hands in his lap and those durned handcuffs on. Oh, Daddy, she thought.

It had been like pulling teeth to get Terry to go out to the farm to find Dustin. "How do you know that's where the kid went?" he'd said, rubbing his face at the table. They were fighting in the kitchen, trying to keep their voices down. She'd let Carl Albert stay home from school. "It's bound to be," she'd whispered. "Where else would he go? He's just a little boy, Tee. What if something happens? What if he gets snake bit?" "Oh for crying out loud, it's February!" "Please, just drive out and take a look. I got to get ready to go to the arraignment." "All right, all right!" He'd downed the rest of his coffee and stomped out the side door, and she'd hurried to the bedroom to give Mr. Bledsoe his eardrops. It was only after Terry left that she realized she didn't have anybody to stay with the old man except her son.

"State versus Jesus Garcia!" the clerk called out, pronouncing the name Jee-zus, not Hey-soos, and everybody jumped. The chunky pastor stood quietly in front of the bench while the clerk swore him in and Judge Yates read him the charges, but when the judge asked, "Do you understand the charges against you?," Pastor Garcia made no answer. The judge repeated the question, and still he didn't answer, not even so much as to shake his head. "Mr. Garcia, do you have an attorney?" No answer. "Sir, do you understand English?" The judge looked out over the courtroom. "Does anybody here speak Spanish?"

Sweet raised her hand.

"You speak Spanish?"

"No, sir, I was just going to—"

—tell him that Pastor Garcia understood English as well as she did, but the judge waved her off. "Does anybody here speak Spanish!" Nobody said anything. The judge, clearly exasperated, smacked his gavel. "Defendant is hereby remanded to custody until we can get a proper translator! Next case." A little ripple went through the men in orange as Pastor Garcia returned and sat down.

"Case number CFO-3-5673, State versus Robert John Brown!"

Sweet watched her father march forward with his head high, shoulders squared: a small, compact man feeling the attention of the whole courtroom upon him. "Robert John Brown," the judge said, "you are hereby charged with transporting, harboring, concealing, and sheltering undocumented aliens in furtherance of their illegal presence in the state of Oklahoma, a felony. You are further charged with interfering with a peace officer, drunk and disorderly conduct, and resisting arrest, all misdemeanors." Drunk and disorderly, my foot, Sweet thought. Her father hadn't had a drink in thirty years. Her heart did a quiet flip. Had he? "Do you understand the charges against you?"

Her father stood mute.

"Mr. Brown, do you understand the charges?"

When her father still said nothing, Judge Yates looked at him real steady a moment, then he droned quickly through the rest of the business, with the court reporter frowning up at him, typing as fast as she could. When he got to the part that said, "Do you have an attorney?," Sweet thrust up her hand. The judge acknowledged her with a chilly look.

"Your Honor, may I approach the bench?" She'd heard that on *Law and Order*. The judge nodded her forward. "He does have a lawyer, sir."

"Where is he? Or she."

"Well, we're getting him one."

"And just when were you expecting this attorney—"

Right then the chorus of "Jesus, Take the Wheel" jingled into the room from inside Sweet's purse. "Shit," Sweet said. She hurried back to her seat, but by the time she dug the phone out, it had quit ringing, and when she turned back to the judge, she thought, This is not good. Judge Yates's face had gone from stern to downright stony. She offered a small apologetic shrug, started across the courtroom toward him, but he stopped her with a look. Then the judge leaned forward and peered down at her father.

"Mr. Brown, how do you plead, Guilty or Not Guilty?" He repeated the question, waited just long enough for it to be clear that the defendant refused to answer before announcing for the record, "A plea of Not Guilty is hereby entered on behalf of the defendant. Preliminary hearing is set for Thursday, March sixth, at nine thirty. Please advise your attorney of the date, Mr. Brown. If you intend to petition the state to appoint an attorney for you, you'll have to have the application filed by Friday." He turned to the D.A.'s table. "What's the State's recommendation concerning bail?"

The assistant district attorney shuffled some papers. He didn't look up. "Defendant has established ties to the community, Your Honor, no criminal record. State has no objection to his release on supervised recognizance."

It took Sweet half a beat to understand, then she jumped to her feet with relief. They were going to let him go home! The judge glared her back down. Then he sat pulling his upper lip, peering at the assistant D.A., who still didn't raise his head. The guy's skinny throat bobbed as he swallowed. He looked actually uncomfortable. Sweet didn't know what that meant. At last the judge said, "Defendant is hereby released on his own recognizance with supervision. The clerk will draw up the papers. Mr. Brown, you may take your seat." A rap of the gavel. "Next case."

Her father stayed where he was.

"Have a seat, Mr. Brown. You can sign the release papers at the end of today's hearing."

Her father remained standing before the bench, motionless, silent. Sweet couldn't tell anything from his back. A flurry of whispers swept the courtroom. Even the boys in orange sat up straighter, paid attention. "Mr. Brown," the judge said, "if you don't return to your seat, I'll have the bailiff remove you." No movement. "You're risking a contempt charge, sir." Still nothing. Judge Yates whacked his gavel. "Robert John Brown, you are hereby charged with contempt of court. The fine will be five hundred dollars." No response. "One thousand dollars!" Not even a flicker. "Two thousand dollars, and defendant will be remanded to custody until such time as he is willing to show respect for this court! Deputy!"

The deputy started to get up, but her father swiveled on his heel and walked back to his seat. Just before he sat down he turned his bright, proud gaze her direction, and immediately Sweet's heart sank. He wasn't going to do it. He wouldn't sign the papers, pay the fine, nothing. Not that her daddy had anything like two thousand dollars to pay a contempt fine with anyway—but that wasn't even the point. The point was that, just exactly as Brother Oren had said, her father had no intention of getting out of jail. Sweet's phone started singing again, and she jumped up, squeezing her purse tight like a baby she wanted to hush, and hurried out of the courtroom.

Two missed calls, one from home, one from Terry's cell. She tried him back but the call went straight to voice mail. Sweet stood staring at the phone's face. Wait or try again? She and Tee could spend ten minutes trying to call each other back. Whichever one of them made the call was supposed to be the one to call again and the other was supposed to wait so they didn't just keep getting each other's voice mail, but half the time Terry didn't remember, and anyhow, she couldn't just sit here. She pushed the speed dial but got his voice mail again, then listened to the message, irritated as always by the fake-pleasant female voice: *You have one unheard voice message. First unheard message,* Terry's voice: "Hi babe, he's not out here, I checked every place, but there's something weird going on. Call me." *If you would like to delete this message, press—*

Sweet flipped the phone closed, almost immediately opened it and called home. Her son answered with his mouth full and the Disney Channel blaring in the background. She'd forgotten to tell him he was grounded from TV. "Did Daddy get back?"

"Nope."

"Did he call?"

"No. I'm hungry."

"How's Mr. Bledsoe?"

"Fine."

"What's he doing?"

"Sitting here. There's no peanut butter left. The milk's all gone."

"I'll stop at the store. Listen, when Daddy gets home—"

"How about tacos?" Her son's voice ticked up in his *I'm-being-good-Mom* lilt.

Sweet hesitated. Yes, all right, she thought. She didn't have time to go grocery shopping now anyway. "Okay. Tell Daddy to call me."

She tried Terry's cell again, no luck. She didn't know whether to be mad or worried. She had the feeling he'd quit looking and had gone on back to work, knowing him. Sweet glanced around the empty lobby, not sure what to do next. It didn't make sense to go back to the courtroom; the judge was mad enough, she wouldn't be helping things there. Go to the bank to see about cashing in their CD? What good would that do? She'd seen in her father's eyes that what Brother Oren had told her was true: Bob Brown had come to a conviction in his heart. When her daddy got convicted about something, well, there just wasn't any changing him. Witness his leaving the church three years ago without one word of explanation. He'd got a conviction about something there, too, and he'd been carting that boy to every you-name-it church all over three counties ever since. Sweet glanced at her watch. It was almost time for Mr. Bledsoe's pain medicine. All right. She'd go home and figure out the next step tomorrow.

She was halfway to the highway before she remembered the tacos and had to turn around and drive back to La Abuelita. The restaurant was right on Main Street, by far the most popular place to eat in the county, and always crowded, especially through the noon hour, but the empty parking places out front made her hopeful they wouldn't be too packed. She angled her Taurus nose-front to the high sidewalk, checked her wallet to make sure she had enough cash, but when she got out of the car she saw that something was wrong. The big plateglass windows were dark. The sign said OPEN, but the door was locked, and when she peered in a window she saw chairs stacked upside down on the tables.

"They're closed." A large girl with several shades of spiky brown hair stood smoking a cigarette outside Kayla's Klip'n'Kurl next door.

"When did they start closing on Mondays?"

"No, like, *closed* closed." The girl tossed her cigarette toward the street. "They hadn't been open since Friday. My boyfriend says all the Mexicans are leaving Oklahoma. I guess that includes Diego and them."

"But—" Surely this didn't mean the folks from Abuelita's? They'd been here for years, those efficient dark young men who showed you to your seat and motioned somebody to bring the chips and salsa and took your money at the register without ever glancing at a ticket or making a mistake, all the shy silent busboys, the deft young women who took your order and smiled and spoke better English than half of Latimer County. They couldn't be illegal; they were fixtures—they belonged here as much as, well, as much as Indians or somebody. Why would they just up and leave?

"On account of that law," the girl said, as if answering Sweet's thoughts. "Larry says they aim to run every Mexican in this state back to Texas."

"Texas?"

"Well, yeah, or wherever. Won't be a place fit to eat in this town." The girl turned and went back inside the shop.

Monday | February 18, 2008 | Evening

Brown's farm | Cedar

The truck gears grind, scream out a bad sound, going up and up
the side of the mountain, and then down, rocking side to side,
swaying, the diesel motor roaring, too fast around the curves, his
bones bumping the hard floor; there is not enough air, the space
is too hot, too dark, why do the exhaust fumes come inside but
not the air? *Bang!* A wounded sound, *thup thup thup thup thup
thup*. Slower, slower, slower, until they are still, waiting for the
door to open, waiting for air, waiting to hear the sound of iron
tools, waiting, waiting, but there is only the soft swish of traffic
far off. *Bang!*

Luis jerks alert, his senses trembling. He holds his breath,
listening, remembering where he is—not in the dark closed truck
on the journey but inside the dark closed bin inside the barn. He
has arrived in the North, yes, but still he is hiding. *Bang!* Carefully Luis raises his head to see between the slats. The light is
dim on the barn floor. *Bang!* A splintering, chopping sound. A
choked voice. Not the man. The little boy. The english words are
harsh and thick. Then there is a quick scuttle of running feet,
and sudden murky light bursts in as the boy lifts the bin lid. Luis
cannot prevent the startled yip that snaps from his mouth, but
the boy does not cry out. His eyes within their bruised circles are

red and swollen. He holds the heavy box lid with both hands. He seems to be looking past Luis, or beneath him. With a grunt the child hoists the wooden lid completely open; it falls back against the wall. He says something to Luis, an accusation. An angry question.

Pardon me, Luis says. *I dont understand.*

¿You dont speak english? the boy says.

Luis shakes his head no. But the boy speaks spanish. How good. Luis reaches for the lip of the bin, pulls himself to a sitting position, his body stiff from being so long without moving.

¿Where is—where is the—how do you say? The boy makes the motion of digging, both hands furiously spading the air.

¿The shovel? Luis says.

Yes. Shovel. The boy talks english then, spitting out the short sharp words between his small teeth. He turns and walks away very fast, but then he stops in the barn doorway as if the space outside will not let him go forward. His small figure is outlined in the square of lavender light. His shoulders are shaking. The smell comes to Luis then, a familiar smell, sickening, a little sweet. Stiffly he climbs out of the box and goes to where the boy stands. On the ground outside is the dead animal, a dog, yes, the carcass still holding that shape although the black coat is coming off in clumps. Luis can see the trail of black hair all the way from the fence line, where the boy has dragged it. The dog has been dead a long while; its eyes are gone, the skull almost naked, the teeth bared. The smell is bad but not so bad as a thing dead only a few days. Clamped on one of the hind legs is a steel trap; the spike on the end of the chain is crusted with dried clay. Above the exposed bones and matted hair, the black tail is perfect, a sleek dark whip, tipped with white hairs at the end. The lavender sky is turning purple.

We will bury him, Luis says.

The boy looks up. He swipes an arm across his eyes, wipes his nose on his sleeve. It is clear he does not understand. Luis makes the motion of digging. *We will bury him,* he says again.

The boy nods, his jaw trembling. He is shaking with sobs, but also with cold. *The shovel,* the boy says.

Yes. Luis looks inside the barn. In the dimness he can see the big metal toolbox upside down near the horse stall, the tools flung everywhere, a claw hammer, a sledge, many screwdrivers, a pry bar, a hand saw, other tools he does not know the name of or what they are for. The blade of a small chopping axe is stuck in the wood of the horse stall. There are many chop marks in the wood. On the floor nearby, a hoe and a yard rake with a broken tine. He picks up the hoe, walks outside to the fading light. *Show me where to dig.* The boy looks up, his eyes cloudy. He does not understand the words. Luis steps over the dead dog and walks out beside the fence and begins to chop the hard winter ground. The boy comes to stand beside him. Again the choked words come from the boy's throat.

I cussed and cussed Mr. Herrington, but it didn't help. I know it's a
sin to cuss somebody, but it's a sin to kill somebody's dog, too! Just set
a stupid trap in the woods where any animal could get in it, and for
what? A blamed coyote? Look how she died! I can't stand to think of
how long she suffered, barking and whining in the woods with her
leg broke, gnawing at it, starving—I wish we'd shot her! I wish my
grandpa had just shot her that day they killed the rooster, it would've
been better than dying like that! Why didn't Grandpa hear? I bet
she barked for days. I bet she barked and whined and cried for me to
come get her, I was supposed to take care of her, she trusted me to
take care of her, and instead I was stupid in town fighting with my
stupid cousin over his stupid Gameboy while Tipper was starving
and hurt and crying for me to come get her and I didn't know it. I
didn't hear. I'd like to kill him! If I had my grandpa's .22, I thought,
I'd go right to his stupid damn house! And I just kept cussing Mr.
Herrington like that the whole time the man dug a hole big enough
to put Tipper in.

He was older than the other Mexicans, maybe almost as old as
my grandpa, but he was strong. He cut the ground with the hoe
like an axe chopping pond ice, and pretty soon the hole was big
enough. He asked me something, but my Spanish ain't that good.

Then he went inside the barn and came back with an armful of old hay and an empty feedsack. He spread the hay all inside the grave, then he went and scooted Tipper onto the sack and picked her up, I mean picked her right up in his arms no matter how bad she stank, and he carried her over and laid her in the grave. The man said some more words, bowed his head and mumbled the Spanish words really fast. I couldn't stop crying. When he was done, he crossed himself, and then he held the hoe out to me like he wanted me to take it. He made the motion for me to scrape the dirt and grass back over her, so I started but then I was crying too hard and the man took the hoe and finished. He motioned me to the yard hydrant and turned it on, oh, that water was freezing, but we both washed because Tipper was so nasty. That's another thing that made me so mad. She'd laid there and rotted since Christmas! Crows and buzzards won't hardly eat a dead dog—my grandpa told me that a long time ago—but she was almost all gone anyhow, even cold as it's been.

"Tienes hambre?" the man said. I shook my head. I'd felt hungry before I found Tipper, but I wasn't hungry no more. "Hace frío," the man said, and I nodded because he was sure right about it being cold. He motioned me to come with him, and we went inside the barn. I followed him to the feed bin in the back, and he reached inside and got an old smelly coat and handed it to me. Then he shut the bin lid and we sat on it while outside got even darker, even colder. How am I going to get to the cemetery now? I thought. Uncle Tee took the bridle. I was watching from the woods when he found it and carried it back to his truck, so then I set out walking. That's how I found Tipper. It was the smell first that stopped me, and then I seen the white tip of her tail on the ground under the cedar thicket on the far side of Mr. Herrington's land.

"El hombre," the man said. "Es tu padre?"

"Hombre?" I thought he meant Grandpa. He motioned outside where Uncle Terry parked his Silverado. "Oh. Mi tío," I said. The man said a bunch of words then but I couldn't understand them except *tu tío*. He touched under his own eye, nodded at my face. It was pretty dark in there but I could see his hand and his head move, and I knew he was asking if it was my uncle who gave me the shiners. "No," I said. "Mi . . . mi . . ." But I didn't know the word for *cousin*. "Un muchacho," I said finally. The man said nothing. We just sat. I started thinking about my mother.

Everybody believes I don't remember her, but I do. I can't tell sometimes if what I remember is from pictures or from really seeing her, but I know I remember how good she smelled and what it felt like going to sleep with her hand rubbing my back really soft. I know I remember that. We lived in Tulsa then. Me and Misty Dawn and my mom. I was a real little kid. Of course, I didn't know it was Tulsa, I only know that now because Grandpa told me. He's the only one that ever talks to me about her, and he don't really like to, except sometimes when he's in a mood, so there's a lot I still got to find out. But here's what I know already: her name was Gaylene Carlotta Brown and she had long straight black hair almost down to her butt. I think she was part Indian. Well, I'm not sure if I heard that or if I made that up, but if you ever saw a picture of her, you'd think she was Indian. She was beautiful, too. She died in California but I don't know what town. My sister, Misty Dawn, might know. I was already living with Grandpa then. That was the first time everything went from bad to worse. Some people might not think it was worse but they would only be people whose mother didn't die when they were little.

Grandpa rode a train to California to get my mom after she died. That's one of the things he told me. He had to drive to Fort Worth to take the train, and when they got back, he hired some people in a truck to haul the coffin up here from Texas so she could be buried at Brown's Prairie with the rest of our kin. Aunt Sweet's mom is buried there, too. She was Grandpa's first wife. She died when Aunt Sweet was just little. I guess that's something me and her have in common. I don't know where my mom's mother is buried, or if she's even dead. Grandpa don't talk about her at all. He's the one takes me out to the cemetery to visit. If I sit next to my mom's grave, she talks to me. My grandpa don't know that. Anyway, it's not like she talks in words or anything, just feelings, but I really needed to listen, I needed to hear her, because I felt like things were going from bad to worse again.

But it was dark out already. I'd stayed too long in the woods beside Tipper. I couldn't get the trap off her leg and it took forever to dig the stake loose from the ground, but I wasn't about to leave her rotting under the cedar trees like that. Ten miles is a ways to walk, I told myself, but I'm going to have to do it. Not tonight, though, I thought. It's too late and too cold. I didn't even want to walk back to town.

So I was glad, sort of, when I heard Aunt Sweet's car coming. You can't miss that old turquoise Taurus since the transmission got rebuilt. Me and the Mexican man both heard it the same minute, and we sat looking hard at each other in the dark. I couldn't see his face, only feel what he was saying: Por favor.

"Quick!" I said and jumped up to open the bin. He got to his feet as fast as he could, which wasn't all that fast, but still we had time for him to climb in and lay down and me to close the lid and go stand outside the barn door before Aunt Sweet's headlights cut the yard. She got out of the car and came at me in such a rush I put my head down and braced myself. She grabbed me in both arms and hugged me till she practically squeezed the breath out of me. I tried to wriggle out but she just kept squeezing. "What the *hell* did you think you were doing?" she said, her chin knobby on the top of my head. "I got half a mind to beat the living daylights out of you!" So I knew then she wasn't going to whip me. I got in the car and didn't say nothing all the way back to town, till just right before we turned onto the highway toward Sweet's house. Then I remembered I still had on the old guy's coat. So I guess that's basically when I started lying.

Telling lies is one sin my grandpa will get really worked up about, so I can't even act like I didn't know it was wrong. But I started talking about Tipper, and the two parts that were lies were, one, I wasn't really crying, I was just making the sound. I was done crying by then but I pretended because I figured if I could get Aunt Sweet to feeling sorry about Tipper before we got inside the house where the light is, most likely she wouldn't pay much attention to that coat. And, two, I didn't say *we* buried her, I said *I* buried her. Well, I am one of the ones that buried her, I told myself. But you can't get nothing past Carl Albert. The minute me and Aunt Sweet came in the kitchen he looked up from licking his sandwich and said, "Where'd you get that ugly coat?"

I said, "You ain't never seen Grandpa wear this coat?" I glanced up at Aunt Sweet, but I could tell she wasn't really listening. She was staring at me the same way Grandpa stared the day the dogs killed the rooster, like she was seeing me and not seeing me, like she was there in the room and also someplace else.

"Pee-*yew*!" Carl Albert said, holding his nose. "You stink like cow pies!"

"Can I make a sandwich?" I said, never moving my eyes off Aunt Sweet's face.

"Go wash up. Here, give me that." And she took the coat off me and held it away from her while she carried it out to the carport. I looked dead-on at Carl Albert when I started for the bathroom because I knew if I didn't, he'd know. He might not know what, but he'd know something. I cut a wide path across the room by the pantry so he couldn't reach out and pop me, but I never flinched my eyes from him once.

So it wasn't till real late in the night, when I was laying on the air mattress listening to Carl snore with his adenoids, that I understood why my grandpa says there's no such thing as a white lie or a little sin. He says one sin leads to the next on the road to perdition, and I could see for the first time how it's really true. Because I'd started out with cussing and went from there to lying, plus stealing, and I thought, No telling where it's fixing to lead me next. Because when Carl Albert pinched my arm while we were brushing our teeth in the bathroom and whispered, "What'd you do with my knife, Dusthole?" I didn't say, *Hey that knife's not yours, it's Brother Oren's and I'm going to give it back to him,* the way I'd meant to. I spat toothpaste in the sink and looked my cousin straight in the face and said, "I don't know what you're talking about." He jumped me then, got me down on the floor really bad, till Aunt Sweet came in and pulled him off me, but I still didn't tell.

I thought about that a long time while I waited for the house to get completely dark, completely silent, till I felt sure nobody was going to wake up, so nobody would see me take the Swiss Army knife out of my sneaker where I'd hid it and carry it out to the carport to put it with the Mexican man's coat. Aunt Sweet had laid the coat on top of the old washer she uses for Uncle Tee's greasy work clothes. I stuffed that smelly coat down behind the washing machine where nobody would find it. I told myself I could always get Brother Oren a new one later, if I could ever get a job for some money, and if I could find out where they sell knives like that, which I didn't know where, someplace in Fort Smith maybe. My grandpa would know.

Sweet had the boys up, dressed, combed, cerealed, and in the car before daylight. When she went back to check on Mr. Bledsoe, she found him deeply asleep, curled on his side like an ancient, bald little fetus, the extra pain pills doing their work, and yes it was terrible, probably even sinful to dope the old man, but she didn't know what else to do. She needed to get to Tulsa today. The boys were quiet in the backseat as they drove along the dark Main Street, where a couple of mud-crusted SUVs stood parked in front of the old mercantile that housed Heartland Home Health. Sweet glanced inside the lighted window at the two women in loose smocks drinking coffee at the desk. She knew good and well Mr. Bledsoe would qualify for home health if they'd just put in for it, but Terry wouldn't let her. *His* family wasn't taking any government handouts, he said. Oh, but if she just had an aide coming in once a week to help, maybe she could manage to get a few things done. Drive to Tulsa to get Misty, for instance, without having to dope the old man. Or medicate him rather. *Medicate* was a better word.

At the end of the street she turned right, drove around behind the rock elementary building, and parked beside the prefab cafeteria in the back. Three yellow buses idled nearby, puffing white exhaust into the cold morning air. "Y'all sit here a minute," she said.

"Where are you going?" Carl Albert whined.

"I'll be right back."

Mrs. Johnson and Mrs. Hale were stirring up powdered eggs and biscuits in the steaming kitchen. Mrs. Johnson frowned under her hairnet, but Mrs. Hale smiled. "Why sure, bring them on in here. We'll feed them with the country kids."

"Oh, thanks," Sweet said. "They've already had breakfast."

"Did Mr. Travers say it's all right?" Mrs. Johnson wanted to know.

"I'll go check to make sure." Actually, the notion hadn't occurred to her to talk to the principal, but she realized that maybe she ought to do that. She could explain about the boys missing school yesterday, give an excuse for Dustin's bruises. She stepped outside and motioned them to come on. Her heart caught when she saw her nephew climbing out of the car. His nose was still so swollen. The skin below his eyes looked like mashed blackberry pulp. Why hadn't she thought to smear a little makeup on him? Cover some of that color, at least. Carl Albert raced up the steps and ducked beneath her arm holding the heavy metal door open. Dustin came slowly behind him, head tucked, hands in his pockets. "Hurry up, Dusty," she said. "I can't stand here all morning letting cold air in."

After she got the boys settled—Dustin hunkering in on himself at one of the long cafeteria tables, Carl Albert hanging over the serving window watching the women work—Sweet went back to her car and sat a minute, glaring at the closed cafeteria door. She'd seen the look the two cooks exchanged when they saw Dustin's face. She felt like marching right back in there and saying, *What are you people staring at?* Or she wanted to give some reason: he'd walked into a door yesterday, he fell down playing basketball.

What she did not want to say was, *Yes, my son did that to his little cousin who is half his size and weight.* Sweet's chest hurt, a deep searing burn radiating from her breastbone up into her throat. A sound escaped her then, a clutched, choking noise, not quite sob, not quite groan; it seemed to come from the same place where her heart burned. Sweet turned the key in the ignition, drove around to the front of the school.

She sat in her car staring at the administration building, a two-story octagon of jigsaw-puzzle-fitted native stone flanked on either side by the grade school and the high school, all built by the WPA back during the Depression. Little had changed since Sweet was a student here twenty years ago, except the classes were even smaller now because the town was shriveling to nothing, and the teachers she'd gone to school to were all retired now, or dead. But the beautiful old buildings looked the same. They would last till the Rapture if somebody didn't get a state contract to come bulldoze them down. Behind the buildings the sky was getting lighter, striated orange and pink. Sweet tried to make herself go in and talk to the principal, but she couldn't think of any calm sensible words to explain why she wanted to drop the boys off at school an hour early, or for them being absent yesterday, or for the bruises on Dustin's face. The cooks' judgmental glances returned to her. She put the Taurus in gear and drove out of the lot.

It wasn't until she was well north along Highway 82, navigating the twisting curves over the Sans Bois ridges, that Sweet remembered she'd left her cell phone plugged into the charger on the kitchen counter. She thought about turning around to get it, but a quick glance at the time dissuaded her—she was already getting a late enough start.

*   *   *

The whole drive to Tulsa Sweet alternated between praying and practicing what she was going to say to her niece. She had tried calling Misty Dawn last night but got a recording saying the number was unavailable. That meant a two-hour drive to Tulsa this morning because she didn't know any other way to contact Misty except that TracFone number. Actually, Sweet had felt a little relieved when she heard the recording. At least she wouldn't have to explain why she'd waited four days to let the girl know her grandpa was in jail.

Traffic on the expressway heading into Tulsa slowed to a crawl. A wreck or construction up ahead, or something. Sweet watched the time tick away. See, Lord? she told Him. Why can't there ever be an easier way to do things! Though in fact Sweet knew she would have driven up here today anyway, even if she'd been able to reach Misty Dawn on the phone, because the only way to talk the girl into coming back with her was to do it in person. What she'd been practicing for two hours on the slow drive from Cedar was how to make it seem like Misty Dawn's idea.

It took another forty minutes before Sweet turned onto a run-down side street in North Tulsa, drove half a block, and stopped in front of Misty Dawn's house—a tiny yellow rent house with a low roof and blue trim set well back from the road in the middle of a huge half-acre lot. Sweet hadn't been here since last August, for the baby's third birthday, when the yard had been filled with over-large, overdecorated pickups and charcoal smoke and tinny fast music blaring from speakers. Now the yard was winter dead and empty except for two resin lawn chairs stacked together, a pink-and-lavender tricycle tipped on its side, and Juanito's big white Dodge Ram parked close to the house. Sweet was relieved to see the truck. The cops had impounded it when they arrested him in November, but apparently Misty Dawn had managed to come up with the money to pay the towing and storage fees. Sweet cringed, remembering; that had been the topic of their last phone conversation, actually. Her niece had called just before Thanksgiving wanting to borrow five hundred dollars to get the truck back. Sweet didn't have it to give her. Misty had said she understood, but had she really? A flicker of curtain in the front window caught Sweet's eye. That was the trigger, finally, that made her get out and go to the door.

She rapped on the frame—no answer, so she opened the screen and pounded on the wood. "Misty Dawn, it's me, hon! Aunt Sweet!" The house only had four rooms, the small kitchen and bathroom here on the left side, a cramped living room and bedroom on the right. There was no way Misty Dawn didn't hear. "I saw the curtain move!" Sweet called. "I know you're up." Still it was several minutes before her niece opened the door. A big girl, solidly built, with a beautiful face and long sand-colored hair, Misty Dawn stood in the doorway in jeans and a black T-shirt. "Hi," she said, her voice faint, almost bored sounding.

"Hi," Sweet said. There was an awkward pause. Misty Dawn held the door partway closed, the way you'd try to ward off Jehovah's Witnesses. The blank look on the girl's face confirmed what Sweet had expected—she didn't know anything about her grandpa's arrest. "I tried to call last night," Sweet said, "but it didn't go through."

"I ran out of minutes. I got to wait till payday to get another card."

"Oh. I was worried you'd had to get a different phone." Her niece stared at her. Not a good start. Last night, when she'd heard that recording, it had occurred to Sweet that the cops might have confiscated the TracFone, too, same as the pickup, when they arrested Juanito. The point being: How many times had Sweet tried to call Misty Dawn since her husband got deported three months ago? Up until last night, actually, not once. "Can I come in?"

Misty slid her gaze past Sweet's shoulder to the Taurus parked in the yard. "I was just getting ready to go to the store."

"Okay. I'll take you. But I gotta come in first and use the bathroom. I'm about to pop."

Her niece pulled the door open, and Sweet hurried through the narrow kitchen into the bathroom. She could hear Sponge-Bob's goofy voice burbling in the front room. Moments later, pumping liquid soap into her palm at the tiny lavatory, she was struck, as always, by what a meticulous housekeeper her niece had turned out to be. The thin towels and washcloths were lined up perfectly on two shelves, color coordinated in greens and turquoises and purples that matched the shower curtain with its seahorse motif, which in turn matched the plastic soap dispenser she was using, with its floating array of purple seahorses and blue starfish. The medicine cabinet mirror had been recently Windexed; she could smell the ammonia. The sink was spotless. It was remarkable, really, when you considered how chaotic the girl's life had always been. Or maybe it was because of that, Sweet thought. Maybe the best order her niece could make of things was to keep her washcloths and towels color coordinated and stacked by size.

In the front room Misty Dawn was crouched by the worn loveseat trying to get the baby to let her put on her shoes. Sweet had never been able to bring herself to call Misty's little girl by her given name. Concepción was just too, well, Mexican. Not to mention Catholic. Not to mention plain icky—who wanted to think of such things every time you said a kid's name? Sweet had tried calling her Connie, but Misty Dawn always corrected her, so Sweet just went on thinking of her as the baby, even though

she was three and a half years old. Misty Dawn swore her daughter could talk when she wanted to, but Sweet had never heard
her speak a word of English or Spanish, either one. The child
had no trouble making her wishes known, though. She shook her
head fiercely at her mother, her thick mat of dark hair tossing
side to side; she pulled up her legs and tucked them beneath herself, stared unblinking at the television. "Concepción María de la
Luz!" Misty said, and then rattled off a long string of Spanish,
ending with " . . . or I'll wear you out." Then she sighed, hoisted
herself up from the floor, and went to the bedroom.

"Hey, those are really cute shoes," Sweet said. "Is that Cin-
derella? Or no, I guess it's Snow White. Is it Snow White?" The
little girl continued to gaze at the television with unblinking eyes.
She was, there was no other word for it, exquisite. Her features
combined the best of both parents, Misty Dawn's perfect nose and
rosebud lips, Juanito's brushy lashes and dark eyes, except that the
child's eyes were not brown but a smoky color halfway between
gray and green. Her hair wasn't quite as black as her father's, but
it was similarly thick and straight—Indian hair, Sweet would call
it—and right now it hung in her eyes and looked like it could use
a good wash. Quit, Sweet told herself. She had promised herself
and her Savior the whole way here that she was not going to judge.

In a moment Misty reappeared in a denim jacket, carrying a
white puffy coat for the baby. She'd put on makeup, dark eyeliner, mauve shadow, her lips glossed a soft pink, her cheekbones
brushed with blush. "You want fruit pops?" she said. The little girl
cut her eyes from the TV to her mother, held her grave look a moment, then her face lit with a gorgeous smile and she scrambled
down from the loveseat, came and took the coat from her mother's
hand. "You gotta put your shoes on," Misty said, and the girl sat
obediently for her mom to strap on her Dora the Explorer sneak-

ers. Misty Dawn stood up and pulled a hairbrush from her back pocket, held the brush in one hand, a fuchsia elastic band in the other, looking at her daughter with eyebrows raised. The little girl jumped up, turned around to stand in front of her, and Misty Dawn swiped the brush through her hair a few times, gathered it in a loose ponytail.

Driving along in heavy traffic, following Misty's chirped directions, Sweet tried to find the right opening. She wanted to ease into the news slowly; she didn't think it would be helpful to just blurt it all out. Misty Dawn had always been really close to her grandpa. He'd raised her until she was almost nine, until Gaylene waltzed home from Oregon one day and announced she'd come for her daughter and then moved the girl up here to Tulsa with that grease monkey dope fiend from Sand Springs. Not Dustin's father. The one before him. Sweet waited, but Misty Dawn had switched from mopey silence to nonstop chatter, and she couldn't find a place to jump in. Misty Dawn said she'd started working nights at a pizza place and the job wasn't too bad, except her boss was a jerk, but she was thinking about trying to get a different job anyway, she could maybe work as a translator or something, it might pay better, or have benefits at least, but she didn't know where to try, and anyhow you'd probably have to have a diploma, didn't Sweet think you'd probably need a diploma? "Um, well," Sweet began. Anyway, Misty said, she'd been thinking about getting her GED, except then she'd have to pay somebody to watch Concepción while she went to class, Blanca worked days so she couldn't keep her in the daytime, did Sweet remember Blanca? Juanito's cousin from the party? She was legal so that wasn't a problem, but she worked all day at the Motel 6 so nights were all she could do, but Misty had been thinking maybe they had night classes for GEDs, that was a possibility, except she never knew what her schedule was going to be, the boss switched it around every week, and anyway she had to get in as many hours as she could, they were just barely getting by with her working thirty, or sometimes she worked thirty, sometimes the boss stiffed her, put somebody else on the schedule, he just did that, Misty Dawn thought, to keep everybody on their toes, plus he was a jerk. "Take a left here," she said. "There it is." Misty pointed ahead to a giant discount supermarket in an ocean of asphalt crammed with parked cars. "Usually I just walk to the bodega on the corner, it takes so much gas to come all the way out here."

"Yeah, I can see that." Sweet turned into the vast lot and started hunting for an open space. Not once in twenty-five minutes of driving had her niece asked her what she was doing here.

"Quit now, Lucha," Misty said, half turning to the backseat. "You leave that seat belt right where it is till we get parked!"

"What did you call her?" Sweet asked.

"What? Oh, Lucha. It's like a nickname." Misty tugged down the visor to check her face in the mirror. "Her daddy calls her that. For Luz, you know. María de la Luz. That was Juanito's grand-mother's name, did I ever tell you that?"

"I don't know. It's cute, though." Lucha. She liked *Connie* better, but *Lucha* was at least a name you wouldn't be embarrassed to say out loud in front of company. She navigated the Taurus into a narrow parking space about a mile from the store door. "Y'all ready? Lucha, honey," she said, trying it out, her voice light, "hold Mommy's hand."

Up and down the aisles they went, Misty pushing her somberly staring daughter in the shopping cart, rattling away the whole time—hey, that's a nice display, did you ever try these? you gotta read the labels though, they put all kinds of crap in there—until Sweet understood that the breathless monologue wasn't due simply to her niece's astonishing self-absorption. Misty Dawn was nervous. She kept dropping things, fumbling with her shopping list, reaching into the side pocket of her purse to rifle through a handful of coupons. Sweet thought about suggesting she not buy too many perishables, but there was no need. They sailed right past the produce section. Even with her husband gone, Misty Dawn was still buying Mexican—a big jar of picante, giant bags of Goya rice and beans—but she also loaded up on frozen French fries and Hot Pockets, artificially flavored Popsicles, sugary cereals, basically anything the child pointed to, except when they passed through the candy aisle and the little girl waved wildly toward a brightly colored package. "No, mami. Not today. We got your fruit pops, remember?" Then she said something else in Spanish, and the little girl lowered her arm as her mother pressed on.

"Lucha?" Sweet said. "You want Gummi Bears, honey? Aunt Sweet will buy you some." She doubled back and grabbed a bag off the rack, returned to where Misty stood in the aisle sorting coupons. "Okay, well, that's it, I guess," Misty said, glancing around vaguely; then she headed toward the checkout.

When the cashier deducted for the coupons and gave her the total, Misty slipped a brown plastic card from her back jeans pocket and swiped it. Sweet recognized the card immediately, and her jaw clenched. Of course she'd known money must be tight, but still, it mortified her to see her own niece using food stamps. "Oh, man," Misty said, frowning at the display. She swiped the card again. The middle-aged cashier didn't try to hide her disdain. "You don't have enough balance," she said, pointing at the register screen, as if the girl couldn't see that for herself. Misty Dawn tugged her plastic wallet from her purse and flipped it open, slid her finger along the empty fold. The side of her face flared a bright blazing pink as she started taking items out of the sacks and setting them back on the glide belt. She reached to take the bag of Gummi Bears from her daughter, who let out a shriek and started wailing.

"No, here!" Sweet said. "I was going to get that." She pulled out her billfold. "How much?" The cashier glanced at her register. "Thirty-six fifty-two. Not counting the candy." Sweet threw a couple of twenties onto the glide belt—a chunk out of this week's grocery money, but never mind; she'd figure a way to make up for it. "Count the candy," she told the cashier, and she had to bite her tongue to keep from saying something else incredibly nasty.

"Here, baby," she said as they rolled through the pneumatic doors, "let Aunt Sweet open those for you." The child surrendered the bag, which Sweet tore open with her teeth and returned to her and, for the first time that Sweet could ever remember, the little girl looked up directly in her eyes and smiled. Misty Dawn walked on ahead of them, stood waiting at the back of the Taurus for Sweet to pop the trunk.

Wordlessly her niece loaded the bags into the turtle hull while Sweet strapped the baby in the backseat. Misty Dawn had shifted into silent mode again. On the way home she spoke only to give driving directions. A dozen times Sweet opened her mouth to begin, but getting started seemed even harder now. She turned onto North Peoria. "You know, hon," she said.

"I should've brought my calculator," Misty said.

"It's not a problem."

"I'll pay you back."

"You don't have to."

"I wasn't trying to get you to pay for it! I lost count."

"No, I know. I wasn't—"

"I'm going to get a different job."

"I didn't mean that. I know it's hard with Juanito gone." Sweet pulled into the yard and Misty Dawn jerked open the door handle before they'd come to a complete stop. "Wait!"

Misty sat staring straight ahead. "We're making it fine. I don't need any help."

"Your grandpa's in jail," Sweet blurted.

"What?" The girl looked not so much surprised as confused. "What are you talking about?"

"Don't you ever watch the news?"

"Not really." Misty's voice had the faint, half-bored sound Sweet had heard earlier, but she could see now it wasn't boredom that caused her to sound that way. It was fear. "Why didn't you tell me?"

"Well, I did. I mean, I am. That's what I'm doing here."

"I can't believe it. What happened?"

"Let's get these groceries in the house."

All while they toted in the sacks and Misty Dawn put things away and Sweet opened a can of soup and tried to take the Gummi Bears away from the baby and gave up finally and set her on the loveseat to watch cartoons with her sneakers on and a pink afghan in her lap and the whole bag of candy in her hands, Sweet related the story. Misty Dawn sat in a folding chair at the card table in the kitchen, looking dazed. After a while she started mixing a jug of Crystal Light, stirring and stirring, saying nothing. Sweet poured up a bowl of chicken noodle and set it in front of her, but Misty Dawn just kept stirring the drink mix. "Who was it?" she said faintly.

"Arvin Holloway and his damn deputies. Pardon my French."

"No, I mean, who'd they get? The Mexicans."

"How should I know? Good grief. Are you listening to me? Your grandpa is sitting in the Latimer County Jail this minute! You need to come home."

"What? I can't. I . . . I've got to work tonight."

"Tell your boss you've got a family crisis."

"I can't do that."

"Why not?" Sweet's list of persuasions came back to her: "It'll be like a vacation, see? You won't have to work. And the baby can stay with you, she won't be having to go stay with strangers—"

"She's not a baby," Misty Dawn said evenly. "And Blanca is not a stranger. She's the best friend I've got." She got up and went to the front room. Sweet followed, stood in the doorway watching Misty wipe her daughter's sticky face and hands with the tail of her shirt.

"A week," Sweet said. "Not even. That's all I'm asking. Just till Sunday. They'll let us see him on Sunday, I'll talk some sense into him then. Or *you* can. He'll listen to you."

"If it wasn't for Blanca and Enrique these past few months," Misty said, "I don't know what I would've done."

"I'm sorry," Sweet said. "About the truck. I really didn't have the money, I wasn't lying."

"It's not that."

"What then?" No answer. "One little week out of your life is not going to kill you!" Sweet caught herself, shifted to a lighter tone: "I'll drive you back up here on Monday. If your boss won't let you off, I'll stay and help you look for a new job. Okay? We can use my gas to go around."

"Hold still, mami." Misty fussed at her daughter, who kept pulling her face away so she could see the TV.

"When we come back," Sweet said, "I'll help you get enrolled in school. In a GED class. Like you mentioned."

Misty Dawn's expression was flat and closed. Sweet had seen that same look on Gaylene's face a thousand times when they were kids. Not refusal or defiance but a fixed, shut-down expression that said no power on earth was going to make her do what she didn't want to do—which in those days had generally been whatever it was Sweet wanted her to. Misty Dawn didn't have Gaylene's coloring or physicality, but she had surely inherited her mother's willful stubbornness. Sweet bit her lip. Please God. Don't tell me I drove all this way for nothing. She watched as Misty Dawn took her daughter onto her lap. The child nestled against her with two fingers in her mouth, her beautiful eyes drowsing closed.

"Last summer," Misty said, stroking Lucha's hair, "when we had the party. He's the only one who didn't act like they were, I don't know, poison or something."

"What are you talking about?" But Sweet knew. The memory unfolded fast: the baby's birthday party in August, all the Mexicans on one side of the yard and her family on the other, and her niece traipsing back and forth, back and forth. That was the first time Misty Dawn had tried to blend the two families, and it hadn't exactly worked. The Mexicans weren't, strictly speaking, Juanito's family—except for this Blanca person, apparently, although Sweet couldn't remember which one she was. Mostly they were guys he worked with, Misty said, fellow roofers and their families. After a grinned hello and handshakes all around, Juanito had gone back over to the Mexican side and stayed there, turning the chicken pieces on the grill, handing around beers. To Sweet, everything had seemed so foreign: actual beer cans in people's hands right out in the open, and that rapid accordion-filled music, trilling voices, all the dark-haired men standing around their big pickups in cowboy boots and snap-button shirts and the women in lawn chairs in full skirts and high heels, talking high and fast. The only English she'd heard over there had come from the mouths of the dozen or so children shouting and chasing each other—all except the baby, who'd trailed silently after her mother in a frilly red dress with so many layers of netting the skirt jutted out from her thin legs like a bell. It had been one of the longest afternoons of Sweet's life. Her husband acted awful, leaning against the church van all day with his arms folded—they'd borrowed the church van for the trip so they could bring Mr. Bledsoe's wheelchair—refusing to eat anything or even drink an iced tea, and Carl Albert had acted just like him, except that her son ate plenty and drank lots of pop.

And then, after an hour or so, Daddy had left their side of the yard and gone over to the Mexican side. He didn't speak Spanish—or not enough to not have to try to show what he meant by using a lot of hand gestures and acting everything out—but that didn't stop him. After that, Misty Dawn had just seemed to shine. She would go stand next to her grandfather and translate for him, and when she'd finished, the Mexicans would all laugh. Then she'd step back inside the little house and bring out more chips and salsa or whatever, come over to Sweet's side of the yard to see if they needed anything, go back to the Mexicans and rattle along in Spanish, make them laugh again. Sweet remembered one moment in particular, when Misty picked up her little girl and perched her on her hip, the frilly dress spilling out over her arm like a giant red poppy; she'd come sashaying broad-footed toward them, smiling, her wide heart-shaped face lit with happiness, like this was the day she'd been waiting for all her life.

Was that it? Sweet suddenly thought. Was that day of the party when her daddy's weird save-the-Mexicans thing started? Daddy had always had such a soft spot for Misty Dawn—the same as he'd had for her mother, Gaylene, and for Gaylene's mother, Carlotta.

An old hard bitterness rose up in the back of Sweet's throat. She shut her eyes. Opened them seconds later to see her niece picking up the remote and aiming it at the television.

"I need you to come take care of Dustin." Well, there it was. All that prayerful practicing, and still she'd blurted it straight out. But Sweet's needs weren't anything that would move Misty Dawn, or Dustin's needs, either. The two siblings weren't even all that close—so much difference in their ages, different fathers, different raising. They hadn't lived in the same house, or even the same town, since Dustin was a toddler and Misty Dawn a young teen. What *would* move her niece, Sweet believed, was her love for her grandfather. She tried again. "Misty, this is your family, hon. Your grandpa needs you." But Misty Dawn sat staring at the television, where a bold-featured blonde in a clingy dress and too much makeup pleaded tearfully in Spanish with a disdainful dark-haired man. Sweet looked at her watch. It was after one o'clock. She had to get on the road right now, or the boys would be home before she got there. She prayed that Mr. Bledsoe was still asleep, that Terry hadn't been trying to call. That she would get home before Dustin and Carl Albert did.

Stepping back to the kitchen for her purse and keys, Sweet asked for the right words, the last word, something, her mind awhirl with every line she could think of to guilt Misty Dawn into coming for the sake of her grandpa. But of course there was nothing Misty could do to help him—it was Sweet who needed the help. It was Dustin. She had to get the boys separated! She'd seen what her son did to him, not just that fistfight on Sunday, but last night, in the bathroom, when Dustin yelped and then went suddenly silent. She had rushed in to find Carl Albert, all hundred thirty pounds of him, pinning his little sixty-five-pound cousin to the floor, with his knee, the full terrible weight of him, pressing on the boy's throat. Dustin's face was turning blue, his arms flailing in that horrible silence, his bruised eyes wide with fear. The urgency and pain surged through her. She turned back to the living room. "Come home with me! Please."

"I can't." Misty was breathing hard and deep, the dozing child rising and falling with each breath.

"Yes you can! Give me one good reason why not!"

Misty Dawn shook her head. Her eyes were brimming red, her cheeks wet. She wouldn't look at her aunt, wouldn't say anything. She just kept shaking her head no.

Sweet was trembling so hard she could barely hold the steering wheel. Her shakes were partly due to fear, partly fury, and partly the fact she hadn't had a bite to eat all day long. Traffic on the expressway was snarled, though, and she had to claw together every part of her brain to concentrate on driving; she couldn't surrender to all the junk cartwheeling through: worry, fear, anger, at her niece, her husband, her father, the Oklahoma state legislature, the Tulsa police, her dead sister, her son. This whole mess was Gaylene's fault anyway. The end result of her not raising her kids. Gaylene's mother, Carlotta, had left her, and Gaylene had left Misty Dawn and Dustin, and here was Sweet having to clean up after them, having to clean up after her sister, like always. Teeth gritted, hands clamped, a taste in her mouth like a rancid walnut, Sweet maneuvered through the dense traffic. Carlotta. That's who you could really trace it back to.

Sweet had no recollection of her own mother, who'd died when she was a year old, but she would never, as long as she lived, forget the night her daddy brought Carlotta home. She was just six then, staying with the neighbor lady Mrs. Billy through the week while

Daddy worked the pipelines down south. One weekend he didn't come home, and Sweet was terrified because Mrs. Billy couldn't answer her questions, and then the next weekend he did come, bringing Carlotta with him. "Your new mommy," he'd said, his eyes and teeth shining, the dark-eyed woman beside him smelling of sweat and powder, smiling without meaning it, her palm on the back of Daddy's neck. Carlotta had stayed long enough to change Daddy from a laughing man to an angry man, long enough to get him to quit the pipeline and go back to farming because she couldn't stand to spend the nights alone, but even that wasn't enough, and so Carlotta had stayed only a little while longer—just long enough to deposit the tiny dark-eyed baby girl in the bassinette in the middle bedroom—and then she was gone. After that came the bad years, the terrible years, Sweet trying to take care of her baby sister while her daddy was off on one of his tears . . . oh, he would try, she would know he was trying, he'd hold off a while, months even, and Sweet would start to hope—until Daddy would come stalking into the kitchen some evening and tilt up the unplugged percolator with the spout in his mouth and pour the cold coffee down his throat, or he'd grab the Tabasco bottle off the table, shake the burning red sauce straight onto his tongue, and then she would know that the thirst was back on him. She would know, even as a little girl of seven and eight and ten, that her daddy was getting ready to drink again. And he would. The next night, or the next, he'd start trashing the front room again, or he'd be . . . hush! Quit. Don't think of it. That was a long time ago.

Her hands wouldn't stop shaking. I need to eat something, Sweet told herself. I need to check on the boys. It was three fifteen already. They would be home from school. She stopped to get gas at a QuikTrip in Muskogee, bought a Diet Dr Pepper and a Slim Jim at the counter before heading to the pay phone in the back. She ripped the plastic wrapper off the jerky with her teeth as she walked, ate quickly while she plugged in the quarters. She prayed that she might at least get home before her husband did so he wouldn't know she'd gone off and left Mr. Bledsoe alone. The phone rang eight times before her own voice answered telling her she'd reached the Kirkendalls, who couldn't come to the phone right now, but please. Leave. A message. God, she sounded like she was talking to a two-year-old. She had to change that greeting.

"Carl? Hi, honey." She paused. Maybe he was in the bathroom. "Dustin? It's Aunt Sweet. One of y'all pick up the phone." She plucked back the pull tab on the pop can, took a long swig. "I, um, I had to run some errands, but I'll be there pretty quick. Fix yourselves a sandwich, okay? There's some Oreos in the jar, you can have two apiece, no more." She waited. Maybe they were outside playing? "Go back and check on Mr. Bledsoe when you get in, see if he needs a drink or anything. And, Carl, if Daddy calls, tell him I'll call him later. I forgot my phone. All right. Y'all be good. Hear me? Don't forget to check on Mr. Bledsoe. I'll be there afterwhile." Reluctantly she hung up. She had a bad feeling.

The feeling unfurled from that tight bud of worry into dark full-blooming dread as she drove south. By the time she turned off the highway in Cedar, she wasn't a bit surprised to see an ambulance pulling out of her driveway, red lights rotating, and the preacher standing in her carport looking dazed and excited, with the boys skulking next to him, both of them scuffed-up looking and scared. But the bad feeling had started an hour ago: Why was the ambulance just now leaving? And why wasn't it using its siren? And why was it going so slow?

"Well, now, looka here, little lady," Monica Moorehouse drawled in bitter imitation. "Looks to me like you're sittin' in some mighty high cotton in this here picture, *ma'am*."

"Shittin'," Charlie said.

"I beg your pardon?"

"I believe the term of art is 'shitting in high cotton.'" Her husband gouged a slug out of his porterhouse.

"Good God, that's worse!"

"Oh, I'm sure he said *sittin'*, babe." Charlie poured out more A-1. "Dennis Langley wouldn't use profanity in the presence of a lady. I'll guarantee ya. *Ma'am*."

"Oh shut up." She took a bite of her naked baked potato, no butter, no sour cream, no tastier than warm cardboard, really. At least the steak was good. When Charlie suggested they drive down to the Stockyards for dinner since she didn't have to go to tonight's reception, she'd reluctantly agreed. She would have much preferred to eat at the little Italian place near their apartment, but Charlie said it would be a good opportunity to be seen in the afterglow of the six o'clock news. "Seen by whom?" she'd said. "Anybody," Charlie said. "Just folks." She smiled *no thanks* at the ancient waitress heading toward their booth with the iced tea

pitcher. The folksy history on the back of the menu said, "Cattlemen's Café opened its doors to hungry cowboys, ranchers, cattle
haulers and the like in 1910." It appeared to Monica that their
waitress had been on duty since day one. Her fellow lawmakers
were no doubt picking at cold chicken salad on stale croissants at
the moment. Forking up a dry chunk of iceberg from her salad
bowl, she muttered, "Langley's probably strolling around the reception hall this minute, gloating."

"He's probably strolling around wishing he had a quarter of
your press contacts and an eighth of your good looks. Pass the
butter, babe."

Tonight's reception was being hosted by the Family Planning
Council, and Leadership had decided to make a statement by having her and others on the Health and Human Services Committee bow out. It was frustrating though, really. The press conference
had gone so well. Kevin had refused to permanently fix her color
(*God, no! Six weeks minimum, darling! It will* kill *your texture!*), but
she had pleaded piteously until he'd grudgingly agreed, the little
fascist, to shampoo in a temporary tawny rinse. She'd been wearing her lovely new aqua Hugo Boss jacket, which looked fabulous
on camera, and she had only been stumped for one tiny second by
one lousy question, a pushy reporter from the *Tulsa World* wanting
statistics about the cost of defending against lawsuits. Fortunately
that little exchange hadn't made it onto any of the news programs.
Charlie had TiVoed all the local stations, plus the *Oklahoma News
Report* on OETA, and the clips had been nothing less than stellar.
Unfortunately she was going to have to wait until tomorrow morning at the capitol to bask. "Shitting in high cotton," she murmured.
"I'll never cease to be amazed by these people."

"How many times do I have to tell you not to say 'these people.'"

"I kept my voice down."

"Babe, you got to believe me: you never know who's tuned in." Charlie reached across the table for her Texas toast. "You going to eat this?"

She shook her head, turned to survey the nearby booths and tables crowded with businessmen in three-piece suits, ranchers in string ties, young people on dates, middle-aged couples sharing dessert plates. At the counter drinking coffee sat a handsome old gentleman in tooled boots, black cowboy hat, floor-length leather duster. He caught her looking at him and gave a solemn nod, touched two fingers to his hat brim. Was he somebody? She couldn't place him but he certainly looked well heeled. She dipped her head, smiled warmly, as if she recognized him.

"Representative Moorehouse?" A short, dumpy woman stood at her elbow with a whining, squirming toddler in her arms. "I just wanted to say how much we all appreciate what you're doing. Those people hang around the Home Depot parking lot on Shields every morning of the world waiting for somebody to give them a job. It's about time somebody did something. You're not my representative but I wish you were."

"Thanks so much. It's very kind of you."

"Have you thought about running for Congress?"

Monica gave her practiced self-deprecating laugh. "Right now I've got a big job to do for the people of the Eighteenth District. That's all I'm thinking about at the moment."

"Well, if you ever do decide to run, you'll get my vote. You'd get the votes of a whole lot of folks in this state who're fed up with things."

"Thanks." She shook the woman's hand, patted the little boy's leg. "I'll be sure to remember that."

"My husband says you're the only one with guts enough to do anything. He says what this state ought to do is rent one of those

big Air Force cargo jets out at Tinker and load a bunch of these
spics in it and fly out over the ocean and open the doors."

Monica couldn't think of anything to say. She smiled. The
woman turned and made her way on toward the restroom, and
Monica looked over at Charlie.

"Tell you what, babe," he said, lifting his red plastic iced tea
glass in a toast, "that Latimer D.A. is going to be falling all over
himself tomorrow announcing that felony charges are going forward. Mark my words."

"Well," she said, still a little taken aback by the woman's comment, "I hope you're right."

"How often have you known me to be wrong?"

"Almost never. Here, you want the rest of this?" She pushed her
half-eaten petite sirloin across the table and motioned the waitress
to bring her a cup of coffee. "Maybe I shouldn't have said anything
to Langley about moving the trial. I mean, that would be perfect,
but I'd rather they came up with the idea themselves."

"Don't worry, by the time all the publicity takes hold, that
D.A. will be begging to move the trial to McAlester."

"What makes you so sure? District attorneys aren't exactly
known for their aversion to publicity."

He gave her his sly look.

"Yes, all right," she said. "I believe you." She relaxed. She didn't
know what he was feeling sly about, but whatever it was, if he was
that certain, she could be certain, too. Not that she was in such a
hurry to get back to McAlester, but surely a trial wouldn't start before the end of session, when she'd have to be down there anyway.
Most legislators hurried home to their districts on weekends, but
Monica only did so when she had some Rotary Club breakfast or
FFA calf-judging event to attend. Oklahoma City was provincial
enough, but McAlester—well, what could you say about a town

where the nonchain dining choices were Tex-Mex, Tex-Mex, Tex-Mex, and Ball Barbecue? Still, she would shine in McAlester. She always had. The place had been good for her career, as Charlie so enthusiastically, and frequently, reminded her.

She'd thought he'd lost his mind when he came home one day, spread the Rand McNally on their kitchen table in Indianapolis, and stabbed his index finger in the middle of the national map. "Right there, babe," he'd said. "This little town is your destiny." She'd squinted. The black dot was no bigger than a pinprick. McAlester? Oklahoma? Where and what the hell was that? He'd had to educate her: a small town with a huge political legacy, McAlester had sent a governor twice to the state mansion, a local legislator to the state capitol for nearly as long as the building had been standing, and a U.S. representative to within a heartbeat of the presidency when Carl Albert became Speaker of the House back in the 1970s—a long time ago, Charlie said, granted, but so much the better. Lots of lost glory for folks to look back on. Nostalgia was as good as Crisco for slicking open wallets when it came to fund-raising, he said. And here was the kicker: the district was on the brink of a massive political shift straight out from under the feet of a locked-in good-old-boys yellow dog network in place since FDR days that was about to wake up on the wrong side of guns-God-and-gays and the fate of unborn babies—and none of them had seen it yet. But Charlie had seen, all the way from their apartment kitchen in Indiana.

He'd proceeded to lay out the path that very afternoon: first a run for city council, then maybe she'd do mayor for a few years, maybe not; it depended on how soon the incumbent representative looked vulnerable. Charlie had a timetable in mind. She might have to do a stint in the state Senate, he told her, after she got term limited out of the House, but hopefully that wouldn't be necessary.

Hopefully, she could make the run for national office directly. She'd be one of the youngest female members in Congress—maybe *the* youngest, if they could move fast enough. "Easy pickings, babe," he'd said, rubbing his thumb down the crease in the center of the map. "The political opportunity in this little town couldn't have been dreamed up on a platter."

Well, and everything had unfolded according to plan. Her husband might have grease spots on his tie and less than lovely table manners, but the man was a political genius. He'd developed his own media consulting business by now, served as strategist for several others in state office, but it was Monica's career that showcased his keenest instincts—and with such marvelous success. Here she was, barely into the second year of her first term, recognized not just by her own constituents two hundred miles away but by strangers right here in the middle of Cattlemen's Steakhouse in the capital city. The press talked about her "meteoric rise in state politics." She had, she'd been told, the highest profile of any politician in the state save the governor himself. Not too shabby for an underclass girl with a two-year degree from Ivy Tech Community College.

But then Charlie had predicted this all along. He'd seen her potential from the beginning, all the secret *star power*—his words—that she'd secretly known she possessed. He'd been her fill-in poli-sci instructor one semester: a Texan new to Indianapolis, fifteen years older, an adjunct lecturer with actual political experience. He'd bragged on her political "gifts," those evenings drinking beer at the Speedway Tavern, described the trajectory of her future career. So far the process had held considerably less glamour and far more work than she'd expected, but that was starting to change. Thank God she hadn't had to run for mayor. Four years on city council had been more than enough, thank you. Even sitting here in the grilled-meat-scented restaurant, her mind could instantly re-create the beige scent of that beige room in the beige Municipal Building in McAlester, the utilitarian beige carpet, faux maple wainscoting, fire-retardant-treated upholstery, and oh good God, the droning voice of the city clerk calling the roll for every vote, ward by ward by ward, meeting after meeting after meeting, ordinance-resolution-sanitation-sewage-permit-fees . . . her eyes glazed over just thinking about it.

At the state capitol, things were different. You could count on an audience, for one thing, whether for committee meetings or full session, and you didn't always know who the people lining the back of the room were, so there was that air of unpredictability and mystery; plus there was always the stir and excitement outside in the halls, all the deliciously complicated undercurrents, exchanges, personalities, history—much of which she'd understood intuitively from the get-go, and what she didn't understand or couldn't decipher, she'd had her mentors to explain to her. Plus there was Beverly and the rest of staff to do most of the grunt work, way more than city government. The fact is, from the moment she passed security in the mornings till she came home exhausted from whatever lobby-sponsored reception she'd attended that night, Monica loved her job.

"Folks," Charlie said, slurping coffee.

"What?"

"The *folks* of the Eighteenth District. Not people."

Monica sighed. "Right." The man in the duster was looking at her again. A rich rancher, she told herself. Or one of those wealthy oilmen-cum-cowboy wannabes, judging by the turquoise on his fingers. The state was full of them. She smiled. He looked away. Monica stirred sweetener into her coffee but then pushed the cup aside. She was going to have a tough enough time getting to sleep tonight, what with all the excitement at the press confer-

ence, the excellent clips on News 9 and OETA, and everything—
everything!—coming together like cream, including her new bill
ready to be introduced next week, that lovely little coup de grâce.
"Son of 1830," the pro tem had called it. Too cute by half, but she'd
take it. How frustrating that she wasn't going to see anyone who
mattered before eight o'clock tomorrow morning! It was tempting
to stop by the reception on the way home. But no, she couldn't
do that. Leadership would not approve. She slipped her lipstick
out of her bag, uncapped it, but then, glancing around, decided
against freshening her color at the table; she grabbed her purse and
excused herself to the ladies' room. She ought to take a look at her
hair anyway.

The old rancher leaned forward as she passed. "Miss Moorehouse." She paused, offered her smile. In the shadow of his hat
brim, the man's face was more handsome and wind worn and also
older than she'd thought. "I want you to know you've cost me a
hell of a lot of money. You're costing business all over this state
a lot of money. You don't know what you're messing with." He
touched his fingers to his brim again, swiveled back to face the
counter. She was speechless. She didn't know what to do but walk
on to the restroom, where she stood in front of the mirror poking
at her hair, growing more and more furious, her mind running a
tirade of everything she should have said. Of course he didn't like
it! That smug old man no doubt used illegal labor for his damn
cows or soybeans or whatever, stealing good jobs away from real
Americans, which was just exactly what her legislation was designed to put a stop to! And she would say that to him right out
loud here in public! But when she returned to their booth, the
leather stool at the counter was empty. Charlie was finishing off
a piece of coconut cream pie. "I didn't think you'd want any," he
said with his mouth full.

"Did you hear what that man said?"

"Who?"

"That old rancher in the duster."

"What rancher?"

"Never mind. Let's go." She reached for her coat. All the way back to the apartment, she fumed—and not just at the insult and the insolence of the old man, but also at her husband's obliviousness. She tried three times to explain the moment, but Charlie just shrugged.

"What d'ya expect, babe? You know you're going to get criticism any time you put yourself out there. You know that. If you can't take it, you'll have to just stay home and be talented in your room."

Stay home and be talented in your room. How she hated that line! If Charlie had used it once over the past fifteen years, he'd used it a thousand times. At the apartment she flounced up the stairs, flung her coat onto the hall chair, and stormed into the living room, where she fixed herself a drink and turned on the television, tuning it to Fox 25 Primetime News at 9.

In the thickening dark Luis sits at the table with his head in his hands. His thoughts run this way, that way, but every direction carries him to a street without exit; he cannot see where the road from this place will go. He is hungry, a little cold, though not so cold as inside the barn. He did not climb through the window this night but walked into the house through the door where, yesterday, the boy cut away the yellow tapes. Inside the kitchen Luis stood in the cold light with the refrigerator door open, looking in. No food on the grated shelves or in the drawers. He knew this already, he had eaten already the last apple. He uncapped a jar of yellow paste, dipped his finger, but the paste was sour, made his belly hurt worse, and he carefully screwed the lid down, set the jar back inside, shut the door, groped his way to this room, where he sits now waiting for the clouds to open in the night sky outside. Then maybe the moonlight will slant through and show him where to search in the black kitchen. There will be tins of beans somewhere, he thinks, and soup maybe. But the night is thick dark, and Luis cannot seem to thrust away from his chest this despair.

The clouds will not part, the despair tells him, and his sons will not find him, because they do not know he is here, and he will not find them because he had only the word written down, the strange name of the town somewhere in this Oklahoma, but the boy took the coat where the paper was hidden, and Luis cannot remember the name of the town, something like stupid monkey or hand, a name told to Beto on the telephone at the taqueria in the last message, delivered on the day Luis was readying to leave on his journey. His sons were traveling to a new town, they told Beto, a new job. They do not know that the tire broke, the truck stopped on the roadside with the people inside, no food or water, no toilet, no air—and so much time lost. By the time Luis arrived at the chicken plant where he was to meet them, his sons had been gone to the new town already a long time, and so they do not know about the men in their tan shirts and straw hats swarming the barn here, yelling, herding the people in clumps, the young women weeping, the faces of the young men steely and blank—this Luis saw from between the slats, his chest galloping, his breath knotted hard—or if his sons do know, they will think that their father has been bused back to Mexico with the others.

Maybe that is the best thing. Maybe he should put on the electric lights in every room, let the gringo sheriff with his round belly come. Then they will conduct Luis on the bus to the border and watch him walk across. All the world knows that this is how it is done. Unless they discover from the ink marks on your fingers that you have been carried to the border already many times, and then they will put you in their jails for many years before they ride you to the border again and push you out onto the street and watch with their hands on their holstered guns while you walk across the bridge. Then you will be in Matamoros or Tijuana or Ciudad Juarez, maybe five hundred miles from your village, maybe nine hundred, with no money and no means to go there except your two feet. Some of the people will telephone their families and ask for money for the bus to return home, but there is no one in Ar-

royo Seco for Luis to call. His wife, Margarita, has been dead almost ten years, and his daughter, Ausencia, is also dead now, since
the summer. Cut down on the street by gunfire. Cut down for
no reason. Her children scattered to live with the relatives of her
husband, who has been working in the North for three years. No
family now in Arroyo Seco. No reason, he thinks, to return there.
He could die here this night. Inside this cold house. It would be no
different than if he disappeared in the desert. He will be one of the
vanished ones. His sons will wonder a little maybe—so the despair
tells him—and then they will forget.

No! Luis chastises himself. This is a sin, not to hope.

He leans forward, presses his forehead against the hard table,
prays now the same as he prayed on the journey inside the creaking truck, the supplications repeated then without ceasing, without count because he had no beads to count them, until the peace
would come in his heart, until he could breathe, until he was not
oppressed by the small space and the smell and the darkness. Then
would he see Margarita as she had been when she was young, in
the cornfield, on the path to the water well, in the churchyard, her
shy eyes looking sideways, smiling. He would see his daughter,
Ausencia, as a tiny girl, and his seven sons, each one a little size
smaller than the last, Cesár, Eduardo, Mateo, Hedilberto, Tomás,
Federico, and the youngest, Miguel, whose face Luis held longest
before him, though he has not seen Miguelito since he was a youth
of thirteen years riding away in the back of a hay truck, as the
others had ridden away, one by one, year by year, in a wood cart,
a produce truck, a bus, and who would have believed that Luis
himself would one day make the journey? But it was Miguel who
had written the letter soon after Ausencia was killed: Come, Papa,
there is work here, our cousin owns a good business, Eduardo is
here, Tomas says he will maybe come from California. What is

there for you in Arroyo Seco? Come live with us, come work with us, you can send money home for the children, and when they are older, we will bring them here, we are their uncles, they will work with us, they will know their cousins in the North, our sons and daughters, you will know them, too, your grandchildren, come, Papa. Please come. And Luis had been persuaded, not knowing that he is too old—not too old to work, no. He is still strong, he can work as well as his sons, he knows this. But there was not a way for him to understand until it was too late that he is already too old for the journey. *GodSaveYouMaryYouAreFullOfGrace TheFatherIsWithYouBlessedAreYouAmongAllTheWomenAnd BlessedIsTheFruitOfYourWombJesusSaintedMaryMotherOf GodPrayForUsSinnersNowAndInTheHourOfOurDeath.*

In the dark place behind his eyes she looks the same as on the walls of the church, hands clasped in prayer, golden rays circling her crown and blue robe. This is not a holy vision. Luis knows that he is not humble enough to receive a holy vision. It is an imagining, brought on by his hunger, but the image brings peace in the same way the images of his young wife and daughter and sons brought peace on the journey. Inside his chest the weight eases. He turns his face to the side. The room is lighter now, a tiny lifting of the darkness. In the next moment he knows what he must do. Very simple. He must find the boy. He does not know how this will be, but he believes that Our Lady will show him. Because the boy has the coat, the coat has the paper, the paper has the name of the town where his sons are working, *guaymono, guaymano,* Luis cannot remember how it reads, but the boy speaks a little spanish, he will tell Luis where this place is. Maybe he will tell him how he can go there. Maybe it is not very far.

He hears a small sound then, and his heart jumps. He sits up rapidly, prepares to run. On the far side of the table stands the boy.

Luis thinks at first this must be a new imagining, materialized from his hunger, but then he smells the coat the boy holds in his hands. The odor is vivid, real. Not an imagining.

I have your coat, the boy says. He starts forward, but Luis flinches. *Pardon me,* the boy says. He places the coat on the table. The odor is familiar, the smell of manure transferred from the corral to the coat when Luis fell as the people pushed and shoved climbing into the truck. The scent is not sharp now, as it was in the beginning, but muted, soft. How strange, Luis thinks, to be glad for the smell of old cow dung. *Thank you,* he whispers.

I have food for you also. In the . . . The boy gestures outside toward the barn. *I look there but I dont see to you. The food is in my . . .* He shakes his head, makes the motion of putting his two arms through straps and hoisting something heavy onto his back. *I dont know the word.*

Backpack, Luis says. He reaches across the table for the coat, searches the pockets for the paper, and holds it out to the boy. *¿You know this name?*

The boy carries the paper into the kitchen, opens the refrigerator door, lifts the paper to the cold light so he can read. Guymon, he says, and looks back at Luis.

¿Is a town?

Yes. I think so.

¿A town or a city?

A town, I think.

¿Where is this town?

I dont know. The boy returns to the table, gives the paper to Luis. *Is possible I can say to some person to tell me.*

¡No! Please. If they know I am here it will go badly for me. For my sons also.

I dont speak nothing, no problem. I . . . The boy blinks, pushes his hair back from his eyes. *Tomorrow I bring more food. If I am able. Is difficult. My aunt and my uncle . . . they are living me when my grandfather . . . while my grandfather . . . I dont know the words. The . . . police take him.*

The police. Yes, I know. I saw this with my eyes. ¿Then the old one is your grandfather?

The old one. I suppose. He is not much old. A little old. Like you. The boy talks in english then. Luis shakes his head to show he doesn't understand. The boy looks around a moment. *It makes cold, ¿no?* He steps back into the kitchen, clicks the refrigerator door closed, and returns, bringing a box of matches. The boy disappears into the next room, which is very dark. In a moment Luis sees through the archway an orange glow. *¡Come here!* the boy calls. When Luis goes to the next room, he can see the shapes of chairs and a large sofa in the steady glowing light from a gas stove on the wall. The boy stands in front of the stove holding his flat palm in the air above it. He passes his palm back and forth. *Warm,* he says. *Very . . . pretty.* Luis goes to the stove, stands beside the boy, warming his hands. *¿How are you called?* the boy asks.

Luis Jorge Ramirez Celayo.

My name is Dustin.

I heard your uncle calling. Luis cups his hands, makes the voice of the uncle softly: *¡Du-u-s-tee!*

Dustin or Dustee. The boy shrugs. *The other or the other.*

If you want to capture the mare you will have to move more slowly, and then very sleek and fast.

The boy looks up. *¿What do you call her?*

Mare.

¿Not horse?

Horse is one word, but mare is better. Mare is the right word for the female. She was teasing you. She wanted more sugar. A cowboy must learn to move suavely. I worked many years with the horses. I could show you. The boy answers rapidly in english. *Pardon me,* Luis says. *I dont understand.*

A moment, please. Is necessary I have more words. I have a book. He crosses the room, makes scrabbling noises in the drawer of a small table near the door. He flicks on a tiny flashlight with a narrow white beam and goes into the dining room. After a moment Luis can hear him in the far part of the house: thumps, small thuds, another sharp word in english. The boy returns with a small fat yellow book in his hand. He sits on the sofa and shines his little flashlight on the pages. Slowly, tediously, using bad spanish grammar and many turnings of the dictionary pages, he makes Luis understand: His mother is dead. He lives here in this house with his grandfather but his grandfather hides the mexicans and he will be in the prison a long time. The cousin of the boy has told him this. He wants to capture the mare but he has one big problem. His uncle carried away the bridle. Now he must walk to see his mother.

But you said your mother is dead, Luis says. The boy goes suddenly silent. He sits with his hands in his lap, unmoving, his head lowered, as if he is ashamed to be caught—doing what? Telling stories? Luis does not want to shame the boy. *Maybe I didnt understand,* he says. *I dont hear very well.* The boy says nothing. After a moment Luis asks quietly, *¿She is alive then, your mother?*

The boy shakes his head no. He doesn't look up.

¿A ghost?

¡No, not a phantom! She is . . . He flicks on the flashlight, thumbs through the pages. *A voice.*

¿You can see her?

No. I hear only. My mother is . . . a spirit voice. Suddenly the boy stands. *I go now. I think my aunt . . .* He speaks rapidly again, his fingers plucking fiercely at the thin pages of the book. The only word Luis recognizes is *hospital*.

¿Your aunt has sickness?¿She is in the hospital?

No. Yes. There is a man who my aunt . . . ¡oh, I dont know the words! This night my aunt goes to the hospital with a person. Later, when she arrives to her house, if she is not able to see me, she wants . . . to see for me here.

¿She will come search for you here?

The boy nods. *If my aunt sees you also, is maybe a problem more big.*

Luis takes out the paper with the name of the town written by Beto. *I must go here, where my sons are working.*

Guymon, the boy says.

Gai-mun, Luis repeats after him.

¿But how? the boy says.

Well, Luis says. *This is a problem.*

I have a good idea. When I bring more food, I bring also . . . He looks through the dictionary. *Ah*. He points to the page. *Is almost the same word. ¿See? In the english and the spanish.* Map.

Sweet smiled again at the sheriff, who lifted two fat fingers as the phone rang. Holloway plunked his boots down from his desk and pivoted a half turn in his chair so he could talk with his back to her. Sweet took the opportunity to peer at the small gray monitor on the side wall, carefully watching the shifting, grainy black-and-white images. So far none of them had shown the inside of a cell, just the empty cinder-block hallway in front and the base of a row of bars. The camera switched to a second view of the concrete floor, different angle, then a third view—what good was that? A prisoner could be hanging himself inside his cell this minute, or shooting dope, or slitting another prisoner's throat, you could be looking right at this thing and never know it. Lord, what made her think such awful stuff? She watched too much TV. She hadn't slept hardly any. Sweet rubbed her eyes. When was her daddy going to come to his stupid senses?

"Well, you heard wrong, buddy," Sheriff Holloway said. "I don't know where you're getting your information, but we don't pull that kind of shi—shenanigans around here. All right. Yup. Uh-huh. You bet." And the sheriff hung up, swiveled around to face Sweet again. "You're up bright and early, little lady."

"Yeah, I know. I didn't even know if you'd be open."

"Always open, always open. Crime don't ever sleep. So, what can I do you for?"

"I need to see Daddy."

"Well, all right. Men's visitation starts at one thirty Sunday.

"No, I mean I need to see him today. Now. This morning."

The sheriff snorted. "You know I can't do that." The phone rang again. He winked at her, wheeled to face the back wall. "Sheriff's office. Yes, ma'am. Oh, he's still here all right. Well, now, I really couldn't say. That'd be up to the district attorney. All right. Yes, ma'am, I sure will. You, too." He turned back to Sweet. "That daddy of yours is one popular fella."

"Popular."

"Lots of folks wanting to know how he's doing. That just now was an aide to one of our state representatives, if you can believe it. Had a reporter from Tulsa down here yesterday, and then I got a call from an ACLU lawyer last night about seven, said he wanted to represent him. I said he's welcome to represent him but I was going to have to get an okay from Mr. Brown first, and far as I could tell Bob Brown don't aim to get himself a lawyer, that's what he told me. But I took the guy's number, got it around here someplace if you want it." The phone rang again. The sheriff grinned. Sweet tried to listen, but her ears were roaring. A lawyer, a reporter, a state representative . . . this was crazy. She heard Holloway say something about a press conference—a press conference! Good Lord. She got to her feet. The sheriff glanced at her. She sat back down. "We'll be talking to you," he said, clapped the receiver down. "Never seen anything like it."

"Ten minutes, Arvin. That's all I'm asking."

The sheriff tilted back in his chair with his thumbs in his belt. His tight little potbelly strained his khaki shirtfront like he had a prize watermelon under there. "You know I can't be playing favor-

ites, Sweet. Let one family bend the rules just because I grew up
with their daddy, but then don't let somebody else. I'd be out of a
job in no time."

"Can't you make an exception?"

His gaze poured over her, chest to thigh to boot, back up
to her face again. Arvin Holloway had a reputation for a lot of
things, good politicking, bad rule breaking, a twitchy trigger
finger—he'd shot at least three men in the line of duty—but one
thing he was really known for was his womanizing. Sweet had
even heard he slept with women prisoners for favors, though she
wasn't sure she believed it. Surely the old fart was smarter than
that. "I don't know about exceptions," he said. "What kind of
exceptions?"

Sweet gritted her teeth and smiled. "Five minutes, Arv," she
said. "I promise I won't tell a soul. I'll, uh, I'll bake you some
cookies."

Holloway barked out a laugh. "Cookies, eh? You slay me."
Again the raking look. Sweet held on to her smile. "All right
then." Holloway chuckled as he hoisted himself out of the
chair, came around the desk, brushing unnecessarily close as he
strolled to the door. "This way." He led her to a cramped break
room painted the same cobalt blue as the hall, where a greasy-
looking microwave sat on the counter next to a burnt-smelling
coffeemaker. "Help yourself." He nodded at the half-empty pot.
"Sweets from the Sweet," he said, still chuckling, and left.

She waited a long time, pacing up and down, her mind scat-
tering like barn cats. When she left the house this morning, she'd
had a simple plan: cash in that retirement CD, pay the fine, make
her daddy sign those papers and come home! But she'd gotten
to Wilburton too early, the bank wasn't open, and now here was
all this other stuff, these phone calls, a state politician, what did

that mean? Sweet stood in front of the bulletin board reading the same words on the same posters again and again, FBI's Most Wanted, a notice to employees to clean up after themselves. Her jaw ached. She had the same reeling feeling she'd had yesterday in the ER waiting room, like everything was snowballing, piling in, piling up. A broken hip. That was the beginning of the end for old people; she'd heard that a hundred times. The guilt was horrible. The guilt was too much. And the boys suspended from school for fighting, the preacher said—suspended! And of course she couldn't get Terry on the phone, of course she couldn't. The doctor showed her the X-rays, right femur at the hip socket, it was going to need a metal plate, he said, maybe a rod implant, anyway surgery too complicated for this little Wilburton hospital—they were going to have to take Mr. Bledsoe on to McAlester Regional, and Sweet had stared at the doctor's face, thinking, Why? What the hell *for*? He can't walk anyway! He can't talk! He's got to be bathed and diapered and fed with a spoon from a Gerber baby food jar, please explain to me what is the point! Aloud she'd said, "Yes, all right. When?" And Doctor Woodson had answered, his voice puzzled, "Why, right now."

She'd looked then at her son slumped in the waiting room chair, a bad nick on his chin, his bottom lip jutted, and the preacher next to him trying to get him to play hangman on the back of an old church bulletin. Dustin was sitting outside on the curb, no jacket on, his shoulders hunched; she could see him through the glass doors. It wasn't their fault, Carl Albert kept blubbering from the backseat all the way to Wilburton: "Them kids jumped *us*! They called us honky wetbacks, they said our grandpa's a beaner smuggler! Where *were* you, Mom? We couldn't get you on the *phone*! Where's Daddy? When's Daddy coming? I think my chin is broken, I might have to have a operation, it wasn't my fault!" Thank goodness the preacher had followed them in his car, she'd thought when she saw the ambulance guys wheeling the gurney toward her with the old man on it moaning *oh, oh, ohhhh*. She'd felt like tossing his Medicare card at them, saying, *Take him!*, but of course she couldn't do that; she had to send the boys home with the preacher and follow the ambulance on to McAlester Regional, because what if they ran a blood test and saw how much painkiller he had in him? But then the old man was groaning so pitifully on the gurney that she'd thought hopefully, Well, if he's hurting this bad, maybe the meds are all gone from his system—oh God, oh God, she hated remembering that!

Sweet whirled away from the bulletin board, stalked to the dirty cabinet, and poured herself a Styrofoam cup of coffee, tasted it, dumped it in the sink. The break room door opened.

He wasn't wearing handcuffs. He had on the orange coveralls. His glasses were smudgy but his hair was combed. The sheriff came in behind him and went to the coffeemaker. "You want one, Bob?"

"No, that's all right." Her father sat down at the little table. "Morning, Sweet," he said like it was a normal day, a normal morning, like the world wasn't falling apart. The sheriff poured himself a cup of the bitter stuff, leaned back against the counter, sipping it, watching Sweet over the white Styrofoam brim.

She didn't bother with the smile this time. "I'd like to talk to him alone if you don't mind, Arvin."

"Oh, I mind," Holloway said. The gun in his hip holster rode low at his side, the tight mound of gut pouching over. "I'm bending the rules far enough for y'all this morning. How do I know you're not fixing to slip him a weapon or something?"

"Give me a break."

"I am," Holloway said. "That's just exactly what I'm doing."

She looked to her father, who said, "Sit down, Sweet." He nodded at the grime-smeared plastic chair opposite him. She was furious, but there was nothing she could do. She sat. After a moment she leaned forward and said in as private a voice as she could manage, "As soon as the bank opens I'm going to get the money for that contempt fine."

"How's Tee?" her father said.

"What?"

"Your husband. What's he up to this morning?"

"He's at work, what's that got to do with anything?" She lowered her voice again. "Daddy, you got to sign those papers and come home now. Dustin ditched school and ran off the other morning."

At that moment the girl who minded the front desk stuck her head in the door. "Sheriff, I think you better come out here a minute. There's people with cameras."

"What kind of people?"

"Like, that woman from Channel 2 that goes all over?"

It seemed to Sweet that Holloway's strained khaki shirtfront strained harder to meet over his puffed chest. "Be right there, Cheryl. Sorry, folks, interview's over. Y'all are going to have to visit on Sunday afternoon like everybody else."

"Just two more minutes," Sweet said. "Please."

"They're waiting to talk to you, Sheriff," the girl said.

"All right, sugar. Go get Beecham, tell him to come escort the prisoner." Holloway swaggered to the door, turned and pointed a finger at Sweet, made a little clicking noise at the back of his teeth like cocking a trigger. "Oatmeal raisin." He laughed his greasy laugh and strolled out, leaving the door open to the empty hall.

"Ran off where?"

"Back out to the farm. Me and Terry both drove out there looking, he hid from us the whole day, I didn't even find him till way up after dark! I can't take care of him, Daddy! You've seen how him and Carl Albert fight, and then on top of that, yesterday afternoon—oh never mind. Just come home, that's all. I'll get you the money for that contempt fine. I'll take it out of savings, you can pay us back."

"No, now, it's going to take a little more time, hon. But me and Jesus got to see this thing through."

"Quit calling him that!"

Her father gazed at her quietly a moment, then he stood up and went to the cabinet, poured himself a cup of coffee, brought it back to the table. "Let me know when your snit's finished," he said.

Sweet was so furious she almost bolted right then, but her troubles came swarming, and she took a deep breath, stilled herself. Her voice was controlled, if shaking, when she said, "All right, Daddy. Why don't you just tell me. What is this 'thing' you and that . . . pastor have got to see through?"

"And Jesus."

She crimped her mouth.

"I'm not making a joke, honey. I mean it, the Lord Jesus and Brother Jesús and me, we're all in this together. Things just took a kindly unexpected turn."

"What turn?"

"Arvin Holloway raiding my farm Friday evening, for one thing. But we decided to just go with it."

"Who decided? You and that Mexican pastor?"

"And the Lord."

Oh, if that wasn't her daddy all over. A man of faith, yes, no denying it, but somehow her daddy's faith and the Lord's name always seemed to cover just whatever the blue blazes he felt like doing. "You tell me how you sitting in jail helps the Lord! Or any-body else, for that matter."

"Somebody's got to stand up to that law."

"Oh, for crying out loud—and meanwhile you're just going to let Dustin run wild? He got kicked out of school yesterday, you know. For fighting. He was defending *you*." She'd been holding on to that bit of information for her trump card, and she could see it working on her father, his jaw tightening. She surged toward him. "See, that's what I mean! I can't control him."

"Bring him up here and let me talk to him."

"The sheriff's not going to let a ten-year-old boy come in here! He barely let me."

"Never mind about Holloway, he'll be all right. Have you talked to Misty?" Her father ran his fingers back through his thinning hair. For the first time she saw the blackened scab on his scalp, near his bald spot.

"What happened to your head?"

"Nothing. It's fine. Georgia, honey, listen. I didn't ask for this. A thousand times since Friday I've prayed for this cup to pass from me, but apparently that ain't the way the Lord wants it."

"How the hell do you know what the Lord wants!" Sweet bit her lip. "I'm sorry, Daddy. I'm sorry." But the next instant she flew mad again. "You absolutely *did* ask for it! How did fourteen Mexi-cans get in your barn? The Lord didn't fly them in there on gos-samer wings!"

"I wasn't out hunting up folks in need of shelter, Sweet. They came to me."

"How?"

"You don't need to know that."

"I need to know something! I need to know what in the world you think you're doing! It's that Mexican preacher, right? Garcia.

He's the one put you up to this nonsense!" This is what her husband kept saying, and really, it's the only thing that made sense.

"What did He say?"

"Who, Terry?"

"The Lord Jesus. In the Olivet discourse. Matthew twenty-five."

"I don't know! He said a lot of things! Most of which nobody in their right mind could live up to!" She reached for her keys. "I'll be back as soon as the bank opens."

"It's too late, Sweet. But don't worry, hon. Please don't. 'All things work together for good to them that love God.'"

"This is not *good*, Daddy. It's a freaking mess!"

"I'll talk to Dustin. He'll settle down."

"It's not Dustin! It's you! What's the matter with you? The judge was all set to let you go, and then you stand there like a dope and piss him off!"

"You don't want to plead Not Guilty to a charge that's bogus to begin with."

"*I* wouldn't want to put myself in a position to have to!"

"No," her father said. "I guess you wouldn't."

She glared at him. "Terry's right. You've spent too much time with those people. They've got your mind all twisted."

"Reckon he would know."

"What's that supposed to mean?" Sweet said.

"Ask him."

A deputy was standing in the doorway, the same hulking guy who'd sat in the courtroom. Her father got to his feet. "I'll square things with Holloway," he said. "Bring Dusty on up this afternoon." The deputy stepped back for her father to walk in front, and they disappeared down the hall. Sweet stood confused and furious. But nothing's settled! her mind cried out. We didn't get anything done! She looked around vaguely, then wandered along the corridor to the front of the building, where she waited for the girl behind the glass to buzz her out.

Coming out into early morning sunlight was like stepping out of a dark movie theater. She blinked, saw the logoed van in the alley, turned quickly the opposite direction, and nearly smacked into Sheriff Holloway talking to a pretty brunette holding a microphone. "Well, here's his daughter right here," the sheriff said. "You might want to talk to her."

Bob Brown followed the broad khaki back of Deputy Beecham along the cobalt hall. The Olivet discourse. Probably his daughter hadn't known what he was talking about. For such a strong Baptist and Christian, Sweet's biblical knowledge was sadly lacking, in Brown's opinion. He attributed this primarily to some of the larger failings on his part. That, and the fact she hung around that bunch who preached Salvation like a house afire but sorely neglected the Master's teachings. Maybe if he'd said "Sermon on the Mount of Olives" she'd have known, though probably not the right verse: "I was a stranger, and ye took me in." He should have been clearer.

At the end of the painted hallway he stood with his teeth clamped and his shoulders squared, waiting for the big deputy to unlock the steel door. He dreaded going back to the drunk tank— all that cold concrete, the relentless light and noise, the absolute boredom, no matter how much they prayed and sang. Not that he hadn't been through it before, or would have turned back now if he had the choice. Still, just dawdling in the outside hall a few minutes felt good. "What's today, Darrel? Thursday?"

"Wednesday."

"Huh," Brown said. "Time passes slow."

"That's what I hear." The deputy swung the steel door open,

motioned Brown into the cinder-block passageway. The drunk tank was here at the near end, no need to walk past the crowded, noisy main run where they'd started out their first night, him and Garcia, sitting on the cell floor next to the reeking urinal, praying and singing hymns—until one of the tattooed young men jumped Bob Brown halfway through the fifth chorus of "I Have Decided to Follow Jesus," cutting the top of his head with his bare knuckle. Garcia had tried to help, several others mixed in it, and soon the jailer was running along the hall, yelling, with his hand on his baton. That was when Brown and Garcia got moved here to the drunk tank, and here they remained. "Reckon y'all are going to need your tank back come Saturday evening?" Brown said.

"Might could." Deputy Beecham unlocked the cell door. "We generally get a few takers along about time the Hartshorne bars close." He shut the cell door behind Brown, relocked it. Garcia watched from his cement bunk, his round, shiny face expectant. This was the first time either of them had been let out since Sunday. Brown waited for the deputy to leave. When the steel outer door clanged closed, he sat on the second bunk—a poured concrete slab jutting from the cinder block. Everything here was designed to be easily hosed down. "That was Sweet come to see me," he said.

Garcia's face showed his surprise. "The sheriff will allow visitors in the week?"

"Arvin Holloway does things just however he wants to."

"This is true." Garcia studied his friend's lowered gaze, his creased frown. "How is your boy doing?"

"Not real great, Sweet said. But then Sweet tends to the hysterical." Brown began scraping one laceless work boot back and forth on the cement floor. "Tell you what, amigo," he said after a moment, "this standing mute is a lot harder than it looks."

"This also is true."

Early on that first night a redheaded kid from Clayton had leaned toward them from his steel bunk. "*Pssst,* dudes," the kid said. "When that judge asks how you plead? Keep your mouths shut." The kid had canted his eyes around the cell to see if anybody was listening; he was doing a two-year bid for possession. He fancied himself a pretty shrewd jailhouse lawyer. "Standing mute, they call it," the kid said. "You're like telling them this is bullshit, see? The charge is bogus. These proceedings ain't legit." At once Jesús Garcia and Bob Brown had looked at each other. Was this not evidence of the Master's hand? Jailed for violating an un-Christian law and already, hardly an hour into their jailing, they'd been given a quiet Christian way to make a stand. The Lord speaks in many ways, through many people. Might he not speak through a young drug dealer in a jail cell as well as anyone else?

Later, after they'd been moved here to the drunk tank, the two men had knelt on the cold floor and made their prayerful vow: they would bear all things, believe all things, hope all things, endure all things, in surrender to the Father's will in this matter. Plus, they would follow the advice of the redheaded kid from Clayton. So far they'd had no reason to doubt.

"Dustin will be all right," Brown said. "I told Sweet to bring him up here and let me talk to him."

"The sheriff will allow this as well?"

"I don't know." Brown stared at the floor. After a moment he added, "That prelim's sure looking a mighty ways away, ain't it? What is it? Ten more days?"

"Fifteen."

This, then, had been their plan: to stand mute to the charges and remain jailed until the preliminary hearing as a way to deny the legitimacy of that law—the redheaded kid from Clayton had explained this all to them, although he'd used coarser words—and meanwhile the outside attention would gather. If they pleaded Not Guilty at the arraignment, bonded out, went home to fight the law with lawyers and all the regular ways, well, what kind of attention would that get? Neither of them were political men, but you didn't have to be political to know that jailing a Pentecostal pastor and a Christian white man would make some news. And Bob Brown had had enough run-ins with the law as a young man to know that if a fellow couldn't make bail, well, there in the jailhouse you sat. It had come as a complete surprise to him in the courtroom when the judge started to release him. He'd gone on staring at the judge in silence, not because the idea of a contempt charge had occurred to him, but because he'd set out to stand mute and hadn't figured out what to do next.

But then, it had worked, hadn't it? More evidence of the Lord's hand. They'd been remanded to custody—Brown on the contempt charge and Garcia until the court could come up with a translator for a new arraignment hearing—and already the publicity was starting to build. Hadn't he just heard there was a reporter outside talking to Holloway this minute? Things were working together for good, just the way the Lord promised, because he and Garcia had aimed all along to stay in jail, and Arvin Holloway wanted it that way, and now, as a matter of fact, so did District Attorney Tom Waters. Each man had his reasons—the D.A.'s, political; Brown's and Garcia's, principled; and Sheriff Arvin Holloway, as Brown told himself, so he could keep his fat nose in the public eye to show off.

So. Two more weeks until the preliminary, Brown thought. Dustin could hold on that long. After that, they would see what the hand of the Lord would do. Maybe He'd throw the law to the courts, hang it up there. This was the suggestion of Garcia's church friends in Texas. Or maybe He would send them a high-powered attorney to help them fight it. They had discussed the different possibilities.

That law. Even before the sheriff's raid last Friday, Bob Brown had despised it, although he'd understood almost nothing about what it contained. But from the day it took effect last November he had seen the growing fear, in the Heavener church services, among the busboys and wait staff at La Abuelita. And then came that night just before Thanksgiving when his granddaughter called, sobbing so hard on the phone she couldn't get the words out: her husband had been taken. Brown remembered standing in the kitchen, trembling, the phone pressed tight to his ear, all the pain and grief and rage in his granddaughter's voice pouring through the line, and him powerless to do one thing in this world to stop it or fix it. Looking back, Brown knew that was the moment that changed things. "This ain't right, Lord," he'd whispered after he hung up. "You know it ain't. Somebody's got to do something!"

Well, and he'd have done something himself, if he'd had any notion of what to do, or how. There was nothing he could do for Juanito now, even if he'd had the kind of money it takes to pay an immigration lawyer. About all the help he could think of to offer Misty Dawn was to send a little money order now and then, whenever he could scrape together a few bucks. He'd griped pretty loudly about the new law to some of the local men sitting around drinking coffee in the snack bar at the E-Z Mart, but that was sure enough spitting in the wind. Useless. Helpless. Bob Brown had done nothing but fume and pray and wait on the Lord Jesus to do something.

Which He did. Of course He did. No mistaking the Lord's hand when He sets it in motion, Brown believed. And so that blustery winter evening, a little over a week ago, when his friend the Pentecostal pastor Jesús Garcia drove over from Heavener to ask for his help, Bob Brown hadn't hesitated. "Sure thing," he'd said. "Bring them on over. You reckon you could get hold of some cots? Maybe a few extra blankets?" The pastor nodded. "I think it will be only a few nights," he said. "Possibly two or three. But perhaps you will want to pray about this first? Because this new law, you know, it makes harsh penalties to anyone sheltering un-documented workers."

No, Brown had not known that. He knew it now. He definitely knew it now. The image seared through him: Dustin coming down the back steps, the deputy's hand clamped on his shoulder. "Unh," Brown grunted aloud. Abruptly he pushed himself up from the bunk, walked the few steps to the thick glass block that served as a window. The glass was set deep in the wall and frosted opaque, the view further obscured by four thick steel bars embedded in the cinder block on this side. Still, Brown stood squinting at the murky square as if he could see through it. "Dustin's a good boy," he murmured. "He'll do all right."

"Maybe you could pay the fine and be released," Garcia offered gently. "We have been here five days now. Perhaps this is all the Lord asks."

Brown shook his head. "You know Holloway's liking all this attention too much. It's not going to be that easy now." He turned from the window and began to pace the small perimeter of the cell again. After a few turns he stopped, stood with his hands gripping the bars, staring at the empty hallway, then he reversed direction, walked the square counterclockwise.

In silence, the pastor watched him. The two men were as different in their temperaments as they were different, in some ways, in their faith: both were born-again believers, both prayed aloud to the Father in the name of the Son. But Bob Brown talked constantly in his mind to the Son Jesus, while Jesús Garcia communed in silence with the Holy Spirit. He'd been raised a Catholic in Texas, but he had come to his true faith in a great ecstatic surrender at the age of thirty-one. Baptized once in water at a tiny storefront Pentecostal church in Waco, he'd been baptized many times since in the gifts of the Spirit. This was the source of his peace.

Their first night here, as they'd sat on the floor next to the foul urinal singing hymns and praying, Bob Brown had remained agitated, fidgety. A dozen times he'd gotten up to make his way around the crowded cell, drawing the jeering attention of the young men, but Garcia had sat serenely. If an earthquake had come along at midnight to shake open the cell doors, as happened for Paul and Silas at Philippi, he would not have been surprised. Signs and wonders continue unto this day, the pastor knew that. The fact that the people had been in Brown's barn in the first place, that was the first sign. How else explain why Garcia himself had been warned that the raid was coming? Not the raid by the deputies on Brown's barn, but the first one, by *la migra*, on the poultry plant in Heavener.

More than a week ago he'd received a phone call from a white Methodist minister in Oklahoma City, a prayerful man whose secretary's brother's first cousin happened to work on the cleaning crew that serviced the Immigration and Customs Enforcement offices in the capital city. And so when ICE agents stormed A-OK Foods in Heavener last Thursday, they'd found the processing plant running at half capacity, utilizing a skeleton crew, and when they checked the green cards of the remaining workers, they found them all in order. The manager had blustered a confused story about workers having been laid off "due to a sudden nation-wide reduction in demand for chicken parts," and meanwhile, the undocumented workers were already safe in Brown's barn—safe, that is, until the county sheriff and his men pushed their way inside Friday night.

Garcia's heart was gripped for a moment, remembering the khaki-clad men with their loud voices and freckled hands, how they'd brandished their pistols, corralling the people, prodding them into the two waiting vans—even the pregnant girl, her large belly telling the men to take care, but they did not. Yet even in this Pastor Jesús Garcia could see the workings of the Holy Spirit. Not the manhandling! No. That would be the work of the Devil, mani-fested, he believed, in the bullying, bellowing person of the county sheriff. But it could not have been coincidence that the people had been kept safe from *la migra* in Heavener only to be taken by local officials from Brown's barn.

No simple coincidence that Garcia himself happened also to be there—running late, yes, a flat tire on an unpaved back road, the long wait for a stranger to come along with a tire jack to help him, because the pastor had loaned his own jack away. Then the bumpy drive to Cedar, more than an hour, so that Garcia arrived not in the late afternoon to make arrangements to move the people from Bob Brown's barn, as he had planned to do, but well after dark. The sheriff and his men poured into the barnyard only a few mo-ments later. And so, Jesús Garcia believed, their arrest and jailing, his and Brown's, must be because the Holy Spirit willed it. And why would that be but that they were to serve as the public faces to test this new law that struck such fear and separated families? Bob Brown's face because his was white. Jesús Garcia's face because his was not.

Brown's gritty voice broke the silence. "'And we know that all things work together for good to them that love God,'" he quoted the apostle.

"'To them who are the called according to His purpose," Garcia completed the verse in his Spanish-tinged accent. Brown returned to the cement bunk and sat scraping his boot against the concrete floor. After a moment Garcia said, "If you decide to go, my friend, this would be all right. Don't you think? Much has already been accomplished."

"Such as what?" Bob Brown asked.

A good question, though not one the pastor could readily answer.

Sweet slammed in the house, said not one word to the boys eating cold cereal in front of the television. If Terry wanted their son grounded for fist-fighting, he could blame well do it himself. She went straight to her room and took a shower, standing in the cramped stall sobbing while the water pounded down. She didn't care anymore. She did not give a damn! She wrapped up in her robe and sat in the front room watching cartoons with the kids, and she did not call the school to set up a parent-teacher conference, or even to find out how long they were going to be suspended, and she did not call the preacher to tell him Mr. Bledsoe's surgery was scheduled for eight o'clock tomorrow morning so he could get the prayer chain going, and she did not, *especially* did not, try to reach her husband on his cell phone. Instead she fixed the boys peanut butter crackers and instant oatmeal and tried not to think about the empty room down the hall or what she'd said to that reporter.

She told herself she wasn't going to watch, but when noon rolled around, she picked up the remote and switched channels, told her whining son he could like it or lump it, y'all go play in the bedroom; then she sat in her husband's chair, gnawing her cuticles through the newscaster's cheerful promise of freezing rain in the forecast, plus details on the latest Tulsa shooting, and then, boom, there was Arvin Holloway in his felt Stetson hat with his big nose and his drawly voice making it sound like he was the only thing standing between law-abiding Americans and the masses of river-swimming hordes, which was just stupid—how many Mexicans lived in Oklahoma even before that law? Not many. And now there were less. Then the camera's eye swung toward a redheaded woman sneaking past with her jean jacket buttoned crooked. It took Sweet a second to recognize herself. God. She looked like Reba McEntire on a bad hair day. "Miss Brown," the reporter chirped, "is it true your father intends to serve as a test case for House Bill 1830?" Sweet's face scowled on the screen. That moment had felt like an eternity when it happened, but on the clip it only lasted a second before she turned and walked away. The reporter hurried around in front, thrusting out the microphone. "How does it feel as his daughter to be at the vortex of this contentious issue?" Sweet remembered that part, remembered trying to walk on around her; she didn't remember batting her hand at the microphone like that. The reporter's bubbly voice babbled on: "Some have indicated there may be a personal element at work here for your father. Would you care to comment?"

On the screen the person who was at once herself and not herself stopped. She glared at the reporter. "Hell, yes, it's personal!" she snapped. "My daddy's a born-again Christian, he takes that *personally*! Is that what you mean?" The reporter was young, she was pretty, but she was good. She segued without a blink right to the next question: "So you're saying your father is part of the new evangelical sanctuary movement?" "I'm not saying anything! My daddy's got a conviction in his heart! That is all. End of story." Sweet started again to walk away. "Your father's arrest is unrelated, then, to a family member being deported?" the young woman called after her. How do they know about that? she remembered thinking. And then: Don't you dare make this seem small! On the screen Sweet whirled, jabbed her finger in the woman's face. "This is about my daddy's faith! Can't you people get that? He's doing what Jesus said to do—unlike some other so-called Christians in this county I could name!" Then, as if things weren't bad enough, the camera showed her backside as she stomped away. Lord, she'd had no idea her jeans were that tight. A quick cut to the beaming reporter: "As you can see, Glenda, this case is provoking high emotions here in southeastern Oklahoma. Live from the Latimer County Courthouse in Wilburton, Logan Morgan, 2News Working for You."

Later, Sweet would blame it on that bubbly reporter and her questions, plus the phone call afterward, nosy old Claudie Ott wanting to know if Sweet had seen the twelve o'clock news. "My stars," Claudie said, "we never had even *one* person from this town on the Tulsa news, much less *two*—you and Arvin! I wisht my boy Leon had been here to see it. But they'll run it again at five, don't you reckon?" Sweet stood in the kitchen thinking, yes, more than likely they *would* run it again at five, and then it wouldn't be just a handful of stay-at-home busybodies but the whole blamed town who would see it. Especially after Claudie Ott got done calling. Sweet threw on some sweatpants, told the boys she was going to the store and she'd better not hear one peep about them fighting. If they behaved themselves, she said, she'd bring them a treat. Then she left the house, but she didn't turn west on the highway toward Roy's Cardinal Food Store in Wilburton; she turned east, toward the Poteau Walmart. A thirty-mile drive. She needed to clear her head, she told herself. She needed to shop economically for her family.

What she really needed, what she *wanted*, was to escape. If she could have, she'd have just kept going, on around the Poteau bypass to Fort Smith and hopped on I-40, headed east to Memphis, to Nashville, to . . . she'd never been past Nashville, she didn't even know what was out there, but she wanted to go there, go anywhere, just keep going and not have to think back to the drive home from the hospital last night, how she'd found herself humming a praise-and-worship song behind the wheel—humming! rejoicing!—because the surgeon had told her that Mr. Bledsoe couldn't come home, he would have to go to a rehab facility after the surgery. How she'd picked up the boys from the preacher's sweet-faced wife with barely a thank you and sent them off to bed without mentioning what they'd been through that day—finding the old man splayed and bawling with pain in the hall; that was the preacher's word, *splayed*, she could only imagine what that looked like—just so she could sit in the front room and flick through the channels over and over, waiting for Terry to get home. The terrible gaping black feeling like maybe he wasn't coming home again, ever, and worse: the silent hope that he would stay gone. Because how was she going to tell him? What would she say? She couldn't come up with any non-self-incriminating way to start the conversation, and so the minute she heard his truck out front she had snapped off the TV and rushed to the bedroom, crawled under the covers, pretending to be asleep, pretending all was well, all was normal, no need for him to walk back to the rear bedroom and see the empty bed, the turned-over wheelchair, his stepgrandfather gone.

Deceitful, that's what she was. Deceitful and selfish. Irritable. Angry. A terrible mother. A piss-poor Christian. A lousy wife and daughter, if you came right down to it, and around and around her mind went. She envied Catholics sometimes, she really did. They went to confession, said a few prayers, it was finished; they didn't have to keep lugging their guilt around. Carrying it and worrying it, the dadgum gerbil on the wheel. Sweet drove into the Walmart parking lot with her heart racing, her mind tumbling—in complete contrast to the slow, deliberate way she got out of the car.

She walked the aisles at a terrapin pace, reading labels, comparing prices, not because she wanted to go slow but because the store was vast and she couldn't remember what they needed, couldn't think straight, and then there was the long checkout line, the trek back across the asphalt lot like across a frozen desert, the stop at Braum's for milk and ice cream, another stop in Wister to get gas; it had been like one of those dreams—she couldn't seem to get finished, she couldn't reach her destination. The end part was like a dream, too, a bad one, when she pulled into town and saw, yonder in front of her brick house at the intersection where Main Street crosses the highway, her husband's big Silverado parked in the drive.

He was sitting in the front room in his greasy work clothes. The minute she saw his face, she knew Carl Albert had told—not just that Mr. Bledsoe was hurt and in the hospital, but that it had happened when she'd left him alone the whole day. While they argued—and it was not pretty, all the old stuff dragged up and spread around: What kind of woman *are* you, what kind of mother? Don't be blaming *me*, Tee, *you're* the one gone all the blessed time, you expect me to take care of everything! No, come back here, come *back* here, you listen to me: *I'm* the one who takes care of things, *I'm* the one who puts food on the table! Oh, that is sure right, Mister *I*-Take-Care-of-Things, I don't see *you* wiping that old man's behind every stinking morning! You hush that nasty mouth!—and on and on, around and around, and the whole time Carl Albert hunkered like a whipped dog on the divan in the front room. Sweet was so furious and guilty and defensive she paid him no mind until the phone rang in the kitchen. She and Terry glared at each other a beat, and then he went to answer it. Sweet turned her heated glare on her son.

"I don't suppose you *also* happened to tell your daddy about y'all getting suspended from school?" The faintest headshake no. "Go get your cousin. Y'all are going to face that little bit of music right now!" Carl Albert didn't move. Terry came back and switched on the television. Sweet felt an awful dread pulse through her. But it wasn't her own haggard face talking back to the smiley brunette brandishing her microphone. In the yard of the little rent house stood Misty Dawn with her frowning daughter on her hip. She was plainly, Lord help us, in her chattering mode. "Yeah, it could be that," Misty said, nodding. "It could be a lot of things. Grandpa seen how they treated my husband, for starters. Juanito wasn't speeding or anything, they popped him for illegal lights, but everybody uses those blue lights. You've seen them, right? They're just, like, a decoration, they sell them at Walmart, how could they be illegal? But then, you know, he don't have a driver's license or anything, so they arrested him. They promised I could see him Friday—I had to bring our marriage license down and everything—but then they put them all on a bus at three o'clock in the morning and shipped them someplace and when I got to the jail, he was already gone!" Tears welled in Misty's lovely eyes. The reporter nodded sympathetically, then crooned, "Your husband hadn't committed a crime, you say, but there are those who would point out that being in this country illegally is breaking the law." Misty's eyes narrowed; the slow, sullen look slid down. "My husband's been here since he was fourteen. He don't know how they live in Jalisco." She opened her mouth to say more but the clip cut away to the reporter signing off from a parking lot somewhere, not Misty Dawn's yard. The phone rang again in the kitchen. Sweet glanced at her husband, who acted like he didn't hear it, so she went to answer. Ida Coley wanting to know if that was Sweet's sister Gaylene's oldest girl she'd just seen on the Channel 6 News.

"Yeah," Sweet answered faintly, and then for some reason corrected her: "Her only girl. And it's Channel 2, Ida, not Channel 6." She'd already hung up before it occurred to her that Misty Dawn might be on another channel, too. She hurried back to the living room. Terry was on his feet in front of the recliner with the remote in his hand. On the screen Arvin Holloway stood bull-bellied next to the jail with a bunch of microphones before him. The phone rang. She hurried back to the kitchen. This time it was Brother Oren saying he would give the church an update at tonight's prayer meeting, they'd be sure to keep the prayer chain going, was there any word yet about when Mr. Bledsoe's surgery might be? Sweet told him the time, blessed him silently for not mentioning the TV news as she hung up, and immediately the phone rang again. A reporter from the *Tulsa World* wanting to know if he could get a comment for tomorrow's paper. Sweet punched the disconnect button, left the receiver off the hook, stood in the kitchen fuming, listening to the shifting garble of voices in the front room as her husband clicked through the channels.

All at once she realized why her son had been cowering like a whipped pup ever since she got home. She didn't have to walk back through the empty bedrooms or check the bathroom, the bare carport and vacant yard—though she did do these things, twice, before she told Terry—but she knew before she ever took a step out of the kitchen that Dustin was gone again.

"Great," Terry said when she told him. "That's just great."

Sweet stared hard at her son. "What did you do?"

"Nothing!" he wailed. "How come you always think I did

something? Everybody's always blaming me for everything. I been
sitting here the whole time!"

Terry had his keys out. "Do you want to go or should I?" The
steadiness in his voice said *truce*. He looked exhausted. Sweet hesitated one long aching moment, turning from her waiting husband
to her son huddled on the divan, hurting and frightened. The old
familiar tenderness swept her. "It's all right, honey," she said. "I'm
not blaming you." Her eyes met her husband's. "I guess we should
all go."

Sweet called his name until she was hoarse. Terry walked halfway
out to the dump ditch, calling. They honked the truck horn. They
searched Daddy's house, the barn, the smokehouse, the storm cellar, while Carl Albert sat in the truck with his head down, whether
sulking or crying, Sweet couldn't tell. "He'll turn up," Terry said
finally, coming toward her from the back of the house.

"It's getting dark, Tee. He'll be scared. Let's go around again."

"I spent forty minutes out here last time, and him hiding from
me the whole while."

"Just once more. I'll check the barn. You go look in the smokehouse." Sweet started across the barnyard. "What's this?" She
pointed to the ground, the faint groove in the soft dirt she hadn't
noticed before: a single row of bicycle tire tracks running into the
yard from the gravel road, but the track didn't turn and go out
again; rather, it vanished halfway across the yard as if the bike had
been whisked away in midair. "Whose is that?" Sweet said. "Dusty
doesn't have a bike."

They both began to call his name again, louder now, retracing
their steps. Carl Albert got out of the truck and joined them, his
face red and swollen. He tagged after his daddy, stayed right at his

heels. Sweet stopped in front of the open barn door. "Maybe we should call the sheriff."

"No!" Terry stood near the truck with Carl Albert. "We'll find him, honey. He's just playing a joke on us. Right, son?" He had his hand on Carl's shoulder. The boy nodded, his face puckered in the fading light. Sweet flipped open her phone. "What are you doing?" Her husband's voice was wary.

"Calling the sheriff."

"Don't do that!" Terry started toward her. "You can't trust that s.o.b! Son of a gun was supposed to round up Mexicans! Period!" Abruptly Terry stopped.

"Round up Mexicans," Sweet said. "When? What are you talking about?" At once her father's words in the break room rushed back to her. *Ask him.* But Sweet did not need to ask. She stared at her husband standing with his head tucked in the graying light, his old burgundy Farm Bureau cap tugged down over his hair. The puffy pale thumbs under his eyes. The fear in them. Of course. She'd known all along, she just hadn't known that she knew: her husband was the one who'd turned her daddy in.

The confluence was perfect. Monica couldn't have scripted it better if she'd conjured it herself. Her bill sailed through committee,
of course, as she'd known it would, but she was particularly brilliant in her presentation, she thought—passionate, with a touch
of quiet outrage—and the tribal members standing around the
edges of the committee room lent an air of drama to the thing.
It required the greatest delicacy, the most nuanced wording possible, for her to clarify that this new bill, HB 1906, had absolutely
nothing to do with oppressing any minority but only with pre-
serving Oklahoma's heritage and saving taxpayers money. Charlie
had warned her about the rumblings among the state's powerful
tribes over the English Only provision, so when the committee
chair stopped her in the hall to inform her that the Cherokee,
Chickasaw, and Creek Nations had all sent representatives, she'd
merely smiled. "You know and I know that Oklahomans want
this bill, Fred. They want these enhancements. I don't anticipate
any problems."

And indeed there'd been none. Gazing placidly at the unsmiling
brown faces ranged across the back of the room, she had managed
to glide smoothly past the "official state language" provision with
only a brief mention of the positive fiscal impact of eliminating

costs for bilingual services, segueing seamlessly to asset seizure:
"It's no different than properties used in drug crimes," she told the
committee, although her senses were acutely tuned to the varied
audience members crowding the room. "House Bill 1906 will au-
thorize local law enforcement to seize properties used in violation
of HB 1830. Clearly this will also provide a positive fiscal impact
for the counties because the properties can then be sold to help
offset the costs of enforcement."

Then she moved on quickly to the provision requiring school
administrators to report the numbers of undocumented students in their districts. When Representative Jemison, express-
ing tribal concerns about the English Only provision, moved to
strike title, Monica acquiesced graciously: "We certainly have
no objection to framing the measure in such a way as to em-
phasize that there's no intention here of impinging upon the use
of Native American languages—absolutely not. Our concern is
solely for the Oklahoma taxpayer. We simply want to eliminate
the burden of bilingual services and translator costs, but I'll be
pleased to work with you on developing appropriate language,
Representative Jemison. By all means." She couldn't tell if this
mollified any of the Indians, but the members of the judiciary
committee seemed pleased, and the bill passed out of committee
without objection.

But the great fun, the marvelous convergence, was the fact that
at the very moment she was procuring unanimous passage out of
committee of House Bill 1906, affectionately known as "Son of
1830" for how it built on her previous anti-illegal immigration
measures—at that precise moment, the Latimer County D.A. was
giving his own curt little presentation in Wilburton. Florid-faced
Tom Waters read a statement in a deadly dull monotone from the
courthouse steps: Felony charges had been filed against two Okla-

homa citizens arrested under the provisions of the Oklahoma Tax Payers Protection Act, otherwise known as House Bill 1830, the preliminary hearing was set for the next available court docket on March sixth, he would not be taking questions, and then he'd turned and walked quickly back inside the courthouse—all of which Monica had been privileged to witness on the majority floor leader's new iPhone as they made their way toward the Fourth Floor Rotunda.

Today's lunch was being provided by FFA students from all over the state, and Monica was so in the zone she barely groaned when she saw they were having barbecued brisket—again. She smiled warmly at the pimply Future Farmer heaping coleslaw and baked beans on her plate, took the barbecue-slathered bun and made her way toward a crowded table, where she received warm commendations from members of both sides of the aisle. The toughest part, really, was having to drag herself away from all the accolades for the HouseTV interview.

The kid running the camera started to shoot her with nothing but a blank wall for backdrop, and she had to reposition herself so that she was framed by the busy rotunda, but then, unfortunately, she happened to glance over her shoulder and realized that the Indians were standing in the food line behind her, looking just entirely too dignified and offended. Later, when she reviewed the footage on her office computer, she decided that this was what accounted for the slight note of defensiveness in her tone. Well, *defensive* was too strong a word, but she did detect a whiff of self-protectiveness in the way she answered the anticipated arguments before they'd ever been stated: "For too long," she said briskly, "the federal government has shirked its duty by failing to pass laws acknowledging English as the official language of this country. Oklahoma taxpayers have been forced to pay for bilingual drivers' tests and other services. This measure is in support of English, not in opposition to any group!"

And she'd been smiling too sincerely. Charlie was going to nail her on it. Never apologize, never explain.

Well, never mind. She'd been brilliant in committee—he *could* have come down and watched her do that—and she would be even more brilliant on the floor next week when 1906 came up for a vote. She'd have plenty of opportunity to eradicate any lingering taint of defensiveness. Besides, who watched www.HouseTV.gov anyway? Only political junkies and fanatics. It was the public media that mattered, and that little campaign had just barely begun.

Today was Thursday, sadly, a less than optimum news day, but at least it wasn't a Friday—what a waste that would have been. And tonight's reception was being hosted by ConocoPhillips at the Petroleum Club, now, how good a timing was *that*? Ordinarily most legislators would be rushing home for the weekend, but no one wanted to miss such a powerful opportunity for hobnobbing. Virtually every member of both the House and Senate would be there—not to mention all the state's biggest movers and shakers.

True, illegal immigration was perhaps not on the top of the oil bigwigs' to-do lists, but she knew the media glow would still be upon her. She was going to have lots of opportunity for networking tonight!

Charlie came into the bedroom with her iced chai and a plate of cheese as she was reapplying her makeup. She would have preferred a good stiff Tom Collins, but she couldn't take a chance on anyone at the reception smelling liquor on her breath. Lips pursed at the mirror, Monica nodded toward the two outfits laid out on the bed, a dress and a suit in her signature colors. The nod said to her husband: you pick.

When she first came to the capitol she'd worn a lot of red and black, until she happened to look down from the gallery one morning and realized that every middle-aged female on the House floor, all nine of them, wore some version of red and black. The next day she'd switched to the aquamarine-turquoise-sapphire-seagreen motif she'd been wearing ever since, and really, the colors were perfect; they showed off her eyes, highlighted her hair. Charlie stabbed a thumb at the suit rather than the cocktail dress, and of course he was right. In fact, why had she ever bought that scoop-necked just-this-side-of-revealing slinky thing? Well, because it looked damned good on her—but where could she ever wear it? Certainly nowhere professional, and as Charlie so often said, there was nowhere a legislator went that *wasn't* professional. Well, no matter, it wasn't designer anyway; she'd drop it off, tags and all, at the Goodwill drive-through in McAlester this weekend, take the deduction on next year's taxes.

"Did you see Waters's little press conference this morning?" Charlie settled back on the mound of pillows, grabbed the remote off her side table.

"I did," she said.

"What did I tell you?"

"You said he'd be falling all over himself."

"And was he?"

"He was. Which pair?" She held up a set of turquoise-and-silver earrings and a set of plain silver. He nodded at the turquoise. She returned her gaze to the mirror, holding herself in check. Why bother pointing out that it had been her own little jewel of a press conference that had forced the D.A.'s hand? Charlie would only say, Well, of course, babe, what did I tell you? She heard him chuckling behind her. "What?" she said, turning. Charlie wagged the remote at the TV.

"That right there is why Waters is going to want to move the trial to McAlester. You watch." On the screen a stocky man in a brown jacket and tan Stetson stood on the same courthouse steps where Waters had given his terse little announcement. Good grief, Monica thought, can't anybody in this state be even the least bit more creative than to hold every damn press conference on courthouse steps? "That's the sheriff who conducted the raid," Charlie said. "Waters is *not* going to want him holding forth to the media every day, believe me. He's a braggart and a blusterer, you'd never get him to shut up. The media would eat him up with a spoon. If Waters is going forward with this thing, he damn sure wants a conviction, and that fool right there could blow the whole deal."

"Turn it up."

" . . . tracking dogs coming in from Stigler and Talihina," the sheriff said. "Probably thirty or forty volunteers, we're confident we'll find him. But yes, ma'am, you could say it's a challenge. That's rough country down in there."

"What's he talking about? Oh my God, did those men escape?"

"Hush. Hush!"

" . . . no reason to expect foul play. The kid's probably just run off to get attention. The boy's aunt says this isn't the first time."

A female reporter's voice: "There are rumors the boy had been beaten. Can you confirm a beating?"

"No, I don't think that's true, ma'am. I know the boy's family, they're good people."

"Good people, hah!" a voice catcalled from somewhere off camera. "Beaner smugglers, you mean!"

A different reporter, a man's voice this time: "Sheriff, what's the correlation between the grandfather's arrest and the boy's disappearance?"

"Well, now, I don't know as I'd use the word *disappear*. He's probably just hiding out someplace. He'll get hungry and come in."

"Sheriff, why did you wait fourteen hours before issuing an Amber Alert?"

The sheriff held up a hand. "All right, folks, nice talking to you. I got to get back to work." He started down the steps, parting the half-dozen reporters like parting the waters; they scrambled aside, calling out questions: "Can you confirm that the boy was suspended from school?" "The boy's uncle has been deported, isn't that right?" "What about the family, do they have any idea who might want to harm him?" The camera followed the sheriff to his cruiser, and then the screen was filled with the exotic features of KFOR reporter Shoshone Ballenger signing off live from Wilburton, Oklahoma. Charlie hit the mute button. After a long, silent moment Monica said, "Shit, Charlie. What does this mean?"

He shook his head. "I don't know."

A chill rushed over her. Her husband never, ever, said he didn't know.

Part Two

Gone Astray

Sweet sat on the divan in her bathrobe reading her *Baptist Messenger*. From what she could tell reading the article, the all-Christian prison hadn't been built yet—it was just a proposal somebody wanted to put before the state legislature—but the idea gave her hope. Maybe they would have a women's wing, she thought. Then she could go to prison right along with her father and hang out with the Christians after she'd murdered her husband. She threw the *Baptist Messenger* on the floor. Leaning forward over the coffee table, Sweet cupped her forehead in one hand in a prayerful attitude. She wasn't praying. She was trying to make herself get up and go get ready for church.

She'd already skipped Sunday School—the thought of sitting around the long table with the six women in her Dorcas Adult Women's class was just more than she could handle this morning—but she really had to go to eleven o'clock Worship. What would it say about her and her family if she didn't go? Every able-bodied man in town was out searching day and night for Dustin, and the women of the church had been feeding them, and the preacher had been running interference like a lineman for seventy-two hours straight. He'd promised not to let news cameras in the sanctuary, but what if there were reporters waiting outside the church? The ugliness she would have to run through to get up the front steps! She looked at the clock. Twenty till eleven. Brother Oren would be in the Pastor's Study getting ready for his sermon; she shouldn't bother him. Anyway, what was the point of calling to find out if there were reporters waiting? Whether there were or there weren't, she still had to go.

Sweet reached across the coffee table and drew the Bible over, but she didn't open it. The house was so quiet. When she'd kicked her husband out last Thursday, she hadn't necessarily meant to kick her son out as well, but Carl Albert needed to be away from all this. He'd had a complete meltdown when they discovered his mountain bike missing, flinging himself down in the carport, flailing his legs and wailing—with that bunch of reporters filming it from right out there in the yard! She didn't have a big enough family, that was the problem. If she only had some kind of a decent living sister, or an aunt and uncle, or even just a few in-laws, somebody her son could go stay with and be away from this mess. She'd had no choice but to let Carl Albert go stay at the motel in Poteau with Terry. So far, at least, no reporters had tracked them down there.

Terry. God. She didn't want to even think about him. She knew what the Bible said, Thou shalt not kill, and what Jesus said, that to look on somebody to lust after them was to commit adultery in your heart. Probably this meant that if you looked at your husband and truly wanted to kill him, you'd committed murder in your heart. She had done just exactly that, from the very minute she realized he was the one who'd turned Daddy in. "You son of a lowdown skunk," she'd spat. "I ought to wring your neck!" She had turned and stomped back inside the barn, and Terry had followed, hollering like it was somehow *her* fault: "How the hell did *I* know it was going to turn out to be such a big deal! I figured he'd pay a piddly fine, learn a lesson, we'd get rid of a few wet-backs! I had to do *something*, they're spreading like these damn fire ants swarming up from Texas!" When she found Dustin's empty Spider-Man backpack, unzipped and filthy and stuffed down behind an old feed bin, that's when Sweet had become truly terrified. She'd immediately punched in the sheriff's number, with Terry shouting behind her, "Don't do that, don't do that, what the hell'd you do that for?"

Well, it was a horrible fight, both of them ranting and stamping and throwing things around the barn, with Carl Albert trailing after them wailing and blubbering. They were still yelling and cussing when Holloway's cruiser pulled up. After that, it was all out of her hands.

But it had always been out of her hands, Sweet thought. She had tried all week to hold things together, and every day things had fallen further apart. What things? she wondered. Hell, everything! Her life! Or her life as she'd known it for the seventeen and a half years she'd been married. And here she sat, uncombed and cussing to herself on a Sunday morning. Unable to pray no matter how badly she wanted to. Skipping Sunday School on purpose. Late for church. Murdering her husband in her heart. Sweet glanced again at the wall clock. Then she got up and went to the bedroom to put on some clothes.

She had promised herself she wouldn't scuttle, and she didn't. She did, however, walk very fast. The Call to Worship had already started; she could hear the singing as she strode past the KTUL-TV Channel 8 News van and directly in through First Baptist's front doors. Grabbing a bulletin from the basket in the foyer, Sweet kept her same swift pace into the sanctuary. Every-

body was standing, singing, and she felt heads turning as she
made a beeline for her regular pew three-quarters of the way
down on the left, where, thank goodness, she could see empty
space on the end where she and Terry and Carl Albert usually sat
next to Mr. Bledsoe's wheelchair in the aisle. She'd never seen
the church so packed, folding chairs lining the wall on both sides
of the sanctuary. If you didn't know better, a person could think
a mighty bunch of folks in Latimer County had just suddenly
got religion.

Sweet reached for the hymnal in the pew-back holder in front
of her, tried to somehow spread out and fill the pew so that the
absence of her husband and son wouldn't seem so obvious, though
the empty aisle space at the end seemed to gape like a wound. She
flipped through the hymnal, kept her eyes on the page even though
she knew the words to "His Name Is Wonderful" backward and
forward, and she sang as loud as she could. She wouldn't allow
herself to look around. She didn't want to know what people's faces
were saying. Numbly she went through the motions, standing for
prayer, sitting when it was time to sit again, listening to the song
leader Lon Jones make the announcements—potluck dinner in Fellowship Hall after the service, all were welcome, the relief search
party would head out from the Senior Citizens Center parking lot
at two o'clock, the list of new prayer requests, Dusty's name, Mr.
Bledsoe's, "the whole of the Brown and Kirkendall families"—but
it all seemed so unreal, like a script somebody wrote.

During the greet-one-another-in-Christian-fellowship portion,
Sweet remained in her pew and let others come shake her hand,
firm grip, limp grip, sweaty grip, *we're praying for y'all, don't worry,*
they'll find him. The ushers started from the rear of the sanctuary
passing the plates, and Sweet plucked one of the little Special Offering envelopes out of the pew back and took her checkbook out

of her purse. Last Sunday had been her and Terry's tithe Sunday—they tithed once a month, on the first Sunday after he got paid, making sure to write the check to God before their balance got too low—but she'd missed both services last week and her Sunday School class this morning, where she normally turned it in. She was going to have to put it in the offering plate if she aimed to get it in today. Sweet licked the envelope, slashed through the words *Special Offering*, signed her name in bold letters. She was not going to quit tithing. That was one thing she could still do.

The song leader dismissed the kids for Children's Church, and that almost got to her, the sight of all those little ones running toward the door to the classrooms where they would color cut-out Bible pictures and learn about Jesus and the Fishes and drink Kool-Aid and eat cheap store-bought cookies and spoil their dinners as her own son had done for years when he was still young enough for Children's Church. Don't! she told herself. Don't go there. She pawed through her purse looking for some chewing gum. If she let herself get weepy now, no telling when she would quit.

So she made it through that part okay, but then here came the Special Music, young Amber Ann Fields standing beside the pulpit with the cordless mike in her hand, nodding to the kid on the CD player in the back, and over the speakers came the rippling sound of harps and violins like an orchestra, and Sweet's heart contracted—oh, wouldn't you know, wouldn't you just know. "I Believe." They couldn't have picked a worse song. Amber Ann's clear, high, country voice rang through the sound system. How many times had Sweet told people that was the song she wanted sung at her funeral? Because it said everything, all she'd ever known of faith—and, yes, there was Jesus, of course there was Jesus, but there was this, too, believing the Lord sends a flower for every drop of rain, a light in every darkness. She didn't have that

kind of faith anymore, or if she did, it was crammed so low and
deep she couldn't touch it; she couldn't even remember what it felt
like. *I believe for every one who goes astray, someone will come, to show
the way.* Probably the people nearby thought she was weeping because of her nephew being lost, but it wasn't for Dustin, it was for
her. She couldn't really be lost, of course—she'd been saved since
she was a kid—but somehow it was only her head that knew that.
Her heart didn't know. Her heart felt like she was sinking into a
black wilderness and she might be there forever. Her soul felt cold
and empty, like there just might not be any point in anything. Her
throat felt like it could burst wide open. "I be-lieve, " Amber sang.
"I—I be-lieve."

When the music finished, the amens were many and loud, and
so was the clapping, which never failed to aggravate Sweet. You
weren't supposed to clap for somebody singing in church, she'd
been taught better than that. It was like applauding a sermon,
like you were giving credit to the human person instead of the
Lord. In her opinion there were entirely too many new Christians who hadn't been taught proper Baptist etiquette. She blew
her nose, opened her Bible to where Brother Oren told everybody
to turn. Matthew 18:12–14. "When you find it, say amen," the
preacher said. Several scattered amens stuttered through the sanctuary. "Let's all stand for the reading of God's Word." Some of the
strangers in the folding chairs glanced around, confused, but then
they stood up along with the congregation.

"'How think ye?'" Brother Oren read. "'If a man have an hundred sheep, and one of them be gone astray, doth he not leave the
ninety and nine, and goeth into the mountains, and seeketh that
which is gone astray? And if so be that he find it, verily I say unto
you, he rejoiceth more of that sheep, than of the ninety and nine
which went not astray. Even so it is not the will of your Father

which is in heaven, that one of these little ones should perish.'
Let's go to the Lord in prayer: Heavenly Father, we come to You
here this morning with burdened hearts. You know our sorrows,
Lord. You know the sorrows of this family. We'd just ask, Father,
that You'd be with us here in this service this morning, guide us in
the seeking of Your Word. Be with the ones who are out searching
now, the ones who'll go out later this evening. Guide and direct
them, Lord, that Your will might be done. We know that not a
little sparrow falls but that Your eye is upon it. We know it's not
Your will that one of these little ones should be lost. Continue to
guide and direct our lives, Lord, and we'll be careful to give Thee
the praise. These things we ask in Jesus' name. Amen."

"Amen," Sweet murmured, along with many others. Brother
Oren was, to be honest, a better pray-er than he was a preacher.
That was one of Terry's biggest gripes. "He talks like a blamed
Presbyterian, he don't *preach*!" By which Tee meant there was
insufficient hellfire and damnation in Brother Oren's sermons.
Sweet had to admit that this was true. His voice was just too
quiet. And monotonous. And he always had to pause to go back
to the pulpit and read his notes. He was a young old man, or an
old young man, with lank sandy hair and a faint little potbelly
showing under his tie. The pulpit committee had found him in
some tiny country church way down around Idabel; she couldn't
think how they'd even run across him down there. He'd been
here five years, and in that time the church hadn't exactly grown,
but it hadn't shrunk much, either. Brother Oren might not be
a great preacher, Sweet thought, but he's a good pastor, a good
shepherd. She couldn't imagine how she would have managed
without him this past week. Out of respect she kept her eyes on
his face, trying to act like she was listening, though her mind, as
usual, began to drift.

Goeth into the mountains. Well, yes, they were doing that. She'd heard that Holloway was getting up a search party to go down into the Winding Stair. They'd already searched every inch of the farm, searched miles out in the valley in every direction, and the boy was not here. "Vanished into thin air," the sheriff kept saying in his many news conferences. After that bad rain Friday night, he'd called in a diving team to search the strip pits north of town. That made no sense to Sweet. Why would Dustin pedal five miles north when the backpack was found at the farm three miles south? Holloway just wanted to make it look like something was happening. But, then, why would Dustin go south into the mountains, either? Why would he go anywhere . . . *And if so be that he find.* If so be. Meaning sometimes it could be that He *doesn't* find the lost sheep. No. Not possible. Not in this case. She wouldn't let herself think it. Sweet must be among the ninety and nine, because she had surely been left behind, because the Shepherd was definitely someplace else—except the ninety and nine went not astray, that's what the verse said, and she *had* gone astray. Somehow. Some way. Astray. A stray. Like Dustin. The little stray orphan. Again the knot swelled in her throat, and she was working it, swallowing hard, trying not to resume bawling, when she heard a faint sound to her left, a tiny, hollow, mechanical *click.* Brother Oren's droning voice stopped. "Who did that!" he said, very loud. Everybody looked around. Sweet was still trying to come to herself when Brother Oren did something she'd never seen him do before. Right in the middle of the sermon, he switched texts. "Would y'all turn with me in your Bibles to the Book of John! Chapter two, verses fifteen and sixteen!"

John two sixteen? Sweet thought vaguely. Shouldn't it be John three sixteen? *For God so loved the world . . .*

"John two!" Brother Oren repeated. "Verses fifteen and sixteen. When you find it, say amen." He didn't wait for any amens, though, but came out from behind the pulpit and held his Bible before him spread open in one hand; he started reading in a loud, clear voice: "'And when he had made a scourge of small cords, he drove them all out of the temple, and the sheep, and the oxen; and poured out the changers' money, and overthrew the tables; and said unto them that sold doves, Take these things hence; make not my Father's house an house of merchandise.'"

Brother Oren paused, looking from one side of the sanctuary to the other. "I believe there's all kinds of merchandise in the world today. Do y'all believe that?" There were a couple of murmured amens. "Back in Jesus' time it might've been sheep and oxen in the temple, might have been doves. These days, though, that merchandise might be something a little different, something you can't put your hands on necessarily but something that's no less real, no less hurtful to the Lord's purpose. Public gossip, for instance. Buying and selling folks' troubles. Merchandising somebody's heartache and pain. Now, we've got members of this church family here this morning that's going through some terrible times, we all know that. The worst kind of times a person can go through nearly, a lost child. Plus other troubles, too, of course—we're not going to speak of that now. But let's listen here to what the Word says: Make not. My Father's house. An house of merchandise." Again Brother Oren turned his head from side to side. "I have asked y'all to keep your merchandising outside the Lord's house. I'm not about to go fixing up a scourge of small cords. All are welcome here. All are welcome. But when I asked folks not to bring cameras into this worship service this morning, I meant that also includes cell phones."

Oh. The little click came from a cell phone. She should have recognized that. Sweet glanced to her left, couldn't tell where the sound had come from. Would it be worse if it was one of the visitors taking her picture or one of her own church members? She didn't know. She felt like she was swimming through cotton. Brother Oren preached a while longer on merchandise in the temple, and his voice was the closest thing to fiery she'd ever heard, and he didn't have to keep walking back over to the pulpit to check his notes. Terry ought to be here to see this, she thought.

The rest of the sermon was short, though, and the invitation even shorter. Nobody went forward. Nobody wanted to go rededicating their life or anything, lest others in the church body think they'd been changing money in the temple themselves. So they just sang two soft choruses of "I Surrender All," and then Brother Oren asked Clyde Herrington to pray the benediction. Then he did something else out of the ordinary: instead of slipping quietly up the aisle during the prayer so he could be at the front door to shake everybody's hands as they came out, Brother Oren stopped beside Sweet and tapped her shoulder. She'd had her head bowed and eyes closed, so naturally she jumped. Brother Oren put his finger to his lips in a shush gesture, stepped back, and his little low-key wife, Vicki, came and took Sweet's arm, and the two of them ushered her silently toward the door to the right of the altar that led to the attached prefab building that housed Fellowship Hall.

Sweet hadn't planned on going to the potluck dinner—for one thing she wanted to get to the jail early, and for another, she didn't want to have to answer questions about why her son and husband weren't in church this morning—but it didn't matter what she wanted. The preacher and his wife, plus three women from her Dorcas class, put her at the head of the buffet line in front of the slow, messy children. Vicki kept hold of her arm like she was afraid Sweet might fly off while Brother Oren asked the blessing, and after Sweet filled her plate, they guided her to a table in the far corner. They brought her an iced tea. They brought her three kinds of desserts. They asked if she wanted coffee. Sweet picked at her broccoli casserole. Something was wrong.

Well, everything was wrong, yes, but there was something really off-kilter about how three women from her class sat down on either side and across from her, and the others carried their plates to the opposite end of Fellowship Hall and sat at the farthest table next to the glass double doors. The song leader and his wife came and spoke to her, said they were keeping the family in their prayers, but the head deacon Kenneth Spears shot glares at her from the kitchen, where he was helping the women serve. Her husband's friend Wade Free came and stood by the table with his ball cap in his hands. He and Tee worked together at Arkoma; they'd graduated school the same year. She expected him to ask about Terry, but he just stood awkwardly a moment, his throat working, then he bobbed his head once, slapped his cap on, and left through the glass doors. Gossipy old Claudie Ott waddled up behind her to whisper, "Don't you worry, Georgia Ann, they'll find him. My boy Leon has been out looking since before daylight."

And so it was throughout the dinner: about a third or so of the congregation hovered around her like worker bees around a queen; the rest of them avoided her like a plot of poison oak. The hall was so packed that several people were eating standing up. Sweet saw members from Cedar Church of Christ, Assembly of God, and both the Free Will and Missionary Baptist, which was unheard of, everybody crossing denominations like that. Plus all the strangers! Folks she'd never seen before in her life. She would've laid it off to them being here as search party members, except there were as many women as men, and teenagers, too, all of them watching her.

That was maybe what bothered her most—how some of the ones from her own church kept their eyes averted, like they didn't know her, while most of the strangers stared straight at her and gawked. The only bit of relief came from the fact that nobody asked about Terry and Carl Albert. It became plain after a while that people just assumed they were out searching. She was glad enough to let them think it. Glad enough to surrender to the ministrations of the preacher's wife and the women from her class, who seemed to be running interference for her the same way Brother Oren had positioned himself between her and the reporters, to protect her. Sweet was grateful. She was grateful, in fact, that she could even feel grateful—at least there was that.

The whole thirteen miles to Wilburton she tried to imagine what she was going to say to her father. She worried she might have to be the one to tell him about Dustin—she didn't know how much news reached the county prisoners—and she would promise herself to lead up to it gently, but then she'd find herself saying, *Oh, Daddy, if only you hadn't* . . . Other times, in her mind, she just flat chewed him out: Dustin running away. His fault. The church folks acting weird. His fault. Misty Dawn blabbing to the world. His fault. The family separated and going broke. His fault. Sweet losing her everloving mind. His fault, his fault, his fault. Lips crimped, throat tight, her chest cold with dread, Sweet turned off the Wilburton main street, drove past the courthouse, circled around and parked inside the covered breezeway at the side of Jones-Hawkins Funeral Home across the street from the jail.

The sheriff had the alley cordoned off so that the news vans were all corralled to one side. There were three of them, even on a Sunday when nobody hardly watched the news. The cold clamp on

Sweet's chest screwed down tighter. She sat in her car eyeing the different jail visitors as they stopped to talk to the reporters. Dyed-blond overweight young mothers holding stringy-headed kids, for the most part. One guy in overalls and a ball cap, no jacket. A sad-looking older couple who walked on past the news people and didn't stop. The rest of them, though, seemed tickled to stand and talk. What could they possibly be saying? Those girls didn't have one thing in this world to do with her family! If everybody would just ignore the reporters and their stupid cameras, maybe they'd all go away.

In the beginning, of course, last Thursday, Sweet herself had been willing to talk. Spreading the word about Dustin could only help, she'd thought. The TV reporters asked for an appeal from the family, and Sweet had repeated into the cameras what they told her to say: "If there's anybody out there who knows anything, who's seen anything, please call the Latimer County Sheriff's Office. Please. We just want our boy to come home." But when she watched the news later, she was mortified at how stiff and wooden she appeared, like she was faking it, and not even faking it well. She'd looked about as believable as one of those country and western singers trying to act in a movie. And she hated how the newscasters shaped things—they kept trying to make it sound like it was all of a piece: "The boy's grandfather, Robert John Brown, arrested and jailed one week ago on felony charges of harboring and transporting illegal aliens"—*aliens,* they all said, not Mexicans, like those people had landed here from outer space—"the boy's grandfather Robert John Brown, currently in the Latimer County Jail without bond . . ." They acted like there was some kind of human smuggling operation going on in southeastern Oklahoma. On one Tulsa channel the anchors did a little happy talk about the meth labs and marijuana patches down in these mountains—

well, good grief, that stuff had been here for ages! Illegal commerce wasn't exactly new in these parts. That didn't have a thing
to do with Dustin being gone. Sweet kept feeling like she was in
a weird movie, her family's story played out on the local news, but
they didn't get half their facts right. Or if they got the right facts,
they didn't get the right *intention*. The back door of the jail opened
and the boys in orange jumpsuits filed out, began lining up along
the fence. Where was Daddy? And Pastor Garcia? Even with the
media cordoned off, Sweet was not about to go over there until
her daddy emerged. At which time she would let him have it. She
really would.

But when she saw him finally, small and defeated looking,
walking out blinking in the sunlight, she knew she couldn't chew
him out. The heartbreak etched in her daddy's features was awful.
Oh, he knew about Dustin all right—and more than that, he understood his part. Her father stood at the fence scanning the beat-
up cars and pickup trucks parked in the alley; he turned to check
the VFW lot next door. It hadn't occurred to him, Sweet could
tell, to look across the street to the funeral home where her Taurus
was half concealed in the covered driveway. Pastor Garcia stopped
behind Daddy and put his hand on his shoulder, said something
to him, then bowed his head to pray. Daddy didn't bow his head,
he just kept scanning the parked vehicles—looking for hers, Sweet
knew that. The camera operators were shooting from behind the
yellow line. They probably had zooms on those cameras, Sweet
thought. They were probably capturing every molecule of pain
on her daddy's face. In close-up living color. For tomorrow's early
morning news.

Go, she told herself. Get out of this car and go over there.
What was wrong with her? This was her chance to talk with her
daddy in private, or at least without the sheriff listening; they

could make a plan together that would solve everything, and she wouldn't condemn him or ask why. What they needed to do was figure out about Dustin. *What should we do, Daddy? You know him better than anybody, where would he go? What would he do? Yes, yes, we've looked there, we've looked everywhere, but where else? Can't you think of where else?* Because this wasn't like Gaylene. Gaylene had done the same thing, run away, vanished, nobody saw or heard from her for six months. But Gaylene was fifteen, not ten, and pregnant, as it turned out, and she'd only gone as far as Okmulgee. *It's not your fault, Daddy,* Sweet had told her father back then.

"Not your fault," she repeated now, aloud in the cold Taurus. She wouldn't switch on the motor to warm up the car. Her daddy might hear. He might lift his face, see her, and then she would have to walk across that empty cold street by herself, all the cameras turning, the smoking mothers and orange-clad meth cookers and the fat deputy in his chair, all turning to look at her, and Daddy's eyes, too, turning, holding up the truth to her, where she couldn't help but see. Who was it that had been supposed to be taking care of Dustin? Who doped poor old Mr. Bledsoe and went off and left him? Whose husband had turned whose daddy in?

Sunday | *February 24, 2008* | *11:55* P.M.

Latimer County Jail | *Wilburton*

Deep in the night Bob Brown lay with his arms over his face, listening. The main cells had quieted, the only sound now the hum of the fluorescent lights overhead, the electric heater outside in the hallway, and, in the nearby bunk, at slow, regular intervals, the pastor's snores. Will you not watch with me one night? Brown thought. Watch and pray. He turned heavily onto his side, the cement slab hard underneath him—hard as the fist-sized rock in his chest. His bones ached. No meat on them anymore, nothing to cushion the ache except old, drying flesh. That's how he felt now, old, dried out. A skeleton. An old scrawny spook. One week ago he'd come in here a young man for his age. Now he was old.

Jesus Lord, don't let anything bad happen to him. Send Sweet back here. Don't let her get up on her high horse. Soften her heart.

That afternoon, when the deputies tweeted their whistles to signal the end of men's visitation, Brown had heard at last the familiar high-pitched whine. He'd turned and spied his daughter's old blue-green Taurus bumping down out of the funeral home parking lot across the street, turning east, driving away. She *had* come, and watched, and left without talking to him—without him being able to talk to her. And that's the main thing he'd been wanting to do ever since Arvin Holloway appeared on the other side of the bars, casually cleaning his fingernails with a nail clipper, saying, "Your grandson's run off." Nonchalantly. Not much of a problem.

And really, in those first hours, that first day, it hadn't seemed like a problem, because Sweet had told him, hadn't she? On Wednesday. That Dustin had gone back out to the farm—but what would you expect? The boy would want to be home, even without somebody there to take care of him. But Dustin could take care of himself, better than your average ten-year-old, Brown knew that. He hadn't become truly worried until last night, when that squeezed-fisted feeling had suddenly kicked up in his chest. He kept seeing the boy coming down the back steps with the deputy's hand on his shoulder, or he'd see him standing in the jail parking lot beside the preacher's car, his hands cupped, the bright blood pouring—oh, if Sweet would have just brought him up here like he'd told her to! Why wouldn't she come talk to him this afternoon? What was she doing parked yonder at the funeral home—spying on him? Surely she hadn't joined sides with her husband.

Please, Jesus, don't let it be that.

Arvin Holloway was the one who'd brought that news, too—early on, when they'd only been here two days. Bob Brown himself couldn't have made it up. If anybody had ever said to him: your son-in-law is going to one day betray you, and here's how he's going to do it, Brown would have answered, Yes, sir, when hell turns into an ice-skating rink. But here he sat in jail on account of Terry Kirkendall—

No. It wasn't that. Things had turned as they turned. They were doing the Lord's will. They had followed as they'd been led.

Didn't we, Lord Jesus?

He listened, his arm crooked under his head for a pillow, his

eyes closed against the light. For thirty years Bob Brown had
trusted the quiet voice, the peace that passeth understanding,
ever since the day he came out of a blackout in a lousy no-name
motel somewhere in Louisiana, sick to his soul, hating himself
beyond all ways he had ever hated. He had stumbled to the bathroom and looked in the scaly mirror at his unshaven stinking foul
miserable self; he'd thought of his two little girls at home with
nobody but a Choctaw neighbor lady to see about them, and he
decided fully in his heart he was not going to do this anymore.
But how many times had he said that? A hundred times. A thousand. But that miserable rock-bottom morning in Louisiana, he
got down on his knees on the filthy motel carpet and said maybe
the first real prayer he'd ever said in his life: "Lord Jesus, I can't
do this. I can't. Help me." At once the peace had entered him—
and with it a slim hopeful sense that maybe this time, *this time* he
would make it. He hadn't touched a drop of whiskey since. For
thirty years he had tried to walk as the peace led him. The still
small voice. If things turned as they turned, wasn't that because
the Lord willed it?

   But not this, Lord. Not Dustin.

Brown groaned softly, pushed himself up from the cold slab.
He felt for his eyeglasses on the floor, put them on, sat with his
hands clasped, shielding his eyes. The unyielding light was as bad
as the concrete. On the nearby bunk the pastor snored on. Brown
had not slept at all the past two nights—not since that knot of
fear came and fisted up inside him. The same thoughts nagged
him over and over. Where would Dusty go? The boy would want
to . . . what?

Go home. So why wasn't Dustin out at the farm? Or maybe he
was there but just hiding . . . but where would he hide that they
couldn't find him in all this time? Not the barn, not the house;

they'd gone over the whole place with a silver comb, Holloway
said.

Holloway. That son of a bitch.

Forgive me, Jesus. Forgive him.

Brown took off his glasses, rubbed his eyes. He couldn't stop
seeing the picture: Dustin coming down the back steps, blinking
through his too-long shaggy hair, the deputy's paw on his shoulder
steering him toward the barnyard, where the silent Mexicans were
being cursed and prodded along toward the waiting van in the
midst of all the flashing lights, the radio squawks and yelling, and
Dustin looking at them, looking around for his grandpa, and Bob
Brown locked in the backseat of a cruiser with his hands cuffed
behind him and the windows shut, unable to signal to his boy that
the Lord was in this, the Lord was in this, everything happens for
a reason. All things work together for good . . .

Help my boy, Jesus! Protect him. Keep him safe.

The boy standing beside the car. The bright blood pouring. The
deputy steering him down the porch steps. The big paw clamped
on his shoulder. The confused fear on his grandson's face.

*If I've failed Thee, Lord Jesus, if I've misunderstood, if I've been self-
ish and pigheaded, it's not Dusty's fault! Protect him, Lord Jesus. Hold
him in the cleft of Your hand. Thy will, not mine. Thy will, not mine.
Show me, Lord, what You would have me do.*

Brown stopped his breath. Listened.

Garcia's snores. The electric hum. Nothing more.

Monday | *February 25, 2008* | *2:57 A.M.*

Sweet's house | *Cedar*

Sweet dragged the covers up over her face, lay quiet a moment, trying to breathe; then she slung the bedspread to the side and lay staring at the black ceiling. She felt like that drawing of Simon Peter denying Christ in her son's Youth Bible: a scruffy-bearded man in a striped cloak skulking guiltily at the base of a clay wall while a rooster crowed from the top of it. That was Sweet. Denying her daddy. She flopped over onto her stomach, pulled the pillow onto the back of her head. Once again she went over the scene trying to make it come out right, but no matter how she tried she couldn't dredge up the image she longed for: herself striding boldly across the street, ignoring those reporters and walking right up to the cyclone fence to talk to her daddy. What she saw instead was a picture of herself scurrying along the church sidewalk like a chased armadillo, which was not an image she'd dreamed up—she had seen the blamed thing. On television. On the Channel 8 evening news.

The red numerals on the night stand glared at her. 2:57. Too early to get up, too late to be awake. She wriggled over to Terry's side of the bed. Oh, the middle of the night was the worst. The absolute worst. At least in the daytime she could do something useful, clean the oven, sort out her junk drawer. Maybe she'd get up and go do that. But she needed sleep. She really, really needed sleep. She pondered the idea of getting up to take one of Mr. Bledsoe's pain pills. She'd seen how effectively they knocked him out, but then, truly, she didn't want to add drug addiction to her list of family problems. Had she called the hospital to check on Mr. Bledsoe? No, she had not. Not since day before yesterday. Sweet added that to her list, another little Lincoln log of guilt.

When she heard the knocking at the door, her first thought was that it was another blamed reporter. Of all the nerve! At this hour! But then she realized the soft pounding was coming from the kitchen door, the one to the carport. The one the family used. But Terry would use his key, wouldn't he? Then she thought: Oh, thank God. Dustin! She scrambled from the covers.

In the dark carport Misty Dawn stood crying.

"What?" Sweet said. "What happened? Oh, my God, where's the baby?" Misty shook her head. These weren't silent tears like before, but deep, wrenching, guttural sobs. Sweet pulled her inside the lighted kitchen. "Get hold of yourself!" She made her voice as gruff as she could. "Sit!" she said, pressing the girl into a chair. "Talk!"

Between sobs Misty said, "Go look. See if. Anybody followed me."

Sweet peeked out into the carport, where she saw nothing but the dim outline of the Taurus. "There's nobody. How'd you get here?"

"Check the front."

Sweet went to the front room, spread two blind slats apart with her fingers. All was quiet, a night-empty main street in a dying small town, nothing out of the ordinary. "Where's the baby?" she demanded again when she returned to the kitchen.

"In the truck." Misty pulled in a ragged breath. "She was sleeping."

"Where's the truck?"

"At the farm."

"You mean to tell me you left that baby alone out in the country in the middle of the night!"

"Of course not! Her daddy's with her."

"Her daddy. Who—Juanito?"

Misty Dawn looked up. "I didn't know where else to bring him."

It took a second for Sweet to comprehend what Misty was saying: Juanito had snuck back across the border. "Oh, no. Oh, *no*. Oh, Misty. This is bad."

"No, it isn't! We had to! It would've been, like, ten years or something before they let him even *try* to come back! Concepción would be practically grown!"

"If he gets caught, he could get sent to prison, don't you know that?"

"He can't get caught," Misty said. "That's why we had to get out of there."

Sweet sat down at the table. "The farm's not a good place, hon. It's crawling with reporters."

"Nuh-uh. Nothing like *our* house. Anyhow, we parked in the barn. There's nobody out there."

"If they're not there now, they soon will be. We've got to . . ." Sweet's voice faded. She looked around the kitchen. Got to what?

"Got to what?" Misty said.

"I don't know." Sweet rubbed her forehead. "Damn it, Misty. What'd you bring him here for?"

Misty Dawn stared at her in silence a moment. Then she stood up and started for the door.

"No! Wait! I'm sorry. I'm sorry. Sit down. Let me think a minute. I just need to think."

The girl hesitated, came back and sat. She hunched forward,
shivering, her bottom lip quivering. She had on the same denim
jacket she'd worn to the store; her mascara was smeared, her long
hair tangly around her face. "You want something to eat?" Sweet
said.

"I'm not hungry. Juanito might be. And Lucha, she'll be hungry when she wakes up. I didn't have time to fix anything. I just
seen the coast clear for the first time in, like, *days*, so I ran out and
started the truck. Oh, Aunt Sweet, they've been—they been . . . I
can't even describe it."

"I know. Same here. Okay, let's just . . . here, get up and help
me fix some sandwiches." Because what else was there to do? As
they slapped together peanut butter and jelly, bologna and cheese,
Sweet tried to see her way clear. Feed them first, yes, but then
what? She couldn't bring Juanito to her house! Reporters still
showed up in her yard ten times a day trying to get Sweet to
talk to them. Sometimes they'd just stand out there and film the
empty porch. She filled the thermos with water, grabbed a couple
of juice packs from the fridge, dumped everything in a plastic
Walmart sack. "Come on," she said, wishing she had a real garage
with a proper door instead of an open carport. If there did happen to be anybody around at this hour, they'd for sure see them
sneaking out to the car.

"Are you going like that?" Misty said.

Sweet looked down at her nightgown and bare feet. "No. Wait
here a minute. Do *not* go outside without me!" But of course when
she returned to the kitchen in sweatpants and a sweatshirt and
carrying her purse, Misty Dawn was already outside sitting in the
dark car. The girl was born to disobey, that was the fact of the mat-

ter. Just like her mother. Sweet should have told her to go get in
the car, maybe then she would have waited in the kitchen. Sweet
started the motor and backed out of the drive.

Misty Dawn sat tense and silent beside her as they drove the
three miles of smooth humming blacktop. When they reached the
turnoff to the farm, the Taurus's tires crunching the gravel, the old
transmission whining, Sweet said, "I meant it, Misty. You all can't
stay out here. Those reporters are here all the time because . . ."
She didn't want to finish. *Because the farm is where your brother disappeared.* She tried to think what excuse she could make for not
getting in touch with her about Dustin. Sweet hadn't tried the
TracFone number again, hadn't even considered making another
drive to Tulsa, but Misty Dawn had to know about her brother
going missing anyway. You would have to live under a rock to not
know. Or watch only the Spanish language stations. "You . . . I
guess you know about Dustin."

"Yeah," Misty said, very softly. "That's what the reporters keep
asking. Even more than about Grandpa." A beat of silence, then:
"I *couldn't,* all right? Juanito was on his way, I didn't know when! I
couldn't just come down here and not be home!"

"I didn't say anything. Did I say anything?" Sweet was more
than willing to let her niece's guilt trump her own. She wheeled
into the yard, stopped in front of the barn. The heavy wooden
door had been tugged closed. It had been standing open for
days—ever since the raid. Reporters often made their broadcasts
right in front of it: "This is where the boy's backpack was found
mysteriously abandoned," they'd say, or, "This decrepit barn is
where Dustin Lee Brown's grandfather Robert John Brown al-
legedly harbored fourteen illegal aliens . . ." The shut barn door
was like a billboard shouting, *Hey, look in here! We got something
to hide!* She had to get these kids out of here—tonight. It took all

of Sweet's strength, with Misty Dawn helping, to slide the rattly old thing open. The inside of the barn was very dark. "Black as midnight under a cast-iron skillet"—that was one of Mr. Bledsoe's old sayings. Back when he used to talk. Poor Mr. Bledsoe. She hadn't been to visit him not one time since his surgery—but how could she? When could she? Another log of guilt.

"*Cariño!*" Misty Dawn called softly, and in an instant Juanito materialized out of the darkness. Sweet couldn't really see him, only hear him, half sense him. The two whispered hard and fast in Spanish. Were they arguing? Maybe not. People talking fast in Spanish always sounded to Sweet like a fight. Her eyes had begun to adjust a little. She saw the ghostly white bulk of the pickup a short distance away; she made her way toward it, feeling along the right side to the passenger door. When she opened it, the dome light came on. The baby was asleep in her car seat in the middle of the cab, breathing slow and even, her brushy thick lashes stark against her pale skin. *Lucha,* Sweet reminded herself. She really was going to have to quit calling her the baby. The child was long limbed as a colt, her feet dangling to the hump in the floorboard. The soft pink afghan was wadded in her lap. Sweet could see a Sleeping Beauty appliqué on her lavender sweatshirt, the beautiful blond princess asleep in her tower. Sweet reached in, brushed the thick mat of dark hair from the child's face.

"She's been asleep since Broken Arrow," Misty Dawn whispered behind her. Turning, Sweet saw Juanito clearly now in the glow from the dome light. The top of his head just cleared Misty Dawn's shoulder. He was thinner than ever, and browner, Sweet thought, like the sun in Mexico these past months had baked him darker. The Indian blood really showed in him, except he was only about half the size of most of the Choctaws around here, short and wiry, smooth faced, and he looked so young.

Sweet was always struck by that, every time she saw him. He looked like a teenager to her, though Misty Dawn said he was a year older than she was, which would make him twenty-four. Juanito nodded at Sweet but didn't offer his usual quick smile. His shirt was worn and ragged. He didn't have on a coat. Both of them watched her expectantly.

They're the ones made this mess, Sweet said to herself, and now they're waiting on me to figure a way out of it. "So," she said briskly, "what are y'all aiming to do?" She knew perfectly well they didn't have a plan. They'd never had a plan, so far as she could tell; they'd met, slept together, produced a child, got married. And it had been nothing but a heartache ever since. Well, no, that wasn't fair. She'd seen them together at the birthday party last summer, holidays before that. Love was part of it, too, no doubt, although why Misty Dawn had to fall in love with a Mexican was beyond her. And an illegal one at that. Sweet didn't even know how they met. Misty had just called up her grandpa out of the blue four years ago and told him she was bringing somebody to meet him. Juanito didn't speak English then. Well, he didn't speak it now, actually. Misty claimed he did, that he was just shy to talk in front of her family, but Sweet had never heard him say anything except Hello, How are you, See you later, Okay. "So?" she said again. "What's the plan?"

Misty Dawn reached around her, pulled the afghan up, and tucked it around the baby's shoulders. She said something to Juanito. Juanito answered. "What's he saying?" Sweet asked.

"He says you're the smartest American woman he knows."

"Really." Sweet very much doubted that's what he'd said. "All right." She sighed. "Okay. Let's think this through. First of all, first thing, the farm is out, and my house is out. Tell him that."

Misty translated. "What about those friends of yours? That girl who keeps the baby? Can't y'all stay there?"

"Blanca and Enrique?" Misty glanced at her husband. "No," she said. "That's no good."

"Why not?" Silence. Misty Dawn wouldn't look at her. "What?"

"Blanca's brother," Misty said finally.

"What about him?"

"He lives with them."

"So?"

"He's not legal. Anyway," Misty rushed on, "it'd be really bad for them. You know, like, if anything happened."

"Right, but it's okay for me?" And with that, Sweet realized for the first time that it wasn't only Misty Dawn who could be charged with harboring and transporting; it was Sweet, too. Why hadn't she thought of that? This wasn't some joke about doing time in a Christian prison with her daddy—the law was real. She had to get them out of here! Not just out of town, but out of the whole blamed state. She could lose everything—her reputation, her voting privileges, her home. She had a son to raise. "We've got to get you kids out of Oklahoma," she said, "that's the first thing. How about you stay in Fort Smith tonight, then we'll figure out what next." Arkansas wasn't exactly the most progressive state, but the border was only fifty miles away and at least folks there weren't out beating the bushes to find illegal Mexicans. She didn't think.

"Stay where?"

"Fort Smith."

"No, I mean like *where*. With who?"

"I don't know. A motel. Have y'all got any money?"

Misty looked at Juanito, who rattled off a long answer. Misty turned back to Sweet. "He had to use everything for the *coyote*. We borrowed from Blanca and Enrique even. He's got like three dollars left. I spent my last eighteen bucks on gas in Muskogee. This truck just eats gas."

Sweet sighed. "Okay. I'll go back to the house and defrost my credit card. But listen, Misty, we can't leave this truck sitting here, you never know when somebody might come snooping around. We'll hide the truck, y'all stay in it, eat your sandwiches, and keep quiet till I get back. Have you got a flashlight?" Misty spoke to Juanito. He reached in and tugged the seat forward slightly, retrieved a large yellow square-shaped Energizer from the floorboard behind the seat. Sweet took it from him, switched it on and off a couple times. The battery was weak, but it would probably last long enough. "You remember where that old trash dump is?" she asked Misty. "Out by the fence at the end of the pasture?"

"I think so."

"Drive out there and park, but don't use your headlights. One of you needs to walk in front with the flashlight, shine it low on the ground in front of the tires, don't be waving it around. Hear?" Misty nodded, told Juanito. Sweet could see the quick comprehension in his face. He slipped around the front of the truck and climbed up, started the motor. Sweet guided him in backing out with low sweeping motions of the flashlight, then handed it to Misty. She waited until the truck rumbled around the side of the barn and disappeared into the dark pasture. Good thing that battery's low, she thought. A passerby wouldn't even notice the dim light bobbing along close to the ground—though who she thought might be passing by at this hour, she couldn't say. Just *them* somehow. The strangers who'd been hounding her. She didn't use her own headlights until she was well out of the yard. Her mind was moving fast.

The main thing was money—well, wasn't money always the main thing? But in this case it really was. She didn't like using the credit card; they'd gotten into such a mess, her and Terry, but that was a few years ago, and it was almost all paid off now. Sweet had cut up all their cards, including their ATM cards because they'd both gotten in a bad habit of stopping at the E-Z Mart to get cash and paying those stupid fees, and then they'd end up broke before the end of the month and have to start charging gas and groceries on the credit cards again. So she'd cut up everything except their two VISA cards, which she'd put in an empty Cool Whip tub and filled it with water and stuck it in the freezer. They were only supposed to thaw them out in case of an emergency, but what would you call this if not an emergency?

When she arrived at the house, though, she couldn't find the container. She took everything out of the freezer, every tray of chicken legs and tube of Jimmy Dean sausage and box of frozen peas, laid them all in the sink, but the white tub wasn't here. For a moment she panicked, thinking somebody had broken in, until she realized it was Terry. At the Black Angus Motel in Poteau. Using the credit card. *Their* credit card. She thought back to their final fight Thursday evening, Carl Albert sobbing and hiccupping in the hallway, Terry stuffing his things in a duffel bag in the kitchen, yelling at Carl to get what he wanted from his room because they were not coming back! She'd been pacing and fuming in the front room and she didn't watch him, but of course he would have just grabbed the whole Cool Whip tub; he wouldn't have taken time to stick it in the microwave to thaw it and retrieve only his own card. Hardly.

Now what? she thought. Now what. She sat on the wooden stool at the kitchen counter with her hand on her purse. She didn't need to take out her check register; she knew what it said. The number would not have magically improved since she wrote their tithe check yesterday morning. But that deposit wouldn't have been made yet, would it? She could call Brother Oren. A wave of relief swept her. Yes. She'd call the preacher as soon as it got to be a decent hour, ask him to hold on to the check till next week, and when the bank opened in Wilburton she'd go to the drive-through and get cash. It'd be broad daylight by the time the kids got on the road, but that couldn't be helped. They couldn't go without money. Sweet doubted they even had enough gas to make it to Fort Smith. She began to gather a few items. They would have a long wait in the truck. She unplugged Terry's rechargeable flashlight from the pantry outlet, grabbed a bag of chips and an unopened jar of salsa, stopped by the hall closet and got down an old quilt, then snuck out to her Taurus and coasted back out of the driveway with her lights off.

As soon as she hit the gravel turnoff to the farm, she knew she'd made a mistake. In the rearview she saw not one set of head-lights but two. How dumb could she be? She should have told the kids to drive on to Wister, she'd catch up with them there. They were hemmed in now—the pasture fence was all grown up with briars and those ugly little wahoo trees; Daddy hadn't sprayed or cleared it in years. The only way out for Juanito's truck was back here through the barnyard. Sweet pulled over close to the house, thinking maybe she could draw the reporters this direction. Her mind clicked fast, trying to come up with some kind of a story for what she was doing out here in the dark at this hour, alone.

But when the vehicles pulled in and parked, they turned out not to be news vans but big F-350 pickups pulling horse trail-ers. What in the world? Baffled, Sweet sat in her car. In a min-ute Clyde Herrington tapped on her window. She turned the key, glided down the glass. "Where's Terry?" Clyde said. Sweet half opened her mouth, couldn't think of anything. She shrugged. "When he gets here," Clyde said, "let him know he's welcome to ride that red mare of mine if he wants. I'm not gonna saddle her till I see if we need her." He withdrew into the dark yard. Another truck and horse trailer pulled in. Soon there were seven trucks and trailers. Sweet could hear the thunk and rattle of shod hooves on metal flooring as the men backed their horses out of the trailers, the chink and clink of bridles, the soft creak of leather, murmured voices. Holloway's cruiser drove into the barnyard then, red and blue lights flashing, followed by a white Latimer County Sheriff's Department pickup and, yes, five TV news vans. She knew without being told that Arvin Holloway had hatched up this little showcase, a horseback search party, something showy and western, for the big-city news. She'd bet anything he'd contacted the stations himself.

Soon there were floodlights revealing a dozen or so ranchers in cowboy hats and Carhartt jackets milling about, coughing in the morning air, sharing thermoses of coffee. She prayed the kids would stay put across the pasture. Surely they wouldn't try to come back here. All this light and noise here at the barn, truck doors slamming, generators humming. Please, honey, Sweet said in her mind to Misty. Y'all be still, be silent. Be smart. Please, God, let the baby sleep. Don't let her wake up and get scared and start crying. The sheriff sauntered to the barn and positioned himself in front of the open door, waiting for the floodlights to be set for the cameras. At least with all these trucks and vans, Sweet thought, the tire marks from Juanito's pickup will be wiped out. But what about inside the barn? She quickly got out of the car and hurried over, halting just outside the circle of light. "Morning, Sheriff," she said, running her fingers back through her uncombed hair.

"Well, if it ain't Sweet Georgia Brown herself. Come out for the mountain search, did ya?" Holloway looked past her toward the milling ranchers behind her. "Where's that ornery husband of yours?"

"Oh, him and some of the guys he works with are covering the south pasture." She was amazed at how easily the lie came to her. "They're fixing to head on up over the ridge from there."

"In the dark?"

"They wanted to get an early start."

"I don't know how much earlier start a person needs than five A.M." Clearly Holloway didn't like anybody getting a jump on him, stealing his thunder in any possible way. He eyed Sweet in her bulky sweatpants and bunchy sweatshirt. "Hadn't seen them oatmeal cookies you promised."

"I've had a few other things on my mind, Arvin." She tried to hold the dislike out of her voice; it wouldn't help to make him mad.

"Is that right." His face suddenly became very serious and official looking. He barked at a passing deputy. "Hector! You bring them graphs and maps like I asked you? Well, get 'em the hell over here! What d'ya think I'm standing here for, waiting on you to get in the blame mood?" Positioning himself in the glow of the portable lights, Holloway made a great show of unrolling the topographical maps, holding them up and pointing to the squiggly lines and whorls, ordering this bunch to cover this ridge, that bunch to cover that one, while the cameras hummed ever so faintly.

"Mrs. Kirkendall?" It was the brunette from Channel 2. "I wonder if you'd be willing to say a word for us? Maybe, you know, make an appeal from the family?"

"I already did that," Sweet said.

"Yes, ma'am," the reporter said. "But 2News Working for You has such devoted viewers. Isn't it possible one of them might have

seen something?" She lilted the words, coaxing gently. "They might
catch you on tonight's broadcast and come forward. Sometimes
an appeal from the family can really help." She glanced toward
the barn where Holloway was holding forth on how rough the
terrain was—too rough for vehicles, even jeeps, he said. A four-
wheeler or a four-footed mule, that's what you needed, and even a
four-wheeler couldn't get through the underbrush, them searchers
would have to get off their fat fannies and walk. He was looking
at the ranchers when he said it, but they were all local men; they
didn't need to be told how rough this country was. The sheriff's little speech was meant for the TV crews, who were lapping it up. As
Sweet watched, the Channel 2 news reporter very studiedly turned
her back on the sheriff; she held her microphone a respectful distance from Sweet's face, nodded almost imperceptibly to her cameraman, who adjusted his lights, started shooting. Sweet thought
to herself, Keep them occupied. Keep them busy. Don't give them
any reason to go wandering around. She kept her eyes on the reporter's face. A pretty girl, not much older than Misty Dawn, with
good skin and perfect teeth and two last names, Logan Morgan,
Morgan Logan. A girl who'd almost certainly never had a member
of her family arrested. Or deported. Or lost.

"My nephew is a little innocent child," Sweet said. "He didn't
have anything to do with those Mexicans, or with his grandpa
helping them. But folks have been saying terrible things. Do you
know some of the things they've been saying?" The reporter smiled
encouragingly. "I don't care what the law is," Sweet said, "that little
boy doesn't *deserve* to be missing. This family doesn't *deserve* it.
Wherever Dusty is, he's probably so scared. We had that bad rain
night before last, he's probably out there in the woods alone, cold
and frightened . . . looking for shelter." A thought struck her then,
so crisp and clear it was almost like somebody said the words in

her brain: the old coal mine. Maybe Dustin had taken shelter in that old mine. Sweet almost called out to Holloway to ask if they'd thought to go inside the mine to look, but she caught herself. The mine was sunk into the ridge on the south side of Cedar Creek, and the low-water bridge that crossed the creek to get there was only a couple hundred yards past the place where Misty and Juanito were hiding. "We appreciate what the sheriff is doing," Sweet went on, "all the volunteers, but they're fixing to head south into the mountains on horseback. I don't know why my nephew would go there. I think it's more likely he went west."

"West?" the reporter chipped, a quick, bright-eyed sparrow. "What makes you say that?"

"Well, Wilburton's west of here. That's where his grandpa's in jail. I can't see Dusty going some other direction. I think he might've set out for the jail on one of the back roads. There's lots of woods between here and Wilburton. My husband is out there searching now. We tried to tell this to Sheriff Holloway, but it's hard to get him to listen." For the first time ever, Sweet smiled at Morgan Logan, Logan Morgan. "You're a pretty girl," she said. "Reckon you could get him to listen to you?"

Monday | *February 25, 2008* | *7:00 A.M.*

Hunter's Ridge Apartments | *Oklahoma City*

"You're going to have to go down there, babe," Charlie said, reaching for the jelly. Monica got up from the breakfast nook, carried her plate to the sink and scraped her untouched poached egg into the disposal, put the plate in the dishwasher. She stood looking at the television across the apartment. There was the kid's face again, that same grade-school picture. The banner underneath read:

BREAKING NEWS **WHERE IS DUSTIN?**
SEARCH FOR TEN-YEAR-OLD OKLAHOMA BOY CONTINUES.

Monica turned and poured the rest of her coffee down the sink. "You got to grab back the reins," Charlie was saying. "Tell it your way."

"I know that! Don't you think I know that?" She stepped across the room and fumbled under the scattered newspapers for the remote. As long as the coverage had stayed local, the spin had remained positive. Local media understood that Oklahomans, certainly the hefty majority of white Oklahomans, supported her law. But then the kid had to go and disappear, and once the news went national, the whole story line changed. They kept running this same picture of the kid over and over, his sad eyes and shaggy hair, that almost smile. On the screen an overly serious female reporter was intoning about "little Dustin Brown, who vanished from the family farm in southeastern Oklahoma after the arrest of his grandfather . . ." intercut with aerial scenes of the search site. The anchor's talking head reappeared framed by changing boxes showing the kid's picture, the sheriff in front of a microphone, men on horseback, a stock-footage view from the upstairs gallery of the empty House floor. Monica switched off the TV, went to the bedroom to finish dressing. She heard the television click back on. Charlie and his damn clicker. She grabbed her green velvet jacket from the hall closet. Charlie was staring into his open laptop on the coffee table. "Good luck, babe," he said, without looking up.

The drive to the capitol was too short; she needed more time to get her presentation together—not her presentation for House Bill 1906, which was coming up for the floor vote this afternoon and for which she'd practiced diligently all yesterday evening, but her presentation of Oklahoma State Representative Monica Moorehouse: her calm, unruffled answers, her self-deprecating smile. She pulled into a Starbucks drive-through. Four cars ahead of her. Fine. She tugged down the visor mirror. Oh, the cucumber slices Kevin recommended had helped not at all. She patted the fatty skin under her eyes. It wasn't supposed to go this way. How had she lost control of the narrative? Her absence. Her silence. That's what Charlie kept saying. But House Leadership wanted her to keep a low profile until after today's vote—and yes, all right, she'd been glad to acquiesce. She'd spent the weekend on the phone with the Speaker and the majority floor leader, or walking Penn Square Mall in headscarf and sunglasses, or lying in bed with cucumber slices on her eyelids.

On Sunday morning she told Charlie to go on to church without her. "No way, babe," he said. "Then they'll know you're in town." Which was true. Her technique for avoiding church more often than she could bear it was to let the people at Saint Luke's Methodist in Oklahoma City think she was at church in McAlester, and the congregation at Grand Avenue United Methodist in McAlester assume she was staying in the city this weekend. This way she only had to put in an appearance at one or the other every third or fourth Sunday during legislative session. This weekend was supposed to be one of her appearance Sundays, but like Charlie said: no way. She had called Kevin in the afternoon to ask if she could stop by (*Ah, no,* mon ami, *I've got* tres, tres *special company!*), did the brisk-walking routine at the mall again, worked a dozen find-the-word puzzles, went to bed straight after *60 Minutes*.

The last several days had been like a yo-yo, up and down, up and down. It was so hard to tell what people were thinking—especially Leadership. Everybody was so maddeningly tight-lipped, waiting to see which way the political winds were going to turn. Well, everybody who counted was mum, that is. There were plenty legislators from both sides of the aisle who were more than glad to rub up against her, metaphorically speaking; they loved all the national attention. But the real powers that be realized that this much uncontrolled media glare had the potential to go against them. Oh, everything would have been fine, absolutely fine, the immigration issue nothing but a win-win for them, for the state, for future elections—if not for that damn kid.

Would they never get gone? Sweet thought. It seemed to take forever for all the ranchers to mount up and head out in the rosy predawn light, three deputies riding with them. The cameramen were still coiling up their lengths of electric cords, repacking their equipment, when Holloway strolled over to where she sat in her car with the motor running and the heater on. She cracked the window as he bent down to peer in. "Why'd you tell that sassy reporter we oughta check the back roads? You know we've done searched this whole valley." Sweet didn't answer. "You might as well go on home," Holloway said, his voice decidedly unfriendly. "We'll call if we find anything."

"I'll wait here."

"Suit yourself." Holloway squinted at her a moment as if he expected her to say something, but Sweet turned her face to the windshield, stared at it until she heard the sheriff's cruiser start and drive off. Still for another few minutes she waited. She didn't trust but what Holloway would turn around and come back, just purposely trying to catch her at something.

The longer she sat waiting, the more convinced she became that Dustin really was hiding in the mine. It made some kind of crazy sense. He didn't want to be found. He thought he could stay hidden until people quit looking for him, and then he'd walk back here to the farm and stay by himself—and the old coal mine was a perfect hideout. She'd bet anything he liked to play there, the same way Sweet and Gaylene used to play there when they were kids. If their daddy found out they'd been in the mine, he would have a fit—the place was too dangerous for kids to play in, he said—but Sweet had usually managed to make sure he didn't find out. She had loved that place, she and Gaylene both. The clean, dry, shaley space at the mine's mouth, their perfect little room with its clear stream running through the center, and the air wafting out of the dark cave behind, always the just-right temperature, warm in winter, cool in summer. Sweet swallowed deep, put the Taurus in gear, headed across the barnyard toward the south pasture, her eyes skimming the rearview and side mirrors, checking all around.

Near the edge of the trash dump she stopped the car and got out. She couldn't see Juanito's truck anywhere. The tire marks were distinct along the rim of the gully right up to the wide sandstone place where the grasses gave way to rock and hardpan, and there they disappeared. She eased carefully along the edge of the gully. All the old junk was still here: rusting carcasses tipped along the ledge and down into the ravine, the dead water heaters and empty water cooler casings, worn-out pieces of farm equipment, the ancient white wringer washer she could remember from when she was a kid, and all the old bald tires and empty oil cans and plastic bleach jugs, and in the bottom of the gully piles and piles of blackened residue from the burn barrel dumped for decades from the back of Daddy's truck. But the huge white Dodge Ram was nowhere in sight. "Misty Dawn!" she called softly. "Juanito?" She listened, heard nothing. "Hey, you kids!" she said a little louder. "It's all right now. They're gone!"

At last she heard the crunch and break of sticks, the rustle of dried oak leaves, and soon Juanito emerged from the tangled underbrush on the other side of the ditch, way down to the left. He was carrying the baby, her lavender-clad legs dangling almost to his knees. Misty Dawn was behind him. Good Lord, how did they get all the way back in there? Sweet called across to them: "What did y'all do with the truck?" Misty Dawn motioned toward the creek. They came on, and Sweet made her way toward them until they were directly across the ravine from each other. "What was that all about?" Misty panted. "Who was it?" The girl's fear wasn't masked by fake boredom now—she was breathing hard, her face red and puffy, her eyes huge.

"Folks looking for your brother. They're gone now. Hey, it's good you hid the truck, though." Sweet scrambled down into the gully. The bottom was pure muck—tannish wet clay mixed with God knew what kind of gunk. She reached up a hand and Juanito helped her climb up. "How did y'all get over here?" she said, scraping muck off her boots with a stick. Misty Dawn pointed farther east along the ditch to where it grew narrower and shallower as it ran under the old barbed-wire fence. A little farther along past that, the fence was down, and Sweet could see broken underbrush where the truck had busted through. The tailgate was just visible through the scrub. "Hooray for four-wheel drive," Sweet murmured. "Listen, hon, y'all are going to have to stay here while I run to Wilburton and cash a check. I couldn't find my credit card." She held up her hand at Misty's protest. "Not long! Forty minutes, tops. But let's drive over and take a look in the coal mine first."

"What for?"

"Your brother."

"Dustin's in the coal mine?"

"I don't know. I just . . . got a feeling. Come on." She squeezed past them, began to wind her way down the old abandoned mining track toward the creek. The kids stayed close behind as she picked her way through the scraggly young cedars and scrub oak growing up in the road, but Sweet could hear, before she saw, that they were going to have to go back and get Juanito's truck. The rock low-water bridge was ordinarily dry, the creek a sluggish brown moccasin flowing underneath, but a good rain like they'd had on Friday could turn the creek into a torrent. If Dusty did go to the mine, Sweet thought, he couldn't have gotten back to this side if he'd tried—and pray God he hadn't tried. The water wasn't exactly a torrent now, but it was well up over the bridge, muddy as creamed coffee, and rushing fast. It could sweep a person away easily, especially somebody as light as Dustin—or Misty's skinny husband, for that matter. Sweet motioned them to turn around and go back. The baby stared at Sweet over her daddy's shoulder as they retraced their steps. Juanito unstrapped the car seat and set it in the truck bed while Sweet tried to tell him that he should let her drive, she knew the old track, exactly where the bridge was, but he acted like he didn't understand. He climbed into the driver's seat and started the truck. Misty sat in the middle holding the baby, her thighs jammed up high because of the hump under her feet. "No, mami," she said. The child was squirming, trying to wiggle off her lap. Misty Dawn rattled off some Spanish, but Lucha wouldn't quit wriggling.

"Come here to Aunt Sweet." Sweet reached for her and took her on her own lap, and the little girl settled down with two fingers in her mouth. The truck bumped hard as they started down the steep, washed-out track. "The bridge is there," Sweet said. "See where the water's swirling? See the rock ledge?" Misty Dawn repeated the words in Spanish. Juanito inched the truck slowly forward. Sweet tried to remember how much water it takes to swamp a vehicle. Two feet? This didn't look like two feet. Did it? The little girl snuggled against her, leaning toward the window so she could

see the water; she didn't look scared, merely interested. And somber. *Do not drive into moving water.* Sweet knew that. Everybody
knew that. The officials were always warning idiot people, who
were always doing it anyway. Like us, she thought. We are driving
into moving water. She kept a tight hold on the child, her right fist
on the door handle. If they got swept away, she would try to save
the baby. She would try.

"*Cuidado*, Juanito!" Misty Dawn's fingers were clamped tight
on Sweet's knee.

"It's fine," Sweet said lightly. "We'll be fine." The driver's side
suddenly dipped as the front tire dropped into a washed-out place,
and Misty Dawn screamed. Sweet grabbed her hand, dug her own
fingers under the vise grip, held on tight, her other arm clamped
around the child's waist. Juanito eased the tire up out of the hole,
steering a little to the right, and Sweet cried, "Watch out, watch
out! You're driving off this side!" Juanito straightened the wheel,
kept easing along, slow and steady, until they made it across, started
up the far bank, which was steeper and even more washed out than
the first. The truck swayed and bounced like a tractor.

At the top of the track, in under the cottonwoods, they stopped.
"See?" Sweet exhaled long and deep. "I told you we'd be fine." Her
voice was shaking. She let go of her niece's hand. "God. That was
scary," Misty said. She reached to take her daughter onto her lap.
"Plus, now we got to go *back*."

"Tell him to drive yonder." Sweet pointed to the knot of pur-
plish shale showing like a bruise on the side of the ridge through
the leafless trees. Misty rattled the Spanish, and Juanito put the
truck in gear, headed across the bumpy ground, seesawing between shrubs and thicket, the truck bouncing worse than ever as
they neared the slate-colored boney pile at the base of the ridge. A
deep blue-black gash slashed from the mine mouth all the way to

the foot of the ridge, carved right through the boney by the clear, constant stream. "This is probably as close as we're going to get," Sweet said, and at once Juanito put the truck in park. She cut him a look. He understood English when he wanted to.

Misty said, "I thought they supposedly searched this whole place already, all Grandpa's land."

"They might not have thought to look inside," Sweet said. "I'll be right back." She got out and began to climb along the side of the coal-colored gash until she reached the mine entrance, a black, low square, timbered across the roof and along both sides; it was so much smaller than she remembered. From the dark mouth the familiar soft breeze wafted. Sweet held still a moment, smelling the earth smell, the water smell, the pure stream. God's breath. She cupped her hands. "Dusty?" The sound came out choked, too soft. She cleared her throat. "Dustin Lee!" *Lee, lee, lee, lee* . . . The brief, hollow echo, then nothing. Only the sound of trickling water and, far back in the depths, a slow constant plink. Water dripping. She remembered the dripping.

Abruptly Sweet crouched over and squat-walked in. Beyond the timbers, the ceiling was higher, and she could stand, but she couldn't see anything past the first few feet. The smell was overpowering, though, sweet and earthen, so familiar it made her chest ache. "Dustin?" she said softly. "Honey, it's all right. We're not mad. We just want you to come home. Okay? Dusty?"

She listened again, heard only the continuous rippling song of the water. Their little river, that's what she and Gaylene used to call it, although it was never more than a few inches deep, clear as glass, flowing out of the darkness across the smooth shale floor. Outside in summers: the parched land, the fierce glare. Inside, the cool dark. They would bring flashlights and play house here in summer, or school, or Belle Starr and the outlaws. In winter, most often they used candles and sat in the warmth and told ghost stories, or Sweet told the stories, and Gaylene huddled against her, listening, thrilled. Sweet stared into the blackness. Why hadn't she thought to grab Juanito's flashlight? Even that weak beam would have been something. "You're not in trouble, honey," she said toward the darkness. "I promise."

Far back in the black depths she heard a child's voice: *Jaja, come heah!* Her breath stopped. The sound of water. "Dustin?" No, it wasn't Dustin, couldn't be Dustin. The only one who'd ever called her Jaja was Gaylene, when she was very little and couldn't say Georgia, couldn't pronounce the *r*. At once Sweet felt her little sister beside her, the wiry tense pliable presence, Gaylene waking in the night, frightened, reaching across the bed for her, the soft word whispered. *Jaja?* Because Daddy would be in the front room, yelling, stacking the furniture, stumbling from wall to wall, cursing, weeping, and Sweet would lay her arm outside the covers for Gaylene to hold. *You're dreaming, Sissy. Go back to sleep.* But Daddy was honking the truck's horn back at the house, calling them, they had to get home, fast! They had to—

Sweet blinked, shook her head, a fierce pinch-me-awake shake. "Dustin, if you're here, honey, answer me. It's Aunt Sweet." Only the water echoed. The earthen empty blackness. The boy was not here. Nobody was here. She could feel her certainty draining away. Why had she believed so hard he would be here? But she knew why. Her aching throat told her. The old hurtful longing. The quiet. The scent of earth and water. Her baby sister. God's breath.

Far away and faint, the truck horn sounded again. She hadn't dreamed it—it *was* their daddy's signal, the one-note tattoo he used to call them home for supper. For an instant her heart lifted, until she realized it couldn't be Daddy. It was Terry, sitting in his truck in the yard at Daddy's house, calling her the same way she called him in from the deer woods: when she needed him during deer season, she would drive up as far as she could get in the mountains, park at a gas well pad site, and honk out Daddy's same staccato rhythm so that Terry would know it was her and not some other wife trying to reach her deer-hunting husband. Sweet's first impulse was to ignore him, wait until he gave up and went away. But then she remembered her Taurus sitting at the trash dump, its nose pointing directly to the torn fence where Juanito's pickup had rammed through. She couldn't let her husband find that.

She bent double again, scuttled back outside, stood blinking in the sunlight, cold and clear, a brilliant crisp February morning. Then she scrabbled and skidded back down the ridge. The kids were outside the truck now, Misty Dawn holding the baby. "Who's that honking?

"Uncle Terry." Sweet walked past them, tossing the words back over her shoulder. "I gotta go back to the house for a minute. Y'all stay here."

"Why can't we come with you?"

"He might not be alone." Which was true, actually—Carl Albert would be with him, and no telling who else—but that wasn't why. "Y'all sit tight. I'll be back in two shakes."

She kept walking. In another second Juanito's truck started, and soon he pulled alongside her. "El agua," Juanito said, "es peligroso." Sweet stopped, squinted up at him. How to explain all of it? That her husband couldn't be trusted. That her husband might as soon turn him in as look at him. Juanito gestured toward the distant creek. "I drive you, okay? Then I come for my wife."

"No, you don't come for your wife," Sweet said. "You come stay with your wife! You get me?"

"Sí, claro." He beckoned through the window. "Come."

The trip back across the creek was harrowing but not so bad as the first. Nothing's ever as bad the second time, Sweet thought. The horn sounded again as they climbed the far bank. Sweet swung the truck door open before Juanito had hardly got stopped; she hurried around to the driver's side. "Go back and stay with Misty." He had his head turned away, looking through the back window to see how to turn around. "Juanito!" His smooth face swiveled to her. Sweet bounced her two open palms in a "stay" gesture like you'd give a dog. "Stay," she said. "You and Misty, stay. Understand?"

"Okay. See you later." He started to back up.

Okay. See you later. She hurried along, picking her way through the scrub brush until she reached the gulley and scrambled down. Terry wasn't honking in rhythm now, just one long continuous blare. *HONNNNNNNNK*. She ran to her car, considered tapping out an answer—but no, that would only draw his attention this direction, not to mention provoke such questions as What the hell took you so long? She started the car and headed toward the house. She had to get Terry to go home. No. No! Not home. Back to Poteau. Because she was going to have to hide the kids at the house and wait for dark—what else was she going to do with them? She'd make them all lie down in her backseat for the drive to town. How she would sneak them from the carport into the house in broad daylight she didn't know, but she'd cross that bridge when she came to it. Sweet snorted. Cross that bridge.

Her husband's large Silverado looked oddly small in comparison to the giant horse-trailer-hauling pickups parked all around. Terry himself looked small, standing beside the open truck door with his burgundy cap in his hand. Their son wasn't with him. Sweet glided her window down. "Where's Carl?"

"At the preacher's. I went by there looking for you. He said you must have come out here for the mounted search." He glanced behind her toward the pasture. "What were you doing?"

"Just, you know, looking around. For Dustin."

"Hadn't they been out there already? They been all over this property."

"I know, I just, you know. Killing time. Waiting on the searchers to get back."

Silence. After a moment, Terry said, "How you doing?'

"Good. Good," she said. "You?"

"Good."

"How's Carl?"

"He's good."

Another silence. Tee stood in the crook of the truck door, examining his frayed cap brim, turning it in his hands, plucking at the loose threads. After a long time he said, "I'm . . . I'm . . . I really hate it that it turned out like it did for your daddy. And for . . . everything."

"Okay," she said. That was the nearest she'd ever heard him come to saying *I'm sorry.*

"Me and Carl, we . . ." Terry glanced up. "He needs to be home, Sweet." Her husband waited, gazing steadily at her now, the bags under his eyes thicker and paler than ever. When she didn't answer he looked back down, gave the cap another turn. "We oughta . . . we got to be in this together." He raised his sad brown gaze. "I need to be at home."

Seventeen years. He was a good man. She loved him. "Just . . . not right yet, Tee," she said, wavering. "Carl Albert don't need to be in the middle of all this. Let's wait till things settle down. Till after Dustin comes home."

"We'll deal with it," Terry said. "We're a family. I'm, I really am . . . aw, honey, you know I didn't mean for things to get messed up like this."

"You didn't."

"Not for your dad! Not for Carl Albert, or Dustin!"

"Just for the Mexicans?"

"It ain't every Mexican, just the wetbacks! Just ones coming here to take people's jobs! You know how many men been laid off from Arkoma in the last year? Nineteen! Look, I come out to borrow your dad's trimmer for the bar ditch. His truck was gone so I went to the barn to get it, the place was crawling with them, they scattered like a bunch of minnows! Not a damn one of them could speak English. They couldn't even tell me where your daddy was at! Face it, Sweet, he's a fanatic. I'm sorry, but he is. You seen how he acted last summer at that blamed whatever it was, that party at Misty Dawn's house!"

Yes, she remembered; in her mind's eye she could see her father on the Mexican side of the yard gesturing around with his hands, acting out the words, while Terry leaned against the church van with his arms folded, watching him—and yes, all right, it had bothered Sweet, too, honestly, to see how cleanly her daddy fit in over there, but that was him. That was just Daddy, a man who would go to a Mexican church in Heavener the same as he'd go to a black church in McAlester, or a Catholic church, even, just . . . whatever. Daddy just had that weird streak. She remembered how Terry groused the whole ride home, talking low, barely over the van's motor, so her daddy wouldn't hear from the back. If Sweet wanted to go to any more family shindigs in Tulsa, he'd muttered, she could blamed well drive herself. This was the last time he was putting up with such crap! Sweet had wondered in silence what was so terrible that he'd had to put up with—a little trumpet music and barbecue smoke? Her daddy trying to act like he knew Spanish? Aloud she'd said only, "All right, you won't have to go. I'll drive next time."

But there hadn't been a next time. The police had stopped

Juanito a few months later for—what was it? Some sort of driving infraction, illegal lights or something; Sweet never quite got the whole story. It had happened so fast. By the time Misty called Sweet, sobbing hysterically on the phone, Juanito was already in the Tulsa County Jail. And then he was gone.

A cold thought struck her then, sinister, sickening. Had Terry turned in Juanito, too? Sometime after the party? But why would he do that? Oh, surely, surely to goodness the man she had lived with all these years was not that low-down ordinary skunk-ugly mean. She looked at him now, scratching his chin under his beard, rubbing his forehead; she knew the signs. He was starting to lose patience. He suddenly tugged his cap on, reached in and swiped his keys off the dash. "I hate that frickin' motel," he said. Then he leaned in and jabbed the truck key in the ignition, which started to buzz. The door dinger dinged to announce that it was standing open with the key in the ignition. Terry straightened, stood peering down at her, a firm, settled look. "We're not waiting till Dusty comes home. He might not ever come home. He might be—"

"Shut up!" She whacked him on the chest. "Don't you *dare* say it! Don't you ever, *ever* say those words!"

"Aw, honey, no. I don't mean that. We'll find him, sure. Right now today, this morning. They might've found him already." He reached for her. She let him pull her toward him, let him put his arms around her back, but she didn't soften against him. "Don't worry, honey, he'll turn up." Terry tried to make his rough voice soothing; he stroked the back of her head with his big paw. "He's probably just, who knows, wandering around. The sun's out, he'll get his bearings, he'll come on in, the men'll find him, don't worry, it's all right, it's all right . . ." The buzzer buzzed, the dinger dinged. After a time Terry reached in and unseated the key. In the silence Sweet heard a motor coming up the gravel road. She twisted around, and Terry released her as she turned toward the approaching vehicle—a mud-spattered SUV filled with men. Her heart lurched. Back already. That was good. Maybe that was good. Or bad. She didn't recognize the fellow climbing out of the driver's seat. She couldn't tell a thing from his expression. Terry took her hand, held tight while they waited.

"Did the sheriff get here yet?" the man said.

"We don't expect him till the teams get back," Terry said.

Sweet looked beyond the man's shoulder at the five men in red hunting caps inside the Explorer. She didn't know any of them, either.

"Deputy in town told us to wait here for the sheriff," the man said. "He don't want folks going out unless him and his men co-ordinate it."

"Y'all haven't been out searching?"

"Got to wait on the sheriff. But they said he'll be here pretty quick. Soon as he can get things organized."

"What things?"

"I don't know. Communication lines. Or paperwork, maybe? I really don't know. They're moving search headquarters out here from Wilburton, they said. Sheriff wants everybody heading out from one location, wants it all centrally coordinated. Makes sense, I guess. How about we pull over and park next to that GMC? That won't be in y'all's way, will it?"

Monica had felt all morning like she was sleepwalking through her committee meetings. Present in body, absent in mind. Her grande extra-shot skinny latte had failed to help. Half her attention was focused on trying to rehearse her bill presentation, the other half kept looking over her shoulder, wondering who was talking about her, and what they were saying. Lunch was no better. Prepped and served by a clutch of student dieticians flanked by homemade signs advocating healthy eating, the food would have ordinarily suited her—baby carrots, chunks of broccoli and cauliflower, ranch dressing, fruit cups, little cartons of 2 percent milk—but today she had no appetite whatsoever. And where were her brains?

Tanked up on caffeine and no food, by the time session started, Monica Moorehouse was grinding her teeth. The speaker pro tem's voice reverberated over the sound system: "The House is now in session! Clerk will call the roll!" Everyone kept milling and milling and gossiping and laughing, which irritated the bejesus out of her. Nothing out of the ordinary, just the regular early-session roving, but the chitchat and commotion further frazzled her nerves. Things weren't helped when the representative from the Nineteenth District stood to introduce his special guests, the assistant chief of the Choctaw Nation and a whole row of tribal elders. And wouldn't you know, the Doctor of the Day just had to be named Gonzalez.

"The House will come to order! The House will come to order!" Her desk partner, Representative Thompson, strolled in, laid his two cell phones on the desk, clicked his laptop awake. His BlackBerry buzzed and he picked it up, strolled out again. Numbly she listened to the session unfold: Speaker recognizes Representative Renegar for questions on the amendment . . . Thank you, Mr. Speaker . . . Members of the House, prepare for debate . . . without objection . . . roll call, final passage House Bill 1727 . . . Representative McDaniel, you are recognized to explain your bill . . . Thank you, Mr. Speaker . . . Members of the House, please come to order! Debate is in progress . . . Roll call, final passage House Bill 1893 . . . Will there be debate? Seeing no debate . . . Representative Cox votes aye, Representative Wright votes aye . . . Members wishing to vote or change their vote . . . prepare to declare the vote . . . having received 73 ayes and 26 nays, the chair declares the bill passed . . .

It seemed forever before she finally heard the pro tem call her name. "Representative Moorehouse, you are recognized to explain your bill."

When she rose from her desk, she felt the gallery's eyes on her, as well as the eyes of almost all her fellow legislators, a kind of watchful attentiveness rare on the House floor. But the effect of so much audience steadied her, and she proceeded fluidly, making every point she'd practiced, even after she'd glanced up at the south gallery and spied in the padded burgundy row directly below the Indians a small clutch of middle-aged Hispanic-looking men in business suits. This would be the Oklahoma Association of Hispanic Professionals, no doubt. Or possibly members of the Coalition of Latino Clergy and Christian Leaders. But Monica kept right on explaining the provisions of the bill smoothly, efficiently, right through to the end.

"Will the representative entertain questions?" the pro tem asked by rote. This was a point much discussed over the phone with Leadership, and one she'd been uncertain about until this very moment, but a kind of bold confidence rushed through her. "Yes, Mr. Speaker," she said, and she remained standing, microphone in hand, fielding the opposition's barbed but politely veiled inquiries about "unintended consequences" and "negative fiscal impact" if the state had to defend against federal lawsuits with House Bill 1906 as they were still doing with the bill's predecessor HB 1830, et cetera, et cetera. Monica maintained her frozen smile throughout the minority's irrelevant commentary about crap that had almost nothing to do with the current bill.

"My constituents in western Oklahoma," Representative Johns declared, "have contacted my office numerous times about how badly they're hurting for workers. We've got a real labor shortage since this bill's predecessor went into effect—not just farm workers but skilled construction labor, too, I'm told."

"The simple solution for that, Representative Johns, is for them to hire citizen workers."

"Thank you, Representative Moorehouse. That's very good advice. But they tell me every citizen in my district that wants to work is already working. Contractors are having to turn down jobs on account of they can't get workers. Now, now," he said, raising his hand as if to fend off an assault, "I promise you, nobody's advocating for illegal workers. But one of the unintended consequences of this bill's predecessor is how it took whole work crews out of the state, whole entire families, many of them here legally, maybe even the majority. This bill's predecessor, House Bill 1830, created such a climate of fear that folks left in droves, and that has produced some real problems in my district. So my question here this afternoon, Representative Moorehouse, is this: Couldn't one of the unintended consequences of House Bill 1906 be to create such an inhospitable environment—"

At which point Monica waved her microphone avidly at the pro tem, who immediately recognized her. "An inhospitable environment is just what we *want* to create for lawbreakers, wouldn't you agree, Representative Johns? We intend to roll up the welcome mat for these lawbreakers, just as we intend to quit having Oklahoma taxpayers pay to educate their children! And to that end, I believe that the education notification provision in House Bill 1906 addresses the issue very well . . ." And she went on to pull the focus back to the bill at hand.

Another member, from one of the Tulsa districts, stood to speak of the recent negative national publicity creating a damaging image of the state, but Monica fended that off with, "Representative Howe, what is your question?" She received plenty of support from fellow majority members in the form of friendly leading questions, the answers to which tripped off her tongue, including debate on the touchy English Only provision—touchy solely because of the Indians, but she had that part deftly rehearsed. "Oklahoma is infinitely proud of its Native American heritage, we *are* Native America, as everyone in this august House knows, and certainly we would never want to do anything that would in any way impinge on that great proud heritage . . ." And so forth.

Still, she was unsure, really, until the voting was well started just how it would go. But the bill passed—with less of a resounding margin than 1830, it's true, far less of a margin than she'd hoped for—but a respectable number of minority members had voted aye, and she knew that the Senate vote, when it came up in a few weeks, was a shoo-in; everybody knew that. House Bill 1906 was a done deal. Unless the governor vetoed. But how could he, when he'd so ceremoniously signed 1830 into law? Anyway, they had the votes to override a veto, she was sure of it. Elated, she was smiling her thanks to several nearby lawmakers when she spied one of the Senate assistant floor leaders motioning to her from the outer hall. Flush with triumph, she went out to see what he wanted.

"Congratulations, Representative Moorehouse. Fine work." Yes? Then why did he look so sour. "I don't want to take a bunch of your time," he said. "I've just been visiting with some people from my district who drove over from Sapulpa this afternoon. They told me a bit of, I don't know, some disconcerting news I thought I'd pass along. It would seem that the Latimer County sheriff is going to be on *Larry King Live* tonight. The promo clips have been rolling all morning."

If she hadn't been so in the zone right then, Monica probably would have groaned out loud. The sheriff was a media hog and an egotistical fool, like Charlie said, and every time he opened his mouth he made Oklahoma look worse. But *Larry King Live*, good God, couldn't somebody have prevented that? It wouldn't just be a cringe-producing sound bite, it would be a whole goddamn interview. She held on to her smile. "Well, that is unfortunate news, Senator. Thanks for letting me know. But I'm sure it'll be fine."

"Yes, well. Apparently the reason he's going on is to defend his arrest techniques. The clips show him denying that that child's beat-up face had anything to do with the initial raid or the boy's treatment at the hands of his men."

"Are you kidding me?"

"I wish I were."

"I thought that was a dead story!"

"If it was, it's been resurrected."

"But the man's an idiot! That's only going to give it legs!"

The senator shrugged. Monica heard the chair finalizing the bill. "Oh my God. Excuse me, Senator!" And she rushed back onto the floor, but she was too late. The minority whip had already captured her bill. This time she did groan audibly, if faintly. Never once had she failed to recapture one of her own bills—that small bit of procedural housekeeping that ensured she'd be the only one permitted to bring it up again. Now the opposition had captured it; they could bring it up for reconsideration, in the meantime having tried to work the floor to make the vote tilt their way—or at minimum adding language that would nullify the bill's intent. Leadership would *not* be happy. She tried to tell herself it would be okay, but the pass margin had been too slim; she couldn't quite convince herself there was no reason to worry.

Dear God, Sweet said to herself, not prayerfully, as she sat in her car watching the men standing around her daddy's barn smoking cigarettes and spitting brown Skoal streams on the muddy ground. Those poor kids out yonder, she thought. What must they be thinking by now? Terry had been stuck to her side like beggar's lice all morning while more and more vehicles filled with searchers poured in to her daddy's yard. A couple of times she had managed to stroll to the corner of the barn and peer nonchalantly across the pasture toward the dump, but she saw no sign of Juanito's pickup. Surely they wouldn't come in with all this activity in the barnyard? Surely if they'd tried, they would have seen from a distance what was happening and stayed put. She couldn't figure out how to drive back to them without raising Tee's suspicions, much less conjure some smooth way to sneak that big white Dodge Ram past this passel of men. And these guys weren't going anywhere, at least not until after the sheriff got back. And then, well, the sheriff would be here. Strutting his banty walk, preening for the cameras, holding court in front of the barn.

Through the windshield Sweet watched her husband talking with the others, one steel-toed work boot propped on his tailgate. He wasn't in hunting clothes and he wasn't chewing tobacco—

she'd made him quit that before they got married—otherwise he was indistinguishable from the rest. The brimmed cap. The serious, concerned frown. The secret excitement. Each of them wanted to be the one to find Dustin. Sweet felt she could see both parts in them: how truly bothered they were by this situation— the lost boy could be their own boy, their own grandson—and so they had to act gruff in order to not let their emotions show. They *had* to chain-smoke, spit tobacco juice, talk about the weather and the brambly terrain in low, grumbling voices, so as not to let their throats catch.

But at the same time, Sweet thought, there was a little thrill in the back of each one's mind—maybe he'd be the one to save the day. For the boy's sake, of course, and the family, too, sure. But still. Maybe this very day he himself, the searcher, would turn out to be a hero. They were all secretly thinking it, Sweet believed. She loved them. She hated them. She wished they'd all go home. No. She wished they'd just go out and look for Dustin, comb the hills and the valleys, everywhere, everywhere, except across the creek, the south ridge that held the old mine. But nobody was leaving. And her husband stood there among them, his face grave and concerned, just like the rest, and he meant it, he really did. He *was* worried. He loved Dustin. She knew that. He loved Dustin, and he loved her, and maybe in some ways he even loved her daddy. And still he had done what he did.

Suddenly Sweet swung open the car door. Terry turned to look at her. "Where you going, babe?" "Nowhere," she answered. "I just feel like sitting on the front porch." And that's what she did, walked around the house and climbed the front steps and sat in the heavy iron lawn chair somebody had dragged up there from the weed-ridden yard. She looked at the overgrown field beyond the fence in front of the house, the blue humpbacked hills in the distance. Her chest was heaving, not with sobs, or even gulps of air, just a slow, steady, up-and-down heave, because she knew now that she was going to leave her husband. Not a temporary separation, not a little secret heart murder that she didn't honestly mean, but for real and all. The sense of ending, the completeness of it, was a little bit like death. After a moment, Sweet put her hand on her breastbone, pressed hard, harder; then she stood up and went in the house.

The familiar smell hit her—linoleum wax, linseed oil, the musty spidery smell creeping up from the cellar—and for a second she almost broke down. She didn't break though, but gritted her teeth and went directly to Daddy's room at the back of the house. Quickly she opened the cedar chest at the foot of his bed and pulled out several mothball-scented quilts, stacked them on the bedspread, and then went to the kitchen. Damn it, she thought, opening and shutting cupboards. There's nothing here. She opened the fridge, stared at the empty shelves. What was her daddy doing, starving the boy? Chicken broth and tomato paste and three cans of Pet milk. Fat lot of good that was going to do. Sweet tasted salt at the corner of her mouth; she licked back the tears, plucked a couple of black trash bags from the box on the shelf and returned to the bedroom to stuff the quilts inside.

From the wall closet she pulled out Daddy's tan feeding jacket for Juanito and a bumpy, slick red down vest for Misty Dawn; she was thinking that they'd just have to wrap the baby in quilts to keep her warm, when she spied her daddy's rifle standing butt down in the dark closet corner. With hardly a thought she carried the gun to the bed and stuffed it barrel-first in the trash bag with the quilts. Then she lugged the bags to the front room, where she paused to grab the two hurricane lamps off the mantel. But no, that would be way too obvious if she toted those outside. And she couldn't stuff them in with the quilts and jackets, kerosene would leak all over everything. Another vehicle was coming up the drive; she could hear the motor, the crunch of gravel—might the men from this morning be coming back? Sweet stepped to the side window. Two men in insulated coveralls and orange hunting vests were getting out of a dark green Jeep Grand Cherokee— newcomers.

Sweet went back to the kitchen. Silent tears began sliding down her cheeks when she tugged open the cellar door and made her way down the splintery steps until she could feel for the light string overhead. The yellow bulb showed the shelved rows of dust-rimmed Mason jars full of home-canned green beans and tomatoes and okra and blackberry jelly and pickled pigs' feet and shredded pork. She gathered as many jars as she could carry and went back upstairs, where she grabbed the cans of chicken broth and con- densed milk from the pantry, fished some spoons and forks and a can opener out of the kitchen drawer, and then began emptying the cleaning supplies out of a beat-up brown Rubbermaid tub she pulled out from under the sink. Sweet had to pause to wipe her face on her sleeve as she set the food jars and cans inside the tub. She dumped the Lipton packets out of the tea canister, found some more trash bags, and in the living room she knelt and unscrewed the globes from the two hurricane lamps, poured the kerosene into the tea canister, tightened down the lid, set everything in the rub- ber tub and cushioned it as well as she could. The slow silent tears were still running when she went into the bathroom and retrieved a couple of hand towels to wrap the globes in, still running as she swaddled the filled tub in layers of black trash bags, but by the time she stepped out onto the back porch, the tears had stopped. She took a deep breath, went down the back steps toward her hus- band.

She smiled when she got close. "I cleaned out the fridge, a bunch of old food garbage and stuff. I'm going to take it out to the dump before it stinks up the house."

Terry was distracted. "Need any help?" he said, but his gaze was on the first fellow from the Explorer who was now explaining things to the two newcomers.

"It's not that much," she said, and got in her car, drove to the back porch. She would have liked to drive around to the front where nobody would see her putting the trash bags in the car, but that would most likely just draw suspicion, so she backed up to the rear porch steps, parked as close as she could. She was surprised, really, at her own calmness as she loaded the trash bags in her trunk. Maybe it wasn't true calm, just exhaustion, but somehow it didn't seem to matter now how any of this turned out. Whether she went to jail or not. Whether they caught Juanito or didn't. Whether her daddy came home or got sent to the McAlester state pen. She waved a little friendly wave at her husband as she passed the barn.

Driving slowly across the pasture, her tongue thick and metallic tasting from too many hours without food, she considered that maybe her calmness was not just fatigue but also hunger. The only thing that seemed to matter, really, was Dustin, and even that, she thought, was going to be all right. Or it would be what it would be. She passed the old dump in a kind of daze, drove around the downed barbed wire where Juanito's truck had broken through. Now, though—*now* her heart quickened.

The moment she started down the steep track toward the creek, those old fight-or-flight self-preservation hormones, or whatever they were, rushed a fierce heat through her veins. Her chest burned. Her mind raced as fiercely as her blood. All this time, she realized, ever since this whole sorry saga began, she'd been thinking in old ways. And the old ways were gone, her old life was gone. There was nobody at home she had to go fix breakfast for, nobody to drive to school or clean house for, nobody to bathe and diaper and spoon-feed. For the first time in seventeen and a half years, she was alone. The bottom of her car scraped and bumped against the high humps as she descended toward the water; she did not have four-wheel drive, she did not even swim all that well. She stared at the muddy creek sweeping fast across the invisible bridge, but she did not hesitate, just glided the Taurus straight into it, because there was one other thought going round and round in her mind, eddying like the brown swirling water churning beneath the car's chassis: this had all been arranged.

By the end of the day State Representative Monica Moorehouse
was hungry, angry, lonely, tired. Not necessarily in that order. She
waited in her office with the door closed until she heard Beverly
leave at last. The outer hall had been quiet for hours. Still, Monica
sat in her Aeron chair, tapping her nails on the mahogany desktop.
Her cell phone buzzed. She ignored it. The thought of going home
to Charlie and his TiVo and his clicker and his advice and questions and rehashed commentary from all those Internet bloggers,
well, it was unbearable. Smiling through tonight's reception would
be no better, two hours of club soda and stale hors d'oeuvres while
she wondered what people were saying behind her back. She pulled
her desk phone toward her, but then slowly withdrew her hand and
reached instead into her bottom file drawer for her Coach bag. She
dropped her cell phone in the bag, dug out her keys. She wouldn't
call ahead, she decided. She would just show up.

Kevin's apartment was in a fine old high-ceilinged home in
the Paseo District not far from the capitol. The neighborhood was
artsy and run-down, most of the beautiful old homes divided into
apartments, but the area was on a gentrification upswing. Kevin
had taken the ground floor of a decrepit three-story monstros-
ity and turned it into a cream and chrome gem. Monica consid-

ered that he might not be home this early, but his black Jetta was parked in the drive, and when she climbed the steps to the broad porch, she could hear Phoebe Snow singing "Poetry Man" in the living room. Kevin and his retro-everything taste. She rang the bell, waited, rang again. Disappointed, thinking that perhaps his Special Company was still here, she turned to leave, but the door opened. Kevin was barefoot, wearing jeans and a soft dove-gray sweater. He studied her quizzically a moment, shook his head.

"What?" she said.

"When are you ever going to believe me that I know what looks best on you?"

Monica resisted the urge to reach up with both hands to cover her rinse-dulled hair. "How's Sniffy?"

"Sniffy," Kevin said, "is perfect!" He opened the door wide for her to come in, motioned her to the cream-colored sofa, where his long-haired teacup Chihuahua lay nestled on a throw pillow, and continued toward the kitchen, flinging over his shoulder, "We're looking a tad furfuffled, aren't we?"

"Bitch of a day," she answered. Sniffy was gazing up at her with his dark marble-round eyes, his too-long tongue protruding, as always, from his too-tiny mouth. "What was wrong with him?" she called out. Kevin's muffled voice echoed from the far side of the kitchen.

"Pancreatitis."

"Aw, poor baby." She heard cupboard doors opening and closing.

"He's fine now," Kevin called. "Thank God for modern medicine."

"Hey, Sniffy," she said. The dog's little rump quivered; she reached for him and settled him in her lap, stroking his silky beige hair. He was extra teeny even for a miniature, but he didn't *yip-yip-yip* like most little dogs—not because he was so well trained but because his too-tiny mouth and too-big tongue kept him from it. He was like a little plush toy, except that he was warm and could move on his own and his coat was infinitely soft. His little doggy poops were no bigger than a baby's thumb. He was always silent. This made him, in Monica's view, the perfect pet.

Kevin appeared in the breezeway holding up a box marked Good Earth Chai Tea in one hand, a bottle of Grey Goose in the other. She pointed to the vodka—she wasn't going to the reception anyway, she could do as she bloody well pleased. Monica relaxed, leaning back to admire the room, its clean lines and sleek surfaces, the minimalist colors: cream and white and brown and beige, here and there an accent of lacquered red or black. The faux fireplace, with its natural gas flames flickering and dancing among the logs, was the most realistic fake fire she'd ever seen. She could smell the pine incense Kevin always burned when he had it lit. Phoebe Snow whined and trilled on the Bose player sitting atop the glass and chrome bookshelf, *I—I—I wish I was a willow*, and Kevin waltzed in, singing accompaniment, with two enormous frosted martini glasses and a bowl of green olives on a chrome tray.

"Okay, babycakes," he said, settling beside her, leaning over to take Sniffy from her lap. "Talk to me. What is it makes our bitch of a day such a bitch?"

"Long story." She wasn't sure if she wanted to talk about it. Maybe she just wanted to sit here and relax. "I didn't know if you'd be home yet."

"No civilized person works past cocktail hour. I told you. Didn't I tell you? My twenty-ninth birthday present to myself: no more cuts after four, no more foil wraps after two thirty."

"Oh, right, I forgot," she said. A little wave of guilt swept her.

Kevin's birthday last week was the first she'd missed since she'd known him. But he'd held the celebration in the Copa bar at the Habana Inn! She couldn't be seen going in there. He knew that. "Lovely," she murmured. He'd been telling her for months he was going to start curtailing his hours, which he had the wherewithal to do now, he said, because, in case she hadn't heard, he was, according to the *Gazette's* Best of OKC Awards, officially *the* hottest stylist in Northwest Oklahoma City! "How was your weekend?" Monica asked, meaning, *How did it go with your* tres, tres *Special Company?*

"Shall we say . . . disappointing." Kevin suddenly plopped Sniffy back in her lap, jumped up to change the CD player, punching buttons till he had the song he wanted. Chet Baker's too-sweet, breathy voice crooned into the room. "I Get Along Without You Very Well." Monica leaned back, closed her eyes, caressed the dog. Kevin was perpetually disappointed. Or pretended to be. He was always declaring that he wanted a steady relationship, but Monica knew better. The fact he hadn't found a steady boyfriend in McAlester back in the day made sense— the pool was too small. But he'd lived in the City for nearly five years. The gay community here was relatively large, and most definitely avid. He could have found a partner by now if he really wanted one. Kevin was like her, Monica thought, only interested in a certain sharply defined type of intimacy. Emotional intimacy, that is. Physical intimacy was quite another matter. And never the twain shall meet, Monica thought, taking another sip of her martini.

The kind of intimacy she preferred was precisely the kind she shared with Kevin: comfortable old-shoe familiarity, with none of the sexual tension of male-female relationships or the jealousies and rivalries of same-sex friendships. For years they'd been privy to each other's secrets. They each knew that the face the other presented to the world was but a fragment of the whole—and usually not the most telling fragment. Their relationship, for instance. He was positively her closest friend—far closer, in many ways, than Charlie—but she could hardly present *that* to the world. And Kevin, who'd spent the first sixteen years of his life disguising his truest self, understood her need for discretion. This was part of why their friendship worked, she thought. Neither made the least demand on the other. She rolled her head, releasing the tension in her neck, sipped her drink. What a relief it was, just to sit here.

"How many ways can I say it?" Kevin reached for the plate of olives, crossed his long bronzed feet on the coffee table. "Champagne is *your* color. Why won't you trust me?"

Well, except, for this, of course. How he tried to instruct her where his sense of style was concerned. Yes, it was true, he did have great taste. Everything about the apartment worked. Everything about Kevin worked: his simple, expensive, muted-color clothes, the small jasper stud in his left earlobe. But he didn't understand politics. Or that wasn't fair—he understood well enough; he just preferred living contrary to the flow. Back when he worked at Supercuts in McAlester, his hair had been flaming-lips red and he'd kept it picked out in a fiery, wiry, Afro-looking halo. Now he wore it in a sleek, close-cropped wavy cut, the color a perfectly highlighted, burnished chestnut. Back then, he'd plucked his brows to a deep arch and worn tons of jewelry, as if he had to be as outrageous as possible in a place that tolerated no outrageousness. Now, he maintained a perfect airbrushed tan year-round, was otherwise unadorned, completely subtle and sexy in his soft, slim-fit clothes. He'd embedded himself in a community where he could have presented himself as flamboyantly as he might want, and so he no longer needed to. "Champagne Ice," he said. "It brings out your eyes."

Monica sighed. "I told you, Kev. It's too dramatic."

"Since when is dramatic bad? Come here, baby." And he took his dog back. Monica didn't trouble herself to repeat what she'd said already so many times—she had a conservative image to uphold. Kevin pooh-poohed image, even though he groomed his own as carefully as any *Entertainment Tonight* personality. She leaned over and whisked away the olive plate he'd balanced on his stomach next to Sniffy. "I have three things to say about Champagne Blonde." She popped an olive in her mouth. "Malibu Barbie. Dumb blonde jokes. Norma Zimmer."

"Who's Norma Zimmer?"

"The Champagne Lady on Lawrence Welk."

Kevin laughed.

They'd met the first month after Charlie moved her to McAlester. She had been dismayed to discover the dearth of hair salons as well as restaurant choices and had stalked into Supercuts in the strip mall that day in a fit of pique, anticipating a total hack job—she would show her husband just what he'd done, moving her to the effing outback! But Kevin, delighted to find someone from "back east" in his small town, had waltzed around the beautician's chair and within ten minutes had given her the best cut she'd had since she used to travel to Chicago to get her hair done. They'd been buddies ever since. One day, over sandwiches in Jana's Tea Room on Carl Albert Parkway, their twice-weekly ritual, she'd said offhandedly, "You're too talented to stay in this little podunk town, Kev." "Yes," he'd answered. "Too talented, and entirely too queer." She'd never dreamed he'd go off and leave her. Two weeks later he'd announced that he was moving to the City to work and save money for the big move, New York or L.A., he hadn't decided yet which. In Oklahoma City, though, Kevin had found a place, a life; he'd quit making plans to flee to the coast. "Why would I? I've got everything right here! Everything but a steady boyfriend—and the cost of living is so cheap!" Stroking Sniffy's back now, he narrowed his eyes critically, examining her crown. "At least let me put some highlighting back in. You look like you've had your head dipped in an iced tea vat."

"All right!" she said. "I'll call Sherry tomorrow and make an appointment."

Mollified, he reached for his martini. "So tell me again. What's got your panties in such a twist."

"You've seen the news."

"You know I only watch *Dancing with the Stars*."

She started to tell him how cable news had glommed onto the story and wouldn't leave it alone, but Kevin interrupted her before she'd got past describing the kid's picture. "I keep telling you, darling—why don't you leave those poor Mexicans alone?"

She frowned at him. The problem was the kid, not the Mexicans, but she began her presentation list: how illegal aliens don't pay taxes but use taxpayer-supported public services, how they take jobs from legal citizens, how much it costs the state to educate their children . . . her voice trailed away. She felt incredibly bored. Maybe she'd repeated it too many times. "Kevin, for God's sake, it's not about them, it's about me. I'm the focus of too much hyped press, or my work is. I've just got to finesse it."

"Well," he said soothingly, "this calls for fortification." He tucked Sniffy in her lap again, cupped a martini glass in each hand and went to the kitchen to fix them another. She watched the archway a moment, glanced up at the large chrome abstract Roman numeral clock dominating the west wall, then hunted around until she found Kevin's remote where he'd secreted it in a console drawer. She pointed it toward the small flatscreen in the corner, but didn't click it on. Before Kevin returned with fresh drinks and a plate of cheese and grapes, she'd replaced the remote in the drawer, kicked off her heels, and was sitting with her eyes closed and her stocking feet on the coffee table, petting Sniffy. She opened her eyes, smiled. She was, she decided, a little drunk. Nevertheless, she accepted the martini. "Thank you, good sir."

"You are welcome, good lady. Something else is nagging your little gut. Speak."

"Nothing. It's nothing." She tilted her glass, peered through it at the fireplace. "Charlie wants me to go down there. To McAlester at least. Take back the narrative, he says, like anybody could do that. It's a freaking freight train." She took a languid sip. "He wants me to hold a press conference. On the steps of the county courthouse, no doubt. Like every other original thinker."

"And? This is a problem?"

She shook her head. Of course not. Press conferences were her forte. She was just . . . tired. And the focus was so unpredictable. And Leadership was so skittish. Charlie thought the whole thing was great. Of course, Charlie was one who believed there was no such thing as bad publicity. She wished she could say the same for House Leadership. She snorted a laugh, thinking of her husband hunkered over his laptop last night: *They're foaming at the mouth, babe! You've got to harness their energies, their passion. It's perfect, babe!*

"What?" Kevin said.

"Oh, nothing. Charlie's just so sure it's a win. He's got his finger on the pulse of the conservative blogs, but I keep trying to tell him, they're not the whole public. They're the most passionate, like Charlie says, and they're right, of course, but, I don't know . . . it could be dicier than he thinks. I'm a little worried."

"Well, you should be," Kevin said. "You cannot compete with an adorable, brown-eyed ten-year-old."

She shot him a look. "I thought you only watch *Dancing with the Stars*."

"Oh, occasionally I might switch over to Anderson Cooper during a commercial break. Speaking of adorable."

"Anyway," she said. "It's not about competing. It's about shaping the narrative." She closed her eyes, almost drowsy, repeating the little mantra aloud: "Never say the word *problem*—these are *challenges* we face. Never use the word *can't*. We are making *positive progress*. It's not reality, Kev, it's perception that matters."

But this was one narrative that was too hard to shape; there was too much attention, and the mix was too potent: illegal Mexicans, state politics, broken family, missing child. Not to mention the quote-unquote "colorful sheriff." Nobody could leave it alone. If the story had only fit into one of the preworn narratives, it could have been controlled, but the whole thing was too contradictory, too confusing; it kept everything in turmoil. Who was the villain here? Who was the victim? Every-damn-body had an opinion—except Fox News, who so far had maintained a most disconcerting silence. And why did the kid have to be the kind who, as one of the women on *Headline News* said, you just wanted to hug and take home with you? Maybe something horrific would happen somewhere soon, Monica thought. Nothing so terrible as a terrorist attack, of course, but maybe something like a pretty teenager disappearing on her spring break, just *something* to compete with that kid's grade-school picture. And yes, they would occasionally intercut grainy images of Mexicans sneaking across the border, or an old studio portrait of the kid's grandfather—and why couldn't they use the guy's mug shot instead of that formal suit-and-tie, church-directory type of thing?—but none of that seemed to curtail people's sentiments. In fact, Monica feared, it seemed to make things worse. Then there was that sappy footage of the kid's weepy aunt begging for the public's help, and the hick sheriff and his endless press conferences and . . . oh, everything would have been fine! she thought, draining her drink. Absolutely fine. If not for that kid.

She sat up, held out her empty glass. "What do you say, shall we have another little drink? A teeny little small one. Here, gimme." And she reached for Sniffy. While Kevin was in the kitchen she petted the dog with one hand, fumbled on the floor beside the sofa with the other. She really, really ought to call Charlie. She located her handbag, pulled it up, and plunked it onto the coffee table, but somehow she couldn't make herself dig out her silenced phone to see how many times he'd called already. She just didn't feel up to listening to him: "Get down there and remind people how this unfortunate situation came about! Or no, not unfortunate—tragic. Don't forget to say tragic. Don't bad-mouth the kid. Don't bad-mouth the granddad. Stay on message: This tragic, truly tragic situation is just one more example of how the unbridled presence of illegal aliens is ripping our country's social fabric apart! Turn the tables, babe. Grab the narrative! Make it about the illegal aliens!" She'd heard his instructions so many times she could quote him in her sleep. She sat stroking the dog, listening to Chet Baker's tender voice, his mellow, raggedy trumpet, *this isn't sometimes, this is always.* A wave of melancholy, or something like it, swept her. Fortunately Kevin waltzed back in: "Here we are, darling. Two tiny little drinkie-poos."

"Kevin. Those are not tiny." Nevertheless, she accepted the drink, leaned across the table for the plate of cheese and grapes. "What do the Nichols Hills ladies think about it?" she asked, referring to the wealthy matrons who made up the majority of his clients.

"About what?"

She waved the plate toward the blank television. "This whole . . . deal."

"I doubt they think about it at all."

"Seriously?"

He gave her a piercing look. "Why would they? What's it got to do with them? Let me tell you who thinks about it, darling. One." He ticked off the numbers on his slim fingers. "The story-hungry media. Two, people such as yourself who have some kind of stake in it. Three, presumably, the little boy's family. And four, those poor Mexicans you're so intent upon hounding."

"Kevin! That is not true." He met her gaze, his bronzed handsome face inscrutable. "How can you say such a thing? And anyway," she went on, "*hounding* is such an ugly word."

"Is it? Come, baby." He scooped Sniffy off her lap and set him on the floor, where the little dog tottered over to the little doggie pad spread open on the hardwood floor in the hall to do his little doggie business.

When she got home, Charlie was fit to be tied. "*Where* have you been! Why the *hell* didn't you answer!"

"Why, hello, wife," she said. "And how was your day? And how was the floor presentation, and oh, by the way, dear, did your bill pass by any chance?"

"I know the goddamned bill passed! I'm talking about where you've been all night and why you haven't been answering your phone for the past three and a half hours!"

"I stopped by Kevin's, had a glass of wine on an empty stomach. I needed to eat something before I drove home. We sent out for Thai, it took a while. Look, Charlie, I'm sorry. I've got a splitting headache—"

"It's not just the fact I had to embarrass myself by calling Jim Coughlin at the reception, assuming, of course, that you were there but had your phone off. It's not even the fact you seem to *want* to jeopardize everything by hanging around your little faggot friend. No, it's the fact you are missing everything. Check this out." He unmuted the mute button. Across from Larry King sat the sheriff with his bulbous nose and his slicked-back hair, saying in his embarrassingly thick Okie accent that the rumors his men had beat a pregnant Mexican woman as well as the Brown kid were just that, vicious rumors, he had no idea where these lies got started, he'd known the Brown family his whole life—

"I know all about this, Charlie. It'll pass, they'll get onto something else. I'm going to bed."

"Where are your political instincts, girl? You don't get what this is at all, do you?" She frowned at the television. "The sheriff is there, right?" Charlie said. "In CNN's Los Angeles studios. He flew out this afternoon." So? she thought. "So," Charlie said, "if that ass is in L.A., who's heading the search mission? Who is here in Oklahoma watching out for the interests of that kid?"

What he was getting at finally dawned on her. "That would be me," she said.

"That would be you."

"All right, I already told you I'll go. On Friday I'm going."

"Not Friday. Tonight. You've got to be down there first thing in the morning, before that idiot sheriff gets back."

"I've got to be in session tomorrow! I've got my Appropriations Committee meeting at nine!"

"I cleared everything with Coughlin. The press conference is set for nine thirty." He snapped his laptop shut, unplugged the cord, started rolling it up. "You're going to hold it at the family farm, right in front of the barn where that fool is always blathering. It'll be the perfect contrast, you with your sincere concern for the little lost boy, the sheriff off gallivanting in California."

"But we're on the same side!"

"Not when he keeps making such a goddamn mess of things. Go pack. We won't have time to do much prep in McAlester. The aquamarine suit, I think. No, wait. Levis. Pack a pair of good-looking Levis, not too tight. And your brown suede jacket. We want it to look like you're down there ready to go to work trying to find that kid."

"What, you expect me to go traipsing around the goddamn woods?"

"Jesus, Monica. It's about *image*. You know that. What's the matter with you?"

The morning is cold, but Luis is sweating as he pumps the bicycle pedals, standing. His legs are strong now. The first day on the bicycle his legs hurt very much, and the second day. Now they feel strong. But the boy grows more weak. Luis can hear the small thin coughs behind his shoulder; he can feel the seams of his coat pulled backward as the boy clutches the coat with his good hand. It is necessary for the boy to rest soon, Luis thinks, pumping hard. He must eat something, drink water. He needs to be warm. Panting, Luis peers ahead. In the distance the long, flat-topped hills slice the land north to south. He has been pedaling toward that shape many hours. Strange to think how important the bicycle has become, how necessary. Luis could not have dreamed this when he first saw the boy riding toward him on the gravel road . . .

From inside the barn, all that day, Luis had kept watch. He had imagined the boy walking to bring him the map. But the hour grew late and Luis began to believe the boy would not come. Then the boy came, guiding the bicycle along the gravel road with one hand. The boy stopped in front of the barn, laid the bicycle on its side, took off the black backpack. From the pack he withdrew supplies of food, a jar of coins, the map. He showed these things to Luis, placing them one by one on the straw-strewn dirt of the barnyard. He shook open the map with one hand, laid it on the ground also, pointed to the lower right corner. *We are here,* he said. He pointed to the top left corner. *Gai-mon here. Is very . . .* He started to open his arms wide to show distance, but at once he grimaced, pulled his left arm to his chest, supported it with his other hand. Luis understood then that the arm was hurt. *My sister lives here, in Tulsa,* the boy said, and with his elbow he pointed to a yellow square on the upper right side of the map. *Is not so . . .* The boy frowned.

¿Far? Luis said.

Far, yes. My sister is able to help. I study this. All the night I think this. She is able to know many mexicans, because her . . . man is mex-ican. He is . . . The boy narrowed his eyes, looking to the side, thinking. He shook his head finally to show he did not know how to say what he wanted to say. Then he started walking away across the barnyard to the house.

¿Where are you going?

¡A moment! the boy called back.

Luis reached for the map to refold it. He had prepared the blue truck of the grandfather already, poured in a little oil, added water to the radiator, left it hidden in the place where he had covered it with branches after the grandfather and the others were taken. An old truck, yes, but the indicator showed a good amount of gasoline. His sons would return the truck later: they would know a person to drive it here from the Guymon town, they would pay money to the grandfather, and also leave plenty gasoline in the tank. He would explain all these things to the boy. Luis replaced the food packages and cans and little boxes inside the black backpack, laid the map on top, zipped the zipper closed. The jar of coins he left sitting on the ground. He was glad for the food, although he had not asked for it, but he did not want to take the silver and brown coins belonging to the boy.

¡Please to help me, mister!

Luis looked up to see the boy on the back porch in a thin wine-colored jacket and dark blue cap like the baseball players wear. In his right hand was the yellow dictionary. His other hand, the left one, the boy held to his chest. *¡Come here, please!* the boy called. Luis walked stiffly across the yard. Inside the house, on the kitchen floor, was a sleeping bag with pictures of the crawling red-and-blue man, the same blank-eyed spider man pictured on the backpack the boy had carried food in for Luis the night before. Luis picked up the sleeping bag. The boy motioned him to the hall closet, pointed to another sleeping bag high on the shelf, a dark green one. Luis frowned. *Is necessary,* the boy said. *The house of my sister is very small.* Luis did not know why the boy said this, but he stood high on his toes and pulled down the green sleeping bag, hoisted one bag under each arm. The boy ran to the small table beside the front door for the little flashlight and put it in his pocket. *¡We go quickly!* the boy said. *My aunt comes soon, I think.*

Outside, the boy unzipped the black backpack and placed the dictionary and the jar of coins inside—this was not the worn red backpack with the crawling man, which was still inside the barn, but the clean black new one with cartoon drawings of automobiles on the sides. The boy talked very rapidly in english; sometimes he included spanish words: *my sister, my grandfather, your sons.* He turned and whistled in the direction of the fenced pasture. *I,* he said, and patted his chest. *You.* He pointed to Luis. *We the two. And also the mare.* He made the gesture of holding reins, pointed to the pasture where the red mare stood grazing in the distance. *For the house of my sister. ¿Understand?* With his bruised eyes the boy looked up at Luis. He lifted his hand to brush his hair aside, and immediately made a face of pain, lowered his arm. *¿Who has hurt you?* Luis asked, but the boy shook his head, looked to the gravel road again. *We go now,* the boy said. *In this moment.*

But of course, Luis thought. They would travel together to the house of the sister whose man is mexican. Luis would be able to speak with him in spanish, ask the important questions, discover the best way to go to his sons. Also, of equal importance: he would be able to leave the boy in a place where they would not bruise his face, or hurt his arm. *Good,* he said. The boy at once turned to whistle for the mare. *No,* Luis said. *She is not necessary.*

Then he took the boy with him behind the large smoke-smelling shed and began to uncover the brush and tree branches he had used to hide the blue truck. The boy seemed confused at first, and then very happy. *¡You!* he said. Many times he said this. *¡All the time it is you!* And he laughed a little, shaking his head. He seemed to think this was a very funny joke. *¡We go quickly!* He ran to the passenger door and opened it, but then he released a yip of pain as he reached to climb up. *¿Can I help you?* Luis said, but the boy shook his head. *No problem. We go.* In the barnyard Luis stopped the truck, motioned the boy to stay seated as he got out to put the black backpack and the two sleeping bags in the back. After a moment he lifted the bicycle also and laid it in the truck bed. The boy protested when Luis climbed again into the truck. *¡Is not of mine!* he said. But Luis told him this was necessary, not to leave behind the bicycle, and the boy said, squinting ahead along the gravel road, Okay, okay. *¡We go now!*

Now, on this cold morning, Luis is the person who peers ahead along the road—not pale gravel, this one, but a smooth blue-black ribbon. The sky is thick gray, so thick he cannot see the sun. The land on both sides, all around, is flat and barren. It is a long time now since they have seen a house or a building, maybe one hour since the last vehicle passed. The coughs of the boy are coming more frequent, thin and dry, like the thin air in this flat land. Oh, why do the tabled hills never seem to draw nearer! Luis treads the pedals more fiercely. The sleeping bags strapped to the handlebars make steering difficult. The boy, sitting on the bicycle seat behind him, pulls hard on the back of his coat.

When they reach the shelter of the hills, Luis tells himself, then he will stop for the boy to rest, to warm himself inside the sleeping bag, to eat something, drink a little water. If only the truck had not failed them! But no, Luis reminds himself. He will not regret. He will not doubt. How many days have they traveled on the bicycle? Four. No, five. Luis counts back in his mind. One night driving in the truck and one day waiting for the sister in Tulsa, and then driving again one more night toward the Guymon town, until, as the dawn came, the truck began to shudder and thump and boil clouds of steam. So yes, it is five mornings ago now that Luis put the boy in the driving seat to steer with his good hand and Luis pushed from behind so that the truck would slide off the dirt road into the arroyo. Then he strapped the sleeping bags to the bicycle handlebars, helped the boy to put on the black backpack, and they rode away in the early morning light, leaving the old truck with its clouds of steam pouring, the last of the lime-green water trickling from the radiator hole.

The truck failed them, yes, but Our Lady has not failed them. This is what Luis reminds himself, pedaling, his breath hot and harsh in his chest. Our Lady has accompanied them all the journey, from that first afternoon in the yard of the old grandfather when Luis was thinking only that if the aunt should come, as the boy said, and find the bicycle, she would begin to search for the boy; she would maybe find evidence of Luis inside the barn, she would maybe telephone the police to watch the highways, because of the missing truck. It was not possible for Luis to understand then that he and the boy would need the bicycle in the future, and yet he brought it. A little miracle, he thinks now, standing up on the pedals, pumping hard, watching toward the horizon. A tiny marvel. The first one.

There was nowhere else to turn. She couldn't think of any-place. Anybody. Sweet tapped on the parsonage storm door. She waited, listened, snapped closed her jean jacket against the cold. After five o'clock on a wintry Tuesday evening, it was almost full dark, the temp dropping toward freezing. Behind her the street was empty, the Senior Citizens cooks and Heart-land Home Health workers gone home now. No news vans. No reporters. She pulled open the storm door, knocked on the wooden inside door. It was obvious nobody was home, but she couldn't make herself give it up. She had to get those kids out of that coal mine—tonight. She pounded on the wood. Where was Vicki anyway? The preacher's wife was almost always here. Sweet rattled the metal storm door, let it fall to. She glanced at the empty church porch next door. Maybe Brother Oren was over there in the Pastor's Study.

She came down off the concrete steps and started around the house toward the Fellowship Hall entrance. That's when she saw the preacher sitting inside his old Toyota inside the dim, cold carport. Well, not so much sitting as lying—leaned back almost prone in the reclined seat, his pale, thinning hair mussed, his eyes closed. Was he sleeping? Or praying. Or, God help us, the way things had been falling apart lately—was Brother Oren maybe laying there in the driver's seat dead?

The preacher reached up with one hand, eyes closed, and scratched his nose. Thank you, Lord. Sweet let go of the breath she'd been holding. She rapped on the car window. Brother Oren jumped like a rabbit. He closed his eyelids a second, opened them, blinked at Sweet; then he popped the seat forward, cranked down the window. "Evening," he said, like it wasn't strange, him sitting outside in the dark car.

"I need to talk to you," Sweet said.

"You sure startled me." His voice got excited: "There's news about Dustin?"

Sweet shook her head. "Reckon we could go inside a minute? It's cold."

"Vicki and the boys are at her mother's. I just got back from running them over to Stigler." No further explanation needed. A preacher couldn't invite a woman inside his house if his wife wasn't present. A smart one wouldn't even counsel a female member in the Pastor's Study unless there were other church members around and he kept the door open. "Let's go in Fellowship Hall," Sweet said, and left the carport, hurried along the angled sidewalk toward the glass doors leading to the prefab addition attached to the side of the old church. She stood shivering on the dark walkway while the preacher got his keys and came on. The warm blast of central heat made up for the ugly fluorescent glare when Brother Oren flipped on the lights. Sweet crossed to the long table nearest the kitchen counter and sat. Then she got up and went into the brightly lit kitchen and started making coffee. The lowest nick on the inside of the forty-eight-cup urn said twelve cups, so that's what she made. The preacher stood on the other side of the counter looking baffled, and awkward, and worn out.

How to start? Sweet asked herself. How to start. She clamped the lid on the coffeemaker, plugged it in, and remained facing the outlet, her back to the preacher. The lights buzzed overhead, the kitchen sink dripped a slow quiet plink. After a moment the coffeemaker began its low burble. Sweet turned around, crossed her arms, rested her tailbone against the kitchen counter. "I need your help," she said. *Hiss, gurgle, glub* went the coffeemaker. The preacher's bland hazel eyes asked her to please not ask anything more from him, but Sweet opened her mouth, and the words poured.

The story was all jumbled, out of order, not even half explained—those kids *had* to come out of there *tonight,* she said, there was freezing rain in the forecast and the creek was probably down by now which was good but that made it worse really because that made it more likely somebody might go out there where she'd had to hide them because Misty Dawn showed up in the middle of the night with her husband who got deported last fall and maybe Tee had turned him in too like he'd turned in Sweet's daddy, which was only part of it really, and she'd been meaning to talk to the preacher about that because she knew divorce did not really go with Baptist doctrine but there were plenty of divorced Baptists, all you had to do was look around, only she just hadn't had time to make an appointment but she was going to do that just as soon as this mess was finished and the truth of the matter was she'd like to wring that khaki-headed woman's neck she really would but the biggest problem was the ice storm headed this way those kids couldn't just stay out there in it but they couldn't stay at her house her yard was also crawling with reporters—and the whole time she was rattling on, Sweet watched the preacher's young-old face to see if she was making sense. She must have been, she decided, because Brother Oren sat down at the nearest table and buried his face in his hands.

A minute passed. Two. The coffee machine burped behind her, went silent. A click told her the red light had come on. Still the preacher sat motionless with his hands covering his face. Quietly, as if not to wake him, Sweet opened an overhead cupboard and got down two stumpy white mugs and set one under the black spigot, flipped the handle forward. She poured both mugs full, came out from behind the counter, set one in front of the preacher, seated herself on the opposite side of the table and a couple of chairs down.

When Brother Oren finally uncovered his face, he looked at his watch. Then he pulled the mug toward himself, sat with both hands wrapped around it. "Which woman is that?" he said quietly.

"What? Oh, that carpetbagger from McAlester. That Monica Moorehouse."

The preacher looked confused at first, then relieved. "Ohhh. Right," he said. Uh-huh, Sweet thought. The preacher had been at the farm this morning; he'd seen how she acted. Brother Oren stared down at his coffee, nodding. "I'm sorry. I thought you meant Terry was . . . Well, that's good. Okay." He blinked, rubbed his palms up and down over his face. "I'm not sure I got this all straight. Whose baby are we talking about?"

"Misty Dawn's. She's not a little baby-baby, we just call her that. She's a little girl."

"And who's Misty Dawn again?"

"My niece in Tulsa."

"She's in Tulsa."

"No, she's here. At the coal mine."

"The coal mine?"

"On Daddy's land!" Sweet stopped herself. Brother Oren wasn't ordinarily this dense. Maybe he was just tired. He looked tired. "Out there on the ridge behind the house," she said more reasonably.

The preacher nodded again, but his face didn't show much comprehension. "And her husband's illegal, I take it."

"I don't know. I guess. Yes."

"He's been deported."

"Well, he was. But he's back. He's out at the mine with her and the baby, that's the whole point! I mean, that's what I'm saying."

"What about Dustin?"

"What about him?"

"He's with them?"

"No! Where'd you get that idea? Good grief, we wouldn't be in this mess if we knew where Dustin is! Half the state wouldn't be camped out at my daddy's farm, and the other half wouldn't be parked in their dadgum news vans across the street from my house!"

The preacher began to draw on the butcher paper with his finger. "And what you're asking is . . ."

"If they can stay here."

"Here? At the church?" Brother Oren looked scared—not quick, startled scared, like when she tapped on the car window, but slow, fathoming scared, like he knew this was coming. Like he'd been dreading this moment his entire short middle-aged life.

Sweet waved her arms around. "Look, here's a kitchen. There's a bathroom. It's warm. I'll fix them a pallet. Just for tonight. Just till the bad weather is past." She saw the faintest movement of his head, the beginnings of a tiny side-to-side wag. "Brother Oren," she whispered, "that little girl's only three years old."

The preacher was silent a beat too long, and when he spoke, it seemed like he was changing the subject. "They called a special deacons' meeting for tonight. Clyde Herrington came by this afternoon to tell me." Sweet frowned. What did this have to do with anything? "Ken Spears called it."

"Kenneth Spears?" The chairman of the deacons, that old bachelor retired schoolteacher, and a retired marine before that—a time-and-rules-stickler who, in Sweet's opinion, would have been a whole lot better off if he'd ever had a wife to keep him from sticking his nose in everybody's business. Then she realized what Brother Oren was saying. "You mean they called a deacons' meeting without you?" The preacher nodded. "Oh," Sweet said. "They're fixing to fire you."

"Deacons can't fire the pastor, you know that. But some of them want to call for a vote of confidence from the church body."

"Oh. That's bad."

Brother Oren went back to tracing invisible lines on the table. He wouldn't meet her gaze. "I got to explain something to you, Sweet. I'm not just only your family's pastor. I've got a whole flock to consider. I got my own family."

A cold spitty rain was falling. Her wiper blades were shot. Sweet hunched forward to peer through the arc of smeared road film, working hard to hold to the unmarked blacktop. She wanted to be mad, she just couldn't. That was so strange. Oh, she could get her hackles up at that woman politician easily enough, but right now it was the preacher Sweet wanted to be mad at, and somehow all she could dredge up was disappointment, and pity, and fear. What was she going to do now? She'd had a more or less workable plan, but the preacher had nixed it, so, well. Just go. That's all she knew. Go out to the mine where the kids were waiting. She would get past all the people in the barnyard somehow.

Not that she'd figured out how to do that yesterday, or this morning, or this afternoon. Her daddy's yard had looked like a tribal casino parking lot for two days now, and Sweet hadn't yet finagled a way past all the vehicles and the people milling. When she took the supplies out there yesterday, she'd found them waiting fretfully inside the pickup the baby whining, the kids frowning. She had explained everything to a sulky Misty Dawn—searchers headquartering at the farm now, the sheriff due back soon—but when she told her they were going to have to wait inside the mine till the coast was clear, the girl snapped, "No way! We're not doing that!" Sweet said, "Suit yourself. If you want to take a chance on the sheriff finding your husband . . ." and Misty Dawn had immediately climbed out of the truck and started helping her lug the black trash bags up the ridge toward the mine mouth. Juanito drove the Ram in under a cedar thicket to hide it, where Sweet showed him, and then she'd lit the lamps, gotten the kids settled, told them she'd be back for them as quick as she could. She'd never dreamed it would take this long.

But what could she do? There'd been even more men hanging around the barn when she went back by there, everybody waiting on the sheriff, waiting and waiting. Sweet had stayed as long as she could stand it, and then she told Terry she was leaving, she would let him know when he could bring Carl Albert home. Tee's face was baffled at first, and then furious, but she drove off without giving him a chance to lay into her. She went home, hurried into her house past all the reporters, sat in the front room with the phones off and the blinds shut all evening, watching cable news. When she went back to her daddy's farm this morning, that woman politician was holding a press conference in front of the barn, and the milling crowds were even worse. And it wasn't just news people and searchers, either, but every kind of old gawker and hanger-on—now, what was that about? People's giddiness and hunger for excitement, Sweet figured. Their ambition. How they all wanted to be on camera.

No, of course that wasn't it. People wanted to help find Dustin. Truly they did. Why was Sweet's spirit so mean? She tried to think nice thoughts, grateful thoughts, but somehow in her mind's eye all she could see was that bunch of strangers milling around her daddy's house this morning, crowding up the kitchen and the front room and both porches, jamming the narrow hallway while they waited in line to use the bathroom, and who were they, anyway? Search team leaders, somebody said. Volunteer firemen from all over eastern Oklahoma. Preachers of apparently every stripe and denomination. The Wilburton mayor and the Cedar school superintendent and that khaki-headed state representative and her froggy-eyed husband and that long drink of water Senator Langley, plus all those church women trooping in with their covered dishes and then hanging around way longer than necessary just to drop off a pan of cowboy bean casserole, not to mention more deputies than you could shake a stick at. Everybody trying to act like they didn't see the reporters or that film crew from *Disappeared!* Everybody talking in those self-conscious voices, creasing their brows in those fake worried frowns.

Sweet reached up to give the fogging windshield a swipe. When we get to the end of days, she thought, we're going to find out the video camera was actually an invention of the Devil. Something sneaky and innocent looking he dreamed up to entice folks into sinning—like line dancing or Powerball lottery. And that Monica Moorehouse was the biggest camera hog of all. Sweet found herself working up a good fury right there in the car, thinking about that woman standing in front of the barn this morning in her fake cowboy-cut jacket, drawling out her fake concern in her fake Okie accent, saying the same things to the cameras over and over, the same exact words, the same phrases—"our hearts go out to the family," "cannot surrender to this illegal alien invasion," "leave no stone unturned," "despite special-interest groups and drug traffickers who want to turn our state into a sanctuary for illegal aliens," "these heroic men," "this tragic situation," "very important not to confuse the two issues," "our thoughts and prayers are with the family," "cannot let this deter us from the fight"—all totally rehearsed, smiling that fake smile every minute—*smiling!*—with that mouth full of bleached teeth. And there wasn't a thing in the world Sweet could do about it. She couldn't even vote against her in the next election; the woman's district was the next one over.

Not that Sweet was much of a political person anyway, but she did vote. Usually. Most of the time. In presidential elections anyway. Terry was the one who paid attention to that stuff, and that was because he came from a political family, or anyhow his own daddy, Carter Kirkendall, had worked on the county election board practically till he'd had one foot in the grave, and Tee's great-uncle, Gene Kirkendall, used to be a corporation commissioner right up till the time he got sent to prison for bribery and corruption when the state attorney general was sending all those commissioners to jail years ago. It had been Terry's daddy's idea, in fact, for them to name their son after an Oklahoma politician, and Sweet hadn't argued. She'd figured there would be other children she'd get to pick the name for . . . a daughter, yes. Oh, how fiercely she had longed for a baby girl. How relentlessly she'd prayed.

Sweet sucked in her cheeks, bit down hard on the inside of her mouth. But the old familiar ache, once awakened, wouldn't leave her. It had been a part of her life's rhythm for too many years.

You couldn't even call them miscarriages, not really—a few days late, enough to make her hope, then a heavier flow than usual, that was all. That was the rhythm: two or three days of hope, then one long heartsickening day of lost hope, then the low, tender ache starting, the yearning, the wait for next month. She'd tried, back then, to talk to Terry about it. But he didn't want to talk. And so Sweet had prayed. Prayed and prayed and prayed. Then, the same month Carl Albert started second grade, Sweet had, in a great weeping emotional trip to the altar, rededicated her life at a church revival. After that she'd quit praying for what she wanted and started praying to accept the Lord's will. And the Lord's will must be, had to be, the fact that she was only ever going to bear the one child. The one son.

Oh, Carl Albert. Oh, honey. This was going to be so hard on him. Sweet's chest was working. She could hear her throat making little low-pitched voiced sounds. She swiped at the windshield with her open palm again. She couldn't see. Everything was so smeary. Maybe her defroster had quit working, too. Damn it. The gravel turnoff would be coming up soon. Damn it. Oh, honey, sweetheart, Mommy's sorry. Carl Albert. My baby. She couldn't see. She couldn't see anything! Sweet stopped the car on the pitch-black road.

There was nothing. Only the faint scent of wet asphalt, the oniony odor from wadded-up food wrappers in the back. The *suck swish click* of her worthless wipers. The tortured, hiccupy sound of her own breaths.

In the Gloss Mountains

In the cleft of the dark, glinting hills, Luis opens his coat, uses the knife the boy gave him to cut a rag from the tail of his shirt, pours cold water on it. With the damp shirt-rag he bathes the face of the boy. For one week, he reminds himself, the miracles have come without limit, one following the other following the other. Each time he believed they were lost, the way opened. Each time he grew afraid, Our Lady brought him peace. She has accompanied them every mile, every minute, until this frozen hour beneath a purpling sky in this small sheltered place on the dark plain. But this hour the boy coughs. His skin is hot. The truck is lost. Luis fears that Our Lady has abandoned them. For what reason? He cannot tell.

Please, mister, the boy says. His voice is rough and low, too rough for the voice of a child. *I have thirst.*

Yes, Luis says, and he opens the jar of water, holds the cold mouth for the boy to drink. In the dark cleared space around them the ground glints in the moonlight as though diamond dust has been sifted in the soil. The boy shifts again, restless. Luis touches his forehead. He is burning hot, his hair is soaked with sweat. Tomorrow they must find a town, find a doctor or hospital. The boy cannot travel the cold, gray days any longer. He cannot sleep anymore in the frozen nights, huddled inside the sleeping bag. Luis is afraid, and yet peace accompanies his fear. The peace of surrender. To have traveled so far, and still not see his sons. This is a terrible decision. But of course, there is no decision to be made. If he does not find help soon, the boy will become more sick. It is possible he will become too sick to get well. No. We must not think this. Luis presses the edges of the sleeping bag more tightly around him, says quietly, *I will climb to the top of the hill to see where is the next town.*

¿You return soon? the boy asks in his rasping voice.

Yes. Very soon.

The climb is not difficult. The hills have been coursed with paved walkways, steel rods for banisters—a park of some kind, though with so few trees, no tables or benches or flower beds, Luis does not know why anyone would want to come here. There are signs near the road that tell the name of this place, and also the names of plants and animals beside drawings; he recognizes the animals—a lizard, a tortoise, a rattlesnake, a mouse—but he cannot understand the english names. By the time they arrived here, the boy was already too sick to read the words aloud. Luis climbs to the top of the highest hill; at the crest is a great flat place, like a table stretching far into the darkness, but the ground is rough, broken by gashes in the rocks, mounds of stone, clumps of brush. Looking off, he can see many miles in all directions—a light here, a light there. Lone distant houses. They would have a telephone, Luis thinks. A car. He looks to the east, the flat cold plains across which he and the boy have traveled, and can see a small clutch of lights—the little gasoline store and few houses they passed in the early morning. The distance is, he remembers, very far. In the west, the sky is still violet, but on the dark earth below he sees no clustered lights indicating a town. Still, it seems better to go on than to go back.

We will go as soon as the dawn comes, he thinks. How strange. All the journey they have been hiding in the daylight, moving rapidly off the road each time they heard a car or a truck, lying down with the bicycle in a ditch or some tall grasses until the vehicle passed. Tomorrow they will travel openly on the side of the road, hoping that some person will drive near and stop. We will do this in the early morning, Luis thinks, if the boy is able to ride a little more.

Quickly he turns to feel his way with his feet across the flat hilltop. The way seems more treacherous going down than climbing; he has to hold more often to the steel bars, his feet slide on the little stones, his knees ache, refuse to bend. When he reaches the bottom, he cannot recall which of the small sheltered crevices he left the boy in. *¡Boy!* he calls softly. But there is no need for silence. They are no longer hiding. It would be welcome if someone heard him calling and came in a car to arrest them. He calls again, this time with his hands cupped, very loudly: *¡Dustee!*

Here, the boy answers with that choked scratchy sound.

Luis makes his way toward the voice.

The boy has pushed down the sleeping bag. He lies sweating, his face wet. *¡No, no!* Luis says, pulling up the flannel. *¡You must keep warm!* At first the boy fights him, pushing away his hand; then he turns on his side within the sleeping bag, whimpers, grows quiet. *It is well, my son,* Luis whispers. *It is well.* Overhead the sky is growing darker. Luis wraps the green sleeping bag across his shoulders to keep warm. The moon is high in the sky already, a little west. When they left the farm in the blue truck, Luis remembers, she was a thin white sliver in the afternoon sky.

That first day the boy showed Luis where to turn, and where to turn, until they were driving west on a rutted dirt road in the frozen winter afternoon. He talked rapidly in english and spanish, but Luis understood very little, only that the boy wished to see his mother. Then the boy grew silent. He sat leaning forward, holding his arm, intently watching the side of the road. Luis, too, watched the road, and also the low humpbacked hills to the south and to the north. He liked seeing the blue hills in the distance. They were not majestic like the Sierra Gorda, but they were pretty.

Here, please, the boy said, and gestured for Luis to turn again. They had come to a small cemetery a short distance off the road, very ragged and rough looking, with thorny, leafless brambles crawling over the rock walls. A rusted iron sign arched across the entrance showing english words. As soon as the truck stopped, the boy jumped down, supporting his left hand with his right, and ran to the open gate. Then the boy halted, walked slowly through the cemetery till he reached a shiny black headstone near the back. Luis had never seen a black headstone; it seemed a strange thing. Was it a mark of honor in this country to have a black headstone, or was this something bad? Luis pictured the black quarry stone of the Temple of Our Lady of Guadalupe in Arroyo Seco. On the front of the unfinished temple, the black stone was something beautiful and good. Maybe here it was the same. On the far side of the cemetery the boy stood with his head bowed. Luis turned his eyes away to give the boy privacy. The other graves appeared untended, with tall yellow grasses growing on them, obscuring the markings. Some of the headstones had fallen over. They were all gray colored or white, very small. The sun was rapidly descending. Soon dark would come, and the cold would be worse. Luis sat in the quiet truck for as long as possible, but at last he returned his gaze to where the boy stood. His heart bumped. He thought the boy had disappeared. Then he saw the wine-colored sleeve peeking out from the far side of the stone. Luis reached to the floorboard for his coat, climbed down from the truck.

He found the boy sitting with his back against the black head-stone, facing the fiery sun, his cap brim pulled low. After a moment Luis sat beside him, placed the coat on the ground between them. The winter sun swam low on the horizon, a fierce red circle. Luis said, *The night will be coming soon.* The boy said nothing. After a time Luis asked, *¿What does your mother say to you?*

She says my grandfather loves me.

It is the truth, ¿no?

Yes.

Luis could feel the sadness in the boy but knew nothing to help. He used one hand to shade his eyes from the sun. It was already halfway below the ragged line of earth now, one half the red circle. *Night will soon come,* he repeated. The boy shrugged. Luis placed the coat a little nearer to him. *Your arm,* he said. *¿He is broken?*

¿Broken? The boy tilted his head, his bruised face shadowed by the cap brim, the brown hair pushed down flat and parted to each side above his brows. *¿What is this word?*

Luis used his two hands to show the gesture of snapping a stick into two pieces.

Oh. Bro-ken. *I dont know.*

With your permission, I will look. Very carefully Luis reached for the hurt arm. The boy did not yip though he made a face of pain as Luis peeled back the slick jacket sleeve. The wrist was red and swollen, turning bruised. With his fingers Luis felt along the arm, the wrist. *Not broken, I think. Maybe sprained.* Gently he placed the arm back the way the boy held it. *¿How did this happen?*

The boy said nothing. The sun was gone then. In its place a rosy light glowed all along the horizon. The boy, too, was glowing rose, the grave, the stone wall, the stunted trees.

Before the light will be gone, Luis said, *we must study the map.*

Okay, the boy said, but he made no move to rise. The sadness in him was a thick dark wave. After a moment he said, very softly, *I want to see my grandfather.*

This was also a sadness. The grandfather in the prison. Luis did not know the adequate words to say to comfort the boy.

We wait for the night, the boy said. *Is more . . . carefulness. For the police. ¿You understand? Then I talk to my grandfather.*

And Luis did understand. The boy wanted to go to the prison to see his grandfather. But this was not possible. *I cannot go where the police will be.*

Yes. We are able. No problem. My mother say me. You wait in . . . the car. The boy motioned toward the truck. *Then we go. Very later. No problem, ¿okay?*

Luis answered nothing. He sat thinking. Perhaps he would be able to follow the map and find his way to the Guymon town alone, but he could not drive off and leave the boy in the cemetery, in the night, alone. Neither did he wish to return the boy to the place where the people would hurt him.

We go together, the boy said. *To the house of my sister.*

Luis nodded slowly. *Good,* he said. *It is well.* Then the sadness was not so strong, neither in the boy nor in Luis. Another traveling marvel—not a miracle, no, but a little mercy.

They waited long. Luis helped the boy put on the coat. The rose light turned purple, then gray. They moved from the grave to the truck, sat waiting for deeper night. The boy talked a little. He liked to come to this place to hear his mother, he said, but he could come only sometimes. This place was far from his house for walking, even more far from the house of his aunt and uncle. He needed to speak with his grandfather. This was very important. He needed to tell the grandfather that he was not . . . But then the boy became suddenly silent. He did not reach for the yellow dictionary to find the correct word. After a moment Luis said quietly, *¿How will this be? The prison will be closed.* He spoke slowly, with great deliberation. If he talked normally, the boy would sit frowning, shaking his head, but if Luis employed simple words, spoke slowly, the boy very often understood. This time the boy shrugged. *My mother say me* was all he said. The night grew colder. Luis started the truck to put on the heat, but he did not want to use so much of the gasoline, and soon he turned off the motor again. He brought the backpack and one of the sleeping bags from the truck bed, spread the bag open across them, and they ate crackers and flat squares of cheese from plastic wrappers. They had nothing to drink. *I forget the water,* the boy said. *I go too quickly.*

No problem, Luis said. The moon was a thin white cord in the sky before them.

Tuesday | *February 26, 2008* | *6:00* P.M.

Brown's farm | *Cedar*

The sight of the near-empty yard scared her. Where was everybody? All those vehicles camped out at her daddy's farm for two days, now all she could see was one lone Latimer County Sheriff's Department cruiser parked nose-to-tail next to a big six-wheeler up close to the house. Well, the weather, of course, Sweet realized. Sleet and freezing rain coming—nobody wanted to get caught out in that. See? she told herself. See! The Lord *will* provide. She doused her headlights as she came up the drive, steering away from the two empty vehicles and toward the barn. Probably the men had gone inside the house to warm up. She could see the lights on in her daddy's kitchen. Sweet eased her Taurus across the gloppy barnyard, didn't click her headlights back on until she was headed across the pasture, praying to God to not let those men look out the kitchen window and see her, and also to please not let her get stuck. She didn't dare drive with her lights off. Seeing where she was going was tough enough.

She leaned forward to rub the side of her fist against the windshield above the steering wheel, but the icy smears were not on the inside. The needlelike rain was starting to freeze. This is how it always starts, she thought—a little deceitful rain, the thermometer falling, a bit of ice on the windshield, then on the fences and power lines. Then the trees. Before you know it you're in the middle of an ice storm, power outages for days, tree branches crashing, people spinning out on the highways, dying—and there wasn't ever any *storm* to it, she thought. Just a nasty fretful spitting rain, turning mean.

Was all this really necessary? All this effort to keep them hidden? Maybe it wouldn't be so bad if . . . Once again she ran through the scenario as she'd done a dozen times since yesterday, seeing at the end of it Misty Dawn and Juanito in handcuffs in the glare of floodlights, and that little girl, terrified, wailing, clinging to her mama while a deputy's big old ugly paw tried to peel her off. Twenty years, Misty said. Juanito could get sent to prison for twenty years. Could that be true? Just for sneaking back across the border after you'd been deported? What was so terrible about that?

But in some ways it did seem terrible. Or stupid. Or, anyway, the law was the law. Oh, why hadn't they known any better than to do this! Why didn't Misty Dawn know, at least?

Well, but what would Sweet rather have them do? Never fall in love? Never have a baby or get married? Never meet? All that was *done.* So what, then? What could they have tried that would have been any better? Sweet had asked Misty one time, back before all this trouble even started, "Why doesn't Juanito go back to Mexico and get in line, do it legally." "There's no freaking *line,*" Misty Dawn had snorted. "Not for Mexicans!"

"But you're married," Sweet had said. Again the snort. The bitterness in her niece's voice was astonishingly cold. "That don't make any difference," she said. "He'd have to wait in Mexico in that supposed *line* like ten years!"

This is what the immigration lawyer had told them. Or that's what he'd told them before Juanito got deported. Maybe after you'd been deported once, you couldn't even get in line. Either way, that little girl would grow up without her daddy. Sweet remembered watching them together yesterday: Juanito crouched on the mine floor in the lamplight, talking quietly, trying to explain what they were doing, Sweet thought. The child kept her face down, shaking her head, and then she'd looked up and said something to her daddy in Spanish, the complicated syllables floating into the yellowed darkness in her high-pitched child's voice, slow and soft.

That moment was in some ways more strange to Sweet, and more hurtful, than all the strange, hurtful moments that had gone before. This little girl, her own niece, who had never, so far as Sweet knew, spoken a word of English, could answer her father in perfect rippling Spanish. How was that possible? English ought to be in her blood, it ought to be born in her. Everybody in their family talked English, had done so ever since, well, the very beginning—how could this little girl not know her own language? Or if she knew it, why wouldn't she talk it? Sweet understood that it was unreasonable to be bothered by that, but she was bothered—wrenched, actually. The child looked like her mommy and daddy, yes, but she also, Sweet had realized in that moment, watching her in the smoking lamplight, looked very much like her grandmother, Gaylene. She is ours, Sweet thought. Concepción María de la Luz Perez Brown. My sister's granddaughter. One of our own.

In the headlights the old trash dump emerged out of the darkness. She gave it a careful berth, steering past the end of the ditch toward the broken fence. The bottom of the Taurus scraped as she thumped down the bumpy track. Lord, do not let me get stuck. At least the water had receded—she could see the rock bed of the old bridge just ahead. She eased down on to it, was halfway across, going slow, when she heard the first gunshot.

In a heartbeat she realized it came from the mine. Three more shots in rapid succession, a little pause, then a fifth and final shot echoing against the ridge. Oh my God. Sweet gunned the Taurus up the far bank, immediately spun out in the mud. Her car stalled, wedged sideways in the narrow track. Please. No. Please, no, please no please no please no. Gradually she accelerated, but the more gas she gave it, the more the tires spun. She tried rocking, shifting from low to reverse, low to reverse, but she was afraid she'd strip the rebuilt transmission entirely—or worse, that the tires would suddenly find purchase in reverse and she'd go roaring back down into the creek. She paused, listening again, in her mind, to what she'd just heard. The shots weren't light and popping enough for a pistol, but they were too light and there were too many of them to have come from a shotgun. It was exactly what she'd first thought: her daddy's .22 rifle—the one she'd pulled out of the garbage bag and handed Juanito yesterday. For protection, she'd said nonchalantly, thinking of the timber rattler Daddy had killed one time near the mine, though she hadn't used the word *snake*—the kids were nervous enough. But snakes don't go crawling in this weather anyway. Dear Lord, dear Lord, please don't tell me somebody came snooping around the mine and Juanito shot them!

Sweet jerked the steering wheel hard to one side, slammed the car in low, gave it the gas. Her front tires spun, spat mud on the windshield so that her worthless wipers could smear the glass into a worse icy mess. She smelled burning tire rubber, smoking oil from the stressed engine. There was no way she was going to get out of this without help. Probably the deputy and whoever was at the house had heard the shots, too. Probably they would come out to investigate. Probably they would be here in no time. Sweet opened the car door and jumped out into the pricking rain.

She scrambled up the clay bank, slipping and sliding until she was down on all fours crawling, the sickening feel of cold clay against her palms, her boots slick against the mud, her denimed knees cold with muck and wet. Against her neck and hands, the freezing rain felt like needles. The slope leveled off and she knew she'd reached the top but she couldn't see anything; the night was black, black, pitch-black, like being inside the old coal mine itself. She stood up and tried to run, but she stumbled into an invisible thicket, her jacket caught on the briars, and she had to use her numb hands to untangle herself. She felt her way along with her arms out in front of her, tripping over old brush stobs, staggering into shrubs; she moved forward and made no progress, like in a bad dream. Maybe it was a bad dream, a nightmare, she told herself—and she could almost believe that, except for the needles pinging her face, how her chest burned.

Headlights were coming toward her! Not from behind but in front, double headlights, high off the ground and spaced wide. Juanito's truck. Oh, thank you, God. Thank you. The lights were like two blessed eyes in the darkness, and Sweet rushed toward them; she could see now how to avoid the thickets, and even in the ticking, clicking rain she could hear the comforting sound of the big motor. She ran toward the headlights, waving her arms. The truck was coming at her very fast. He wasn't slowing down at all! Sweet waved her arms more wildly. At almost the last minute she jumped to the side, shrieking in the rain, screaming as loudly as she could, "STOP! STOP! MISTY DAWN, MAKE HIM STOP!"

The truck was already past her when it came to a squealing, sliding halt. Sweet stumbled around to the passenger side, opened the door to the sound of her niece and great-niece both wailing. "Where *were* you!" Misty cried. "Why didn't you *come*!"

"Scoot over!" Sweet reached for a handhold to climb up. "Hush now. Calm down! What was that shooting about?" But the girl couldn't stop sobbing. "Juanito, what happened?" He'd already started driving again. "Misty Dawn, quit that now and tell me what happened! Who fired the gun?"

"Juan—Juan—Juanito!"

"Was somebody trying to get in or what? He didn't shoot anybody! Please tell me he didn't do that."

Misty Dawn shook her head. She still couldn't talk. All Sweet could make out in the dim dash light was the outline of Juanito's profile, his arms wrapped over the steering wheel as he leaned forward in concentration. Misty Dawn was still shudder-breathing beside her, holding tight to the baby, bracing herself against the dash with her free hand as the truck lurched and swayed. Juanito steered fast between the clumps of scrub brush, hurling them across the pasture toward the creek.

"You can't get across," Sweet tried to tell him. In the headlights she could see the ice already crusting the shrubs and tall grasses. They were going too fast, they were liable to skid headlong down the bank right into her car! "We can't get across, my car's in the way, tell him, Misty!" Misty Dawn rattled off some Spanish, but Juanito did not slow down. "Tell him to stop!" They were bouncing almost to the bank, with Misty jibber-jabbering and the baby wailing and Sweet yelling, "Stop! Stop! Stop!" when Juanito finally jammed on the brakes and the truck slid sideways to a stop. He turned his face toward her, and Sweet could see then in the grim dash lights that he wasn't just concentrated—he was furious. At her.

He said something, and Misty Dawn took up the tune: "Why didn't you *come*? I *told* him you'd come, I promised! I kept promising! He said maybe you're lying, maybe you're just tricking us like the others, you're going to bring *la migra*, I said no, you're my *aunt*, you mean to *help* us, but you didn't come! And that stinking lantern went out! And we couldn't find the matches!" Misty

Dawn was rising again toward hysteria, her voice hitched with sobs. "And that thing started to come in, we didn't know what it was! We couldn't see, we could just hear it, and smell it, it was so big, and the damn flashlight was dead, and it was making this horrible sound, I never heard anything like it, it was horrible, horrible! It was like screaming or something! It came right in the cave with us! He shot it, he had to keep shooting and shooting, my God, you never heard such a horrible sound! It was *huge!*"

"What? What!"

"A big old damn coon! We didn't know *what* it was, I thought it was a panther or something, oh my God, it was so mean, you should have *heard* it, it was like screaming. Like meowing and screaming, like snarling, after he hit it, he didn't know he hit it, he just had to keep shooting. We couldn't *see!*"

"All right, all right, hush. Look you're making the baby worse." Sweet tried to reach for her, but Lucha scrambled over onto her father's lap. "Okay," Sweet said. "It's all right now, it's done. I'm here now. Listen, my car's stuck, see it down there?" She pointed to the dark hump just visible in the truck's headlights below the edge of the slope. "Juanito, you're going to have to get out and help me. I'll get behind the wheel and rock it. You can push from outside. Tell him, Misty."

And her niece made the translation while the baby settled back against Juanito's chest, cutting her eyes sideways to glare at her great-aunt Sweet. The ice pinged on the windshield, *ticktickticked* on the top of the cab and the truck's hood. The freezing rain was turning to sleet. And we're going to drive to Fort Smith in this mess? No, Sweet told herself. Not *we*. *They.* The Ram had four-wheel drive, after all. She'd give them what little money she had for gas, they were just going have to make it on their own; there was no way she could drive her car to Arkansas on this ice.

Nothing can drive on ice, her good sense told her. Not safely. Not even a four-wheel-drive truck. And no gas stations would be open anyway, not in the middle of an ice storm. Sweet looked at the child sitting in her daddy's lap, her two fingers in her mouth again, her little face frowning in the glow from the dash lights. Okay. She would figure it out. She would figure something. What they had to do right now was get her Taurus out of the way. "Come on, Juanito," she said, reaching for the door handle just as Lucha popped her fingers out of her mouth. "*Mira, Papa!*" the child said, and pointed.

There, through the winter bare trees, on the far side of the creek, at the top of the track, red and blue lights stuttering side to side, coming slowly toward them—the white cruiser. Oh, wouldn't you know. Wouldn't you just know. "Listen, Misty," Sweet said, "do not move from this seat. Do not move this truck. Tell him to turn off the headlights—no, wait. That'll look too suspicious. I need them to see by, anyway. Y'all stay here and don't do any-thing!" She leaned forward to peer around her niece. "I want you to understand something, mister," she said. "I did not bring the law. You did. By firing that gun. At a stupid dadgum coon. Now, I'm going to go talk to these people, I'll figure out something to get them to leave, but I want you to know that I do not appreciate your attitude. Not one bit. Tell him, Misty. Every blessed word I just said." Sweet jerked open the door handle and climbed down into the spitting sleet.

Tuesday | *February 26, 2008* | *Night*

In the Gloss Mountains

Each night since that first night the moon has swelled a little more big. Tonight, looking up, Luis considers that she is almost half. She makes good light in this dark place. He can see the sloping ground nearby, the two low feet of the hillside like two sheltering arms. He looks again at the face of the sleeping boy, wet with sweat, frowning. Now, in his heart, Luis is afraid only. No peace accompanies his fear. He must pray. To pray is difficult when a man feels abandoned, but Luis repeats the words. Sometimes just the rhythm of praying . . . *OurFatherInTheHeaven SanctifiedIsYourNameYourKingdomComeYourWillBeDoneOnThe EarthAsInTheHeaven. . .*

He has been too long without the sacraments. It is like an ache in him, how long the time has been. He last attended mass the morning he left Arroyo Seco, so now it is almost three weeks since he received communion. Perhaps this is why he cannot feel the presence of Our Lady here in this dark place. He cannot envision her image anymore. But how could he have attended mass here in the North? And where? Who would hear his confession, offer penance, absolution, place upon his tongue the sanctified host? *Forgive me, Father, I have sinned.* After he takes the boy to a doctor, if the authorities do not arrest him, he will find a church. He will go to confession. He tries to remember his sins. Theft, yes, he will confess that, make the penance, because the abandoned truck cannot be returned. And when did he swear by the holy names, lose his faith, lose his patience? Maybe he did a wrong thing, to come with the boy. Or to bring the boy with him. Which is the truth? Which way did it go? Him bringing the boy? The boy bringing him? Luis tries to remember. They seemed to decide to go together. They seemed to both hold the same hope.

When did this happen? At the white jail? Luis had not wanted to go there; he was afraid to be seen by the police, the officials, but the boy could not be persuaded, and so, very late in the night, Luis started the truck beside the cemetery and drove as the boy instructed, bumping along the dirt road until they arrived at a medium-sized town, not so big as Arroyo Seco, with dark sleeping houses and one street of stores, all closed. He stopped on a dark side street where the boy showed him. In the distance he could see the white building—not a prison, as the boy had called it, but a small jail in a not-so-big town, illuminated in the night, with a steel fence around the back and razor wire along the top. *¿How will you see your grandfather?* Luis asked. The boy used his good hand to make the shape of a square in the air of the dark truck, then cupped his palm around his mouth as if speaking a secret. *¿A window?* Luis said. The boy nodded. Without a word he opened the truck door and jumped down.

Luis watched the boy walk along the fence, disappear around the corner of the building. He was gone from sight for many minutes, then his small figure appeared at the first corner of the fence, and again he walked along it, disappeared around the corner of the white building once more. Luis did not count how many times the boy did this, maybe five or six. The light was very strong all around the building, shining down from tall poles on every side. The boy was taking too long! Someone might see him. Very quietly Luis got out of the truck and crossed the road to the steel fence. When the boy rounded the corner, Luis stopped him, making a gesture to ask the boy to be careful. The boy was crying. With a hurt wrist and bruised face, the boy did not cry. With cold and thirst, the boy did not cry. Now, however, there were choking sobs in his breath. *I cannot speak to my grandfather,* the boy whispered. *Please to help me, mister.*

Walking rapidly, looking toward the bright parking area, the shadowed street behind them, Luis accompanied the boy around the jail. But in all the square building there were no windows of any good size to let in light and air, only small blocks of thick glass in a few places, sealed inside the concrete walls. Like a cave it must be. Like a tomb. He touched the shoulder of the boy to pause him. They were beside the fence again. *I dont see how you will speak to your grandfather, my son,* Luis said. *I think we must make a new plan.* The boy lifted his head.

Now, as he keeps watch under the glittering stars and sinking moon, Luis remembers the mysterious thing that happened in that moment, the first night of their journey, beneath the arcing lights outside the white jail. He had called the boy *my son.* At once the boy lifted his face, looked up steadily at Luis. Then the same trust that Luis had placed in the boy already—trust that was necessary, although he had scarcely known he had given it, because the boy spoke a little spanish but knew all the english, because the boy had brought food to him, and a map, and a jar of coins—that same trust seemed to turn and return, like a boomerang, whirling in the air from the boy back to Luis again.

Yes, okay, the boy said, no longer crying. *Plan. Is the same word, in the spanish and english. A new plan.* He waited then, looking up at Luis, his face calm, expectant, beneath the dark brim of his cap. *Come*, Luis said, and he and the boy walked rapidly across the road to the truck.

Sweet scrambled sideways down the bank, using her frozen muddy hands to help, squeezed past the Taurus turning white now with sleet. On the bridge the ice was really starting to build. Her boots were impossible. Why hadn't she thought to change to sneakers when she heard the weather report? It's not like she didn't know that the absolute worst thing to wear in this weather is cowboy boots. She made her way across in the middle of the bridge, very slowly, very carefully, crouching a little so that if she fell she wouldn't hit the ground with too much force. The main thing was to not go sliding off into the creek. The cruiser was stopped at the top of the track with its front end tipped down enough that the headlights helped her see. They also showed her looking like a fool no doubt, scrabbling across with her arms out and her hair plastered to her head and muddy smears from one end to the other. The quick-flashing red and blue lights turned the ice a brilliant violet color, made her sick to her stomach, a little dizzy.

The lawman was standing outside the car when she got to the top of the bank—a big hulking deputy with linebacker shoulders hunched up to his ears against the sleet. He'd left the cruiser's door partway open so that the interior light showed another guy in the front seat. The deputy held the rear door open, Sweet scrabbled into the car, and the deputy got in the front and slammed the door against the cold. He reached up to click the dome light back on. She recognized him then as the deputy who'd escorted her daddy away from the break room last—God, how long ago was that? A week? A lifetime. "Man," she said, trying to catch her breath, "am I glad to see you."

"What're you doing out here, ma'am?" He was too big to turn easily in the seat, so he was looking at her in the rearview. The radio squawked and stuttered with distant voices; she couldn't make out what they were saying. The other fellow wasn't a cop, or anyway he wasn't wearing a uniform but a bulky plaid insulated jacket and a hunter's cap. He did turn around to look at her. He had squinty eyes and a big mustache. "What was all that shooting?" he said.

"Well," she panted. "You're not going to believe this—hold on." She held up her open palm. "Let me catch my breath." She could feel them looking at each other while she gasped loudly, stalling for time. "Well," she said again, "My, uh, cousins were out searching, you know, and I, I came out to tell them the weather report and I got my car stuck. Then we thought we saw something. I mean we did. See something. A . . . a . . . well, we think it was a bobcat. My cousin tried to shoot it but we think he probably missed."

"You sure got yourself in a mess." The deputy gestured across to where the cruiser's lights showed the whitening trunk and tail fender of Sweet's poor Taurus. She felt a kind of sadness toward it, like it was a very old dying pet.

"Yes, sir," she said. "Reckon you could call us a tow? I'd just leave her there till this weather's finished but I got to get my cousins back to the house."

"Motion 'em to come on. We'll drive y'all into town."

"Well, no, my cousin, he's got to get to work, he needs his truck."

"Where's he work at?"

"Tulsa. I mean, Muskogee. Well, just, you know, one place and the other. Construction."

"Ain't nobody driving to Tulsa or Muskogee either one in this weather, ma'am."

"No, I know, we just want to get it out and be ready for him to leave in the morning when the roads clear."

The deputy grunted. The ice crystals in his brown crew cut had melted to water droplets now. "I imagine they're pretty busy, what with roads like they are." Nevertheless he picked up the radio mouthpiece and made the call. The man with the mustache kept glancing back at her, his frowning face sort of a cross between skepticism and concern.

Sweet said, "You suppose you could turn off the red lights? They kind of give me a headache." The deputy reached over and switched them off. At once the flashing, violet tension bled away. The car seemed quiet, though the motor was running and the radio was still spitting its muffled squawks. Sweet pondered the rolls of fat at the back of the deputy's neck, how they showed through his crew cut, swelled over his jacket collar. Carl Albert had little rolls like that starting. She'd suggested to Terry that maybe they could let him grow his hair out, not keep it buzzed so short, but Tee wanted it short like that, even though he kept his own hair as long and scraggly as he liked. She could feel the pain in her solar plexus starting. "All right, thanks," she said and reached for the door handle—which was nonexistent. She patted all along the inside door panel. "Uh, could you let me out? I'll just go tell them yonder what's going on."

"It's awful cold out, ma'am," the deputy said. Like she didn't know. He hoisted himself out of the front seat, opened Sweet's door. "Bring 'em on over here, why don't you. We might as well all go back to the house where it's warm. It's liable to be a while."

"Okie-doke." She had no such intention. "Thanks so much." She gave a little backhanded wave as she started the slip-slide scramble back down toward the bridge. The crossing seemed easier without the strobe lights, but when she climbed back into the cab she was both wetter and colder. Juanito had turned off the motor. They were almost out of gas, Misty said. Sweet told them about the tow coming, said not to worry, the deputy didn't have any idea who was here in this truck; they just had to wait till the Taurus got pulled out of the way, then Juanito could drive straight on out. "Y'all keep going, no matter what happens. If that deputy tries to flag you down, just drive on. When you get to the blacktop, turn right. Don't go back to town, Misty. Hear me? Just keep going to the next section line road and pull off the blacktop and wait for me there. I'll take care of the tow operator and come on as quick as I can."

"And then what?"

Sweet shut her eyes. "Then we figure out the next step," she said, entirely uselessly, but it seemed to satisfy Misty, who rattled off to her husband what they'd be doing next. He leaned forward to see around Misty Dawn and the baby. "Thank you," he said.

Sweet nodded. "You're welcome."

The wait was long. The baby was bored and fretful, and it was so cold. The more Sweet rested from her exertion, the colder she got. Her teeth were chattering, her jaw trembling. It didn't do any good to wrap her arms around herself, her jacket was soaked through. After what felt like hours but was probably more like twenty or thirty minutes, the cruiser's headlights came back on. Worse, the red and blue lights started flashing again. Uh-oh,

Sweet thought. That deputy's mad I didn't come back. He's going to come over here to find out why not. She knew she'd better get out and head him off—but oh, oh, how she dreaded going back out in that freezing rain! Then another set of headlights sawed through the trees, came rolling up behind the cruiser. Oh, thank God. Of course. The tow truck. That's why the deputy had put his lights on—to flag down the driver. Well, with the tow here, she had to go. "Okay, what's the plan?" she asked Misty Dawn through clenched, chattering teeth.

"Soon as your car's out, we go across and keep going, no matter what, turn right at the blacktop and wait for you."

"At the next section line."

"Uh-huh," Misty said.

Sweet ached in every part of her being as she climbed down and started back across the bridge. It's almost over, almost over, almost over, she promised herself with each sliding step. Where were the yellow emergency lights on the tow truck? She couldn't see past the flashing red and blue ones. She climbed the far bank using her hands, squeezed past the cruiser, squinting, shielding her eyes with her hand till she was past the lights and could see the deputy's big outline, leaning down to talk in the window of the preacher's little tan Toyota. Sweet's fatigue zipped right out through the top of her head. *No!* she screamed in silence to Brother Oren: *Don't tell him!* She ran toward them, slipping, calling out, "Hey, hey, hey! Hello!" The deputy stood up from the window, flattening his hand over his head, like that was going to protect him from the sleety rain. Sweet went as fast as she could to the passenger side of the Toyota and got in. "Thanks for coming, Brother Oren! We're good, Deputy!" she shouted across at the open window. "We'll take it from here!"

"I was just telling the preacher—the dispatcher called and said it might be three or four hours yet. There's folks off the road clear to Hartshorne, she said it's real bad in Wilburton. Matter of fact, I got to get back. Sheriff called us in, said there's too many wrecks for just the town officers to work."

"No problem!" Sweet chirped. "Really. I appreciate everything you've done. We'll just, uh, Brother Oren can drive me into town."

"What about your cousins?"

"Oh, they're good. I mean, well." She looked at the preacher.

"I came out to help, Darrel. We'll be fine."

The deputy leaned in. "How'd you hear about Miz Kirkendall getting stuck?" Sweet couldn't see his expression. Was he suspicious?

"Well . . ." the preacher started.

"Claudie Ott's police scanner!" Sweet finished for him. "Isn't that right? We'll just back up and let y'all out."

"This sure ain't the best kind of car to be driving on ice in," the deputy said.

"It's got front-wheel drive," the preacher said. "We'll be all right."

"Thank you, Deputy," Sweet said. "Really. Thank you so much." The preacher rolled up his window, braced his arm on her seatback as he put the car in reverse. All through the exchange of positions, while the deputy backed past them, with the mustached hunter in the passenger seat pressing his face to the window to try to see out, and then while the cruiser slowly turned around and started across the pasture, Sweet was afraid to speak. Brother Oren edged his car forward to the top of the slope. "Better stop here," she whispered. The preacher's headlights showed up her mired Taurus extremely well. "I got stuck," she said pointlessly.

"Yeah."

"They're over yonder. "

"Uh-huh."

"Sitting in Juanito's truck." The preacher was silent. "What should I tell them?" She heard him take in a long shaky breath, but his voice was real calm when he answered.

"Maybe I'd better come with you. Y'all might need somebody to carry the little girl."

Tuesday | *February 26, 2008* | *Night*

In the Gloss Mountains

The boy talks aloud in his fever, asking questions, but Luis does not understand the english words. *It is well, my son,* Luis answers. *It is well.* Sometimes the boy thrashes about on the cold earth, coughing, pushing down the damp sleeping bag. Sometimes he moves his hurt arm and cries out. Sometimes he grows alarmingly still. Luis repeats the Our Father, the Hail Mary, the Glory Be, the Our Father again; many times over he prays while he bathes the forehead of the boy to make him cooler, or tugs the sleeping bag around his throat to keep him warm. Luis remembers how, when they drove away from the town with the white jail, the boy was completely silent as if he waited for something, or listened. But there was no sound except the loud grumble of the truck motor. Luis, too, said no words. Neither were there any lights of houses, only the black asphalt highway winding before them—a mountain road, similar to the roads near Arroyo Seco, but not so steep and winding, and the dark slopes of hills on both sides were only a little high. After a long time Luis said over the loud motor, *When we arrive to the house of your sister, we will ask her to telephone to your grandfather to say you are well.*

The boy did not answer. Luis remembers how he glanced at the boy then, but the truck was dark and he could see nothing except that the boy was still holding his wrist. The road began to descend, going down out of the hills, and soon they arrived at an intersection where it was necessary to turn to the right or the left. Luis waited for the boy to tell him, but the boy leaned down and fumbled inside the backpack on the floorboard. He withdrew the map and the small flashlight, held them out to Luis. *I dont know the good streets to go.* With the narrow beam Luis studied the map. The boy pointed to the town where the jail was, this road going north that they were on. But now they must choose which way to turn. Luis tried to ask if the big roads would be safer from the migra or the small ones, but the boy did not know, or perhaps he did not understand what Luis was asking. Looking at the map, Luis decided to turn left.

There were several hours of driving then, many wrong turns, many stops for consultations of the map. They drove on two-lane roads in darkness, sometimes through small towns without stop-lights. They saw few other cars. The journey was taking very long. Luis stopped to look at the map again, decided to go to one of the big roads. They passed through a town with plenty of streetlights, and outside the town, on the big road, many cars and trucks going north. Luis understood that it was the hour already when people were driving to work. The dark sky was thinning when the boy said, *¡Look! Tulsa.* The lighted buildings of a large city rose up in the distance. The vehicles were passing the truck on the both sides now, going so fast. Sometimes they honked at Luis driving slower and slower as the tall buildings drew nearer. The boy sat forward, watching. *I cant remember the way my uncle comes.* Luis saw an exit and drove down it. The boy shook his head. *This doesnt maybe be correct.* Then for a time they were driving aimlessly, looking at the tall buildings surrounding them, stopping again and again to wait at the red lights with many other cars. The indicator showed that they were going to need to buy gasoline soon. With what? The coins from the jar? The boy said, *Im sorry. I think I am able to know how my uncle goes but . . . is not the same. Maybe we come a different street.*

Your sister has a telephone, ¿yes? We can call her.

I dont know the number. The boy tucked his head forward, looking up. *I dont see these buildings at her house. Of her house.* He frowned, looking all around. *I think is possible we come this . . .* He pointed straight ahead. Luis drove as the boy pointed. Soon they were not among the tall buildings but driving deserted streets between low brick buildings like warehouses or factories, and then they were passing wooden houses and a few empty parking lots with closed stores. The boy seemed very lost. *Im sorry,* he said, many times, and each time Luis said, *No problem, no problem. It is well.*

The bodega, the boy said suddenly. He sat forward, pointing with excitement to a small building on the corner. *¡Here, this is the street here!* He smiled hugely at Luis. *¡I dont believe this!*

And how, Luis thinks now, would anyone believe it, except they believe in the guiding hand of the Virgin? They had not had to drive very far from the tall buildings, it is true. Nevertheless, it was miraculous that Luis had driven to the street where the boy recognized the little store—which was not, Luis could see, a true bodega selling wine but a small spanish grocery. On the window was written *Food and Beer.* His heart leaped to see the familiar words. But the store was not open. Luis turned at the corner and drove along the street as the boy directed to a small yellow house almost at the end of the block. The boy indicated Luis should drive into the big yard. There were no cars here. The white curtains on the windows were closed. But the morning was early, and Luis still retained hope as the boy climbed down slowly from the truck and walked, supporting his left arm, to the front door. Many times the boy knocked and called out a name that sounded a little like his own name. After a time he returned to the truck, wearing an expression of pain. Luis came around to help him climb back into the seat. *Your wrist is hurting.*

A little. Without doubt the boy had been hurting all the night, but he had not complained, and still he complained nothing, but his face showed pinched in the gray morning light. *I think that my sister is not here.*

We will wait, Luis said. *¿You have hunger?* The boy shook his head. *¿Thirst?* The boy nodded. Luis turned then and walked around the house, looking at the base, until he found what he wanted, a spigot, and on the ground beside it, disconnected, a coiled water hose. He screwed the hose on, carried the nozzle to the truck. The boy climbed down and drank a long time, and Luis drank. The water was very cold, metallic. He coiled the hose on the ground again, unhooked it from the spigot. They sat in the truck while the day grew stronger, though not bright, because the sky was overcast. After a time the boy slept, leaning his head against the side window. Luis, too, was very tired, but he did not want to sleep. He needed to keep watch. The truck was cold. If the sun would shine through the windows they would be warm, but the sun was hidden in an iron-gray sky. Luis unrolled the sleeping bag from the seat between them—this was not the bag with the crawling man but the dark green one with drawings of turkeys and deer on the inside—and covered the boy. Good. He would let the boy sleep. When he awakened, if the sister had not yet come, Luis would drive to the little store and buy aspirin for the boy, to help with the pain in his wrist. The shopkeeper would speak spanish, naturally. Luis would ask him for advice. Maybe the shopkeeper would allow the boy to stay inside the store until the sister would come for him. The boy could write a note at the little house to say he was waiting at the store. Then Luis could drive on in the truck to the Guymon town. Yes. A good plan. But there was one problem. The gasoline tank was nearly empty. Just to buy the aspirin Luis would have to use the coins from the jar. How would he buy enough gasoline to go to the Guymon town? Even if he would use all the coins, how much could they buy? To Americans, these coins would be nothing, a small fraction of American dollars, like centavos to pesos, he knew this already. Luis felt then the familiar weight on his chest. Another street without exit. The one most familiar. No money.

Monica Moorehouse paced the dark length of her den in McAlester, stood a moment staring out the sliding glass door at the freezing rain—a trillion tiny glass splinters spilling down onto the cement patio. She turned and paced to the opposite end of the room. The window facing the street was small, chest high, a 1960s relic. She glared through it at the low dark ranch-style catty-corner across the street. No lights on inside. Peaceable Road was peaceable all right—excruciatingly so. No passing cars. No street sanders, of course. Nothing but dead ice-spangled grass, the gleaming leafless twigs of the crape myrtle beside the window, the glittering shards streaming down in the streetlight. She would be stuck in McAlester till who even knew when. Charlie had already gone to bed.

She retraced her worn path between the couch and the darkened flatscreen, which she'd clicked off in disgust during the ten o'clock news. Good God, you'd think there'd never been ice in eastern Oklahoma. Only every damn winter since they got here in 2000—that Christmas ice storm, that was the worst. That's when she'd known for sure her husband had transported her from civilization to the absolute outback. Please, please, do not let there be

another power outage, she thought. Not like that one. They'd been
without electricity for seventeen days. She had very nearly lost her
mind. Monica peered out at the yard. In the patio light the ice
sheath on the Bradford pear tree appeared to be very thin. Maybe,
just maybe—if the temp would only rise a degree or two, if the
falling precip would quit falling—*maybe* she'd be able to get out
of here early tomorrow morning. The front was moving east, as
the hyped-up forecasters kept saying, devastating Arkansas, cant-
ing north into Missouri. They were welcome to it—and may the
nasty thing continue on into midwestern oblivion. Damn it, she'd
told Charlie they needed to get out ahead of the storm! Did he
listen? Did he ever listen? The TV was still babbling in the bedroom at the other end of the house. Charlie was almost certainly
flopped back against the pillows with the remote in his hand and
his mouth open, snoring. She envisioned herself slipping into the
room and lifting the keys off the nightstand, going out to the garage and starting the Escalade, driving across town through the
sleet to turn north on Indian Nations Turnpike, west on I-40—
how far west would she have to drive to get out of the bad weather?

Pausing beside the coffee table, Monica picked up the remote,
held it a moment, then tossed it onto the couch, where it thumped
against the leather. Charlie's Cadillac was still parked at the apartment in the City. She couldn't leave him here without a car. Even
if the roads were clear this minute, she'd still have to wait till
morning. Oh, she was so ready to get back to the capital, the tension, and attention, the buzz . . . she could stop by Kevin's, have a
drink, find out . . .

A drink. What a good idea. Monica mounted the low step into
the dimly lit kitchen, dug under the kitchen sink for the vodka
bottle.

She carried her drink to the couch, sat in the dark with the

lavender-tinged patio light streaming in to her right, the little gray
square of streetlight at the other end of the room, the muted yellow kitchen stove light behind her. She stared at the blank screen
on the brick wall. Charlie had bought a bunch of Jerome Tiger
prints and hung them encircling the television like a war party
attacking a covered wagon. Monica patted along the hard leather
cushion until she'd located the clicker, sat holding it without using
it, like an unlit cigarette in her hand. What was the point? All
evening she'd scanned the channels. Locally, the only news was
the weather. Nationally, it was all about the primaries, a different
kind of gossipy hysteria that interested Charlie infinitely, but not
her, at least not tonight. Even the *Headline News* Furies, the barking former prosecutor and her flared-nostril sisters, were off onto
a new track—some mother had killed her children in Idaho—and
the Dustin Brown story was barely mentioned. Monica couldn't
decide if this made her glad or mad, or merely depressed. In her
rapidly shifting emotions, she felt some of all three.

Charlie kept bragging about how much she'd done for her
national profile this morning, but Monica wasn't satisfied. She
couldn't feel it. She wanted to get back to Oklahoma City, hear
what people were saying—damn it, she did not want to miss another day of session! And here she was, trapped again inside this
low-slung mildewed ranch-style cavern to which her husband
had relegated her eight years ago. He'd known perfectly well she
wanted to live in something brand-new, clean and modern, not
a forty-year-old tasteless buff-brick shag-carpeted grotto that no
amount of framed Indian art on the walls was going to help. She
took a sip of her vodka tonic—more vodka than tonic, but who the
hell cared? She wasn't going anywhere.

She shivered, pulled the faux Pendleton blanket from the back
of the couch and wrapped it around herself. This night reminded

her way too much of that first winter, when she'd felt like she'd just made the worst mistake of her life, letting her husband drag her down here to Oklahoma. Not that she'd been so crazy for Indianapolis—in fact, she had more or less hated it—but at least in Indiana the term *winter storm* meant snow—plowable, shovelable, walkable. Here, it meant sleet and freezing rain, and you couldn't do anything about ice, couldn't walk on it, couldn't drive on it. No escape. She took a long sip.

Had she really hated Indianapolis, or did she just tell herself that now to tamp down the little nagging flares of regret?

Yes, well, as Charlie would say: What was there to regret? Her job filing contracts at Superior Finance? Their infrequent trips to Chicago? Certainly there'd been nothing to regret from the years before she met Charlie—what did she have then? A lousy job running the cash register at a Sirloin Stockade and boring night classes at Ivy Tech. The falling-apart house on North Adams. The occasional phone call from her brother in Florida asking about their mother quietly drinking herself to death in the upstairs bedroom. Charlie Moorehouse was by far the best thing that had ever happened to her: she'd known it then, knew it now. He'd been sort of good-looking, actually, back in the day. Dark hair and bedroom eyes, or that's how she'd seen him then, standing at the front of the classroom. She'd thought his Texas drawl was sexy. She hadn't expected his hair to turn lank and thin so soon, or his bedroom eyes to go buggy, or the faint little paunch he'd sported back in the 1990s to become such a gut. Oh, never mind. Never *mind*. Charlie's looks were hardly what mattered.

She set her drink on the coffee table and, with the blanket draped over her shoulders, felt her way to the framed mirror beside the kitchen divider. She could just make out her face in the glow from the stove light. Thirty-seven. Still remarkably young for all she'd accomplished, as Charlie constantly reminded her. People thought she was younger. Reaching up, she fluffed out her hair. Too bad there hadn't been time to get the highlights put in. Kevin had been right about that, as she'd seen immediately in the first clips of herself standing in the shitty barnyard looking haggard and hungover after the mad midnight ride from the City. Iced tea vat indeed. Even so, the ones on the noon news had looked pretty damned good.

Oh, and she had *so* managed to outshine that aw-shucks-ma'am senator, Dennis Langley—him with his shaggy mane towering over everybody in the kitchen, gossiping with reporters, acting like he was just there as a friend of the family. Why, surely he had not showed up at the highest-profile news story since the bombing as a *legislator;* why, he wasn't even any sort of a *politician* at all. Just a friend, ma'am, just a friend. To Monica's infinite satisfaction, the darty-eyed aunt never spent one minute talking to Langley. Some of the local news people acted way too chummy with him, but who did the network camera crews follow around, pray tell? State Representative Monica Moorehouse. Yes, ma'am.

And then, just a little after noon, the sheriff had made his grand entrance, all flabby eyed from his trip, and she had mopped the floor with him, that's what Charlie said. No challenge at all. There'd been such a mass of people milling around, cameras and mic cords everywhere, inside and outside the house, but Monica had had no trouble sorting out who to pay attention to, who not to waste time on—an art the sheriff had obviously not mastered. Anyone with a microphone to stick in his face could get a long blustery self-serving explanation about why the boy hadn't been found. And every tack the sheriff took, Monica followed up with her own color commentary.

She was skilled enough—and she had Charlie's eyes and ears

abetting—so that she could appear to be listening intently to the search team captain, nodding worriedly in her tan suede western-cut jacket and Dingo boots, while simultaneously monitoring every asinine comment the sheriff made. Then she'd appropriate it, give it nuance, make it her own. If Holloway got defensive about the roughed-up kid, Monica implied family child abuse. If he talked about the grandfather's arrest, she'd mention rumors of a "deported illegal alien family member." When the sheriff barked orders like he was the big high muckamuck who had everything under control, Monica would smilingly mention to some reporter how she'd felt it was "important to be here at the search site while Sheriff Holloway had to be out of the state on his recent media visit to Los Angeles." And yes, all right, by five o'clock the local newscasters were already fixated on the weather, but they still gave her good chunks of coverage, and cable news stayed with her right through to prime time. She'd been flawless. Leadership was bound to be pleased. Monica gazed at her pale image in the mirror. She ought to feel happy. She ought to feel *satisfied*, at least. Why did she feel so irritable, and restless, and depressed?

Well, the damned weather, of course. Who wouldn't be depressed?

Retrieving her tumbler from the coffee table, she went to the kitchen to fix herself another drink. When she returned to the den, she resumed her catlike pacing—patio doors to street-side window, street side to patio, behind the couch one direction, in front of it the next. What was there to plan for? What was there to *do*? Read bills for tomorrow's meetings, in case they did manage to get back? No thank you. She was too keyed up to just sit. At the moment the only thing she could have possibly watched on TV would have been news clips of herself, and unfortunately she was off the radar just now. Hah, she thought. Literally. In her mind she saw the pink and purple Nexrad images jerking across the weather map in time-lapse sequence, lurching from eastern Oklahoma into the neighboring Ozarks, again and again. How quickly the media jumped to the next thing! And just precisely when she'd found the perfect note, she thought resentfully. The perfect tone.

Charlie was only half right. Oh, it was about image, certainly—who could deny that? But it was also about sound. He was always on her to use the right words—*folks* of the Eighteenth District, not *people;* Oklahoma *taxpayers*, not *citizens*—but from the very first news clips this morning she'd heard it: the pitch-perfect intonation she'd been striving for. Monica wasn't naturally husky voiced but she had learned how to keep her voice in the lower registers, just as she'd learned how to sound smart but not too smart, how to smile winningly but without flirtation, how to briefly, rarely, and seemingly unthinkingly, refer to her Lord and Savior Jesus Christ. So yes, of course, on the clips, she had looked right, she had sounded right, she had used all the right words. But what most astonished and pleased her was how she had delivered them in the soft, pitch-perfect, almost-but-not-quite Okie drawl she'd been working on for years. And she hadn't even been conscious of trying to use it! She had, she realized, internalized the thing at last. Oh, she'd been shining. In those early news clips she had *owned* the story. Then the goddamned weather swept her off the map.

Glass in hand, Monica stood again at the sliding patio door. The freezing rain had stopped. Had it stopped? She squinted. Yes, she thought so. The arrow on the round plastic outdoor thermometer still pointed at 30, but it was a cheap thing they'd bought at Atwoods years ago; it always took forever to adjust when the temperature changed. The painted-on cardinal still looked startled, taken by surprise, frozen on his white circle. But wasn't that water—plain glorious melted *water*—dripping from the eaves? Oh, hallelujah. She headed for the kitchen.

One more drink, she told herself, then to bed. Even if the roads were clear in the morning, it was still a two-hour drive to the City, and her hair was gummy with the expensive salon product Kevin insisted she use. She was going to have to get up early to wash it. There was no guarantee, of course, that the roads would be clear. She switched on the floor lamp to locate the clicker, stood squinting at the blossoming screen. Well, thank God. The storm had apparently swept on out of Oklahoma—no hyped-up forecaster interrupted Jimmy Kimmel. Not even one of those little logoed maps in the corner showing Doppler radar. McAlester had dodged the bullet—no power outage this time. The roads should be fine by morning. Hallelujah again. She sat down.

It was after midnight. On cable news it was all repeats of the evening shows, excitable analysts analyzing last week's primary. Or was it next week's? They were always on now, the primaries, a constant low-grade fever, a stew pot on simmer. Monica propped her feet on the coffee table, pulled the blanket from her shoulders and tucked it under the full length of her legs, snugged the brightly striped wool over her toes. She unmuted the mute button, took another sip.

Tuesday | February 26, 2008 | Night

In the Gloss Mountains

The moon is low in the sky now. Soon she will be hidden behind the slope of the hill. The coughs of the boy grow thinner, more shallow, as if there is not enough air within him to breathe. Luis sits huddled beside him with the green sleeping bag wrapped around his shoulders, thinking, remembering, trying to stay awake. To keep watch. How very strange, he thinks, the manner in which his journey has turned the opposite way of so many others, and yet the same. All the world knows the stories of those lost in the desert, the ones who walk north and never reach their destination, and yet never return. Their families never see them again, never learn what has happened to them. At the beginning of his journey, in Mexico, Luis had been relieved that he would not have to walk across the frontier because his sons helped him, they paid the money to the *coyote* to bring Luis north in the crowded truck. Never did he expect that his journey would one day become like the others, crossing the long flat plains without protection, without sufficient food or water—and yet his journey is very different from the stories. He travels not to the north but to the west, suffering not heat but too much cold. Traveling with a boy who is very sick, who could become, it is possible, one of the vanished ones.

No! No. This is not true. Our Lady will not withdraw her protection so much as to permit this to happen. This fear is only the fear of Luis, his fatigue and lack of faith. The boy no longer talks aloud in his fever, but lies very still, very pale in the moonlight. Is he perhaps better? *Tomorrow*, Luis whispers aloud to the high plains night, the sinking moon. *Let us protect him until tomorrow. Then we will find help.*

GodSaveYouMaryYouAreFullOfGraceTheFatherIsWithYou . . .

There have been many gifts, Luis reminds himself. Many small miracles of passage from Our Lady of Guadalupe, who has attended the travels of Luis from his home in Arroyo Seco all the way to this place on the night plain. She will not abandon them now. She was with them in Tulsa, when Luis left the boy sleeping inside the truck in the yard of the sister and walked the long block back to the little spanish store.

He had expected the shopkeeper to be a man. When he saw the mexican woman behind the counter, he felt strange, as if he knew her, as if he had seen her many times before. But oh, how he breathed! hearing the familiar words when she asked what he wanted. She was short and round and spoke with a Chiapas accent. Probably it was only her familiar words and coloring that made her seem like a person he had known. Of their conversation he remembers very little. He must have asked for the aspirin to help the boy. Perhaps that was when he told her he was traveling to join his sons. Certainly he asked for the bathroom, and with her permission he went into the cramped ammonia-smelling room in the back of the store. When he came out again, the small bottle of white aspirins sat on the counter and also a tall plastic bottle of Pepsi and a short bottle with water, and the boy stood in front of them, counting out coins from the jar. Had Luis carried the jar of coins to the store? He cannot remember.

What he remembers most distinctly from that day is how the woman said it would be dangerous for him to stay in Tulsa. The migra was strong there, she told him; it was not a good place for Luis. Families had been separated, she said. Many men deported. The woman spoke with the boy in english, with Luis in spanish. So rapidly the woman clicked the english words! And the boy talked just as quickly to the woman. Soon it became apparent that the woman was familiar with the sister of the boy. The woman turned to Luis then and told him in spanish that the husband of the sister had been deported since before Christmas. But now the sister talked with the news reporters, the woman had seen this. Therefore maybe the sister was not trustworthy. She was married to a mexican man, it was the truth. They had a daughter. Nevertheless, she was a lightskin. The woman shrugged, as if to say, *This is no business of mine; you must decide for yourself.* Luis picked up the coin jar and the plastic bag with the Pepsi, and he and the boy turned to leave. The woman called out, *¡A moment!* From the cash register she withdrew an american dollar with the number twenty on it, held it out to him. *Is dangerous here,* she repeated. *Go quickly to your sons.*

So, yes, this was a miracle. Or a mercy. The kindness of a woman who did not know him but would help him go to his sons. He and the boy walked back to the truck. *¿What is this word, dangerous?* the boy asked. But Luis did not know how to explain. Dangerous means dangerous; it could not be demonstrated like a broken twig. Again they sat in the truck. Did they talk? Luis cannot remember. Did they eat? He does not know. Those hours waiting for the sister seemed to last forever, the sky growing grayer, the inside of the truck turning colder.

This was when the fatigue came most hard on Luis. Many times he found his head dipping forward, his eyes closing, and he would jerk himself alert. Finally he crossed his hands on the top of the steering wheel, rested his forehead on them, saying to the boy that he would rest his eyes only a moment. Later he awakened with a quick flash of fear. He could not tell the hour, but he believed that much time had passed. And still the sister had not come. The boy sat reading the yellow dictionary. His lips were trembling with the cold. Luis, too, was very cold. He started the motor, watched as the indicator needle came only a little way above the letter *E*.

He told the boy that they would go now to buy gasoline and then return to wait for the sister, and the boy said okay, but he could not show Luis where to go. They drove around many blocks, but Luis did not want to travel far and become lost; he was also concerned that to keep driving would finish the gasoline. So he drove back to the street of the little house, stopped in front of the spanish store on the corner, thinking he would go in and ask the shopkeeper for directions. But now the sign in the window said in both english and spanish that the store was closed. *Look*, the boy said, pointing down the street to a white van parked in front of the little house. *I think is not of my sister,* the boy said. *I dont see it . . .* He motioned behind himself. *In the past.*

Okay, Luis said.

¿Is good or bad? the boy asked.

¿Who knows? We will wait a little while and watch.

The passenger door of the van opened and a young woman with black hair climbed down. She crossed the yard and knocked at the door of the little house. She knocked many times, looked around the yard, looked back to the van, knocked more. At last she returned to the van, and the van pulled away. But it did not go away. The driver turned at the next corner and parked just at the edge. Luis could see then the brightly lettered words and numbers on the side of the van. The people in the van waited, Luis and the boy waited. More time passed. *¿What do you think?* Luis asked the boy. The boy shrugged. *No idea,* he said.

Then another vehicle passed where they were parked—a police car! Even worse. And the police car, too, stopped in front of the little house. A police in uniform went to the door to knock. He stood with a pad of paper in his hand, waiting. *Dangerous,* the boy whispered. Luis looked over. Oh, of course. The dictionary. *Dangerous for me,* Luis said. His heart was thumping fiercely in his chest. *But not for you. Maybe you can go to him, he will help you.*

¿Help me for what?

To wait for your sister. So you will be in a place where the people will not hurt you.

The boy looked up. His face was very old for such a young boy. *No,* he said. *We have a new plan. I come with you to your sons. Then my grandfather is ready. Then I come home.*

I think is better that you wait for your sister.

I think is better that I come with you.

Luis sat watching the police knocking at the door. Maybe the police would turn and see them, only one long block away. Maybe he would say to himself, I will check this mexican man sitting in a truck with a boy whose face has been beaten. Then all would go very badly for Luis. But how to drive away without attracting attention? If he would go forward, he must pass the police car. If he would turn the truck in the street to go back, the police would see him. If he would reverse the truck around the corner onto the next primary street, this would be even more bad, because the street was busy with the traffic, and the police would know someone in the truck was trying to sneak away. Then, as Luis prayed for guidance, the police returned to his vehicle and drove to the corner, where he turned right, passed by the van, and disappeared, and at once the van followed the police car, easing away out of sight. Luis and the boy looked at each other. The boy laughed out loud. Then Luis laughed. After a moment he said, *Now is possible for you to wait for your sister.*

She doesnt come today, the boy answered, gazing straight ahead. *My mother say me. I go with you.*

Luis, too, stared straight ahead a few moments. This was the same, like in the cemetery. He could not leave the boy alone. To wait might bring more danger. So yes, Luis thought then. They would go together to the Guymon town, and when his sons would return the truck to the grandfather, they would return also the boy. Luis nodded once. Okay.

In this way began their journey together from the city to this frozen place here on the night plain. Many miles, many days and nights of travel, following the red spidery roads they were able to discover from the map, west, toward the Guymon town. And only a few hundred of those miles inside the blue truck.

The boy whimpers inside the damp sleeping bag. Luis puts his palm to his forehead. The heat of the fever rages, and yet the boy shivers. Luis can feel him shuddering beneath his hand. Quickly Luis unwraps the sleeping bag from himself, lays it across the boy. Within moments his jaw begins to clench with cold. If only he had the protection of the truck now! The inside of the truck had seemed insufficient, too battered and small and chilly, but how much easier the journey had been before the truck failed them! It is for this reason, Luis thinks, that the boy became sick. So much time exposed to the freezing weather. It would have been better if he had taken the boy to a police or a church in a town while they were still traveling in the rolling land where the towns were frequent. Luis was then making such effort to avoid the towns, when he should have been seeking their help. But how could he know?

A man can know only the mistakes of the past, the decisions he would make differently if he could remake them. Never is there sufficient knowledge of the future to make the wise choices. What is there to rely on, when a man must make choices? Protection and guidance from heaven. The blessings of the sacraments, if he is able to receive them. Prayers. Miracles and mercies. Faith.

Part Three

Welcome the Stranger

Morning brought headache, dry mouth, and a slight argument with her husband in the kitchen before daylight. "We need to stay here, babe," Charlie said, scratching his belly, his thin hair sticking up like a kewpie doll's. "One more day."

Monica pressed her thumb against the ache between her eyes. "I know *you* can work anywhere, Charlie, but I have obligations."

"They'll understand. They know the roads are bad. Listen, I got a feeling. My old political bone's trembling. I can smell it."

"You're mixing your metaphors," she said, pouring coffee. She pawed through the overhead cabinet for ibuprofen.

"What if something breaks and you're not here to capitalize on it?"

"I can capitalize from Oklahoma City."

"Not the same way. Look, what's the difference between even-numbered years and odd-numbered?"

"Oh, shut up." She took down a glass, ran some water. The difference, as Charlie loved to repeat ad nauseum, was simply that in even-numbered years you had an opponent. Meaning: you are always in campaign mode, whether it's a campaign year or not. You never let your guard down, never quit paying attention to your constituents, the ones who elected you—the people here in this little burg in southeastern Oklahoma and nearby environs who sent you to the People's House. Monica tossed back the Advil, gulped a slug of water, gazed at her husband a moment. "What the people sent me to do is make laws at the capitol to their benefit," she said evenly. "And that's precisely what I'm going to be seen doing. Today." She set the glass in the sink and went to take a shower.

Charlie had the Escalade warming up in the garage by the time she finished blow-drying her hair. His laptop was open on the passenger seat, the connect card winking lazily, his twin BlackBerrys propped in the cup holders. He held the driver's-side door open for her. She didn't really feel like driving—the Advil had only dulled the throbbing, not eliminated it—but it would be less irksome to drive than to be the one to have to monitor Charlie's laptop, the constant influx of e-mails buzzing in on the phones. Less stressful. There was no way her husband could just *drive* somewhere; he always had to be doing six or seven other things—even if it was just fiddling with the radio to track the news on NPR and the Oasis Network at the same time.

They crossed town in predawn darkness. The residue of last night's ice glistened in the crooks of trees in the graying streetlights. The roads were still wet, but clear. A thin line of red broke on the eastern horizon as they turned north on the Indian Nations Turnpike. The farther north they drove, the heavier the ice sheen on the trees and power lines, but the roads remained navigable. Charlie scanned his RSS feeds, read aloud the better blog postings, the relevant e-mails and "tweets," as he called them, some new messaging system that sounded to her like abbreviated fortune cookie renderings.

By the time they reached Henryetta a half hour later, the sun was glaring on the sparkling trees, the ice-spangled fences. Monica squinted against the brilliance as she negotiated the ramp onto

I-40. After that, thank God, the sun was behind them. She listened with only half an ear to Charlie's monologue. Her mind was
distracted. She hadn't heard from anyone yet, not even her most
avid allies, but really it was still early; she might have to wait till
she got to her office to find out how her performance had been
received. She occupied her mind with rehearsals for what she'd say
to the Speaker if he was excited about the way things were going,
and also what she'd say if he was pissed. Not that Coughlin would
ever reveal *pissed* in any overt way—his veneer never slipped—but
she would know. Oh, what was she worried about? She'd been
perfect. Hadn't she been perfect? It was just this hangover making
her feel shaky. She'd be fine as soon as she got something to eat.

The news, when it came, arrived not via one of Charlie's inces-
sant news feeds or blog posts but through an old-fashioned cell-
phone call. "Hey, man," Charlie said. "Yeah. Yeah. Nope, haven't
heard a thing. We're driving." He listened. "Are you shittin' me?"
Charlie listened a while longer, let out a whoop. "Thanks, friend.
You just made my day." And then to Monica: "Turn around, babe."

"What? No. We're almost to Shawnee."

"Huh?" He glanced around. "Oh, yeah." They were well past
the iced area. On both sides of the interstate, the land sloped toward the dark tree line in shades of winter beige. "Okay, okay, no
need to address it from down there anyway, the sighting was in
Tulsa. You're back on the job, right. Working for the Oklahoma
taxpayers."

"Sighting. You mean—the kid? Somebody's seen him?"

"Better than that, babe." Charlie's grin was beyond wolfish.
"They've seen him *and* the illegal Mexican he's traveling with!"

"No."

"*Oh* yeah."

Monica let out a whoop of her own. Her mind raced. "How do

they know it's—oh my God, it's the, uh, uncle, right? Or whatever. That guy they deported?"

"Cunningham didn't say. Maybe. Yeah, could be. All he told me, word came in last night some bodega owner admitted to seeing the kid and a Mexican together in Tulsa last Thursday, and why his detectives just now got around to hauling that shopkeeper in for questioning the Tulsa chief of police is mighty anxious to know."

"Is it out yet? The news?"

"Chief's set to call a press conference later today. Noon maybe. Cunningham said he's got every Tom, Dick, and Myrtle out canvassing the Hispanic section, trying to come up with something solid before the news breaks. Doesn't look so good for them they let this slip by a whole goddamn week."

She drove straight to the capitol, had Charlie drop her off at the east entrance, but then she got stuck behind a battalion of high school seniors with their six thousand cell phones and backpacks; she was late for her committee meeting but nobody cared. The majority whip chaired the committee. The caucus chair served as vote counter. When she walked into the room, she could feel the silent applause. They'd seen the clips; they approved of her performance. The story was playing just fine with Leadership—and they didn't even know the half of it yet.

First Baptist Church | Cedar

Sweet watched her grandniece sleeping peacefully in the church nursery crib. The top of the child's head brushed the yellow baby ducks decaled on the headboard. Her little blanketed feet were curled up against the footboard. Still, the crib had to be more comfortable than the pews out in the sanctuary where Misty Dawn and Juanito slept. Sweet had fixed them up with quilts and pillows the preacher had provided—Misty Dawn on one of the front pews, Juanito in the next one behind—but she'd insisted on letting the baby sleep in the nursery. That little girl needed some semblance of normalcy, Sweet told them—something like furniture, for example, she'd said, pointing to the low child-sized table and toddler chairs, the two baby beds and the rocker. Toys in the toy box. Kids' books on the shelves. And Misty Dawn had agreed, or else she'd been too tired to argue; in any case, after they ate the canned spaghetti Brother Oren brought over, she'd settled Lucha in the crib, left the safety rail down, rubbed her back until she fell asleep. Sweet had dragged the rocking chair over then, whispering "Y'all go get some sleep. I'll stay."

She'd rocked all night under the buzzing fluorescent glare. She hadn't wanted the baby to wake up in the dark and be afraid. Had Sweet herself slept? She thought so. She'd dozed anyway. Much of the night, however, she'd spent rocking and charting what she needed to do today as soon as the roads cleared. Were they clear? She would have to go out to Fellowship Hall to see. There weren't any windows in the nursery. She ought to check the time on her phone. All right, she would do that. Here in a minute. When she felt up to looking at all the missed calls. She continued to rock slowly, staring glassily around the walls at the posters of Jesus Suffering the Little Children, Joseph and his Coat of Many Colors, Noah and his family peering down from the side of the Ark at all the zoo animals marching two-by-two up the ramp, lions and giraffes and elephants. No skunks or opossums, no coyotes or box terrapins, no rattlers or copperheads or armadillos or raccoons. None of Oklahoma's natural wildlife. You never saw those kinds of animals on Noah's Ark. Shoot the gerbil, she thought. Shoot the gerbil. Please.

But Sweet's mind continued to turn in its endless fruitless circle: first she'd have to call a tow truck to come from Wilburton to get her Taurus out so they could move Juanito's truck, and of course she didn't have a credit card to pay for it but maybe they would just bill her or she could give the driver a check, but she still had to get out to the farm to meet the guy and she'd have to stop by the house first to pick up her checkbook, so she wouldn't call for the tow until she was sure what time she could get out there. Brother Oren would be heading to Stigler this morning to pick up Vicki and the kids—he said he'd be leaving as soon as the roads cleared—so probably the first thing she needed to do was see if he'd left yet or if he was back already so she could find out what time he could take her out to the farm.

No, actually, first thing she had to do was get out of this ratty blue plaid bathrobe the preacher had handed her last night and put back on her muddy clothes. Hopefully they were dry now. She'd laid them out on the floor heating grates in the Fellowship Hall kitchen. It embarrassed her to remember coming out of the ladies' room in the preacher's bathrobe holding that muddy mess of wet clothes in her hands, and him standing there in the cramped hall in front of the nursery. So, yeah, she'd go check to see if her clothes were dry straight off.

Then, after she got her car out, she would drive to Wilburton to cash in that retirement CD she'd been intending to use for Daddy's lawyer so she could give the kids enough money for the motel and also food to last a while; hopefully the bank would let her do that without Terry being there—she could always forge his name—plus she'd also have to remember to put enough money in the checking account to cover the hot check she was fixing to write to the tow truck driver because she had totally forgotten to ask Brother Oren to ask the church treasurer not to deposit her tithe check, then she'd come back to town and wait till it got late enough for her to pick up the kids here at the church under cover of darkness and drive them to Arkansas. After that, well, she didn't know. Just take care of the next thing. The next thing in front of her. That's all she could think.

So. Just a few more hours. A little while longer. Half a day. Then she could let Carl Albert come home. Then she could go see Mr. Bledsoe in the hospital in McAlester like a decent Christian woman. Then she could proceed with her normal life, except that her daddy was still in jail and Dustin was still missing, and there was this other strange new condition, something unfathomable, something she'd never considered before . . . she would be single. A divorced woman. A single mom.

No, really, she said to herself, rubbing her face. How did it come to this? She tried to recount events, tracing them from that first Friday night, when the sheriff pounded on her front door and

handed off a scowling, tousle-headed Dustin, all the way through
to this past Monday at the farm, when she'd realized, finally, that
her marriage was over. She couldn't see a through-line, though—
the memories were too jumbled, all mixed and mauled together.
Whose fault? her mind said. Not mine, her mind answered. Not
mine, surely.

Then why did she feel so guilty and heartsick?

Her phone buzzed inside her purse again. Sweet leaned forward and pulled the blanket up to Lucha's chin, touched her
cheek. The child stirred, curled over onto her side with her two
fingers in her mouth. Quietly Sweet pulled up the safety rail and
locked it in place; she grabbed her buzzing purse off the little table,
tiptoed out.

Terry again. Of course it was Terry. She stood a moment in
the dark hallway between Fellowship Hall and the old part of the
church. The phone's face said in bright blue letters, *Terry Cell*. All
right, she thought. No point in putting this off any longer. She
punched the button to take the call as she headed to the kitchen
to make coffee.

"It's about goddamn time!"

Sweet said nothing. Through the double glass doors beyond the
rows of tables she could see bright sunshine. Well, that was good
news.

Tee was making some kind of strange noise. It almost sounded
like he was choking.

"What's the matter?" she said. More choking. A guttural
half-hitched breath that Sweet recognized as a sob. "Terry! What
is it!"

"Dad's dead."

The reactions swept through her in milliseconds—a wrenching pain, a rush of blood, a silent scream, followed by sudden

relief—he hadn't said *your daddy*, but *Dad*. Mr. Bledsoe. Then the sickening guilt. "Oh, my God, honey," she whispered.

If Terry had kept crying, if he'd kept on choking speechlessly, if he'd done almost anything except what he did do, everything might have been different. They might have worked things out. Or this is what Sweet would later tell herself. But what her husband did next was start yelling, blaming, yelling: "This is *your* fault! I'm on my way to Wilburton, I'll be dropping Carl off in a little bit and don't give me any of your damn lip! I been calling all frigging morning, why the hell did you leave the phone off the hook?"

"Is Carl with you?"

"Hell yes, he's with me! What did I just say? He's been with me the whole damn week. One whole week I couldn't go to work because I got to take care of my kid because my wife has gone off her frigging nut! Why the hell didn't you pick up?"

"The reporters . . ." she started vaguely.

"I don't give a shit about reporters! My grandpa is dead! And Carl's having a meltdown, and you can just damn well deal with your son!"

It was then Sweet heard through the roaring road noise the sound of her son sobbing. A warm, pulling sensation went through her, almost like her milk letting down back when she'd nursed him years ago. She wanted to cry, too. Instead she said mildly, "Watch your language, Tee. He don't need to hear you talking like that."

She expected an explosion back from him, but all she heard was a low growl. "We're coming through Fanshawe now. I'll be there in ten minutes." Then the phone went dead.

Immediately Sweet rushed around grabbing her crusty jeans and sweater and jacket from the heat grates. She got herself dressed in about thirty seconds, and the clothes were dry enough, thank God, except for her socks, but everything was stiff as burlap, almost certainly ruined, especially her good cream-colored sweater—how did it get so much mud on it? hadn't she had her jacket snapped closed?—and she threw the wadded bathrobe on the kitchen counter, ran with her mud-caked boots in her hands to the sanctuary, asking herself why she was in such a panic. She didn't have to answer to her soon-to-be-ex-husband Terrence Kirkendall, she reminded herself. Except if she wasn't home, what would Terry think? What would he do?

"Misty Dawn!" She shook her niece's shoulder. Juanito shot up in the next pew, alert, ready to jump, but it took a second for Misty Dawn to come around. "What?' she said sleepily. Juanito was already on his feet. "*La migra*?" he said. Sweet shook her head. "My husband. Misty Dawn, get up now! Y'all go hide in the nursery. Stay there till I get back." She was already hurrying away from them up the aisle. "Tee's on his way to the house, I got to get there before he does. Shut the nursery door. Don't even peep your heads out, hear me?" She balanced herself against the very back pew as she tugged on her stiff boots, wishing she hadn't said that last— saying *don't* to Misty Dawn was such a bad idea. "Brother Oren will be here after a while. Y'all just sit tight, okay?" She pushed through the door to the foyer, suddenly remembered today was Wednesday. She stuck her head back inside the sanctuary: "Take the quilts, Misty! Keep the baby quiet! I think there's a WMU meeting this morning!"

Sweet hurried through town, practically running, grateful that the sun was shining and the ice melting, and simultaneously feeling very, very sorry that it was already this late—because there was Gladys Chester, one of the Senior Citizens cooks, getting out of her car in the center's parking lot. She stared at Sweet, lifted her hand in a halfhearted, confused wave as Sweet crossed hurriedly to the other side of the street. And oh, wouldn't you

know, there sat the two smocked, smoking women frowning out
at her through the plateglass window of Heartland Home Health
as she race-walked past. Nobody walked anywhere in this town.
Well, nobody except mentally handicapped adults and the poor-
est of the poor. Certainly no normal person ran along the old
high sidewalks in muddy clothes and caked cowboy boots with
their hair sticking up like a fright wig, as in her own reflection in
the blacked-out window of the old pool hall. Phones would ring.
Tongues would wag.

She was panting hard as she crossed the highway, watching
east to see if Terry's truck was coming. It was not. She stumbled
across the railroad tracks, cut through the right of way in the dry
crackling weeds. Her chest burned, and there was that stabbing
pain in her side like she used to get when she played basketball in
high school. By the time she reached the carport door, she felt like
her heart was about to burst. She was gasping at the kitchen sink,
running herself a glass of water, when she heard Tee's diesel engine out front. Sweet set the glass down, sprinted to the bedroom
to get out of her filthy clothes. And she almost made it, would
have made it, if her son hadn't pounded into the house so fast,
straight to her bedroom, where he flung himself at her, clamped
his arms around her waist, sobbing hysterically, just right when
she was trying to pull her mud-crusted sweater up over her head.

"What are you—?" Terry stood in the doorway gaping at the
muddy remains flung across the bedroom floor. "What is this,
Sweet?"

"Nothing. I don't know." Sweet held her son very tight. "What
happened?"

"What do you think happened! Dad died! At four o'clock this
morning!"

"Why didn't somebody call? They should've called."

"They did call! They said they tried! Both numbers! Where have you been!"

"Here! I was here, I just left the phone off, I'm sorry. What did he . . . how did it . . . ? I mean, oh, let's— Shhh, honey, it's all right." She hugged her son, stroked his prickly head. He was sobbing so hard she couldn't bear it. "I'm sorry," she whispered. "I'm sorry, hon, it's okay, it's okay." She offered her husband a you're-right-but-please-let's-talk-about-this-later look. Tee wasn't having any.

"They said it was a blood clot or something, but basically you killed him."

"Terry!"

Carl Albert let out a wail.

"That's what happened, isn't it? He died as direct result of you leaving him alone to fall and break a hip! What the hell were you doing? Where were you?" Tee's eyes narrowed. "It's another man, isn't it?"

"Good God, no. Are you kidding? That's the last thing!"

"I want to know what you're up to, Georgia. Look at this!" He waved a furious paw at the muddy jeans on the floor, the caked sweater she was still wearing. His voice lifted in a high sarcastic twang: "'No, Tee, you can't come home, *you* take Carl Albert with you, *you* turned in my daddy!' Well, I might've turned in your weird old fanatical daddy, but you killed my grandpa! Now. You tell me which is worse."

Sweet stared. The anger in her husband's swollen face was fully matched by the pain. Terry loved Mr. Bledsoe. Of course he did. The wash of guilt pouring through her was so powerful she couldn't speak. She backed to the bed, sank down, drawing her son with her. Carl Albert collapsed sideways against her, still bawling uncontrollably, and hiccupping, too, now. Sweet reached for the crocheted afghan on the foot of the bed, dragged it over

and draped it across the boy's shuddering form and her own naked
legs. Terry was making the choked barks in his throat like she'd
heard on the phone. She kept her eyes on the rug.

After a minute Terry got quiet. When he spoke, his voice was
thick. "The folks from the funeral home already picked him up
from the hospital. I got to get to Wilburton and make the arrangements." Sweet nodded without looking up. She ought to go with
him. He'd never made funeral arrangements by himself. Sweet
had been the one to help his father pick out the casket and flowers
and dress for Tee's mom, and then she'd done it all for Mr. Kirkendall himself when he passed. Terry had been too distraught; he'd
gone to the funeral home with her, but on every decision he'd just
said, "I don't know, hon, whatever you think."

"I'll be back in an hour," Terry said. "Then, I'm telling you
something, Sweet. We are going to set a few things straight."

She nodded again. In a bit she heard him leave. She went on
rubbing her son's back, humming "The Old Rugged Cross" like she
used to do when he was a tiny boy. He had finished bawling, was
in the shuddery, raggedy-breaths stage. She knew it would take
Terry longer than an hour to drive to Wilburton and look at all the
coffin samples and make up his mind and go by the florist's and the
Latimer County News to give them the information for the obitu-
ary, if he even remembered to do that, which he might not, but at
the very least it was going to take closer to two hours—definitely
longer than he expected, she knew that. But still, it wouldn't be
near time enough.

Wednesday | *February 27, 2008* | *8:00 A.M.*

Latimer County Jail | *Wilburton*

After breakfast, while the two men sat on their bunks waiting for the trustee to come collect the trays, Arvin Holloway suddenly appeared on the other side of the bars. Bob Brown's heart lurched. He looked over at Garcia. The pastor gave an uncertain shrug. Shakily Brown got to his feet, crossed the small space to talk. Fear and grief pulsed through him. How had Holloway managed to get through the clanging outer door into the echoey concrete hall without them hearing? The sheriff unclipped the jumble of keys from his belt and opened the cell door; he motioned Brown to come out, waving Garcia back when he started to stand, too. Without a word Holloway relocked the cell, nodded Brown ahead of him toward the solid steel door at the end of the hall. Brown stood swaying on his feet as he waited for the sheriff to find the next key and turn it in the fat lock. He was afraid he might faint; he'd had too little to eat for too many days. Every one of those days he had asked to speak to Holloway. The trustees kept saying, "Sheriff ain't here, he ain't here." Now, this early in the morning, and in terrible silence, Arvin Holloway *was* here. It could only mean something very bad.

The sheriff ushered him along past the unmanned front desk and empty break room into his own office. There he shut the door, motioned Brown to sit, hoisted himself down into his roller chair. "All right now," he said. "Talk."

The pause that followed was not, as Holloway thought, because of Bob Brown's stubbornness but his surprise. He'd been expecting the sheriff to tell *him* something, maybe something unbearable, maybe the worst possible news there is. That the sheriff wanted Brown himself to do the talking simply threw him. He shook his head—more to try to clear it than to say *I don't know what you want,* but Holloway took the gesture for refusal. "Goddamnit. Talk!" The sheriff was furious. He'd gotten the first call a little after seven this morning, the last one not ten minutes ago. "You sorry old coot, you'd better start explaining. I mean *now!*"

"Explain what?"

"How your goddamn pickup ended up in Tonkawa!"

"What?"

"State Patrol found that piece-of-crap Chevy of yours in a ditch six miles south of Tonkawa. I want to know what it was doing there."

"I don't know."

"Where's the boy?"

"My God, man. Don't you think I would've said something if I knew?"

"I don't know *what* you'd do. I never expected the Bob Brown I grew up with to be a goddamn Mexican smuggler, either."

"Arvin, you know it's not like that." Brown's voice was quiet, but his heart was racing, his hands trembling. "There must be a mistake."

"They checked the VIN number."

"I don't know. Maybe somebody borrowed it."

"Somebody like that goddamn spic your boy's hanging around

with? Oh, yeah, we know all about that! Sure do." As of seven
o'clock this morning the sheriff had known, anyway—that was
the first call that came in: Tulsa police phoning him at home to
tell him the kid had been sighted in Tulsa with "an unidentified
Spanish-speaking man." Holloway had exploded in fury, flung his
coffee mug in the kitchen sink, where it bounced and broke in half.
He leaned in now toward Bob Brown. "Who is it? That wetback
your granddaughter married, right? He's the one drove your truck
to Tonkawa!"

This was the call that had come in a few minutes ago: the
truck located not just a measly hundred miles away in Tulsa but
all the way practically to the goddamn Kansas border! Holloway's
rage knew no bounds. He jumped up and went to the high small
window, stood seething, his right hand fondling his pistol grip.
Goddamn Tulsa PD, State Highway Patrol, Kay County Sheriff's Office, Oklahoma State Bureau of Investigation—everybody
getting in on the act! The case was set to be ripped right out of
his jurisdiction! Press conferences would all move north. He'd be
relegated to second fiddle, the county sheriff who broke the news
and then botched finding the missing kid. Holloway turned and
narrowed his eyes at Brown. "You got that snively little grandson out doing your dirty work while you loll around in my jail,
is that it?"

"What are you talking about?"

Holloway stalked back to his chair and eased himself down.
"We are fixing to have us a little heart-to-heart, my friend."

"Arvin, we have never been friends. Not growing up. Not now."

"You are one arrogant son of a bitch, did you know it? You
always have had a ton of gall." He pulled a small spiral notebook
over, located a pen. "All right then. We'll start at the beginning.
Who's this spic your boy's running around with?"

"I don't know what you're talking about. Who told you they saw Dustin?"

"Tulsa chief of police, for your information. Some store owner seen them there together, your grandson and this Mexican fella he's hanging around with. So. You ready to volunteer me some help here, or do I have to come around there and smack it out of you?"

Brown's mind scrambled, trying to fit the pieces together. Dustin in Tulsa? Yes, he might have tried to go to his sister's, but how would a little boy travel a hundred miles to Tulsa? Had they checked at Misty Dawn's? "You need to go—" He'd almost said "talk to my granddaughter," but stopped himself in time . . . *this Mexican fella he's hanging around with.* Who could that be? Holloway seemed to think it was Juanito, but Juanito was in Mexico. Only, what if he wasn't? "—talk to Sweet," Brown finished. "She might know something."

"Oh hell yeah, that misbegotten, misnamed daughter of yours, she's real forthcoming. No, I ain't talking to Sweet! *You're* talking to *me.*" He noticed Brown cut a sideways glance at the murky TV monitor, where, in one of the gray rotating screens, the Mexican pastor's tennis shoes and pants cuffs showed at the foot of the cell bars. "Tell you what," Holloway said slowly, "I been thinking I just might have to transfer that amigo of yours to, say, oh, I don't know, Tulsa County. Or back to the main run. Someplace I wouldn't have any way to protect him." He tried to gauge how the threat was playing. "Folks hate beaner smugglers, they really do. Not quite so bad as child molesters, but pretty bad. Especially Mexican ones."

Brown gazed steadily back. There passed a few clicking moments of silence. Beneath the sheriff's bloated features Brown could still make out the face of the small-town bully he'd known as a kid: the chuffy little coward, intimidator, bellowing school-

yard tyrant. Arvin Holloway had translated these lifelong traits
into a fine law enforcement career. He wasn't about to quit as long
as he thought he could bully somebody into telling him what he
wanted—but what could Brown tell him that he didn't already
know? Only to check at Misty Dawn's house for Dustin. But what
if Juanito had snuck back across the border? Misty Dawn could
get arrested for harboring her husband. "How long ago was that?"
he said.

"How long ago was what?"

"When somebody saw Dustin."

"Hell, I don't know! Who's asking the questions here? Me. *I*
am. And you're answering. I want to know what your truck's doing
in Tonkawa!"

"I told you. I don't know."

Holloway jumped up and swooped down on Brown, leaning
over him, forcing his head back, his fist twitching on his pistol
grip. Breathing hard, he said between tight-gritted teeth, "You
sorry self-righteous so-and-so, you *tell* me where that kid is and
what y'all got going with this goddamn smuggling operation or
I'll—"

"You'll what."

"Arrest the rest of your goddamn family," he snarled. "Starting
with that snooty tight-britches daughter of yours."

"Sweet hadn't done anything illegal," Brown said, his voice
steady.

"I'll find something." Holloway backed off a little. "Believe me.
Then I just might have to bring in that hefty granddaughter you're
so proud of."

Bob Brown's eyes flicked away. Well now, Holloway thought.
That got his attention.

"You can't do that."

"I can do any goddamn thing I please, and you know it. In this county I can."

"Misty Dawn ain't in your jurisdiction."

"I can fix that."

"Arvin, listen. I want my boy home safe, I want that worse than anybody. If I knew one thing in this world, I'd tell you."

"Like hell."

"I would. You know I would."

"I don't know nothing except you're an arrogant s.o.b. and always have been. And I know I'm going to be the one finds that goddamn kid if I have to slap half the goddamn county in jail!" Holloway went to the door and bellowed out into the hall: "BEE-CHAM! GODDAMNIT, GIT IN HERE!"

Brown tried to think faster. He needed to talk to Sweet. He needed to tell her to check at Misty Dawn's house—but surely she'd thought of that already? None of this made any sense. What *was* his truck doing in Tonkawa? Or was that even true? Maybe Holloway was just playing him. The deputy appeared in the doorway. Brown burst out, "I can't tell you what I don't know!"

"Get him the hell out of my sight."

The deputy motioned Brown to stand up, guided him in front of him away down the hall.

Holloway reached for the phone, sat a good while with his hand on the receiver, trying to think of who to call to stop all the air being sucked out of the case, sucked up north, to Tulsa and Oklahoma City, where every goddamn thing got sucked in this state. But who would it be? The governor? Tulsa PD? The head of OSBI? Hell no. State Bureau had probably brought in the feds already. Anybody he could think of to call would just make matters worse. Well, maybe the Kay County Sheriff's Department, he thought, lifting the receiver. At least they'd be coequals.

"Sheriff?" It was Beecham again. He looked beat, dark circles under his eyes, his skin splotchy. Hell, they were all beat, the sheriff thought. This business had been going on too damn long. He'd had every man jack working every minute he could get them, and the shake-and-bake meth cookers hadn't just thoughtfully all packed up and moved to Texas simply because Arvin Holloway had a few other things on his mind—that was a good line, he thought. He'd have to remember that one for the reporters. Then that blamed ice storm last night, now wouldn't that gripe you. He'd had to call in his men to help the town officers. The county was going to go bust on overtime this month. The deputy hulked in silence in the doorway.

"What!" Holloway said.

"I thought maybe I better mention . . . well, Phil Hunter, he was out there with me, and he thought—I don't know. Probably it's nothing."

"What, goddamnit! Don't start and stop like a dadgum choked engine."

"Well, we were out at the site last night. At Mr. Brown's place? That's the duty I drew yesterday evening, till y'all called us all in, and, well, his daughter, you know, the one that came to see him last week? Well, she was out there, too. I didn't think much about it, the place being kind of her family's place, but Phil Hunter, he thought it was curious. She got her car stuck trying to cross the creek. Said they were out looking for the boy, she had some cousins or somebody with her, but, well, that freezing rain and all. Just seemed kind of a odd time to go looking. Anyhow, Phil Hunter, he said I better mention it."

Cousins, Holloway thought. What cousins?

"So. Well," Beecham said. "I don't reckon there's any fresh word, is there?

"Word."

"About the little boy?"

"I'll let you know. Go on back to the office, Darrel. Get yourself some coffee."

Hot damn, Holloway thought. That little high-nosed bitch is up to something. Well, well, well, looked like he'd better pay a call on Sweet Georgia Brown this morning after all. Arvin Holloway got up from his chair gracefully, reached to the wall hook beside the desk for his tan Stetson.

As Holloway wheeled his cruiser past the courthouse, he happened to glance to the left and spied Terry Kirkendall climbing out of his Silverado in front of Jones-Hawkins Funeral Home. That was strange. They wouldn't be having a viewing this time of day. He watched Kirkendall walk up the long sidewalk to the white double front doors and thought about stopping to find out who died. But Terry Kirkendall was a pain in the ass who'd been in the office a dozen times already, complaining about them hauling in his father-in-law along with all the wetbacks—well, what the hell did he expect? Holloway was in no mood to listen to that fool's blather. He drove on. When he hit the highway, he flipped on his roof light-bar, picked up speed. The ice was gone everywhere except the shady places. The center of the blacktop was dry as sand. Holloway didn't turn on his siren, but he drove at high speed, east on Highway 270, toward his little old familiar hometown.

Sprinting back through town in sneakers and sweats, Sweet prayed that her son wouldn't wake up—she'd left him asleep on her bed under the afghan, his swollen adenoids making his snores as loud as poor old Mr. Bledsoe's—and also that if anybody saw her, they might think she'd taken up jogging rather than that she was trotting back to First Baptist to commit a felony, and also that Misty Dawn hadn't particularly heard that last order to stay put inside the nursery so that maybe she wouldn't feel compelled to act just precisely the opposite. On this last count, apparently, the Lord wasn't listening.

Because, indeed, it was Wednesday morning at nine o'clock when the Women's Missionary Union had their weekly meeting, and there in the cramped hallway between the church nursery and Fellowship Hall stood Misty Dawn in the preacher's blue plaid bathrobe, her long sandy mane combed, pink lip gloss on, balancing a mug of coffee in each hand as she lectured four baffled blue-haired ladies and the preacher's confused wife about illegal immigration. Vicki Dudley's youngest boy was asleep in her arms. The other wild one was racing around in circles. Sweet could see Brother Oren standing back in the bright kitchen, rubbing his palms hopelessly up and down over his face.

"—*do* pay taxes," Misty Dawn was saying. "That's just another lie, because people don't like Mexicans, when actually there's as many illegal Indians as Mexicans, but you don't ever hear about that. I mean like India Indians, not Choctaws or anything, obviously, but when you think about it, we're *all* illegal immigrants from their point of view, American Indians, only they're the only ones who'll say that, and my grandpa, *he'll* say it, which is probably half the reason he's in jail, nobody wants to hear it—"

"Okay, okay!" Sweet cried, rushing forward to squeeze herself between Misty Dawn and the WMU ladies. "We know, they know, that's fine, Misty, thanks."

"People *don't* know! That's what I'm saying—"

"Hi, Brother Oren!" Sweet waved toward the kitchen. "Y'all got back!" She dashed a quick smile at Vicki. "How's your mom, good, huh? Boy, that was some weather. Glad y'all made it home safe. Misty, why don't you, um, run get dressed—"

"I'm dressed." She opened the robe to show her. "I'm just cold."

"Yes, all right." Sweet beamed at the ladies—and Lord, oh, Lord, wouldn't you know one of them would have to be Claudie Ott. "I guess y'all are fixing to start your meeting, huh? Well, we don't want to hold you up. Come on, Misty, let's just get out of their way." She didn't, of course, actually move out of the way. The nursery door was closed behind her, thank goodness, but she could hear the baby in there talking Spanish to her daddy— Spanish! Probably the elderly WMU ladies were too hard of hearing to detect it, but the preacher's wife wasn't. But then there probably wasn't ever any way to keep this from Vicki anyhow. Sweet looked desperately toward the preacher in the kitchen. He was slouched back against the counter, and his hands were down off his face now, but his eyes were closed; he looked like he might be praying.

"You're Gaylene's daughter, aren't you, dear?" This from the retired schoolteacher Ida Coley. She'd taken Misty Dawn by the arm. "I remember your mama so well, what a pretty girl. I'm just so sorry about your brother. That's your brother, isn't it? Bobby's grandson that disappeared?"

"I always said that child would come to a bad end," remarked Claudie Ott. "Too pretty for her own good. Didn't I always say that?"

"It's a shame," Edna Martin said, frowning hard to tell Claudie Ott to shut up.

"A crying shame," agreed Alice Stalcup.

"Honey?" the preacher's wife called toward the kitchen.

The preacher straightened up from the counter and started toward them just as his older boy, Isaiah, came tearing along the hall making squealing tire sounds. The boy rounded his mother with a wailing screech and slammed open the nursery door and raced inside, causing Lucha to let out a shriek and start sobbing hysterically. Sweet and Misty Dawn rushed forward together, Misty a half step ahead. She clunked down the coffee mugs and reached for her screaming daughter sitting on her daddy's lap. The child clung to her and sobbed and sobbed. Juanito got to his feet, looking worried. Little Isaiah flew around the nursery with his arms out, an airplane now, and Sweet tried to catch him, barking "Quit that now, quit!" Lucha's sobs grew louder, turned into long trembling wails, as if everything, the mine, the dark, the cold, the hunger, her parents' fear, the strangeness of everything had culminated in her little chest all at once. "Shh, baby, shh," Misty Dawn said, walking the room with her, patting her back. The preacher came on into the nursery and picked up his son, who was sputtering motorboat sounds now, his little chunky arms and legs pumping, and carried the boy back out to the hall. The four WMU ladies crowded together in the nursery doorway to see in.

Looking up, Sweet cast her gaze from each old woman's face to the next: Ida Coley's startled eyes and rounded mouth, Edith Martin's creased frown, Alice Stalcup's raised, auburn-penciled brows, Claudie Ott's crimped satisfaction. Oh, what's the use, Sweet thought. It's all over. All over. But she had to go on. "Miss Coley," she said loudly over Lucha's wails, "would y'all leave us a little privacy? It's a family matter. I'll come, well, explain in a minute. I know it looks . . . We just need to . . ." She smiled, trying to act as if the shabby-clothed, coal-smudged Mexican man standing next to her niece might be invisible. Clearly, he was not invisible. Edith Martin's frown deepened as she stared. Claudie Ott's filmy blue eyes never left his face. But Ida Coley, bless her heart, bless her, announced in her trembling turkey voice, "Come on, girls. If we mean to get those Lottie Moon baskets finished, we'd better get started." And she came around in front of the other three like a skinny little cow dog and herded them out the door toward the Adult Women's classroom.

Sweet took in a long breath, listened to the child's wails a moment longer, then she turned on her niece. "Do you see what you've done? Do you *see*! No, you don't see! Because it's never your fault, is it? It's always somebody else's!"

Misty Dawn stared at her, shocked.

"I told you to stay hid!" Sweet snapped. "But you don't listen. You have *never* listened. To anyone! You longhead on, doing just what *you* want to do. Your granddaddy's sitting in the Latimer County Jail this instant because of you and that . . . *husband* of yours. And I don't blame them, Misty, I blame *you*! What have you ever given this family except trouble and heartache?" Fat silent tears were running down the girl's cheeks, but Sweet was too wound up to quit. She stormed around the room. "I'm asking you, Misty. Name me one thing! We all go carting up there for your daughter's birthday, but you can't even a make dadgum birthday phone call to your granddaddy who put his whole life on the line for you! You can't think to send a card to your baby brother, who would not be lost right now this minute if you'd just come home with me like I asked! But no, you got to wait for your illegal husband to swim back across the damn river! Or whatever it is they do. Then y'all show up at my door expecting *me* to fix things, expecting me to give you food, give you money, pay for your gas and whatever, risking my own future, my *own* child's well-being, and then you're going to stand there and lecture those poor old ladies about how people don't like Mexicans! Give me a break! You are so selfish and self-centered, you don't care about anybody but yourself! Look how you're raising your daughter, Misty! Look at her! She can't even speak the damn language of the country she lives in!"

Misty Dawn was crying now as hard as the baby, whose wails had increased in volume and hysteria right along with Sweet's rant. Juanito was awkwardly trying to pat Misty's shoulder. Sweet stood trembling, panting a little, knowing her anger was as much at her dead sister as her self-centered niece. She'd said the same things to Gaylene when she came home from Oregon years ago and took Misty. The same things, and worse. Sweet looked up to see the preacher standing in the doorway. He met her eyes a moment before silently withdrawing. She sank down on the low table. She felt like throwing up. "I'm sorry," she whispered. Three times she said it, even though she knew Misty couldn't hear over the child's wails. Not that it would make any difference if she did hear, because Sweet couldn't unsay the words. Misty Dawn would never forget them. And the preacher—he'd seen her acting like that.

Dear Lord help me, she prayed. Help me be better. The baby kept crying.

Wiping her face on her sleeve, Sweet got to her feet. She didn't look at the kids when she told them to please stay in the nursery, she'd be back in a minute. There was no time now to wait for a tow to get Juanito's truck out. Claudie Ott would be on the phone the minute she got home. Sweet would just have to go ask the preacher for his car keys. If they got caught, she'd tell the cops she stole the car. Maybe that might keep Brother Oren from getting charged with harboring and transporting at least. Sweet's limbs were moving in slow motion, like she was crawling underwater, when she needed so badly to hurry, she really did, because she needed to get this done and get back to the house before Carl Albert woke up.

She walked across Fellowship Hall in a watery dream, reached for the push bar on the glass door, saw then, at the side of the parsonage carport, her coatless, hatless son, in his yellow T-shirt, yawning next to the preacher, who stood in the driveway talking to Arvin Holloway. Sweet's dreamlike stupor vanished in a sudden rush. The sheriff's cruiser was parked behind Brother Oren's Toyota, red and blue lights stuttering. Sweet tried to read the preacher's face. She looked helplessly at her shivering son. What was Carl Albert doing with the sheriff? And what was the sheriff doing at the church?

A big F-250 pickup pulling a stock trailer stopped on the street. Then two more cars stopped. Townspeople wanting to know what was going on. And, oh Lord, here came Claudie Ott tottering along the icy sidewalk from the front door of the church. She went right up to the sheriff, talking excitedly, bobbing her head at the glass doors to Fellowship Hall, where Sweet stood. Sweet didn't wait to see more—she dashed back across the room and around the corner into the nursery, slammed shut the nursery door.

* * *

"Sanctuary," Oren Dudley repeated. Miss Ott's filmy blue eyes peered up at him. The sheriff stood massaging the side of his nose. Carl Albert tugged on his sleeve. "Brother Oren, I'm cold!"

"Say what?' the sheriff said again.

"*Sanc*tuary. We decided to offer . . . or that is I . . . the church fellowship . . . well, I did plan to do a prayer walk. With the deacons, of course. Welcome the stranger, the Lord said."

"Sweet Kirkendall ain't a stranger."

"Well, no."

"It's something fishy, Arvin," Claudie Ott said. "You mark my words."

"Claudia!" Ida Coley came picking her way between the slick spots along the front walk. "What are you doing out here without a coat?"

"Well! I looked out the window on my way to the ladies' room! And what do you think I spied but the sheriff's car!"

"You're gonna freeze a twig."

"I'm fine, Ida. Listen here. Arvin's hunting Georgia Kirkendall, now what do you think of that?"

"Morning, Sheriff," Ida Coley said. She gave a meaningful look to Claudie Ott, but the woman's lip was unbuttoned; there was no shutting her up now.

"I told him, I said she's right *there*—" Claudie stubbed a thumb toward the glass doors. "Right inside the church nursery with her sister Gaylene's oldest daughter and that precious little girl and"—she lowered her voice as if whispering a bad word—"a *Mexican man*." Edna Martin and Alice Stalcup came carefully along the walk from the sanctuary. Vicki Dudley arrived from the

other direction, the parsonage front door. Carl Albert tugged the
preacher's sleeve again. "Can I go see my mom?"

In the street Floyd Ollie got out of his truck and stepped
across the drainage ditch to come find out what was what. Colton
Springer and his little pregnant girlfriend got out of their car;
Tommy Joe Holbird got out of his. Phyllis Wentworth walked
over from her house across the street. Somebody must have
phoned the deacons, because Clyde Herrington and T. C. Blankenship both pulled up, and within minutes a good-sized crowd
had gathered in the patch of yard between the parsonage and the
First Baptist Church. With each new arrival, Claudie Ott repeated her observations, never failing to finish in a hushed whisper: *a Mexican man!*

"Brother Oren," Carl Albert said, "I wanna go see my mom."

Arvin Holloway was pacing back and forth beside his cruiser
with his fist on his pistol, trying to make up his mind whether to
call for reinforcements or just take the suspects in himself. He was
convinced the Mexican man was the same one the Brown kid had
been seen with; he knew he was close on the trail now, and this
whole drama was soon to be finished, starring himself as arresting
officer and hero—but you never knew what you were walking into
in this sort of a blind situation. How well armed they might be, or
how desperate. Might be a drug lord of some kind, or a loco, you
just had no way of knowing.

Oren Dudley put his arm around his wife and asked her
quietly to go back inside the house. "What's this all about?" she
whispered. "Well," he said, "it's a long story. Take Carl with
you. I'll be in in a minute." She could hear their two little ones
screaming gigantically in the living room. She couldn't tell if
they were playing or half killing each other, but she felt like she

ought to go see. "Come on, Carl," she said, and, glancing back over her shoulder several times, she walked away with her hand on the boy's head.

The sheriff, having decided that it would be better to take a chance on getting shot and still garner the glory than to pussyfoot around until OSBI or some other agency showed up, started along the angled walk toward Fellowship Hall. Oren Dudley loped around in front of him and blocked his path. Holloway stood frowning. "You wouldn't be obstructing a peace officer in the lawful execution of his sworn duty, would you, Preacher?"

"No, sir," Oren Dudley said. Holloway started around him, but the preacher did a little sidestep and blocked his path again.

"What the blazes do you think you're doing?"

"Well," the preacher said. Despite the chilly weather, he could feel his forehead popping out with sweat. He'd prayed the whole night long, had searched Scripture till daybreak, flipping back and forth between his Concordance and the verses. No word for *immigrant* in King James, of course, or the New Revised Standard, either; he'd had to look under *stranger* and *alien*, also *sojourner*, and very sorely he had tried, for the sake of his family, he'd really tried to find verses to support doing the opposite of what he was getting ready to do, but unfortunately, on the treatment of aliens, the Bible was just pretty clear: "'But the alien that dwells with you,'" Oren rattled off quickly, "'shall be as one born among you, and you shall love him as yourself,' Leviticus nineteen, verse thirty-four."

"What the—" The sheriff started around the other side, but Oren Dudley sidestepped again.

"'Vex not a stranger, nor oppress him, for you were strangers in the land of Egypt,' Exodus twenty-two, verse twenty-one."

"Get out of my way, Preacher."

"'Do not oppress an alien,'" the preacher said, unconcerned about mixing translations, "'for you yourselves know how it feels to be aliens,' Exodus twenty-three, verse nine."

Arvin Holloway pushed forward. "I'm warning you, man."

Eyes closed, combing over a few damp strands of hair with his fingers, Oren Dudley quoted on: "'And to the strangers that sojourn among you, which shall beget children among you: they shall be unto you as born in the country,' Ezekiel forty-seven, verse twenty-two."

The sheriff was stymied; his hand twitched on his pistol grip. You couldn't just shoot a blamed Bible-spouting Baptist preacher for standing in your path. Not in front of this many witnesses. He turned to look behind. More people had gathered.

"'One law shall be to him that is homeborn,'" the preacher droned on, "'and unto the stranger that sojourneth among you,' Exodus twelve—"

"I got no concerns about strangers and sojourners, Preacher! It's Sweet Kirkendall I mean to talk to."

"Well," the preacher said. "You want to tell me what that's about?"

"Hell no, I don't want to tell you what it's about!" Holloway shouted, but he quickly checked himself. Not good policy to cuss a preacher. "This is official Latimer County Sheriff's Department business, Oren. I'll thank you to step aside."

"Can't do that, Mr. Holloway."

"I'm not here to arrest nobody, damn it. I'm here to conduct an investigation."

"Into what?"

"The disappearance of Dustin Brown, what the hell do you think!"

"Dusty's not here, Sheriff. I promise you."

"I ain't said he was, did I say that?"

"'I was a stranger,'" the preacher answered, "'and ye took me in,'
Matthew twenty-five, thirty-five."

"Get out of my way!" The sheriff's pistol was in his hand, pointing skyward—force of habit, he later told himself, but the gesture
did not sit well with Clyde Herrington and some of the others
gathered in the yard: "Here, Sheriff, what do you think you're
doing!" "Arvin Albert Holloway, you put that away!" "You can't
draw down on a preacher!"

"I ain't drawed on nobody! Y'all stay out of this!" Reholstering
his pistol, Holloway turned and stomped back through the crowd
to his cruiser, reached in for his radio.

Inside the nursery, Sweet stood with her back to the door. "If the
sheriff tries to come in . . ." she started. Her voice trailed off. If
Holloway tried to come in, what? She'd have to let him. What
else could she do? She slumped against the door. Misty sat in the
rocker with her daughter in her lap. Lucha was quiet now, curled
against her mother's chest, sucking her two fingers and staring
solemn-eyed and suspicious at Sweet. Misty Dawn, on the other
hand, hadn't looked at her once since she'd slammed back into the
room and told them the sheriff was outside, nor did Misty translate
for her husband. How much Juanito understood, Sweet couldn't
tell—but enough to make those black eyes of his look mighty serious. Well, it was serious. A serious situation. She needed to know
what was happening, but she didn't dare go back out to the glass
doors. Sweet glared at the poster-covered cinder-block wall opposite. Why would anybody in their right mind build a church nursery without windows? What if there was a fire or something? How

stupid could people be? Well plenty stupid, she knew that. She'd been knowing that a long time. She turned around and opened the door a crack. A faint squeak of protest erupted from Misty Dawn behind her, but she heard no sound outside in the hall. Her senses told her there was nobody out there. She was almost one hundred percent sure of it. But what if she was wrong?

Snicking the door shut again, Sweet scanned the room. Not even a chair tall enough to prop against it. Well, except for the rocker. "Get up, Misty." Her niece was looking at her now, frowning, but she gripped the baby more tightly and got to her feet. Sweet dragged the rocking chair over, tilted it back on its rockers and wedged the wooden edge of the top slat under the doorknob. This is beyond stupid, she told herself, but she could think of nothing better to do. Then she went over to the little kids' table and sat.

"*La migra?*" Juanito asked softly.

"*La policía,*" Misty answered, then a few more words in Spanish, then: "Aunt Sweet, what are we going to do?" Her voice still held a faint note of resentment, but mostly she sounded scared. In her arms her daughter began to whimper. "She's hungry."

"I know."

"What are we going to do?" Misty Dawn repeated.

"Let me think!" But Sweet could think of nothing to do, no action to take. "Wait and pray," she said finally.

"You're joking, right?"

"No." Sweet bowed her head. "Dear Lord, we are really in a fix here. We need You to do something drastic, if it be Your will. We'd just ask that You send the sheriff away from this place, Lord, and also to please shut Claudie Ott's mouth. We know that in You, Lord, all things are possible. Give us this day our daily bread, because the baby is hungry. And deliver us from evil. And we would just ask once again, Lord, that You—" Her voice caught.

She cleared it. " . . . bring Dusty home safe. In Jesus' name, amen."

"Amen," Misty echoed. Sweet looked up to see Juanito finish crossing himself before he reached to take Lucha, who was still whimpering. A light tapping came at the nursery door, and all three adults jumped. The doorknob rattled, and whoever it was pushed against the door. The rocker held. But this wasn't the kind of pounding and yelling Sweet expected from Arvin Holloway. "Who is it?" she called in a low voice.

"Me. Vicki. I need to talk to you."

Sweet went over and stood by the door. "What's going on out there?"

"It's kind of a . . . standoff."

"Between who?"

"That's what I wanted to talk about. Can I come in?"

"Is Carl Albert with you?"

"No. He's fine, though. He's eating a sandwich."

"This little girl here is hungry."

"I'll bring something over if I can."

"*If* you can. What's that mean?"

The doorknob rattled again. "I don't like talking through the door, Georgia. It makes me have to talk too loud."

Sweet cut her eyes at the kids. Misty Dawn shook her head no. Juanito stared back with a kind of wary expression. Well, but it was the preacher's wife, after all. Sweet tugged the rocking chair out of the way, and Vicki Dudley hurried in.

"Who's standing off who?" Sweet said, jamming the rocker back under the doorknob.

"I knew something was wrong," Vicki said. "The whole ride home from Stigler."

"Did Arvin say what he wants?" Then she caught sight of Vicki's round pink face staring at Juanito. "Um, this is Juanito," Sweet said. "And you met my niece, Misty." She decided against trying to explain why Misty Dawn was wearing the preacher's bathrobe. "And this is their little girl, Lucha."

"I *knew* it was something," Vicki said. "He told me he'd be in in a minute. When he didn't come, I went to the bedroom to look out. He's standing in front of Fellowship Hall with Clyde Herrington and T. C. Blankenship. They're blocking the doors. Arvin Holloway is on the sidewalk with Rex Hendricks and Cecil Young and a couple others, glaring fit to be tied. The rest of them are watching."

"Rest of who?"

"I don't know. Half the town. There's probably fifty or sixty people." Vicki's eyes returned to Juanito holding his little girl. "I thought this was supposed to be about Dustin."

"Well," Sweet said. "Not entirely."

"See? This is what happens. He won't talk to me! I said what's a pastor's wife for? It's my burden as much as yours! The whole way home from Stigler I kept asking."

"I'm so sorry, Vicki. I didn't know where else to turn."

"But what *is* all this?"

As quickly and plainly as possible Sweet explained, and she thought she must be doing a better job today than yesterday evening with the preacher, because Vicki seemed to grasp it all at once. She sat down on the low table, nodding. "He's welcoming the stranger."

"I guess."

"No, he *is*. That's what he said. Two or three times, on the way over the mountains. I just didn't understand what he meant."

Misty Dawn edged forward. "How'd you get in if they're blocking the doors?"

"Oh, I went out through our kitchen door, down the back steps, and around behind Mrs. Griffith's. I came in through the Pastor's Study door."

Sweet said, "I forgot there was a door there."

"Is it in the back?" Misty said. "We could maybe sneak out that way."

"And go where?" Vicki said.

"Fort Smith," Sweet and Misty Dawn said together.

"All right, good. Where's your car?"

Sweet and Misty Dawn looked at each other. "Well," Sweet said, "that's one of our problems." After a beat, she said, "My car's sort of stuck. I was kind of hoping we could borrow yours." She held up her hand as Vicki started to protest. "I promise I'll take full responsibility! I'll tell them you didn't know I was going to take it!"

"No, I'm saying you *can't*. The sheriff's parked behind us."

"Oh. Right."

"Mommy, I'm hungry," Lucha said. Sweet shot a look over. The child had her face tucked against her daddy's chest, her long legs dangling. Her daddy said something in her ear, and she answered in Spanish. "She needs some breakfast," Misty said. "She hadn't had anything to eat since last night."

"There might be some saltines in the kitchen," Vicki said.

"She needs *food*, like real food—not crackers."

"Misty Dawn, don't be rude!" Sweet snapped.

"Well, she does."

"Well, whose responsibility is *that*? Miss Mommy."

The bored look slid down. Misty Dawn walked over and took Lucha out of her husband's arms. Sweet could have bit her tongue. Oh, why couldn't she keep her mouth shut? At least till this was over. Vicki Dudley was in the process of unwedging the rocking chair from the door. "I'll see what I can find in the kitchen," she said. "I think that'd be better than my trying to go to my house and back."

"But they'll see you!" Misty cried out. "Can't they see in the kitchen?"

"It's a sunny day out. I doubt they can see inside that far." Vicki opened the nursery door just as Arvin Holloway's voice squawked into the room over a loudspeaker: "YOU MEN ARE RISKING ARREST FOR OBSTRUCTING JUSTICE AND INTERFERING WITH AN OFFICER!"

They heard Brother Oren's answer, slightly muffled because he was turned away, but clearly enough, as he was using his strongest pulpit voice: "'Thou shalt not oppress a stranger!'" the preacher called, "'for ye know the heart of a stranger, seeing ye were strangers in the land of Egypt!' Exodus twenty-three, verse nine!'"

"THIS AIN'T NO JOKE, PREACHER!"

"We never take the Lord's Word for a joke, Sheriff!"

"Y'ALL STEP ASIDE AND LET ME EXECUTE MY SWORN DUTY OR I SWEAR I'LL HAVE EVERY LAST ONE OF YOU IN JAIL!"

There was a brief silence, like a held breath, then they heard roaring car motors coming fast along Main Street, then the sound of squealing tires turning quickly, braking. Then the sound of several slamming automobile doors.

Oren Dudley's hands were trembling. He was trying to keep from rubbing his face, a bad habit, he knew, because his wife often pointed it out. He didn't want to take his eyes off Arvin Holloway. He was worried the sheriff might try to rush them now that he had five deputies lined up with him. Five deputies seemed like a lot. What if there was a crime going on somewhere in the county?

Clyde Herrington, standing next to him, took a little coughing fit.

"You all right?"

"It's nothing," Clyde answered between coughs. "This always happens, I don't know what it is."

"MOVE ALONG PEACEABLE AND WE WON'T PRESS CHARGES!"

"This cold air can't be good for it."

"Aw, he's all right," T. C. Blankenship muttered from the other side.

"I'm all right," Clyde said.

"Well," the preacher said, "I appreciate y'all standing with me."

"I'M FIXING TO GIVE YOU MEN A COUNT OF THREE!"

"I don't know what this is about, Preacher," T. C. said, "but those were some convincing verses."

"ONE!"

"I'll explain it when we get a minute."

"TWO!"

On the street behind the three Latimer County Sheriff's Department cruisers other vehicles were still arriving, all of them belonging to local people, quite a few of whom were members here at First Baptist, Oren Dudley was glad to see. Or at least he hoped he was glad to see them.

"THREE!"

Nothing happened. The air was crisp and clear, the only sound a few motors that hadn't gotten switched off yet. Also the muffled squawk from the sheriff's radio. Holloway was scowling fiercely across the yard, bullhorn lowered, right fist on his hip. Throughout his night of prayer and searching, Oren Dudley had imagined a few different scenarios, but he hadn't anticipated anything like this—him and two of the church deacons facing off against most of the Latimer County Sheriff's Department and four men from the town. The rest of the people who had gathered stood watching in silence, even Claudie Ott. *So great a cloud of witnesses,* Oren Dudley thought to himself. Apostle Paul to the Hebrews. *Lay aside every weight.* "Sheriff," he called out, "I'm willing to talk!"

"Come on then!"

"I'm going to need a few guarantees!"

Why, of all the arrogance, Arvin Holloway thought. He hesitated, raised the bullhorn. "LIKE WHAT?"

"Like you meet me there in the middle!" Oren Dudley nodded at the angled sidewalk. "And your men stay back where they are by the cars."

"I DON'T AIM TO NEGOTIATE WITH SOMEBODY OBSTRUCTING OFFICIAL SHERIFF'S OFFICE BUSINESS!"

"All right, we'll just stay like we are then!"

Well shit fire, Arvin Holloway thought.

"Looka there, Preacher," T. C. said, very quietly, and the preacher glanced over to see his wife standing on the little square back porch of the parsonage. The way the house set, she couldn't be seen by the sheriff and the others out front. She wore a significant look on her face. After seven and a half years of marriage, Oren Dudley could most generally read his wife's faces, but right now he couldn't. He gave a little shrug. Vicki shook her head, opened the door, and went in the house. Unable to think of anything better to do, the preacher called out, "'Be not forgetful to entertain strangers, for thereby some have entertained angels unawares!' Hebrews thirteen, verse two!" He was thinking he might have to start over if this situation went on very much longer; he was getting close to the end of the verses he'd memorized.

Meanwhile Vicki Dudley was rushing through the parsonage kitchen, where little Micah was pounding on his high-chair tray and Carl Kirkendall was hunched at the table, still eating, and

Isaiah was crawling around on the sticky tile floor for some reason, and on into the bedroom, where she grabbed her husband's Scofield Study Bible off the nightstand; she hurried through the living room, calling toward the kitchen "Y'all mind, now!" as she went out the front door. Pausing on the concrete steps, she tried to assess the situation.

The townspeople had arranged themselves into little bunches of sixes and sevens as they tried to find the best location to see from. A few were talking on cell phones. Colton Springer and his little pregnant girlfriend were both texting, it seemed. Her husband and the deacons remained in perfect alignment in front of the Fellowship Hall doors, and directly across from them, the deputies and a few local men were rowed up in front of the vehicles, the sheriff glowering in the midst of them with his hand on his gun belt. Well, Vicki thought, I don't guess he'll shoot me. Nevertheless, she hoisted the enormous black book high over her head like a white flag as she walked it through the crowd and across the soggy yard to her husband. She leaned in a little when she handed it to him, saying, "I wish you'd *talk* to me, Oren."

The preacher said, "I know."

She stepped back then, gave him another significant look, which meant, in her own thoughts, *I've seen them and they're fine but don't take too long with this, those people are hungry,* but which he took to read *I am with you, Oren, always,* and he squeezed her hand. She turned and made her way back through the crowd to the parsonage and went in to see about the boys.

The sheriff hollered, "Preacher, I'm about to lose patience!"

Oren Dudley held the large Bible squarely out in front of himself as if to say, *See, Sheriff? No tricks.* "I just wanted to look up a passage of Scripture!" he called. "Then we'll have a word of prayer! I believe that'll help calm things down a bit, maybe!" Arvin Holloway was boiling, but what could he say? No Bible reading? No praying? The preacher thumbed through the onionskin pages. He didn't actually have a particular passage in mind, but the book was here, and so he thought he ought to use it. As things went, though, a new verse wasn't necessary, because it was at this juncture that Ida Coley detached herself from the clutch of women standing nearest the sanctuary and started toward him. Alice Stalcup followed her. The two permed, powdery, elderly ladies arranged themselves on either side of the two deacons. "Why, I thank you," the preacher murmured. "I truly thank you." Not to be outdone, Claudie Ott and Edith Martin came tottering along the walk and stood, both of them, next to Ida Coley. Then Phyllis Wentworth crossed over and stood on the other side of Alice Stalcup. "What the hell are y'all doing!" the sheriff shouted, then he remembered to use the bullhorn. "WHAT IN THE WORLD DO YOU PEOPLE THINK YOU'RE DOING? YOU CAN'T DO THAT!"

Later some of them would say that they did what they did purely because Arvin Holloway told them they couldn't. Others claimed that they hadn't really known anything about that law; if they had, they might have acted different. Some said they'd just surmised that if the pastor of the First Baptist Church aimed to stand against the law (and here by *the law* they didn't mean *statute* but *officers*), then, by gosh, that was good enough for them. In the long run, there turned out to be a whole host of reasons— conscience, ignorance, rumor, the makings of a good show—but for whatever individual private reasons it started, the order went like this: Curtis Shawcross and his wife, April, then Tommy Joe Holbird, then Gladys Chester, then the Alford twins, then Sue Ann Whitelaw, then Floyd Ollie and Wade Free. These were the names of the next bunch that crossed the scrap of yard to stand in front of the glass doors.

In the late morning light slanting into the bare room, Luis sits in a hard straight-back chair beside the bed. His heart is peaceful, although he is farther from his sons today than last night on the black plain. But this is of no significance. Our Lady has not abandoned him. This is the most important thing. Many hours ago, in the thin predawn light, Luis watched as the boy twisted inside the sleeping bag, coughing, making the small weeping sounds like a cat, throwing his head side to side, his forehead dry and hot, like a stove fired too high with burning wood. Then the sweat returned and his hair was drenched wet again, like a boy swimming in a river. The sleeping bag, also, was soaked with sweat, but the boy did not shiver with cold, only grew hotter and hotter, until, as the light reddened toward the rising sun, the boy suddenly ceased his restless twisting, became very still, his skin bloodless, his features soft and lax. Luis prayed every prayer, but he did not have the good faith then, his heart was not calm. Dead, the despair told him. What a long hopeless time it was before Luis saw the deep ragged breath the boy drew in, the slow calm exhalation. At once Luis hoisted himself to his knees on the frozen ground, praying prayers of gratitude. The boy slept peacefully then.

He sleeps peacefully now, his bandaged arm resting across his chest. Sprained, not broken. Luis had been correct about this. The woman doctor told him when she came to look at the boy. She did not ask Luis where the home of the boy is, who his parents are, although she could have asked if she liked. She speaks spanish. She is not mexican, however, but indian—the same as the man who stopped to help them.

Luis had seen the vehicle coming from the east, very far away, while he stood alone at the side of the road. It did not slow as it passed Luis with his hand in the air but continued on a little distance before it stopped and began to reverse. When Luis saw the brown face of the man through the window, he began at once to speak—the man was like him, indian, or part indian, Luis believed he would know spanish, but the man did not appear to understand. However, he opened the vehicle door and climbed out. Luis saw then that he was a large man, very much taller than Luis, big in the shoulders and belly—too big for the indians of mexico. Maybe it was for this reason, his great size, that the man did not seem concerned that Luis might rob him on this deserted road, or lead him into a trap.

Without need of explanation the man followed Luis, and when they arrived where the boy lay, the big man said words that Luis did not understand—maybe english, Luis was not sure. The man crouched beside the boy, touched the top of his head, frowning; the boy was not coughing then, but he was very hard asleep. Luis said, *He needs to see a doctor. His arm is hurt, but this is not what gives him the fever, I think. He has been coughing all the night.* The man answered nothing. His eyes grazed the boy, the bicycle lying on its side, the empty water jar, the backpack. Then he gathered up the boy inside the crawling man sleeping bag and began to walk the asphalt path to the parking area. Luis followed.

On the highway the man turned to the east—the direction

from which he, and Luis and the boy, had come. Luis was trou-
bled to see they were traveling away from his sons, not toward
them. *¿We are not continuing west?* Luis asked, but the man answered nothing. Luis twisted around to see the boy on the seat
behind. The boy drowsed; once his eyes opened, and he looked
around the unfamiliar vehicle a moment, then he closed his eyes
again and slept. Luis turned back to watch the road. East a little
ways, and then south, the big man saying nothing, and Luis also
was silent, because they had no shared language between them.
He wished he knew even a little english, or that the man spoke a
little spanish, like the boy. He wanted to ask where the man was
driving them, how much distance away from the Guymon town.

It seemed a long time, maybe almost an hour, before the indian
stopped in front of a small gray building in a small brick town
and lifted the boy from the backseat and carried him inside. Luis
followed, sat in a chair beside the boy, and the boy leaned against
him, dozing and waking. Every person in the clinic was indian:
the young girl behind the desk, the people waiting in the plastic
chairs, all ages, men and women and children, and the woman
doctor, too, when at last they were able to see her. The big man
stayed with them while they waited. He talked to the boy in english when the boy was awake, and also to the doctor when they
crowded into the small room where she examined the boy. The
doctor told Luis in spanish that they must take the boy to the
hospital. And so the big indian drove them here, to this small hospital, to the back door where the ambulances arrive. Luis under-
stands that this place is even more far from his sons, but whether
the distance is far or near is no matter. He will see his sons if the
Father wills it. Luis will continue to pray to the Virgin to inter-
cede, and she will continue to offer her mercies. Our Lady has not
abandoned him. For what reason did he doubt? It is difficult now,

in this warm room, to recollect his fear. Fear and faith, they are two sides of the same person. Luis has known this for many years. But the will of the Father is always inscrutable. He has his own purpose. Luis will accept whatever comes, he has promised this. However, he holds hope. There have been now already sufficient miracles. It may be the will of the Father to grant one more.

The first reporter on the scene was Logan Morgan of 2News Working for You. This was due in part, she later said, to her excellent interpersonal community outreach skills (it had been, in fact, her mobile number that Colton Springer's girlfriend was texting), and also the fact it had only taken her twenty minutes to drive the thirty miles from Poteau, where she'd spent the night with her grandmother so as not to be traveling home to Tulsa on last night's icy roads. The instant she reached the church in Cedar and saw what was happening, she got on the horn to the station and called for a camera crew. Then, with excellent foresight, as she would point out to her supervisor, she climbed up in the back of a conveniently located pickup and started filming straightaway with her fully charged iPhone. Thus the first video to hit the airwaves (not counting the grainy, blurred clip somebody uploaded to YouTube) was the one Logan Morgan captured of the five Masons and the two deputies in a showdown in front of the church sanctuary.

The five men weren't outwardly identifiable as members of the Fraternal Order of Masons—it was Logan Morgan's astute investigative reporting that would ferret out this fact—but they were clearly all local men, all of indeterminate age, two wearing ball caps and one in a battered Toby-Keith-style straw cowboy hat. All five appeared at once calm, self-effacing, and resolute (as her quiet voiceover described it) as they eased away from the crowd and strolled casually to the front porch of the church to stand shoulder to shoulder, unarmed, against the two clearly armed deputies who were trying to head in through the church's front doors. She caught the entire dramatic scene, scanned over to the sheriff scowling at the preacher and the handful of citizens in front of the prefab addition, then zoomed in smoothly to the free-standing marquee in the church yard:

CEDAR FIRST BAPTIST CHURCH

"WHERE IT FEELS LIKE HOME"

SUNDAY SCHOOL 10:00

MORNING WORSHIP 11:00

PASTOR OREN DUDLEY

That little clip alone set the tone for much of the coverage, as Logan Morgan would also point out to her supervisor, not to mention netting the station a tidy sum in network usage fees. She would find it necessary to remind her boss of these helpful facts in order to counteract the considerable criticism she received for reporting the events in Cedar, repeatedly, live and on air, as "a Mexican standoff." But, of course, all that came later.

Inside the church nursery Sweet and the kids were eating peanut butter and crackers and drinking cherry Kool-Aid left over from Children's Church. Inside the parsonage, Vicki Dudley was at the bedroom window, holding her youngest child, Micah, and wiping his face with a damp rag, as she peered out. Carl Albert stood next to her. "What are they doing?" the boy said.

"Well. That's a good question."

"Are they fixing to shoot Brother Oren?"

"No. No, it's just a . . . demonstration. Why don't you go watch cartoons with Isaiah?"

"I want to go where my mom is. The sheriff said he was bringing me to see my mom."

"Well, she'll be out in a minute, she's just—hey, quit that! I mean, please don't put your sticky hands on the curtain. How about you go in the bathroom and wash up?"

"They're gonna get a divorce," Carl said, wiping his grape-jellied hands on his yellow T-shirt. "My dad told me."

"Oh. I'm sorry to hear that."

"Yeah, on account of my mom murdered Mr. Bledsoe."

There was a moment of complete silence in the parsonage bedroom. After a beat, Vicki Dudley said again, "I'm sorry to hear that." She looked down, trying to figure where such a bizarre notion had come from. A good-looking, round-faced kid with a close-cropped burr and lots of freckles, the boy watched out the window with careful hazel eyes. "You reckon Dustin's dead, too?" he said.

"No, son." Her heart went out to him. "I'm sure your cousin's fine. Don't worry. They'll find him."

"He took my bike. And something else, too. That belongs to Brother Oren."

"What?" Vicki said, meaning, *What did you say?*, but the boy took her literally.

"Something I found in the glove box. I was going to give it back, but Dustin stoled it. You reckon if he's dead, I'll get my bike back?"

"He's not dead, Carl. Nobody's dead."

"Yes, *sir,* Mr. Bledsoe is. My daddy told me."

Micah was squirming in her arms and starting to squall. Vicki Dudley took a deep breath. "I think we ought to all go in the living room and watch cartoons."

"What's Lon Jones and them doing?"

Vicki pressed her face to the window so she could take in the whole vista. She saw the five local men all moving in a slow wave toward the church porch, and the two deputies shuffling their feet uncertainly across from them on the sidewalk. She saw a dark-haired girl standing in the back of Floyd Ollie's pickup with her phone stuck out to take pictures. She saw the WMU ladies and several others in front of Fellowship Hall begin to lock arms, elbow to elbow, and she realized that her husband, standing in the middle without a coat on, his eyes closed, his two arms holding the Bible tight to his chest, was praying. This is getting serious, she thought. "Come on, Carl," she said. "It's almost time for SpongeBob."

But the boy suddenly grabbed the windowsill and leaned forward to see farther down the street. Then he shouted, "Daddy!," and raced out of the bedroom, and she heard the front door slam. By the time she plopped Micah into his walker in the living room and grabbed her husband's windbreaker from the hall closet and threatened Isaiah within an inch of his life to behave himself and got out the front door, Terry Kirkendall was climbing out of his truck parked cockeyed in the middle of the street. His little boy ran up to him, then halted abruptly, stood mannishly a moment with his hands poked into his back pockets. Then the two turned and made their way between the cars with the same cowboy stride.

"I GOT NO QUARREL WITH YOU PEOPLE!" the sheriff was bellowing.

The faces of the men on the church porch were dead serious,
Lonnie Jones and Wade Free and the others. That's strange to see,
the preacher's wife thought. Lon Jones was generally just so good-
natured, a big smiler, he kept the crowds laughing with his jokes
when he auctioneered the Mason pie suppers. At that point Vicki
Dudley realized that the men on the church porch were all Masons. Well, except there was one Mason not on the porch. Kenneth Spears. That old priss, Vicki thought. He and two other men
were loitering between the two groups, not too close to Holloway
and his deputies, but not standing with their pastor, either. Terry
Kirkendall pushed his way through the crowd. "Holloway, what
the hell is this? Where's Sweet?"

But the sheriff's attention was entirely focused across the yard.
"GET OUT OF THE WAY AND LET ME TALK TO MY WIT-
NESS! Y'ALL DO THAT, WE CAN FORGET ALL ABOUT THIS!"

"'Wherefore seeing we also are compassed about with so
great a cloud of witnesses!'" Oren called back, having run out of
welcome-the-stranger verses, "'Let us lay aside the sin which doth
so easily beset us!'"

"I'LL SIN YOU IN A MINUTE!"

"'And run with patience the race that is set for us! Looking
unto Jesus, the author and finisher of our faith!'"

Well, that did it for about nine more Christians. Two men and
three women and four teenagers all crossed the yard to go stand
with the preacher. Not all of them were members at First Baptist,
Vicki noted, but they were certainly all local churchgoers, all anxious to be looking to Jesus the author and finisher of their faith.
Three more townsmen made their way up onto the porch to join
the Masons. The sheriff's face was boiled as a beet as he hollered
through the bullhorn, "QUIT! QUIT! Y'ALL QUIT!" He's going to
fool around and shoot somebody, Vicki thought. She came down

off the parsonage porch and started across the yard, but the slick navy windbreaker she was holding didn't have the same white flag effect that the Bible had. The sheriff hollered at her to stay right where she was.

"I just wanted to give Oren his jacket."

"Get back up on that porch before I have my men arrest you!"

Vicki Dudley looked across to her husband. The brief gaze that passed between them contained a lengthy conversation: "Go back in the house, honey." "I'm not going to let you do this alone." "I'm not alone, the Lord's with me, and also these good folks here." "I'm coming over there." "No. You've got to stay and look after the boys." A pause. A heartbeat. Vicki retreated to the high parsonage porch, though she did not yet go in the house. She stood awhile wondering to herself, Why are they all doing this? Well, Bob Brown's a Mason, so that might account for the Masons, but what about everyone else? They couldn't know the whole story, that long complicated tale Georgia Kirkendall had just unraveled in the nursery. How could they even know who was in the nursery, who the preacher was protecting inside the church? Or why Oren was doing this? They didn't know, she decided, couldn't know— and yet they'd made that choice.

Brushing cracker crumbs off the front of the plaid bathrobe, Misty Dawn said, "This isn't a whole lot better than that godawful coal mine."

Sweet cut her a look.

"Well, it isn't! I mean, it's still cold, and you can't see out, and we haven't got much to eat. The only improvement I can see is electricity."

"You're free to go."

"That's not what I'm saying."

"No, I mean it. You and your husband are welcome to waltz right on out of here and turn yourselves in. That would save everybody a whole lot of trouble."

Her niece hushed. "I don't know," Sweet said softly after a moment. "Maybe that's the only thing to do, Misty. I mean, how are we going to get out of this? Arvin Holloway's not going to just walk away. I know the man. At some point he's going to bully his way in here, and then what? We're probably just making things worse."

"Worse than Lucha not seeing her daddy for twenty years? Let's just go! We can sneak out that back door the lady was talking about—"

"And do what?"

"I don't know! Go to Fort Smith."

"This town has got like five streets, Misty. We're not going to go sneaking along on foot without somebody seeing! We got no car, remember? And anyhow that door leads out to the other side of the church, not the back. All the sheriff or anybody would have to do is take about ten steps to the left and they'll see us."

"Well, we got to do *something*!"

The stridency in Misty's voice caused Lucha to start crying again. She toddled over to her mother's knee and leaned her face down on the wide blue-jeaned thigh, wailing. Sweet raised her voice over the noise. "See? You think we're going to sneak this crying baby through town? That is *not* going to work, Misty. Nothing's going to work!"

Then she heard Terry's voice outside on the street, coming over the loudspeaker:

"GEORGIA, IT'S ME. COME ON OUT NOW."

There was a pause as if he was waiting for her to answer.

"I DIDN'T MEAN WHAT I SAID. I KNOW IT WAS AN AC-CIDENT."

"What's he talking about?" Misty said. "Don't believe him. It's a trick."

Sweet was standing at the nursery door.

"COME OUTSIDE AND WE'LL TALK THINGS OVER, OKAY? SWEET? HONEY? EVERYTHING'S GOING TO BE FINE! I PROMISE. NOBODY'S GOING TO PRESS CHARGES!"

Sheriff Arvin Holloway glared at that fool Terry Kirkendall. How the hell did he get hold of the bullhorn? The sheriff had been paying too blamed much attention to that arrogant preacher and his bunch across the yard; it hadn't occurred to him to just go over their heads and communicate directly with the suspect herself. Or witness. Or whatever the hell she was going to end up being. He snatched the bullhorn out of Kirkendall's fist.

"LISTEN HERE TO ME, SWEET! YOU GOT TWO MINUTES TO SEND THAT ILLEGAL ALIEN OUT WITH HIS HANDS UP OR I'M COMING IN THERE WITH A SWAT TEAM!"

That wasn't exactly what he'd meant to say, but it seemed a stroke of brilliance once the words were blurted out. Whatever this bunch of do-gooders believed they were doing, Arvin Holloway thought, harboring illegal aliens was no part of it. They would turn on that smart-aleck preacher right quick, he promised himself.

But Arvin Holloway was wrong—just as Vicki Dudley, standing on the parsonage porch a moment earlier, had been wrong. The men and women barricading the church doors *did* know there was a Mexican man inside. Claudie Ott's early pronouncements had seen to that. In fact, there was hardly an adult person present who didn't know, via whispers and text messages and phone calls and plain talk, about the man in the church nursery—although the rumors about who he was and why he was here seemed varied and contradictory. Most folks assumed he was one of those shy, quiet busboys from La Abuelita in Wilburton. Others thought he might be a Heavener chicken plant worker who had somehow escaped the raid on Brown's farm. He obviously hadn't come from Cedar itself, because Cedar didn't have any Mexicans, or any other sort of minority residents for that matter, except Choctaws, who, since most of the white people in town claimed Indian blood whether they had it or not, weren't considered a minority.

There were rumors that the man belonged to that really good roofing crew out of Panola, and some even got it correct straight off—that he was Bob Brown's granddaughter's husband who had been, according to news reports, deported last fall. The main unity to the rumors was how they all had the Mexican man qualifying as a stranger according to the preacher's texts, but one with a local connection. He was an alien all right, but he was somehow their own alien. What turned out to be even more varied and elusive and in the end unpredictable was what each person thought he or she personally, as witness or citizen or civic leader or neighbor or deputy or deacon or American or Christian, ought to do about it.

The observer who got that part mostly right was the enterprising young reporter Logan Morgan filming from the back of Floyd Ollie's pickup. Or in any case, she was the one who came closest to grasping what most of the people standing with Oren Dudley understood themselves to be doing:

"As the evangelical sanctuary movement takes hold here in southeastern Oklahoma," she murmured softly into her iPhone, "these born-again Christians have allied themselves with their

pastor." Panning slowly to the right, she zoomed in on the perspir-
ing face of the preacher. "Who appears," she narrated as quietly
and reverently as a TV golf announcer, "to have offered sanctuary
to one or more illegal aliens sequestered inside the First Baptist
Church in this small town with a population of five hundred and
eighty-one." She'd just googled the last census stats. Easing the
phone around, she captured the sheriff and his megaphone. Her
battery was alarmingly low. "Another local man," she went on in
her hushed tone, "Robert John Brown, was arrested two weeks
ago for harboring illegal aliens, by Sheriff Arvin A. Holloway,
seen here in this riveting Mexican standoff. Brown is currently
being held without bond in the Latimer County Jail on state felony charges." Worried that the battery would soon cut her off, she
turned the phone around to film her own face, signing off soberly,
"Live from Main Street in Cedar, Oklahoma, Logan Morgan,
2News Working for You." It was then that she spied, with great
relief, the Channel 2 news van wheeling off the highway and racing toward the church. Her camera crew.

     She scrambled down from the truck just as Kenneth Spears
and the two men with him moved from the neutral territory in the
middle of the yard over to stand behind the sheriff, clearly align-
ing themselves with the rule of law. Several other citizens joined
them. Then a few more witnesses walked over to join the ones
lined up with the pastor. Then Kenneth Spears, gesturing around
toward the back side of the church, spoke secretively to the sheriff,
who leaned over and gave a quiet order in Darrel Beecham's ear.
Before Logan Morgan could get her crew set up, the deputy was
making an effort to sneak around to the small obscure door in the
far southwest corner of the old building. But Deputy Beecham was
far too large to sneak. Two of the Masons, Floyd Ollie and Wade
Free, came down off the church porch and kept pace with him

around the building, positioning themselves between him and the Pastor's Study door.

By 11:30 A.M. camera crews were setting up from KFSM-TV Channel 5 in Fort Smith as well as Channels 2, 6, and 8 out of Tulsa. A reporter from the *Tulsa World* was milling around, gathering comments, collecting people's names and ages. And a well-equipped satellite van from KFOR in Oklahoma City was racing east on I-40 at eighty miles per hour. Shoshone Ballenger was hoping like anything to get footage beamed back in time for the noon news.

In the crackling bed, the boy stirs. His eyes open. The bruises on his face are almost healed now, only a faint yellow half-moon beneath each eye. *Good afternoon,* Luis says.

Good afternoon, the boy answers. *¿Is the hour more late?*

¿More late than what?

The boy shrugs.

¿Have you hunger?

The boy frowns. *I dont know.*

Luis goes to the door and looks out. The two large women in their pastel smocks are behind the screens at the big desk. They dont look up. They are not indian like the woman doctor. They dont speak spanish. Luis thinks maybe it is better not to ask for their attention. They do not look at him with kindness, though they had kindness for the boy when they came to change the medicine in the clear bag that hangs from a hook and drips into his arm. Here the people are all lightskins, except for the woman who brings the food trays. She is black, a little short. Luis peers down the pale green hall, hoping maybe to see her. The hall is empty, but her cart stands at the far end. Good. He will wait until she comes nearer. Luis returns to sit beside the boy.

The food will come soon.

The boy sits in the bed, looking to the window. *I have much to pay to my grandfather,* he says softly. *Maybe I . . . Is necessary I work to pay to him.*

I and my sons, Luis says, *we will pay for the truck.*

¿After we go to Gai-mon?

I think you will not go there. You will go back to your town. I think the woman doctor will arrange this.

¿How do you know?

I dont know. I think it. Because of the big indian. I think maybe he told her all that you told him when we sat waiting.

¿What is it I tell him?

I dont know. You talked english.

¿How will you go to your sons now?

The indian will drive me.

¿Is the truth?

Luis nods. This is not the truth. The big indian left when an attendant came to the hospital door with a rolling chair to take the boy. Luis did not tell him thank you, because he did not realize the man was leaving.

Then I come with you and the indian, the boy says.

Luis stands and walks to the door again. He will not insist with the boy now—later will be better for that. The short black woman emerges from a nearby room, lifts a tray from the cart, and carries it into the next room. Luis glances the other direction. One of the nurses at the desk is watching him. Her face is very stern. Luis withdraws again. *The little-black-one is very close now,* he tells the boy. *She brings the food.*

This doesnt listen well. No, I want to say . . . sound. This word doesnt sound well in english. The little-black-one. Dont say her that, ¿okay?

Okay.

Sheriff Arvin Holloway had understood he had a situation on his hands, but he didn't know just what type of a situation, or how out of hand it was liable to get, until the demonstrators started showing up. Those news crews hadn't bothered him. He knew how to talk to reporters and still take care of business, give orders, coordinate crowd control. The bullhorn never left his grip. When Clyde Herrington collapsed and everybody gasped or cried out *Oh!*, Arvin Holloway didn't flinch. He let them call for an ambulance, let the EMTs carry the ornery cuss away on a stretcher. He was generous, tough, calm—a good hostage negotiator. Technically speaking, this wasn't a hostage situation, but it had a lot of the same earmarks—an unplanned crisis, unspecified demands, one or more individuals barricaded inside a building—and throughout the fat part of the day, Arvin Holloway remained in charge of the developing situation.

Then the first vanload of protesters arrived. There were only a dozen or so—they said they were from the Muskogee chapter of Outraged Patriots—and really that alone wouldn't have been a problem. Holloway figured these people had a right to free speech, as he certainly mentioned to several reporters, but just as a precautionary measure he told them go stand on the other side of the

street away from the church. He wasn't real happy about how the
news crews all followed them over there, but they behaved themselves, and you had to pretty much agree with the signs they were
carrying: AMERICA FOR AMERICANS, THIS LAND IS *OUR* LAND,
THIS LAND AIN'T *YOUR* LAND, and WHAT PART OF ILLEGAL DON'T
YOU UNDERSTAND?

But then that other bunch showed up, walking along Main
Street from the Senior Citizens Center because they couldn't get
close enough to park. There were seven of them, all middle-aged
Hispanic-looking men in suits and ties, walking close together,
and the sheriff thought to himself, These people are mighty damn
brave or mighty damn dumb. They tried to cross the yard to go
stand with the preacher, but Arvin Holloway told them to get
their butts back behind the drainage ditch. Well, that was when
the Patriot group started hollering "Hey, Hey, Ho, Ho, Illegal
Aliens Have Got to Go!" and Holloway had to send a couple
of deputies over to calm things down, which left him with only
three actual deputies and the seven local men he'd sworn in as
deputized citizens to keep order. Meanwhile Terry Kirkendall
would not shut up. He kept trying to get Holloway to let him go
inside and talk to Sweet, but the sheriff didn't have time to mess
with an irate husband. The yelling and name calling in the yard
were getting worse, with some of the locals jumping in on the act,
hollering taunts not just at that little Spanish bunch in suits and
ties but also at the homefolks around the church. Holloway was
worried he might soon have a riot on his hands. He got on the
radio and told Cheryl to contact the LeFlore County sheriff to
send him some men. "Call Highway Patrol, too! Tell them I need
a roadblock set up on State Highway 270 at both ends of town,
east and west! I don't need any more of these outside agitators
coming in!"

But the troopers took their sweet time getting there, and people continued to pour into Cedar, more outsiders, another news team from Oklahoma City, quite a few unemployed young beer drinkers who seemed to think they were coming to a party. Folks parked their vehicles every old which way all up and down the street, until the entire length of Main Street was jammed full, and the sheriff was having a hard time keeping everybody back out of the church yard. "Damn it!" he yelled at Cheryl on the radio. "Get me some more men here!"

"'Jesus loves the little children,'" Sweet said. "'All the children of the world. Red and yellow, black and white, they are precious in his sight.' And see?" She pointed to the picture in the book. "Here's Jesus suffering the little children. Here's the little Indian boy and the little Chinese girl and the little black boy and the little white girl, and—well, this first little boy might actually be Mexican." She turned the page. Lucha leaned back against her daddy sitting on the low table. Her two fingers were in her mouth. Hardly a moment went by now when she wasn't sucking her fingers. Sweet sat on the floor next to them, trying to get Lucha engaged, or at the least distracted from the hollering outside. Sweet had shown her every toy in the toy box, had tried crayons and stickers, coloring books. Nothing changed the child's expression. Her big somber eyes were wary, watchful. "And look here," Sweet said. "This is the little boy with the five loaves and two small fishes. Can you point to the fishes?"

The child gazed at the book but made no response. She sat on her daddy's lap wrapped in the crib blanket while her pants dried. She'd wet herself earlier; they'd had to put her in Pampers from the stack in the closet. The top of her Sleeping Beauty sweatshirt was grimy with coal dust. A tiny smear of peanut butter showed on one cheek. Her hair was matted.

"And here's Jesus talking to Zacchaeus in the tree," Sweet said. "Do you know that song? 'Zac-chae-us was a wee little man,'" she sang softly, "'and a wee little man was he—'" Lucha turned away, buried her face against Juanito's jacket.

Sweet frowned at Misty Dawn rocking fiercely in the rocker. Her niece stared back at her blankly. They had spoken little since Sweet returned from that last trip out and told her the door through the Pastor's Study was also blocked off. Misty had cried out, "See? I *told* you we had to get out of here!" Well, and there had been words—Sweet's mostly. She didn't want to think about it. She pushed herself up off the floor and began to pace the room.

"Could you not do that?" Misty said. "Please." Her voice was exceedingly polite. They were both very polite with each other.

"This can't go on indefinitely," Sweet said. "Look at her."

"I know." Misty Dawn had stopped her ferocious rocking. Her eyes were on her husband and daughter. Juanito stared back at her, steady. Lucha's eyes were closed, but Sweet didn't think she was sleeping—she was nursing her fingers too hard.

"Let me just take her over to Vicki's," Sweet said. "You two wouldn't have to go, we could—"

"What? Let DHS take her?"

"No, they wouldn't . . ." Yes, they would. That was precisely what would happen.

Lucha had opened her eyes at the sound of her mother's voice, and Misty Dawn raised herself out of the chair and went to get her daughter. She walked the room, patting her back like a crying baby, but Lucha wasn't crying. She hadn't cried for some time now. Sweet could see her glazed, staring face over the back of Misty's shoulder.

"Maybe it wouldn't be for all that long. Maybe—"

"No!" Misty whirled, glaring hard. "I'm not doing it!" Her face held a terrible fierce protectiveness, and that chin-raised defiance that was so like Gaylene's. "What do you think they'd do? We're felons, for Christ's sake! Alls they want is to send you and me to jail and Juanito to prison! And then deport him! And meanwhile strangers will be raising my baby! Forget it! I'm not doing it! Oh, why did you have to go and make matters worse?"

I didn't! Sweet wanted to say. But in fact she feared she had. Her husband's voice had been like a hot nasty wave pushing her out of the nursery and around the corner to the Fellowship Hall doors, where she'd yapped at the preacher through the glass: "Tell that so-and-so I am *not* coming out! Tell him next time he wants to make threats, I'll give him something to get me arrested *for!*" And the preacher had done what she'd said, if with milder words, while she glared across at Terry Kirkendall standing next to Holloway with his thumbs hooked in his belt just like that potbellied blowhard sheriff, and their son, *her* son, standing there precisely like them, like a little bully-in-waiting, and the sight had made her spitting mad, and she'd shoved open the door and shouted, "Arvin Holloway, you are wasting your time here! Go on back to Wilburton, you skunk! You and that Judas-traitor skunk standing there with you!"

Yes, and it was right after that she'd seen Kenneth Spears go over to talk in the sheriff's ear, and within two seconds Holloway sent the big bland-faced, crew-cutted deputy toward the west side of the building. Sweet had wheeled around and raced through the dim hall in the old part of the church to head him off, ran straight to the Pastor's Study, where she'd slid open the latch and pushed the door halfway open, and the fierce sunlight raged in. She'd stood squinting at the side of Wade Free's utterly calm, motionless face. His ball cap was pushed back. The sun was bright on his ruddy freckles. He hadn't turned to look at her but kept a close watch on what was in front of him. That would be the big deputy, Sweet knew. "We're here," Wade Free said quietly. That was all. He was the same age as Terry; they'd gone to school together, there wasn't that much difference between them—gas field workers, churchgoers, family men. Not that much difference—except Terry was out yonder with the sheriff, and Wade Free was here. "Thank you," she'd whispered, and shut the door. Then she'd gone to tell the kids they couldn't get out that way.

"Listen," she suddenly said. "I'll go talk to Wade Free, he's the guy at the side door. I think he's . . . I believe he'll help us. Maybe he can draw off that deputy some way, give us a chance to slip out."

"And go where? You said yourself they can see us."

"Only if they step around to the side. Maybe Wade can draw them way off, like out past the bar ditch or something. I don't know! I'll just go talk to him."

"What makes you think we can trust him?"

Sweet paused with her hand on the doorknob. "Because he's there." She gazed at her niece a long time. The girl's face was red and splotchy, her eyeliner smeared, her sandy hair hanging in her eyes. "I'm doing all I can think of, Misty. She can't stay here like this. She's got to eat. I'll bring in her sweatpants so you can get her ready. Tell Juanito what we're doing. And take off that bathrobe and leave it here. It belongs to the preacher."

Stepping into the hall, Sweet turned toward the kitchen, where she'd laid the baby's lavender sweatpants to dry on the heat grate after rinsing the pee out of them. She passed through the small wedge of open space between the interior hall wall and the kitchen counter, glancing quickly across the room toward the glass doors, where she saw the same hunched backs outside on the walkway, the preacher's hunkered shoulders, beyond which she spied the battered crown of an old Farm Bureau cap. Tee was standing right there talking to the preacher! The fury rushed through her, and she headed straight across Fellowship Hall to tell him he had no business here, he should take their son away from all this! That was when she heard the low, rumbling buzz of a helicopter coming in from the north, closer and closer, until it was directly overhead, circling the church.

That *thwapping* noise made Arvin Holloway nervous. It reminded him too much of Nam. There'd been TV news choppers following the horseback searchers, granted, but they'd stayed high enough, a respectful distance, not hovering down so close they were fixing to blow somebody's hat off. Holloway held his Stetson down with one hand, tried to wave the pilot away using the bullhorn, but that just seemed to get the pilot's attention to circle back in closer—and *what* the hell was Kirkendall doing! He'd told him, "Okay, shut up man, you got one minute to talk that wife of yours into coming out." He hadn't added *or else* because he didn't know or-else-*what*—that was the whole blamed problem. But Kirkendall hadn't even got past the preacher, much less convinced Sweet to come outside. There the man stood, gaping up at the sky like every other blamed idiot, including Holloway's own deputies and that useless bunch from LeFlore County. The sheriff had finally had it. Enough was enough. He marched out across the yard.

Immediately he felt everybody's eyes swing around to him, all the cameras, and that goddamn stupid helicopter dropping down even lower, till you couldn't hear yourself think, much less talk! Standing a dozen or so feet away, Holloway hollered at Kirken-

dall, "WHAT'S THE HOLDUP HERE! YOU SAID YOU ONLY
NEEDED A MINUTE!" He couldn't make out the answer, though
he could see Kirkendall's mouth moving, his hand flapping at the
preacher. "PREACHER!" Holloway yelled. "LET THIS MAN IN-
SIDE TO TALK TO HIS WIFE! AIN'T THERE SOMETHING
IN THE BIBLE ABOUT THAT?" He couldn't make out what
the preacher said, either. Then he saw, in the dim recesses of the
building, Sweet Kirkendall standing on the other side of the glass
doors. "WHAT THE HELL DO YOU THINK YOU'RE DOING,
SWEET? YOU'RE COSTING THIS COUNTY A FORTUNE!"
Terry Kirkendall whirled around to look at his wife just as Holloway recollected what had set this whole mess in gear in the first
place. "I WANT TO KNOW WHAT THAT SPIC YOU GOT IN
THERE WAS DOING WITH THAT KID IN TULSA! YOU HEAR
ME? SWEET!" Well, how could she, with all the blamed noise
overhead? Again Holloway tried to wave the helicopter away, at
which point he lost his grip on his Stetson and it went sailing off
across the churchyard, flipping and tumbling toward the drainage
ditch, and as the several news cameras recorded, Latimer County
Sheriff Arvin A. Holloway jerked out his pistol and fired straight
up in the air—not aiming to hit the bird, mind you, just get it the
hell away from there—and, *thwap-thwap-thwap-thwap,* the chop-
per dipped and bowed and suddenly levitated straight up, headed
back off north. Holloway turned around to continue his conversation through the door, but Sweet Kirkendall was gone.

"I'll be goddamn," Holloway said. He turned his glare on the
preacher, skimming from him to the others standing with him,
the powdery old ladies and emphysemic deacons, the Skoal-bitten
farmboys and their chuffy short-waisted wives. He'd known most
of them most his life, and it really pissed him off that they wouldn't
listen to him. "I'm saying this for the last time! You people stand

aside and let me talk to them witnesses or I'll sling every last one of you in jail!"

"What witnesses?" the preacher said.

"We're witnesses," Ida Coley said.

"Go ahead on, Arvin," T. C. Blankenship offered. "See how well you get elected next year."

"Heavenly Father," the preacher started, "we come now to Your Throne of Grace—"

"All right!" the sheriff exploded. "Let's just see how you folks like standing out here past suppertime when the sun goes down and the temperature drops!" If this wasn't the stubbornest, prayingest, believingest bunch of Scotch-Irish pilgrims in the county, damn it, he didn't know who was. That was when a new notion struck him—right out of the blue, but like so many of his blue notions, it was perfect. Without another word Holloway turned on his heel.

"Brother Oren," Terry said, "would you ask her to just come back to the door and talk a minute?"

"I'm sorry, Tee. I don't think she wants to talk to you."

"Kirkendall! Get over here!"

Terry Kirkendall looked at the sheriff, hatless and furious, standing halfway across the yard now, and beyond him, the line of deputies and local men, and beyond them his own son looking short and scared in front of the crowd of shouting, sign-wagging strangers. "Tell her . . . tell her Carl Albert needs her to quit this nonsense and come home." He followed the sheriff back to the other side.

Sweet grabbed up the baby's lavender sweatpants as she sank to her knees on the tiled kitchen floor. She had never in her life been a knee pray-er, didn't know any Baptist who was, but in this moment she became one. *Help me God, help us,* a one-note pleading to the one Source she believed *could* help them—because she had seen for the first time what was truly happening out front. All that muffled yelling hadn't begun to tell her how many people were gathered, or how riled up they were getting. Or how ugly their expressions might be. It hadn't told her about the news vans, either, although that part didn't surprise her. Clutching the damp little sweatpants to her chest, Sweet pictured again the yelling faces on the far side of the yard, pushing forward, crowded all the way back into the street. She didn't remember ever seeing such hateful looks, not live and in person, only in old newspaper photographs or something. What worried her more, though, was what she'd seen in the features of Ida Coley and Alice Stalcup and some of the others as they lifted their chapped wrinkly cheeks to gape at the helicopter. They were tired. They were cold. They were *old.* Or in any case, the majority of the ones standing with the preacher were old, and the ones who weren't old were just kids on their cell phones, horsing around. They'd be bored soon, if they weren't bored already. It was getting late, and they'd been out there for hours. The old people couldn't hold up much longer. She should have thought to come out and look sooner. If she'd realized how bad it was getting, maybe she could have—what? She didn't know. She didn't know. *Help me, God. Help us.*

When she stepped back inside the nursery, Misty Dawn rushed over. "That was the SWAT team, right?"

"No, just some nosy folks who ought to mind their own business."

"In a helicopter?"

"It's not a SWAT team, Misty! For crying out loud." Then she caught the look on the girl's face. Her voice softened slightly. "Did you ever hear of a SWAT team in Latimer County?" Misty Dawn shook her head. "Well, me neither. They haven't got that kind of a budget. Here." Sweet pushed the sweatpants into her hands and went to the supply closet.

"They're still damp," Misty said.

"They'll be dry in time."

"In time for what?"

"We got to get ready." Sweet gathered an armful of Pampers and the small stack of clean sheets off the closet shelf, grabbed another pastel-striped baby blanket, then she went to the crib and started pulling the sheets off the mattress.

"We're leaving?"

"We're going upstairs. Grab that box of crackers."

"Upstairs! What for?"

"We'll hang out in one of the classrooms in the old part above the sanctuary."

"What good's that going to do?"

"I need to be able to see what's going on."

"See from where?"

"I don't know! A window."

"Aunt Sweet, you are making me crazy! You keep switching plans like every two seconds!"

"I'm trying to be flexible. Let's just go upstairs and keep quiet, see what happens."

"What for?"

"They know we're in the nursery, Misty! This is the first place they'll look!"

"Oh my God, you think they're about to bust in?"

"I don't know."

"How about we just *go*! And that man helps us like you said!"

"We have to wait till it gets dark."

"That's too long!"

"What choice do we have? Don't give me any grief, Misty. Here, Juanito, carry this."

Well, unfortunately, Oren Dudley thought, the sheriff had a point. How *were* these old folks going to stay out here after dark? The preacher himself apparently wasn't that good a judge of what people could handle and what they couldn't. For instance, he hadn't thought that dry cough of Clyde Herrington's amounted to anything until he heard the deacon say weakly, "Preacher, I think I better set down." He'd turned to see Clyde's face pale as pie crust, his hand on his chest, huffing like he couldn't catch his breath. "Oh my word, yes!" Oren had fumbled to open one of the glass doors so Clyde could sit inside, but before he could get it done, Clyde Herrington just sort of melted down onto the sidewalk.

The next little while had been a blur. Oren kept expecting the sheriff to rush them, but instead here came an ambulance wailing toward the church, and next thing he knew the medics were trying to get an oxygen mask on the deacon, with Clyde shaking his head and waving his hand in front of his face, wheezing, "I'm fine, leave me alone, I'm fine," until they rolled him away on a gurney. It was right after that Oren Dudley started asking himself if he was doing the right thing—or, rather, not so much if *he* was, but if all these church members needed to be involved. So many of them were so frail, and it was nippy out, and there was already so much strife and dissension, that specially called deacon's meeting, and the awkward potluck dinner last Sunday. Kenneth Spears and them going over to the other side. Which wasn't a surprise exactly, but it was disappointing. Oh, he wished they'd had time to do that prayer walk. But he *had* prayed, he reminded himself. Considerably. On his knees all night in the bedroom. He'd asked to be led. His wife was standing by him. He'd memorized all those verses.

But then, he still expected some of them were going to want to call for a vote of confidence. Or not. Oren Dudley felt that it was increasingly possible that the one thing he'd dreaded most in his pastoring life could come to pass: he might be the catalyst that would split the church. He would hate that, he really would. He was distracted in his deliberations by Claudie Ott's skittery voice: "Brother Oren, I got to be getting home to start Leon's supper. When do you see this all being finished?"

"To tell you the truth, Miz Ott," the preacher said, rubbing his face with his free hand, "I don't see."

This was, in fact, the question on everyone's mind—when would this all be finished? Those trapped inside the church wondered, as did those linked together in front of the doors. The handful of deputies who were ready to call it a day wondered, and also those who were happy to be standing around doing nothing while they racked up more overtime. Carl Albert Kirkendall and his dad both wondered, the boy because he was hungry and he wanted to see his mom and he thought it might be almost time for *The Suite Life of Zack and Cody,* and Terry Kirkendall because—well, just because.

Vicki Dudley wondered because she wanted to put a frozen chicken pot pie in the oven for her husband's supper and those things take a while to cook. The demonstrators from Outraged Patriots wondered—they had an hour's drive back to Muskogee— and so did the seven representatives from the Latino Council of Clergymen, who would be returning to several different locations around the state. Logan Morgan and Shoshone Ballenger and the other reporters all wondered, because if there was going to be a dramatic showdown, they wished it would hurry up and get started so their live reports could make the evening news.

But there were others following the story who hoped the climax would come later, not sooner. This was true in particular for the two cable news producers in New York who were scrambling to book flights to Tulsa, and also for State Representative Monica Moorehouse, who had contacted those very producers, and who was at this moment standing outside the east door of the capitol building in Oklahoma City waiting for her husband to come pick her up. Representative Moorehouse was praying, in fact, that the standoff would last long enough for her to drop by the apartment and change clothes before making the long drive east on I-40 again.

Deputy Darrel Beecham also had reason to wonder. He was driving as fast as he could. Sheriff Holloway had called him from his post at the church's rear side door and told him to drive lickety-split back to Wilburton and pick up the prisoner. "Cuff him and shackle him good! Make sure that steel is out in the open where these reporters can see it!" The sheriff stood peering west. "Looks to me like we got an hour of good daylight left. If you value your job, Beecham, I suggest you have that son of a bitch here before the light goes, you hear?"

Wednesday | *February 27, 2008* | *Afternoon*

Watonga Hospital

The little-black-one carries the food tray in one hand. She is small and quick and smiling. She talks rapidly as she places the tray on the metal table and rolls the table to fit properly for the boy sitting up in the bed. She speaks as if she knows him very well. The boy keeps his smile when she goes out again. *She calls my name Sugar. ¿Do you want the TV on, Sugar? This is the same like I call the red mare.* The red mare, Luis thinks, remembering how the boy tried to coax her with sugar. What a long time past it seems. The aide returns with a second tray of food, which she places on the small crowded table beside Luis. She blinks one eye at him, raps her knuckles on the wood as if to say, dont worry. Then she goes to the small television mounted near the ceiling and switches it on, turning the knob a few times to a program with large colorful puppets and the young ones with smiling faces. She shows the boy how to use the arrows on the side of the bed to make the sound more loud or more quiet, or to turn to another program. *Thank you,* the boy says in spanish. The little black one answers, *For nothing,* and leaves the room again.

Much later, after they both have eaten and the aide has come and retrieved the two trays, and the day has grown late, the room graying with shadows, Luis, seeing the boy asleep again, pushes the arrows on the side of the bed. He knows he will not understand the words on the television but maybe there is something that will be more interesting to look at than a program for children. He stops moving the arrow suddenly, stands very still. On the small screen is the face of the boy—much younger, yes, but without doubt it is him. In fear Luis looks to the door, which stands a little open. No one must see this!

Rapidly he closes the door, returns to the bed. He thinks to awaken the boy, to ask what the voice is saying, but the picture changes. Now, from the sky, a moving picture of the blue truck of the grandfather, in the same arroyo where Luis and the boy left it, with the hood open. No steam pours from the broken radiator now. Then another picture from above, this one of a church, like a parish church, not a cathedral; he can recognize the small, plain steeple, though it carries no cross. In the street beside the church are many automobiles and trucks and police cars with lights flashing. He can see also, standing among the vehicles, men in tan uniforms like the uniforms of those who came into the barn to take away the young people. The same color as the two uniforms of the two men that Luis sees now walking in through the hospital room door.

Sweet felt as if she'd been led to this upstairs corner classroom just in time to see the big deputy drive off in his cruiser. Did this mean nobody was watching the Pastor's Study door? She couldn't tell from this angle. What she could see, looking down on the street, were dozens of other deputies, the TV vans and reporters, the sign-waving strangers, all those people from town, and the astonishing number of vehicles parked in every imaginable position, including her husband's Silverado sitting cattywampus in the middle of the street. She looked for Terry and Carl Albert, but the thrusting front porch roof blocked part of her view. She couldn't see the sheriff, either, or the preacher and them guarding Fellowship Hall on the opposite side of the church, or the Masons guarding the sanctuary, or Wade Free and Floyd Ollie around at that rear side door. If they were even still back there.

What she could see very well, at the far end of the street where it intersected the highway, were the two black-and-white Highway Patrol cars parked crossways blocking the road, red lights flashing, a row of blue sawhorses set up. Behind her, in the Sunday School classroom, Misty Dawn and Juanito were fighting—not just talking fast Spanish but having a ferocious whispered argument. No mistaking it now. *What* they were arguing about, Sweet didn't know, but the *why* of it she understood acutely: just moments ago they had come to stand beside her. They had looked out the window and seen, for the first time, the roiling crowd, the hateful yelling faces, the officers in uniform rowed up in front of the pickups and cruisers, their guns.

"No, no, no!" Misty cried. "*Tu eres loco!*"

"Hush!" Sweet hurried over to where they were standing at the classroom door.

"Talk to him, Aunt Sweet! He's trying to go out there! He says he's going to give himself up!"

"Keep your voices down! Somebody might be downstairs! Juanito, sit!" Sweet maneuvered herself between the two young people and the classroom door. Misty Dawn started off on a renewed Spanish tirade. "Hush now! I mean it, Misty!"

"He thinks they'll just bus him to Mexico and he can turn right around and come back! *You* tell him! He won't listen to me! Shhh, shhh, baby, it's all right." Lucha was whimpering, reaching up from the floor for her mother, and Misty Dawn swooped down and lifted her in her arms. "It's okay, mami." Juanito looked at neither his wife and daughter, nor at Sweet, but held his gaze on the colorful posters featuring the ABC's of Salvation on the classroom wall. His face was young, solemn, completely unreadable.

"Both of you sit down and be quiet," Sweet said.

They didn't sit, but they no longer argued out loud. Misty Dawn went on in a suppressed voice: "I keep trying to tell him everything's different now. He says he knows, but he *don't* know. I mean, he *ought* to know, from Enrique and them, but he just acts like it's no big deal."

"My daughter," Juanito said. "She is hungry. She is not able . . ." He finished in Spanish.

"He says she can't stand any more of this," Misty said. Then she sank down in one of the metal folding chairs against the wall, pressed her face against the top of the child's head. "He's right," she whispered. "But I can't let them. I won't!" She said a few words in Spanish, and Juanito's voice, when he answered, was extremely quiet.

"What's he saying?"

"That it's better for him to go to jail than for her to be more frightened and hungry."

Another phrase from Juanito.

"He's afraid there might be shooting. They've got too many guns. He says something bad could happen to Lucha."

"*Tú también.*"

"And me."

Juanito looked directly at Sweet. Later she couldn't be sure if what he said was in English, the way she remembered it, or if Misty Dawn translated, and she just remembered it as coming from Juanito's mouth, or if it was simply his expression that told her, but she felt it clearly, what he had to say: It is necessary for me to surrender so that my daughter will be safe. It is better for her to be alive and fed and unhurt, no matter what they do with me.

"Not you," Sweet said. Everything fell into place then. She looked at Misty. "Not him. Me."

"What?"

"I'll let the sheriff know I'm coming out."

"Are you kidding? No!"

"Just listen a minute! When it gets dark, I'll go downstairs where the preacher and them are standing." She snatched up her purse from the table, began to dig for her wallet. "I'll act like I'm, you know, negotiating. I'll, I don't know, make a scene of some kind. Create a distraction." She handed her niece a twenty and three singles—all she had left of last week's grocery money. Misty

Dawn took the money without a word of thanks, shifted the baby to one arm and leaned to the side so she could stuff the bills into her jeans pocket. "While I'm doing that," Sweet said, returning to the window, "y'all slip out through the side door like we talked about."

"They'll see us!"

"That's why we're going to wait for dark."

"Where do we go?"

Sweet turned to look at Misty Dawn, her beautiful, frightened face and smeared makeup, how she held her daughter so tight on her lap, and Juanito standing beside them, thin and small, his sober expression, and the child herself, the crib blanket gone now, dropped somewhere, her long brown legs dangling almost to the floor; she wasn't sucking her fingers, just staring straight ahead, unblinking, from beneath the dark thatch of matted hair. "Y'all are going to have to figure it out for yourselves," Sweet said. "Once I walk out there, they'll take me into custody. I won't be able to help."

"But I don't know where to go! And even if I did, how would we get there?"

"You'll have to ask the Lord, I guess. And also Wade Free, maybe, if he's still outside the Pastor's Study door."

While Misty Dawn changed the baby's diaper and put on her little sweatpants and gathered their things, talking low to Juanito the whole time, explaining what they were doing, presumably, Sweet stood at the window. The street was relatively quiet, people milling around, unfocused. What attention was being paid was all directed toward the Fellowship Hall doors to her far left. The light was glowing amber as the sun lowered behind the church, casting long shadows behind the pickups and cars. Soon the air would turn orange, then ruddy red, then lavender and purple—

then, at long last, it would be dark. How long? Sweet tried to judge. Maybe twenty minutes. Half an hour. For once in her life, Sweet was grateful for the short days in February.

A flurry of movement to her right drew her gaze along the street. Down at the highway intersection one of the troopers was waving a white cruiser around the sawhorses onto Main Street. The cruiser came along fast, navigating between the helter-skelter-parked vehicles until it nosed quickly into the one empty space directly in front of the church. Oh, wouldn't you know, Sweet thought. The big deputy returning. Holloway would send him straight back to his post at the rear side door. A stark urgency pressed on her. Maybe she should go downstairs right now? Yes, before the deputy had time to walk back around there! But no, the kids needed to wait for dark, they *had* to, it was going to be tough enough. Sweet watched the big burred fellow hoist himself from behind the steering wheel, reach for the rear door handle. A little cry popped from her mouth when she saw her daddy being helped awkwardly out of the backseat in handcuffs, his feet shackled.

"What?" Misty said, hurrying over. "Oh, no. Oh, look what they're doing! Grandpa!"

"Y'all stay back!" Sweet said, because Juanito was pushing forward now, too, holding the baby. "Don't jiggle the curtains, we don't want them looking up here!" But nobody on the street was looking up. Their eyes were all on Bob Brown—the camera operators and reporters, the townspeople, the churchgoers, the deputies, the strangers: all eyes homed on the graying rack-thin orange-clad prisoner, shackled and chained waist to ankle, being shuffled forward to where the sheriff waited with his bullhorn. "Oh my God," Misty Dawn whispered. "Aunt Sweet, I didn't know."

"I know. It can't be helped now." Sweet reached up, her own

heart pounding, to rub the girl's back. "But hey," she said lightly, "this a real good distraction. I mean, right? Nobody's going to be paying attention to that back door."

"Listen to them! Do you hear what they're saying?"

Well, Sweet did hear. She had heard it before. The words were little different to what she'd heard earlier, but the faces—they looked, Sweet thought, even uglier, even angrier. Her daddy's presence had totally revved up the demonstrators, and not just them, but also the beer drinkers and the general onlookers, some of whom—oh, this really broke Sweet's heart—were local people who'd known her daddy for years. How could the ones who knew him be so turned against him? What would change people like that?

And the others, those twisted yelling faces, she recognized them now, or rather the looks of them, where she'd seen it before— pictures from an old social studies class, a bunch of white teenagers spitting and yelling at a black girl in sunglasses walking to school. There was one face in particular in that picture, a white girl with a short bubble haircut and a shirtwaist dress, her face twisted as she screamed at the black girl's back—that face had always bothered Sweet the most because the girl looked so much like the girls in the old yearbook pictures on the walls of the ad building at Cedar High School. She looked, to be truthful, a little like Sweet herself. If she'd grown up in a different era. Different clothes, a different haircut, but that spitting girl could be kin to her. The people down below, yelling, they were the same, too—the same kind of kin.

But not all of them! Sweet told herself. What about Brother Oren and Vicki? Ida Coley, T. C. Blankenship, Wade Free . . . there were plenty other people down there, folks from this town, and this church, doing what they thought was right. But the others across the way—didn't they think what they were doing was

right? And the uniformed deputies, the sheriff, they all thought
they were doing right. And her daddy. Oh, Daddy. He looked
terrible. He'd lost so much weight. His shoulders were slumped
in a way she'd never seen before, maybe because of the shackles,
how they had him handcuffed to the chains clanking down to
his ankles. My God, Sweet thought, you'd think he'd murdered
somebody! You'd think he was a dangerous criminal, some kind
of a—what? Felon. *We're all felons, for Christ's sake*, Misty Dawn
had said. Well, we are, Sweet said to herself. We are that.

"Y'all come away from there." She drew the kids from the window just as Arvin Holloway started bellowing through the bullhorn: GEORGIA KIRKENDALL, I GOT SOMEBODY HERE
WANTS TO TALK TO YOU! Sweet stopped on the other side of
the classroom. The kids stood nearby, looking expectant. She really wished they could wait for dark, but they couldn't. She reached
over to brush the hair back from Lucha's forehead. The child
shrank against her daddy. "You be a good girl, okay? Aunt Sweet
will bring you some Gummi Bears next time I see you. Okay?"
Lucha solemnly nodded. "Well, then," Sweet said, looking around
the room. She picked up her purse, stood on tiptoe to hug Misty,
gave a quick awkward kiss on the cheek to Juanito, who ducked
his head, flicked an embarrassed half smile. "Well," Sweet said. "I
guess y'all are on your own, then." She stepped to the door, paused,
raked her fingers back through her uncombed hair. "I'll drag it out
as long as I can."

He had thought he'd come to terms with everything. He had
truly believed that. The story, as he got it from the taciturn mouth
of the big deputy on the drive here, had seemed convoluted, but
Bob Brown had felt like he understood. His daughter was at the

Cedar First Baptist Church with the preacher and the sheriff and, somehow, some kind of a Mexican stranger—a weird mishmosh, but there would be a good explanation. But when they came upon the roadblock and turned and he saw the mangle of pickups and vans and cars on the street, Brown knew, before he was hauled out of the cruiser to jeers and taunts, that he had understood nothing. And when he stood in front of Holloway and saw, behind the sheriff's shoulder, Terry Kirkendall lurking at the edge of the crowd with his cap brim pulled low, Bob Brown realized that there was one thing, at least, he hadn't come to terms with. The sheriff shoved the bullhorn at him, and with a clank Brown took it by the cold metal handle.

"Call her out!" Holloway ordered.

"Do what?"

"Don't give me any bullshit." The sheriff snatched back the megaphone. "GEORGIA KIRKENDALL, I GOT SOMEBODY HERE WANTS TO TALK TO YOU!" He slapped the horn in Brown's hand again, and Brown lifted his shackled wrists to demonstrate that he could raise them only chest high. "Beecham, get over here!" The deputy blocked Brown's view as he hulked in front of him fumbling with the heavy lock at his waist. Twenty minutes ago, inside the drunk tank, Darrell Beecham had apologized for clamping on the steel chain linking the handcuffs to the foot shackles. Now he growled roughly at Bob Brown to hold still. Brown leaned around, trying to see his son-in-law skulking back behind the police tape. Tee wouldn't meet his gaze. Carl Albert stood next to him; he kept peering up into his dad's face and then turning to look at his grandfather. The boy's face was red, wincing, puffy with crying.

"Call her!" Holloway barked as the deputy began gathering up the heavy chain.

"What do you want me to say?"

"Tell her to send that spic out! I want to know what he done with that kid!"

"You mean Dustin."

"Hell, yes, Dustin! Who the hell else? Call her!"

Awkwardly Brown pulled the megaphone toward his mouth, holding it several inches away so that the sound flowed around the mouthpiece more than into it, although his tinny voice could also be heard coming from the closed speaker: "Oren," he called to his former pastor, "could you explain to me what this is about?"

And the preacher called back across the way, "Yes, sir, be glad to, Mr. Brown—" But a burst of heckling from the crowd drowned out the rest of his words, and a helicopter hovered overhead—not so low now as to blow hats off, but close enough to be loud—and some of the camera operators were angling around to get a better shot of the grizzled prisoner in his orange jumpsuit with the black words *Inmate Latimer County Jail* stenciled on the back.

"Put it to your mouth, man!" the sheriff ordered. "Put some goddamn spit in it!"

Brown's sudden cooperation had little to do with the sheriff's instructions and much to do with what he himself wanted to know. "SWEET? IT'S DAD. CAN YOU HEAR ME?" Despite itself, the crowd quieted down. One of the reporters moved out into a little cleared space to wave off the helicopter—they all wanted to catch this. "I APPRECIATE WHAT YOU'RE DOING. COME HERE AND LET ME ASK YOU A QUESTION." No flicker of movement behind the dark double glass doors, but a quick dart of yellow on the street as Carl Albert, having twisted away from his father's grip, ran around the barrier straight to Bob Brown. "Grandpa, Grandpa, don't let 'em shoot her!" The boy was gasping and sniffling. "They're not gonna shoot her, are they?" He turned and sobbed at the sheriff: "Please don't shoot her!"

"Carl Albert!" Terry called. "Get back over here!"

"She didn't mean to kill him! It wasn't her fault!"

"Kill him?" Holloway's ears pricked. "Kill who?"

"Mr. Bledsoe! It was a accident, I promise. Me and Dustin seen it!" Carl Albert turned now and pleaded across the yard to the preacher. "Tell them, Brother Oren! Tell them my mom didn't do it!"

"Come here, son." Terry Kirkendall was making his way around the tape. "Let's go home."

"Kirkendall, what the hell's he talking about?"

"Nothing. Carl Albert, let's go."

"Horace is dead?" Bob Brown said.

Terry kept his eyes on his son. "Passed away this morning. At McAlester Regional."

Brother Oren called across softly: "I'm real sorry to hear that, Tee. If there's anything—"

"What did Sweet do?" Holloway demanded. "Speak up, man!"

"Nothing! My boy's just got things mixed up!"

"This whole blamed family ought to be in the goddamn jail!"

"Shut up, Arvin," Brown said. For a few seconds, in the ruddy glow of sunset, in the midst of the mostly quiet crowd, Bob Brown struggled. There stood his son-in-law not six feet away looking baffled and frightened, looking heartsick, looking weary and maybe even a little ashamed, with his cap tugged low and his grease-stained work coat unbuttoned, his ragged beard uncombed, his hand clamped on the boy's shoulder, the same way he'd stood beside the church van at Misty Dawn's house last summer. It all passed through Brown in a flash: Terry's expression that day at the birthday party, his surly voice in the van on the ride home,

Brown's own shock when the sheriff told him who'd turned him in, his disbelief at that moment, his anger. The same anger that boiled up in him right now—not for what had been done to him or Jesús Garcia or even those poor people in the barn, but because of Dustin. If Tee hadn't made that call, Dustin would not be gone. Jesus said, Forgive. Jesus said, Go the second mile, Turn the other cheek, Do unto others. *As we forgive those who trespass against us,* Bob Brown thought, and then, before he or anybody else knew what he was up to, he leaped across the six feet of soggy yard and took down his son-in-law.

The television cameras captured it all quite well: the elderly, bespectacled inmate on his back on the ground, with the heavy bearded fellow pulled backward on top of him, the prisoner's clasped hands around the bearded guy's neck, choking him with the handcuffs, and the little chunky boy dancing around, screaming, and Sheriff Arvin A. Holloway hollering at the top of his lungs words that nobody could understand while the preacher and some of the senior citizens rushed over from the glass doors and the deputies swarmed, and then the sheriff, still yelling unintelligibly, drew his pistol and aimed it, not overhead for a warning, but directly at the two men grunting and wrestling on the ground. It was only the swift thinking of Deputy Darrel Beecham that saved a worse tragedy from taking place—a truly engaging unsung hero, as young Logan Morgan recognized, shoving her cameraman's shoulder and pointing him to shoot the scene at the very instant Beecham swatted the sheriff's elbow straight up so that the shot went winging up over the top of the parsonage, hitting no one, thank God.

Sheriff Arvin Holloway, in a profound and horrific rage, snatched up the cracked bullhorn from the sidewalk where Bob Brown had dropped it, and his roar, even through the broken microphone, was louder than any of his amplified bellows that had come before: "YOU PEOPLE SHUT THE HELL UP AND GET OUT OF MY WAY!"

There followed then a great hush, except for the two men coughing on the ground, and the hiccupy boy still bawling. All other eyes and lenses were turned toward Fellowship Hall, where on the narrow slab of concrete in front of the double glass doors, Georgia "Sweet" Kirkendall stood with her short auburn hair spiking straight up and dark circles beneath her eyes, a fake leather purse hanging off her shoulder, and both hands in the air.

Wednesday | *February 27, 2008* | *8:00* P.M.

Cedar

By the time the calm GPS voice in the speeding Escalade guided the decidedly un-calm State Representative Monica Moorehouse and her husband over the mountains into the little town of Cedar, the night was full dark. They hadn't come the familiar route via McAlester, which would have taken, according to Charlie, an extra forty minutes, but had relied on that serene disembodied guidance, which directed them south from I-40 over tiny two-lane highways, through dead and dying small towns, across narrow being-repaired one-lane bridges, and finally south along the winding curves and steep ridges of the Sans Bois Mountains—a drive that might have been quite lovely in daylight, Monica observed tensely, but which turned out to be, after dark, damned scary. Her hands were cramping on the steering wheel, she had a splitting headache, and the Escalade seemed to have dropped into some kind of technological black hole where Charlie's laptop connect card could not connect, cell reception was intermittent, and, worst of all, they met several sets of headlights coming toward them on the winding curves— going the opposite direction.

When they turned off the highway at last, Monica was relieved to see a number of vehicles down the street in front of the church.

She sped toward them and parked next to a giant pickup hooked to an empty stock trailer. Streetlights illuminated the broad white face of the old building and the several law enforcement officers milling about, but where were all the reporters? Where were the huge crowds her husband had described from the news feeds? She could see miles of yellow police tape, yes, and discarded soda cans and paper trash and a few hicks in ball caps perched on tailgates across the way surreptitiously sipping from silver beer cans, but where were the demonstrators, the media, the cameras and lights and tension? "What happened, Charlie? Where is everybody?"

Her husband grunted as he hit the refresh button on his laptop, to no avail. He plucked one of the BlackBerrys from a cup holder, glanced up, and pointed. "There."

Monica leaned forward to see. Through the wide glass doors of a brightly lit prefab addition attached like a suckerfish to the side of the church she could see a handful of senior citizens seated at a long table and that fool sheriff striding back and forth in front of them. Then she spied the camera crew filming from the back of the room, "Wait!" Charlie said, punching numbers, "let me find out what's going on!" But Monica left him still trying to connect as she shoved open the car door and climbed down.

She ducked deftly beneath the yellow tape and was at the glass doors before a deputy saw her and called out for her to halt. With a quick smile and a little wave, she slipped in to the hall, where no one paid her the least attention. The senior citizens were all glaring at the sheriff. Well, they weren't all seniors, as Monica could see now; they were just mostly gray haired, except for the soft little round-faced woman standing by the back wall with a wriggly toddler in each arm and the workingmen seated at a second table fidgeting with their ball caps, their arms stretched out on the butcher paper. More to the point: there was only one reporter, the perky young brunette from Channel 2 and her gangly camera operator—oh, it had all taken too long! Charlie had been right. She shouldn't have stopped by the apartment to change clothes.

At the front table a plump lady with a bad perm was wiggling her fingers in the air. "When are you going to let us go home, Arvin? My boy Leon can't wait much longer for his supper."

"I told you! Nobody's going nowhere till I get some blamed answers!"

"You got your answer!" This from a skinny old lady with a wattled neck. "How many times do we have to say it? We don't know what you're talking about."

"Like hell!"

"Please watch your language," a fellow said tiredly from the far end of the front table. "This is God's house." Monica recognized him as the pastor who'd nervously shadowed the smart-mouthed aunt at yesterday's news conferences—but where was she? The aunt? Weren't they supposed to have nabbed her along with the cache of illegal aliens she'd been harboring? Hard to believe, Monica thought from her position near the door: an entire family of more or less middle-class, nominally Christian white people smuggling Mexicans, with, it seemed clear, the support of their church. Likely there was a drug-running operation in the mix, too. "Sheriff!" Monica strode forward to where the camera operator could see her. "Representative Monica Moorehouse of the Eighteenth District!" She put out her hand as if they'd never met, smiled winningly, could almost feel the lens zooming in. "I'm here to offer the support of the entire Oklahoma State Legisla . . . ture . . ." The scowl the sheriff turned on her could've choked a toad. "If there's any . . . assistance you need . . ."

"I don't need *assistance*, lady. From you or anybody else!"

A uniformed deputy stepped into the hall. "We finished the sanctuary, Sheriff. Still can't find any sign. It don't look like—"

"Search it again!"

"Yes, sir."

"And the baptistery! Did anybody check the baptistery?"

"Yes, sir."

"Well, look again. Get down in the dadgum water and feel along the bottom!"

"It's only a few feet deep, sir, you can see the bottom."

"I don't care! Get in there and check it! I want ever inch of that building gone over!"

"The water heater ain't on—"

"Do it!"

The deputy withdrew. The sheriff whirled and made a chopping motion toward the back of the room. "Turn that blamed thing off! I'll tell you when you can shoot! And *what* you can shoot!" He started toward the back, and the young camera operator—baffled, because it had been the sheriff who'd beckoned them to come in—squeaked, "It's off, it's off, I turned it off!"

"Turn out that goddamn light, too!"

"Sheriff!" the pastor said. "If you have to use profanity, let's go over to my house. We can talk there."

"Nobody's going nowhere! Do you people get that?"

In fact, the people did get that—not least because Arvin Holloway had shouted it so many times. They'd been sitting here close to two hours. The first search had lasted only twenty minutes, as there were so many deputies and so few rooms in which an illegal alien might be hiding, but the subsequent searches were taking longer. The deputies had found bits of evidence in the nursery—

cracker crumbs on the table, empty Styrofoam cups rimmed in the bottom with red Kool-Aid, a soiled crib blanket in the corner, a couple of soaked disposable diapers in the trash—but there was no way to tell if these telltale signs were from today or last Sunday. A raggedy blue house robe had been discovered on the floor of the nursery closet, and they'd thought at first that might be a clue, until one of the deputies remembered seeing it on a Wise Man in the Christmas play last December. Nevertheless, they bagged it along with the Styrofoam cups and the diaper and the discarded plastic cracker sleeves they'd collected for DNA testing, should there ever be enough money in the county budget to pursue such a course of action—and provided, of course, there turned out to be reasonable cause. Other than that, the diligent deputies had found no sign of an alleged quote unquote illegal Mexican.

Still, they kept looking, more and more carefully, and this last search, the third, had been dragging on for almost an hour. Every empty moment that passed caused Arvin Holloway's blood to boil more recklessly—to the point of a stroke if he wasn't careful, he knew that, but he could not contain his fury. Not one of these blankety-blank Scotch-Irish pilgrims would admit to having seen a Mexican person, living or dead, legal or illegal, alone or accompanied, anywhere in the town of Cedar or its environs, period, ever, at all: "Don't know what you're talking about, Sheriff." "Don't have any idea what you mean."

At this moment Bob Brown was sitting in the back of the sheriff's cruiser, rechained and badly bruised from his fall, under arrest for aggravated assault and battery with a deadly weapon—the handcuffs—and also for resisting arrest, although he had resisted nothing when the two deputies jerked him up from the ground where his son-in-law lay coughing. Carl Albert had thudded across the yard, crying out "Mommy! Mommy!" as he flung himself at her so fiercely that the startled sheriff, flustered and furious and completely undone, swung his bullhorn on the kid, pointing it straight at him like a pistol. In the few seconds it took the sheriff to realize what he was doing and lower the bullhorn and start yelling for somebody to arrest the goddamn prisoner, Bob Brown had stood staring at his daughter. Sweet met his gaze steadily over the head of her sobbing son. She'd looked disheveled, exhausted, and . . . something else. Settled. Some kind of settled, or acceptant, or . . . it would take Brown several hours, the whole evening, in fact, to glean what his daughter's face said: *We are together in this, Daddy. I get it now. You had your reasons. I have mine.*

Sweet herself was shivering in the backseat of Deputy Darrel Beecham's cruiser. She wasn't chained, but she was handcuffed, and she was most definitely under arrest—for the crime of harboring undocumented aliens in furtherance of their illegal presence in the state of Oklahoma, a felony, as the deputy rattled off when he took her into custody. She had the right to remain silent. She had the right to speak to an attorney. If she couldn't afford an attorney, one would be appointed . . .

And so it was left to the pastor and his wife to bear witness to what the citizen Christians of Cedar were doing—an even smaller group now than had originally stood at the church doors, since the less stalwart of the rebels had made their excuses and signed their court appearance tickets and gone home to supper a couple of hours ago. Floyd Ollie, dragged forth from the rear side door, sat alone under guard in the church sanctuary. The teenagers who had once stood with the pastor were all gone now, too, because Vicki Dudley, at the sound of gunfire winging over her rooftop, had raced down her front steps and across the yard and pushed the four Youth for Christ kids into Fellowship Hall away from potential stray bullets. While the sheriff was arresting everybody she motioned through the glass doors for the kids to slip out through the old part of the church, and then she'd hurried home to get her boys. Therefore, the ones sitting now at the long tables were those who faithfully believed they had reason to be here—beyond just the fact, of course, that the sheriff wouldn't let them leave.

Of this resolute remainder, the only Christians who had directly bald-face lied to the sheriff were the four elderly Women's Missionary Union ladies. Claudie Ott had no trouble prevaricating, prone as she was to exaggeration and embellishment when telling a story, and Ida Coley had certainly felt no compunction about narrowing her eyes at that fool blowhard sheriff and saying, "You are so full of it, Arvin. I never in my life saw a Mexican man in this church." The other two women, Alice Stalcup and Edith Martin, had, early on, sat at the front table wavering and quavering, hemming and hawing, cutting their eyes at each other and jumping nervously every time the sheriff shouted, until Oren Dudley had at length braced himself to hear the beans come spilling out of their two quivery mouths.

But the beans did not spill.

Later, Brother Oren would come to believe that that brilliant white light suddenly flooding the room in the precise moments when Mrs. Stalcup and Mrs. Martin were finding it so hard to lie was like the Light of the World visited in a great beneficent flood upon them. Yes, he understood that its actual nonmetaphoric source was the portable LED light the Channel 2 cameraman had switched on, but the light had burst forth at just the right moment, and wasn't that, Brother Oren asked himself, just exactly like the workings of the Holy Spirit? "Ask and ye shall receive," the Word said, and he and several others had most definitely been asking. The two women, startled, had looked around, met Ida Coley's firm gaze, and at once their quivery mouths firmed up to match hers.

When the sheriff bellowed at them again, they repeated what had become the evening's stock answer: "We don't know what you're talking about."

Thus the investigation had begun with the people standing in solidarity—or, more accurately, sitting—and so it continued. The people were weary, they were hungry, their bodies were sore, but they were determined. They sat up straight in the folding chairs, even the oldest folks whose backs were naturally humped. The WMU ladies led a rousing chorus of "Onward Christian Soldiers" until the sheriff made them quit. Floyd Ollie had been brought in to explain to the sheriff in his own words how Wade Free had been called out on a gas line explosion near Bokoshe, and the Masons, seated in a taciturn row at the second table, murmured their corroboration. Each time an officer returned from the search to admit they'd found nothing, the resolve of the people was strengthened; they made their backs straighter, they smiled, forgot their hunger, repeated their stock phrase, and up to this point, the Channel 2 team had been recording it all.

The other news teams had hurriedly packed up and left forty minutes ago, but Logan Morgan and her cameraman had elected to stay. She still held out hope that the church searches would produce aliens, or, failing that, that the sheriff might yet explode and do something newsworthy. At the very least she planned to get an exclusive interview with the big deputy for tomorrow's *Good Morning Oklahoma*. She observed the deputy standing near the kitchen, legs akimbo, hands clasped behind. That footage of him knocking the sheriff's pistol skyward was some of her finest work. Unfortunately, it had come too late to make the evening news.

In fact, for Logan Morgan, the end of the standoff had turned out to be a disappointment. No shootout, no actual Mexicans, and the little that did happen had happened too late in the day. Her best captured images—the disheveled aunt with her hands in the air, the deputy striking the sheriff's gun—would have to wait for the lower-rated ten o'clock report. The 10:00 P.M. and morning news shows were fine, but it was the 5:00 and 6:00 P.M. spots that, professionally, made all the difference. The question Logan Morgan kept asking herself was this: Would the story still have legs tomorrow at five?

This was a concern she unknowingly shared with State Representative Monica Moorehouse, who at this moment was asking herself a very similar question: Was it too late now for the story to make a political splash? And for God's sake, *where* was that cache of Mexicans? All those cable news people on their way, Monica thought, and not one illegal alien to show them!

This singular lack of aliens was also what had Arvin Holloway frantic and furious and cursing in church—but goddamn it, how was he going to justify the expense of a daylong siege, all that overtime, bringing in extra men from LeFlore County? How could he jail Sweet Kirkendall for harboring illegal aliens if nobody could find the damn aliens she'd been harboring? Most urgent of all, how was Sheriff Arvin A. Holloway expected to achieve the one main fundamental purpose of this whole dadblamed operation— that is, find out where the Mexican man had stashed the missing kid—if he couldn't find the dadblamed Mexican!

"What are you looking at?" he barked at Beecham as he stomped past—he'd kept Darrell Beecham here where he could keep an eye on him—and the big deputy shrugged. Holloway marched to the mouth of the short hallway leading to the old building. "Y'all quit horsing around in there and bring me something I can use, goddamn it!" he hollered, then whirled around and yelled at the preacher: "Don't get up on your high horse with me! I'll cuss when I need to!" The sheriff stomped back to the front of Fellowship Hall.

His fury was intensified by a single suppressed fact he could admit to no one, including his own dimly conscious self: *he* was the one who'd left the rear side door unguarded when he sent Beecham to Wilburton to fetch Bob Brown. It was such a glaring stupidity on his part that Holloway's mind refused it. His mind assured him that the Mexican was still hiding in the old church house someplace. He resumed his pacing and cursing, muttering foully under his breath as he mulled the possibility of arresting Sweet Kirkendall for manslaughter in the death of the old man Horace Bledsoe. He couldn't rely on hearsay, though; he'd have to have facts, the autopsy report, testimony, well, he could get all that, sure, but it was going to take time—and anyway, how was that going to help him find the lost kid? Just then Holloway caught sight of the state representative edging toward the news people at the back of the room. "What the hell do *you* want!" he hollered.

Well, this was perhaps an apt question, but not one Monica Moorehouse could have publicly answered, even had she been so inclined. Which she was not. She stopped, flustered, at a rare loss for words. All eyes were turned to her. It's probable that no one except the representative herself heard the little whirring click as the cameraman switched his camera back on, but Monica Moorehouse heard. She stared in midair. She stammered. She struggled. Helplessly she searched for the proper calm, confident, self-deprecating answer. Her mind was utterly blank.

"Get back over there by the door!" the sheriff bellowed. "I'll have you arrested!"

The representative, incensed, immediately found her tongue. "On what charge?"

"Trespassing, public nuisance, and interfering with an officer!"

"Do you know who I am?"

"I don't give a shit who you are!"

"Arvin, please," the pastor said. "Your language."

Tap, tap, tap, tap. Monica turned to see her husband outside the glass doors, motioning her fiercely to come out. *What!* she mouthed at him. *Let's go, babe, this instant!* his fleshy face said, a study in urgency and excitement. For the briefest of moments, Monica Moorehouse was torn. The camera was on. She could have ripped that fool sheriff apart, rhetorically speaking, but there was some kind of gleaming triumph in Charlie's eyes. At the back of the room the camera operator lifted his platinum umbrella reflector. Instinctively she turned her cheekbones to catch the light. "Goodness, Sheriff Holloway," she said brightly as she edged backward toward the glass doors, "it appears you've misunderstood. As a representative of the People's House here in this great state of Oklahoma, I've simply come to *thank you* for your service. For having the *courage* to uphold the state's laws, no matter *who* transgresses them, no matter how *personally difficult* the circumstances might be . . ." Monica swept the room with her most charming, self-deprecating smile. "The people of Oklahoma appreciate our public servants, we really do. Don't we?" The people at the tables stared back at her. With a final well-practiced, open-palm side-to-side wave, she stepped out.

In the backseat of the deputy's cruiser, Sweet's mind churned—had the kids made it? She hadn't seen any sign to the contrary. She'd watched the deputies shoving her shackled daddy into the sheriff's car, surely she would have seen if they'd caught Misty Dawn and Juanito, too. She had wanted to give them more time, and she would have, truly, if Carl Albert hadn't come tearing across the yard. She remembered that moment, her son's body hitting her full force. She remembered looking over his shuddering head at her husband. Who was going to take care of their son when she got sent to prison? Terry would have custody, yes, but Terry worked all the time. Who was going to watch Carl Albert the sixty or more hours a week his dad was in the gas fields? She thought of Vicki Dudley. Among all the women she knew, the preacher's wife would be the best choice. But Vicki might not want to. She might not be available. She might, in fact, be in as bad a fix as anyone if Brother Oren got charged with a felony, too. Would they do that? Sweet wondered. Hopefully not. Not the good, sweet-tempered pastor of Cedar First Baptist, and the two senior deacons, and those four powdery little ladies from WMU . . . but Sweet had seen the uncontrolled rage of Arvin Holloway, how he'd roared *Halt, halt, goddamnit!* and pointed his busted bullhorn at Carl Albert like an enormous fat pistol he'd like to use to blast the boy off the earth. There was no telling, Sweet thought, what Arvin Holloway might do.

Numbly she watched as the khaki-headed representative emerged from Fellowship Hall and followed her froggy-eyed husband back to their giant SUV. Another pickup pulled in, and a young woman got out and hurried along the sidewalk toward the brightly lit doors. Sweet's gaze followed her, barely registering that it was the girl from the front desk at the Latimer County Jail. Her mind returned to its worn circles. Had she waited long enough before coming out? She had tried, she told herself. Hadn't she tried? She had done what she could . . .

"Watonga," Monica said from behind the steering wheel. She massaged her forehead. "Where's that?"

"An hour northwest of Oklahoma City."

"Oh, Charlie," she moaned, "that's four hours. I don't know if I can make that drive again."

"You can."

"How about we go home to McAlester, get some sleep, and leave early tomorrow?"

"They've got the kid, they've got the Mexican, the media's all halfway there by now! I called Tim Cunningham, told him to meet the network teams at the Tulsa airport and drive them straight out to Watonga. You can't miss this, babe."

Monica pinched her cheek, tried to keep from rubbing her eyes. "I'll drive," Charlie said, and shoved open the door on his side. "*I'll* drive!" she said. Her husband shut his door, hit the laptop refresh button. Monica glanced along the dark empty Main Street toward the highway. "Please tell me we can get a cup of coffee *some*place in this godforsaken town."

"Watonga," Cheryl repeated to the sheriff. "They said he's suffering from exposure and a sprained arm but otherwise he appears to be okay."

"Praise God," Ida Coley murmured.

"Praise Jesus," Claudie Ott echoed.

Oren Dudley looked across the room at his wife. Her look said, *See? I told you everything was going to be fine.* At the second table, Lon Jones sat with his head bowed, his shoulders shaking with silent sobs of relief. The preacher could feel his own emotions welling: relief, yes, and gratitude, and a piercing tenderness deep in his chest. He closed his eyes. *Thank you,* he said.

"The call came in, like, forty minutes ago?" Cheryl was saying. "I couldn't get you on the radio or whatever, so I just drove over. I figured you'd want to know."

Sheriff Arvin Holloway said nothing. He was stunned beyond
fury, beyond indignation, beyond self-justification, resentment,
rage—all that would come later. Without a word he walked out
of Fellowship Hall, across the trampled strip of muddy yard to his
cruiser, and got in.

Sweet watched the sheriff's car in the stillness that followed. She
couldn't see her father in the backseat, though she knew he was
there. Probably cold, like she was, probably sore around the wrists.
The glass doors opened again, and the young brunette reporter
and her cameraman fumbled their way out with their equipment,
rushed toward the news van. The sheriff started his car. So they
were taking her daddy back to jail, Sweet thought. She supposed
the deputy would be here in a minute to transport her, too. She
would be one of those mothers in orange jumpsuits visiting with
their children in the county jail yard. At least until her trial was
over, that's where she'd be. Until she got convicted and sent to the
McAlester state pen. If that's where they even sent felons like her.
Maybe not. Maybe they had special places for women where their
kids could come visit without having to stand around outside in
the heat and cold.

Part Four

Postlude

ONE WEEK LATER

I kept feeling like I was waiting for something, but I didn't know what. Every time I went to the window and twisted the blinds open, there wasn't nothing outside to see. Our whole town looked dead. "Dead as a mackerel." My cousin Carl Albert used to always say that. When me and Aunt Sweet got home from Watonga Monday evening, there was a white news van parked in her yard like the one me and Señor Celayo seen at Misty Dawn's house. Aunt Sweet wouldn't talk to them though, she squirreled us right past into the carport, and after a while the van left. Now nobody bothers us. The house stays more quiet than you could ever imagine. Sweet keeps the sound down on the TV. I said, "Is that lady from the human sources office going to be there when we go see Grandpa?"

"What?" Aunt Sweet said. "Oh. No, of course not. It's human services, hon. Department of Human Services. Please quit messing with those things."

I quit twisting the blinds open and closed and just left them closed and came over to the divan. "How do you know?" I said.

"She won't be there. Sit down, Dustin. Nobody's going to make you go live someplace else."

"How do you know?"

"That judge in Watonga gave his ruling, hon. You heard him. You'll stay here till Daddy gets out."

"When's that going to be?"

"Honey, I told you. We just have to wait and see." She got vague again, staring off at the TV, flicking at the little thumb tabs on the Bible she was holding in her lap. Genesis Exodus Leviticus Numbers Deuteronomy Joshua Judges Ruth . . . I learned them all straight through to Revelation in Vacation Bible School last summer. They gave me a prize, a new Youth Bible and a fake sword. I said, "Is Carl Albert going to be there?"

Aunt Sweet set the Bible on the coffee table, got up and left the room. In a minute I heard the popcorn in the microwave. I try not to say my cousin's name out loud, but sometimes I forget. Part of me sort of hopes Carl Albert might be at the fence when we go to the jail yard tomorrow, and part of me hopes not. For one thing, I don't know if him staying in Poteau with his dad is something else I'm going to have to tell Grandpa. There's a bunch of things I'm going to have to tell him when I see him, including lying, cussing, and stealing. I've been thinking about that a lot.

The cans of pork 'n' beans and other stuff I took from Aunt Sweet's pantry and the map I got out of her glove box and the coin jar I swiped from her dresser drawer—I'm going to pay all that back. Twenty-seven dollars and thirteen cents, me and Señor Celayo counted it. Everything else, though, that's going to be hard. The bike's gone, the preacher's knife's gone, and my cousin's brand-new *Cars* backpack.

When Aunt Sweet came in from the kitchen, her eyes were red, and her nose, too, and she had a wadded-up Kleenex in one hand. She handed me a plastic bowl. I didn't really want any popcorn, but I took it so she wouldn't feel worse than she already looked like she felt. There are a lot of things different now—how quiet the

house is, no Uncle Terry and no Mr. Bledsoe, no dodging the secret hand-pops from my cousin, no arguing with him in the bathroom when we're brushing our teeth—but the biggest difference is
Aunt Sweet herself. She's nicer than she ever used to be. She lets
me stay up till practically midnight, watching TV. She never says
no reading under the covers. Half the time she even forgets to tell
me to brush my teeth. Staying here wouldn't be so bad, except I'd
just rather be home.

I said, "Can we go out to the farm in the morning?"

"We'll see."

"Don't I need clothes to wear to church?"

"I haven't made up my mind yet to go to church."

I cut my eyes over. I never knew Aunt Sweet to just purpose-
fully miss church. Maybe she don't want to go because she feels
bad about missing Mr. Bledsoe's funeral. They had it at First Baptist. I know that because the preacher came by real late the night
we got home from Watonga and told that to Aunt Sweet. He said
it was a nice turnout, and Uncle Terry and Carl Albert seemed to
hold up real well. Aunt Sweet said she was glad to hear it, but she
still didn't ask him to come in. He stood under the porch light
smoothing his hair over the top of his head with his hand. After a
minute, he said, "Well, if you need anything," and she said, "We'll
be fine. But thank you. For everything. Really. I can't thank you
enough." The preacher sort of craned his neck then to see around
her. "You doing all right, buddy?" he said. "Good," I said. "Well,
we're all . . . real glad to see you home." He kept standing there
like he still wanted to say something. Then he blinked a couple of
times and went back down off the steps, and Aunt Sweet shut the
front door and turned off the porch light and she hasn't opened the
front door any more since.

The reason Aunt Sweet didn't get to go to Mr. Bledsoe's funeral

is because she had to be at family court in Watonga with me. That
human sources lady was there, too, the one that drove me over
from the hospital. The lady kept trying to talk to me, she said she
was on my side, she was just there to help me, and I guess she was
nice and all, except she really frowned when the judge said I could
go home with Aunt Sweet. That's why I don't trust her. I was worried she might be at the Wilburton courthouse, too, when we went
up there for Señor Celayo's hearing on Thursday, but she turned
out not to be. The preacher was there though. He's the one who
came in and told us what happened at Grandpa's hearing.

They had all three hearings in Wilburton last Thursday, for
Brother Jesus and my grandpa and Señor Celayo, but me and Aunt
Sweet didn't get to see Grandpa then because I had to be a witness
at Señor Celayo's hearing, and the district attorney said witnesses
aren't allowed to come in until it's time for them to talk, so he
made me stay in his office at the end of the hall. Aunt Sweet stayed
with me. She wanted to go in and watch Grandpa's preliminary,
but it got finished too fast. Before we hardly knew it, Brother Oren
was standing at the office door saying they were letting Brother
Jesus go, but they were keeping my grandpa, and Aunt Sweet got
really upset. "What for?" she said, and the preacher said, "Well,
felony assault," and Aunt Sweet said, "Are you kidding me?" and
the preacher said, "Well, no." So then Aunt Sweet went out to talk
to the district attorney and Brother Oren stayed with me and we
played tic-tac-toe on a piece of paper the secretary gave us until
Aunt Sweet came back.

"Is Brother Oren going to the jail with us tomorrow?" I said.

"Not that I know of. You want something to drink?"

She didn't wait for me to answer, just got up and went to the
kitchen. I heard the icebox door open. Then the dishwasher started.
Aunt Sweet says we'll get on a regular schedule about eating after I

start back to school. I don't know when she's going to make me do that. I didn't ask her yet. I sort of don't want to bring the subject up. In a minute she came in with two Dr Peppers. She popped the rings on both cans, took a drink of hers, and set it down next to her popcorn bowl. I keep thinking how lonesome she's going to be when Grandpa gets out and me and him go back to live at the farm. But maybe if I could get the bike back, Carl Albert might come home and not be mad, and maybe even Uncle Terry, and then everything will go back to being how it's supposed to be.

The trouble is, I don't know where that mountain bike's at. I remember riding it away from the ditch after the truck boiled over. Señor Celayo pumped the pedals and I rode on the seat with my feet out to keep them from getting caught in the spokes. After I got sick, though, I don't remember everything. I remember we stopped and camped in the nighttime. I remember my throat hurt and Señor Celayo tried to get me to drink some water and the sky was really black. I remember my mom being there. That's the best thing I remember. Sometimes I could hear her, like when I used to listen at the cemetery, but after a while it wasn't her voice anymore but just a feeling like she was sitting beside me, watchful, like an angel, except not white and with wings and glowing like you see in the pictures but more dark and soft, like a shadow, but I don't mean something bad by shadow, just something good and nice and warm. Like sleeping in the bed next to her when I was a little kid.

"Dustin," Aunt Sweet said. "Please leave that alone." I quit rolling the doily and smoothed it out flat. My chest was hurting. I had that feeling again, like I was waiting for something. Aunt Sweet leaned over and set the Bible on top of the doily. "Finish your popcorn now and then go get in the shower," she said. "I want you to wash your hair this evening. Can you do that with your arm?"

"I think so."

"Here," she said, and took my arm and unwrapped the stretchy bandage and rolled it up and laid it on the coffee table so it wouldn't get wet. She pressed a little on the top of my wrist. "Swelling's about gone. How does it feel?"

"Okay."

"Then go get your shower and come in the kitchen when you finish. I'm going to trim that shaggy mop." I didn't move. "You want to see your grandpa tomorrow?" she said. I nodded. Aunt Sweet tugged my hair at the back where it's been getting long. "Well, you're not going up there with this mess." I stood up to take my bowl and pop can to the kitchen. "Rinse your head good!" she called after me. "Put on one of Carl Albert's old T-shirts!"

So I went and took a shower and thought about everything. I thought about my cousin. If he's at the jail fence tomorrow, he's going to jump me for wearing his clothes, I know it. I'd rather just go out to the farm in the morning and get my own. Not to mention what he's going to do when he finds out I stole his bike and his new backpack. I could tell him I only meant to borrow them, not steal them, but I don't think that'll do any good. Maybe I could ask Aunt Sweet not to tell him it was me that took them. But then that would be like trying to get her to lie, too. All the lying I been doing, that's the main thing I'm dreading about tomorrow. I *want* to see my grandpa, I feel like I can't hardly wait to see him, but it still makes me kind of sick to think about.

I tried telling the truth. I told it to the sheriff in his office the night me and Aunt Sweet got home from Watonga. I told him it was my idea to go to Tulsa. I said I was the one that swiped the food and the preacher's knife and the map and the coin jar, but he just stomped around and cussed worse than I ever heard a grown man cuss, and then he stuck a pad of yellow paper in front of me and started telling me stuff to write down that never actually happened. So I figured if the sheriff wouldn't believe me, nobody else would either, including the judge at the Wilburton courthouse when we went up there for Señor Celayo's hearing. I've been trying to tell myself it wasn't real true lying I did, or maybe it was just a little white lie, but I can hear it in my mind anyway, my grandpa's voice in the jail yard tomorrow: You know that don't make any difference, son. There's no such thing as a white lie or a little sin.

There are holes in the wall near the floor where the rats run. The room is crowded, dark, the stink bad. But Luis will be here only a few days more, the woman lawyer has told him. Only until the deportation papers are completed; then he will be put on the bus back to Mexico. Luis hopes she is correct. Though the sadness is strong in him, because he has not been able to see his sons, nevertheless, to return to Arroyo Seco will be better than to stay in this place. The stench here is very bad—more bad than the first jail, where the officers in the tan uniforms first put him. More bad even than the second jail, where the police drove many hours to deliver him. They took Luis from the van in handcuffs and delivered him to the gringo sheriff, who walked him along a midnight blue hallway and locked him in a concrete cell alone.

The second jail was where the woman lawyer first came to talk with him. She said that Luis must go to the court the next day and stand before a judge—not for the crime of entering the United States illegally, she said, but for kidnapping the boy and stealing the old truck. Luis asked her what would be the punishment for such crimes. *For stealing the truck,* she said in her clumsy spanish, *many years in the prison. For stealing the boy, maybe the whole of your life*. She shrugged, her shoulders large, her face calm. *But first it must be determined that a crime has been committed. This is the purpose of the preliminary hearing. I will see you in the courtroom tomorrow.* Luis protested then, telling her that he had no money to pay her. *No worries*, she said. *In this country, the law is the law.* Then she left him before Luis could think to ask her about the boy, if he was well, if he was still in the hospital.

In the courtroom the next day, the lawyer talked quietly, continuously, in his ear, making all the translations, and Luis could find no good opportunity to ask about the boy. Her spanish was thick, harshly accented, but clear enough for Luis to understand that the testimony did not go well for him. One police sat in the chair beside the judge and told of finding the truck of the grandfather in the arroyo. Another officer told of arresting Luis in the hospital room where the boy lay very sick. The woman indian doctor told how the boy arrived at the clinic with so much sickness it was necessary to carry him to the hospital. The boy suffered from pneumonia, the doctor said, a bad throat infection, insufficient food, insufficient water, too much cold, an injured wrist. *Yes*, she repeated each time the large man asked the question: *Yes, the defendant, Mister Celayo, was present in the hospital room with the boy.*

 Luis remembers his confusion when all the people in the courtroom turned their heads at the same moment, and so Luis also turned to look, and there, beside the door, stood the boy, with the aunt beside him, her hand upon his shoulder. The boy appeared so small and thin, his clothes too large for him, his hair combed to the side and slicked down. The boy walked alone across the sunlit floor, cradling his bandaged arm. Luis had felt a little sad, but also fearful, because the boy would not look at him as he stood beside the judge with his good hand raised, swearing to tell the truth, all the truth, and only the truth, with the help of God.

Then the large man in the gray suit with the great mane of gray hair stood in front of the boy. He spoke very kindly, asking the simple questions: What is your name? How many years have you? Where do you live? All this the lawyer translated for Luis. The gray man asked the boy where he had been on the night of february twenty this year.

I dont know, the boy answered.

¿Do you remember that night? the gray man asked.

I dont know, the boy said.

It was a wednesday. Two weeks ago. The twenty of february. ¿Do you remember now?

I think so.

¿What happened to you that night?

Nothing. You mean my arm?

Well, yes, all right, we can start with your arm. ¿What happened to your arm?

I hurt it.

How?

I fell off the bike.

The gray man frowned, walked over to his table, looked down at some papers. *¿And what happened after you fell off your bike?* he said.

It was not my bike, it belongs to my cousin.

All right. And what happened after you fell off the bike of your cousin?

I decided to drive the truck of my grandfather to Tulsa.

Then the gray man really frowned. He looked again at the papers, moved them around on the table. His voice, when he spoke again, was not so sympathetic: *¿Did you make a report to the sheriff about the events of that night?*

I guess, the boy said. *He was asking me questions.*

The gray man carried to the boy a piece of paper. *Is this your signature?*

Yes.

Ask that the record reflect the witness has identified his own signature on the Latimer County Sheriff Report.

The record so reflect, the clerk said.

¿And what did you tell the sheriff about what happened that night? the gray man asked

Luis remembers how the boy sat without moving, and still he would not look at Luis, and his voice when he answered was so soft that the judge said he must speak more loudly. In a high clear voice then, the boy said, *I dont remember.*

¿Did you tell the sheriff that you rode in the truck with someone?

I might have said a person rode with me.

All right. ¿Who rode in the truck with you?

Mister Celayo.

¿And is Mister Celayo in the room today?

Yes.

¿Could you show the court which person he is?

The boy lifted his good arm and pointed at Luis. *There*, he said.

Ask that the record reflect the witness has identified the defendant.

The record so reflect.

Then the man in the gray suit asked another question, but Luis was not able to know the question because beside him the woman lawyer jumped up quickly, very red in the face, her hair brown, her shoulders big. The woman called out many rapid words in english. There was a quick, sharp conversation between her and the man in gray and also the judge, until finally the lawyer sat down. She was not happy with what the gray man said, what the judge said. She no longer translated for Luis but stood again and again to say *Ob-jeck-shun! Ob-jeck-shun!* But the man in the gray suit continued, and the judge did not stop him. Then the woman lawyer began once again to tell Luis in her flat american voice what the boy was saying—but not in whispers; she said the words very loud:

Yes, this was my own idea, she said the boy said. *I am the person who drove the truck to Tulsa. I am also the person who drove the truck into the arroyo when the radiator broke. Yes, sir, I am the person. I am not lying. I know how to drive. I have been driving the truck of my grandfather for many years. Yes, sir, I know what it means to swear on the Bible. But I tell you the truth. If someone must be charged with stealing the truck of my grandfather, this should be me.*

The judge was frowning. The man in the gray suit was frowning. All around the crowded courtroom many people were frowning. The man in the gray suit returned to the table, grabbed up a paper, waved it at the boy. He said in a cold voice, *¿What did you declare to the sheriff in this signed affidavit about where the defendant took you?*

¿The defendant?

Mister Celayo.

The defendant didnt take me. This was my own idea. To transport the illegal mexican man myself.

The face of the gray man became very red. *You transported the illegal alien yourself,* he repeated, looking not at the boy but all around the courtroom, as if he could not believe such crazy words. Then he came close to the boy, stood over him, very large and sweating, his face red, his voice loud. *¿And just how was this smuggling operation of yours financed, little boy?*

I stole the money from my aunt.

¡You stole—! ¿Your Honor, may I approach?

Then the woman lawyer too was standing in front of the judge with the man in gray; they were talking, talking, and the boy remained very quiet in the chair beside them, very somber, staring straight ahead with his face that was too old for such a young boy. No one was nearby to translate for Luis. He sat at the table inside the bell of silence of one who does not understand the words being spoken around him. Then the boy turned his gaze. The english voices went on chittering and clicking very loud, but Luis and the boy greeted each other in silence. No expression passed between them, no smile or nod or gesture, but the silent greeting leaped across the sun-swept room, from the boy to Luis, and back again: *Hello, friend. It is well. No problem.* Okay.

Sweet checked the fridge again. Whether she liked it or not, she was going to have to go to the store. They'd been living on canned tuna and frozen pizza and macaroni and cheese all week, but now they were out of almost everything. Well, she'd go tomorrow, after they visited Daddy. Oh, she dreaded it, though—the thought of people's eyes watching her in the aisles at Roy's as she pushed the cart. Watching Dustin. Coming over and trying to get him to talk. But maybe they wouldn't. People around here were mostly decent that way. Or maybe she could just let him wait in the car. But she couldn't keep him protected forever, they couldn't stay cooped up in this house together forever. They had to live in the world. She listened a moment toward the hall. The shower was still running. Well. Maybe they could get by a few days more. She went to the pantry to see if she had powdered milk and cornbread mix. The phone rang. After seven o'clock on a Saturday evening, who could be calling except a reporter, or . . . She rushed to the counter to grab the phone.

"Hey." Misty Dawn's faint bored voice. "Aunt Sweet? It's me."

"I'm glad you called, don't hang up! But don't say anything, okay?"

"Huh?"

"Like location. Or any certain person's name."

"Oh," Misty said, and then after a beat. "Right, okay."

It wasn't probable her phone was tapped, but Sweet couldn't be sure. She felt like she couldn't be sure of anything. "How's it going?" she said.

"Okay, sort of."

"How's the baby?"

"She's okay."

"I'm really glad to hear from you. I was worried. Hey, we've got good news here, you know it? Dustin's home. And things are looking better for Daddy. Or he's got a lawyer anyway. And they dropped the harboring charge. So now it's just, you know, that assault charge, but the lawyer says—"

"Assault? What assault?"

"Oh, just . . . never mind. We're working on it." Arvin Holloway had been furious when the D.A. dropped the harboring charges, even though it was Holloway himself who'd screwed up the paperwork, a bad warrant or something. Naturally he'd thrown the book at Daddy for what he *could* charge him with— felony aggravated assault with a dangerous weapon, which it turned out was way worse than harboring illegal aliens. Her daddy could get sent to prison for ten years, the lawyer said, just for jumping on Terry, but who could even blame him for that, really? Well, a lot of people, actually, the lawyer said. Not to mention the whole scene had been caught on camera. So that was the main problem right now—whether to take the plea bargain or let her daddy take a chance on going to trial. Well, and also the problem of where was she going to get the money to pay for the lawyer. But of course Misty Dawn wouldn't know anything about all that, and Sweet didn't want to go into it right now. "So, y'all are doing okay, huh?"

"Not really. I mean, we're here in this lousy motel by the train—"

"Hush! Don't say anything!"

"Oh. Yeah. Okay. Anyway, you know. There's no money. We got a job though. So that's good."

"That's great."

"Just, he won't—it's going to be a while before we get paid."

"Okay." Sweet checked the caller ID, scribbled the number down on the notepad. "Can I call you at this number?"

"It's a pay phone. The Kum'n'Go on the corner by the—"

"All right!" Sweet cut her off. "Let me just think a minute." The same story, the same story, the same, same old story. "But the baby's all right?"

"Yeah. She's better since we—" This time Misty Dawn caught herself. "Yeah, she's doing good."

"Tell you what, you be at this number nine o'clock Monday morning. I'll call ya. I'll have something figured out by then."

"Monday. That's a long time."

"A day and a half."

Silence on the other end.

"It's the best I can do. There's a lot going on here."

"Yeah, okay." More silence.

"What?" Sweet said.

"Just. We were wondering. All our stuff's at the house."

"What?"

"You know, all our clothes and, well, everything. Everything we own."

The jewel-colored towels folded and stacked by size. The worn, blanket-draped loveseat. The small, dim portable TV.

"We thought maybe you could go up and get it?" Misty said.

"The rent's been due like three weeks. The landlord will probably just haul it off, or keep it. It's everything we got in the world."

"Why don't you have your friends in Tulsa go get it? That Bianca woman."

"They can't. They're not there. Actually, they're down here with us, that's how Juan—how we got a job."

"I can't be seen going in there! No. Just leave it. You can get new stuff. It's not like it's worth anything."

"Our marriage license is there, Concepción's birth certificate. All her baby pictures."

"Oh, Misty."

A sudden coin-dropping mechanical sound, followed by a digital female voice: *Please deposit three dollars for the next minute.* "I gotta go. I don't have any more quarters. Please, Aunt Sweet? I won't ask for anything else, I promise." *Please deposit three dollars for the next minute.* "We need our stuff! We got to be able to prove our baby was born here! You never know from one second to the next if—"

"Misty? Hello?" Sweet pushed the disconnect bar a few times, though she knew the line was dead. She stood blinking at the blank caller ID a moment before she finally thought to redial the number. It rang and rang.

A man's voice answered. "Hello."

"Is, is Misty there?"

"Who?"

"Um, a girl, Misty. She's tall, got long sandy—"

"This is a pay phone, lady. I don't see nobody around."

Saturday | March 8, 2008 | 7:30 P.M.

National Cowboy and Western Heritage Museum
Oklahoma City

Monica steered the Escalade through the asphalt lot of the Cowboy Hall of Fame, as the locals all seemed to still call the place, even years after its name had been changed to something more sophisticated and tourism worthy. She squeezed her SUV between a Lexus and a Mercedes and parked. In the moonish dome light, she checked her hair in the rearview, tugged her bangs down with her fingers, plucked up the crown. Kevin was punishing her. For what reason, she couldn't fathom, but she was certain that he was—and right here before her presentation, too, the traitor. She reached into the passenger seat for her clutch bag.

Two things came immediately to her attention as she stood in line at the check-in table near the museum gift shop. One was that she was overdressed. Or underdressed, rather. Beneath her teal jacket, Monica's shoulders were bare. She'd have to keep her jacket on. The invitation had said business attire, and she had assumed that a simple knee-length cocktail dress would be fine. But as she scanned the people milling about inside the huge entry hall, she realized that everyone, male and female alike, wore some version of a dull gray or black dress-for-success business suit, the men with muted ties, the women in straight skirts and black pumps. She did *not* want to walk up to the podium in the spotlight wearing a quilted jacket. Damn. She should have checked with Charlie. But Charlie was in Denver at a Thunder basketball game, and until this moment, as she stood smiling at the middle-aged frump checking names off the guest list, Monica had been only too glad.

The other attention grabber—and this one was equally disconcerting—was the sight of Senator Dennis Langley talking to someone in front of the gigantic End of the Trail sculpture framed inside the glass atrium on the far side of the entrance hall. Tall as the senator was, he and the man he was talking with were dwarfed to pygmy size by the gargantuan droopy Indian on his sad lank-necked horse. What was Langley doing here? This was not a legislative event but the Oklahoma Spirit/Devon Energy Business Excellence Awards Banquet, where Monica was to have the honor of presenting the prestigious Outstanding Oklahoma Woman Entrepreneur of the Year Award. She seriously doubted the lanky lawyer was being so honored. She paused to grab a glass of white wine off the wine table before heading over.

"Hello, Senator. You're looking rather perky this evening." A subtle dig at his laconic slouch—he looked nearly as droopy as the giant Indian he stood under. "Thank you, ma'am," he drawled. "I'll say the same for you." She turned her smile to the old gentleman standing next to him, silver haired, handsome; the face seemed vaguely familiar. The man touched two fingers to his forehead as if touching a hat brim, and at once Monica remembered who he was—the old guy in the duster eating alone at the counter at Cattlemen's. *You're costing me a helluva lot of money, lady. You don't know what you're messing with.* Oh, good heavens, that rude man. "You know Buck Sherman, I guess," Langley said.

Oh no, Monica thought. Don't tell me. "Why, yes, of course. How do you do, Mr. Sherman? Good to see you again."

The old man didn't bother to grace her with a greeting, merely nodded, excused himself, and wandered over to the wine table.

"Me and Buck go way back," Langley said.

Of course you do, Monica thought.

"He's set to receive the Private Capital Investors Award this evening. I'm here as a guest at his table."

"How nice." She'd heard the name countless times, of course, just hadn't had a face to go with it. Why hadn't Charlie recognized him that night at the restaurant and told her who he was? Because, she thought, Charlie was too preoccupied with his damn porter-house steak. Well, it could be amended; such little gaffes could always be amended. She would speak to him at some point this evening, think of something charming to say to smooth his old feathers. She took a discreet sip of wine and turned to survey the crowd. All those dress-for-success suits spilling down the long east corridor toward the banquet hall. She wanted to plunge in, start greeting people, shaking hands, but she abhorred walking around smiling at strangers without knowing what her hair looked like. She glanced around for a ladies' room.

"I guess congratulations are in order," the senator said. "This has been a successful week for you, I understand."

"Well, some are saying that," she demurred. I should say so, she thought. The final version of House Bill 1906 had passed by a good margin, even after the kerfuffle with the opposition trying to put in their watered-down twist. Her failure to recapture hadn't mattered in the long run; the bill had passed undiluted, with just that little adjustment she'd had to make in the English Only provision to mollify the tribes. Charlie and Leadership were confident the governor would sign. Her new law would go into effect next fall, the first day of November—four days before the election. She'd be sitting pretty again, just like Charlie said, by the time her constituents went to the polls.

"History moves fast, doesn't it?" Langley said, apropos of nothing. "Hard to predict which side of it a person's going to end up on."

Monica held her gritted smile. He was implying, of course, that *she* was going to end up on the wrong side of history. Look around, buddy, she thought. That person would be *you*, I believe.

"Take Buck Sherman over there." Langley bobbed his plastic drink glass toward the old guy, surrounded now by a clutch of balding middle-aged men. "Always been a successful rancher, big-time oil speculator and landowner, but I don't believe I would have ever predicted, back when he started buying up all these natural gas leases from here to Pennsylvania, that he'd someday end up one of the wealthiest men in the country. No more than I might have predicted things would turn out like they did in Latimer County the other day." Langley coughed a short laugh. "Old Tom Waters surely didn't predict it. Never seen the guy so flummoxed. Of course, no smart D.A. goes into preliminary without knowing every word that's going to be said, and Waters is one very smart D.A. But I don't guess anybody could have seen that coming."

"You're saying the district attorney didn't expect that little boy to get up on the witness stand and lie?"

"You think he was lying?"

Hell, yes, he was lying. "Well," she said neutrally, "it's difficult to imagine a ten-year-old coming up with the idea to smuggle an illegal alien by himself."

Langley's lazy drawl drenched her. "I suppose so, ma'am. If you believe that's what happened. And then that federal judge handing down his injunction the same morning, now, wouldn't that gripe you? Looks like a good chunk of that bill of yours is going to be on hold till these lawsuits make their way through the court system. That's liable to take a few years. I don't expect it'll be much of a problem for you in November, though. People's memories are short," he said in that infuriatingly slow, musing tone. "Except when they're long."

"I don't foresee any problems, Senator." She couldn't keep the nastiness out of her voice. "But thank you for your concern."

"We may be on opposite sides of the aisle, ma'am . . ."

. . . but we serve the same constituents, blah, blah, blah, Monica finished in silent unison. Oh, she had half a mind to follow Charlie's advice and go after Langley's senate seat next fall—just to wipe that smug smile off his face! There was no doubt she could trounce him. But her plans did *not* include four more years of Mason pie suppers and 4-H calf judging contests! Two additional years in the state legislature, she promised herself, and then the run for Congress. That was it. That was *it*. Washington, D.C., she thought, here I come.

"Some folks were glad enough about that injunction. Buck Sherman sure was. Lot of folks from the Chamber. Others, though . . . probably not so much. Can I get you another drink, ma'am?"

"No, thanks. If you'll excuse me." She walked away from Langley, away from the crowd, set her empty wineglass on a table and picked up a full one and continued along the empty west corridor in the opposite direction of the gathering, gliding smoothly past floor-to-ceiling portraits of John Wayne and Roy Rogers and Clint Eastwood toward the ladies' room at the far, quiet end where she could tend to her hair and makeup and finish her drink in peace.

Oh, she never should have stopped to talk to him! The man wasn't capable of just pleasantly passing the time of day; he always had to throw in his little aw-shucks-ma'am digs. Well, who the

hell *could* have predicted things would turn out like that? Who
in their right mind would have ever dreamed it? The D.A. and
that fool idiot sheriff—they were the problem! How unthink-
ing could Tom Waters be, to load all three preliminaries on the
same docket? Maybe he'd thought it would be his big fat day to
shine, but look what a mess happened—all those rumors flying,
all those unanswered questions, because somebody leaked it to
the press that there was a problem with the search warrant, that
Arvin Holloway had conducted the raid on Brown's farm without
a warrant in the first place, and then cobbled one together after
the fact—and that cowardly D.A. dropped the harboring charges
before the hearing even got started! All that *Breaking News* hysteria when the Mexican pastor was released. Monica hadn't been
there, of course—it was only supposed to be the freaking preliminary, not the end of the whole case!—but she'd seen enough news
reports to feel like she'd been there: those endless clips of the ro-
tund little pastor coming down the courthouse steps in a suit and
tie, smiling and squinting, and the old grandfather in handcuffs
being walked in a classic perp walk back across the alley to the
jail. At least they'd held on to *him*. Although not for the reason he
should have been held. Not for violating the provisions of her bill!

Monica walked into the empty ladies' room, went directly to
the softly lit mirror covering the wall above the sinks. There's
such a thing as good confluence, she thought, and then there's
shitty confluence—and last Thursday was the worst of the worst.
All those repeated news clips, plus the horrid courtroom sketches
on every blooming channel: the tiny long-haired boy on the witness stand with the giant prosecutor rearing over him, and the
hunched-over Mexican prisoner sitting at the defense table looking old and frail and confused—oh, why on earth would they
allow a sketch artist in a preliminary hearing? Who ever heard

of such a thing? And then that stupid federal injunction issued by that stupid activist federal judge the very same morning!

Which was all for show, she told herself. Because the employer E-Verify provision *would* be upheld in federal court, regardless of what fat cat businessmen like Buck Sherman thought! The constitutionality of every provision of House Bill 1830 would be upheld, and the *new* provisions of her *new* law, too—English Only, asset seizure, the requirement for schools to report undocumented students—they would *all* be upheld! She didn't give a snot *how* many lawsuits those smart-aleck ACLU lawyers filed! *Or* the State Chamber of Commerce, *or* the Oklahoma Restaurant Association, or the Oklahoma Hotel and Tourism—oh, it was infuriating! It was disgusting. It was unthinkable, actually, and she simply wasn't going to think about it anymore.

Monica took a long drink of wine, set her glass on the marble counter above the sink, frowned at her hair. No two ways about it. Kevin was punishing her. But why? He wouldn't return her calls, hadn't been home to her knock for almost a week now, even when his Jetta was parked in the drive. And when she called the shop, he was always busy—booked, booked, *booked*! the receptionist said, but she could fit Monica in with Ginger or Patrice, if that was okay? The fifth time that happened, Monica had shouted into the phone: "Tell that little fascist if he doesn't schedule me an appointment I'm taking my tea-vat head elsewhere, and then blabbing to the whole world he did this to me!" And so he'd squeezed her in yesterday, adjusted her color, given her a fresh cut. You wouldn't say it was a *bad* cut, there was nothing definitively *wrong* with it—it just didn't have any, well, character.

She wet her fingers, fluffed the top. The color was somewhere between plain yellow and flat gold, hardly what Kevin would have accomplished if he hadn't been so busy flirting with that new stylist Javier he'd hired for the next chair . . . oh, the hell with Kevin! She didn't want to think about that traitor. She had other more important things to think about. Her presentation in the banquet hall in a few minutes, for example—on the podium, in the spotlight, with giant sweeping western sunset canvases all around. She slipped out of her jacket, hung it on a stall door, turned to look at herself. Who cared about those business types? Her silk aquamarine dress was going to look lovely under the lights. Lovely. From her clutch bag Monica withdrew the small folded square of paper with her prepared remarks. She didn't unfold the paper but held it between her beautifully lacquered nails, staring straight ahead. She felt herself washed suddenly in dark nameless dread.

She'd been fighting the feeling for days. The empty apartment with Charlie gone didn't help. All she could think about was that there was not going to be any change-of-venue trial in McAlester this summer, no high-profile platform from which to showcase her talents—nothing, in fact, to look forward to after the end of session but the long sweltering summer stretching ahead. Rotary Club breakfast every first Tuesday. Biweekly grocery shopping trips to the Walmart. Friday nights eating out at Western Sizzlin. Charlie had promised her a cruise, but how long could that last— ten days? Two weeks? It would be months before campaign season got into full swing—months of doing nothing but trying to hide out from the miserable heat inside their mildewed grotto. She gazed at her reflection, not really seeing herself. She felt bereft, as if she'd lost her best friend. And, really, maybe she had.

No! She wouldn't look at it that way. Kevin would come around. He would! This was just a temporary little snit. It was sheer coincidence that Kevin's avoidance of her started right when those images of the kid started getting plastered all over the news. Or more likely it was the influence of that cute little

Brazilian stylist Javier. Or Puerto Rican. Or whatever the hell he was.

Furiously Monica stuffed the folded paper back inside her clutch bag. She was too keyed up to study the notes now; she would look them over during dinner. She plucked out her lipstick and comb. At least, Monica thought, uncapping her lipstick, the illegal Mexican is sitting in a holding pen in Pauls Valley this minute. He'd be on a bus back to Mexico within the month—Immigration and Customs Enforcement had assured her of that. One less law-breaking illegal alien in this state. People would remember. And anyway, Langley was right about one thing: history moves fast. Or in any case, news stories do. Already the story about the lost Brown kid was subsumed by the hysteria over rising gas prices, the presidential primaries, that woman in Idaho who'd slaughtered her kids. Monica reached for her wineglass, drained it. She narrowed her eyes at the mirror, turning her crown to catch the light. Oh, really, the color wasn't bad. A little brassy in this poor light, maybe, but she would find a new stylist to fix that.

When she emerged from the ladies' room, she momentarily panicked. Where was everyone? She peered down the long corridor toward the east wing, where servers were clearing away the wine and hors d'oeuvres tables. Oh no, oh no, she couldn't be late! Quickly Monica clicked along the echoing corridor in her new designer heels. She snatched a full wineglass from one of the caterer's serving carts as she passed it and had arrived at the entrance to the banquet hall before she realized she'd left her teal jacket on the stall door. But the crowd was already murmuring within; she could hear the seductive clink of silverware on china, wine bottles kissing crystal goblets. Never mind. She would retrieve the jacket later—after her presentation, on the podium, in the spotlight, with the enormous sweeping sunset canvases all around. Oh, what was it that she supposed to say? She had such a hard time remembering things when Charlie wasn't here to write her speeches. But she would have plenty of time at the banquet table to check her notes, surely. Monica glanced around, stepped into a recessed alcove, where a bronzed sculpture of several wild cowboys on horseback was illuminated on a mahogany display table. For a moment the dark dread rushed over her. She gulped the rest of the wine, bent down to set the empty glass on the floor behind the sculpture. She must have stood up again too quickly, she told herself, because she found herself swaying slightly as she turned to enter the great hall.

When I came back in the kitchen after my shower, Aunt Sweet had an old sheet on the floor underneath the tall wooden stool and her scissors and comb laid out on the counter. "Climb up here," she said. She put a towel around my shoulders. She walked around me a few times, combing my hair down wet over my nose and making it tickle. "All right," she said. "We'll go out to the farm in the morning and get you something decent to wear." I pushed the hair away and twisted around to look at her. "Well, if I don't take you out there," she said, "you're liable to run off again."

"No, I won't."

"You'd better not. Turn around."

I took a big breath. I tried to sit still. I had my eyes closed. "You could come stay at our house," I said. "When Grandpa gets out? We got the middle bedroom that nobody sleeps in."

"We'll see," she said and kept combing my hair down and cutting it. It felt kind of good, her combing my hair down and cutting it, over and over. Almost like I remember from when I was a little kid in Tulsa, laying in the bed next to my mom.

"Aunt Sweet? Do you remember my mom?"

The scissors stopped cutting. I could feel her in front of me, very still. I kept my eyes closed. I thought maybe if I didn't look at her. "Yes," she said after a second. "Of course. She was my sister."

"Was she part Indian?" I said.

It took her a while to say something. The scissors still hadn't started snipping. "What makes you ask that?"

"From her picture."

"I don't know, Dustin. It's possible. Anything's possible." She started cutting again.

Why don't you know, why don't you know, why don't you know. I couldn't say it out loud though. "Is she . . ." I started, but I couldn't say that, either. It was stupid.

"Is she what?"

"Never mind." I had my eyes open then, but I wasn't looking at her. Little snuffs of my hair were all over the blue flowered sheet on the floor. The words that had popped in my mind to say were: *Is she coming back?* I knew how crazy that sounded, and anyway, I knew she wasn't. That's what being dead is. But maybe she wasn't ever coming back the other way, the spirit voice way, like Señor Celayo called it. Because ever since I woke up in the hospital I haven't heard her or felt her, not once. I know that's what I been waiting for.

"Dustin." Aunt Sweet put her hand under my chin and raised it. She looked at me real slow a minute. It was like Grandpa, I had to keep looking back even if I didn't want to. Then she started cutting again. "You favor her quite a bit, did you know that?" She was making her voice light. "She was a skinny thing, like you." Combing it down, cutting, moving around the slow circle. "Gaylene was a chatterbox, though, that's one way y'all differ. And a real wigglewort. You couldn't make that kid sit still."

"What else?" I said.

"Well, um, she did good in school. In the beginning. You know, till, well, till she got older. She was a good memorizer like you are. She was stubborn. I think you take after her that way a little bit, too. God knows your sister does."

"How old was I when she brought me to Grandpa's?"

"Three and a half. And she didn't bring you. Daddy drove up to Tulsa and got you. He tried to get Misty Dawn to come, too, but she didn't want to leave her school. All her *friends*." Aunt Sweet stopped. She rubbed her eyes with the heel of her hand, the scissors sticking out away from her head. "I really don't want to talk about that old stuff, honey. Here, let's look at you a minute." And she stood back and eyeballed me, combed my hair a few times. "Pretty darned good if I do say so." She unwrapped the towel from around me real careful and used the end of it to flap at the back of my neck to get the hairs off. Then she came around and did my face. "Shut your eyes," she said, and brushed the tail of the towel on my forehead and then leaned over and blew really soft on my eyelids, flipped the towel a little again.

"How come?" I said. "How come Grandpa went to Tulsa and got me?"

"Go put that T-shirt in the hamper and get a pair of clean pajamas out of the drawer."

I didn't move and I didn't say anything.

"Dustin, go do like I said now."

I just kept sitting. I had my head down.

"That stool's liable to make for a mighty uncomfortable night's sleeping."

But I still didn't say anything. Then Aunt Sweet dropped the towel on the floor, went over to the other stool by the counter and sat. "Dustin, listen. Your mother loved you, but she couldn't take care of you. She couldn't take care of herself. Or Misty Dawn, either, for that matter. That child was snatched up by the hair of the head, which accounts for a lot. I know that. I try to take that into account."

"What does that mean, snatched up by the hair of the head?"

"She didn't have any raising. She didn't have anybody trying to help her grow up right, Misty Dawn just basically had to raise herself. Your granddaddy wasn't going to see that happen to you."

"Why didn't she have anybody?"

"Because your mother . . . had other priorities."

"What does that mean?"

"Gaylene was a lousy mother. She was no kind of mother at all."

"That's not true! Y'all think I don't remember but I do. She was soft and sweet and good, she rubbed my back when I went to sleep—she was good!"

"Shhh, you're right, Dusty, shhh, of course she was, see, that's why it's no use to talk about that old stuff, it makes everybody want to cry, shhh, it's all right, it's all right . . ." She was trying to hug me but I wouldn't let her. I jumped down from the stool and went along the hall to my cousin's room.

Saturday | *March 8, 2008* | *8:00 P.M.*

Sweet's house | *Cedar*

"Oh no," Sweet said as she watched her nephew disappear into the bedroom. What the devil was the matter with her, blurting out words like that? Hadn't the kid been through enough? She started to go after him to see if she could settle him down some, but then she thought, no, given his nature it would be kinder actually to just leave him alone. She moved the barstool off the sheet, bent down to fold in the ends, gathered the sheet and the towel, and took them out to the carport. She stood behind the Taurus and shook out the sheet. Her feet in her socks were cold. She was trembling a little, her teeth chattering, but she stood a while with the wadded sheet in her arms. Help me, Lord. Help me to be better. Help me to at least for once in my life get some control over the crap that comes out of my mouth.

Inside the house she carried the rolled-up sheet and towel toward the bathroom. Her son's bedroom doorway was dark. She hesitated a moment in the hall. "You okay?"

"Yeah." His voice came from down low, on the floor, where the air mattress lay.

"You want ice cream?"

"No."

"Well, if you change your mind."

He didn't say anything.

"Dustin . . ." But what could she say? To apologize, or lie, would not fix the pain, the trouble, the old relentless facts. "Your granddaddy's sure going to be glad to see you," she said.

The boy didn't answer. Sweet went on to the bathroom and stuffed the sheet and towel in the hamper, returned to the kitchen, and started unloading the dishwasher. The dishes weren't dry yet but she snapped open a dishtowel, swiped hard at each plate and bowl before putting it away. It was because of Misty Dawn's phone call. She'd just been too angry to watch herself, to think what she was saying. Sweet dumped the silverware basket on the counter, started tossing the different utensils into the drawer. It had taken her several minutes before she'd even thought to dig out the phone book and look up the area code she'd scribbled down. 504. Southern Louisiana. What were they doing in Louisiana? Arkansas she might have figured, Texas even. And now Misty Dawn expected her to drive to Tulsa and pack up all that stuff and ship it? No! How would she even get in the house? And what if the police saw her? That could get everything stirred up again. They would want to know what she was doing at the house of an illegal alien who'd recently been deported—and what if they figured out Juanito had snuck back, tried to reinstate the harboring charges against her? No! She wasn't going to do it! She had to get her daddy's assault case taken care of! And Dustin, she had to get him back in school, settle on some kind of a regular schedule; she couldn't be gallivanting off to Tulsa to take care of what should have already been taken care of! A sudden fierce resentment welled in her, old and sickening and familiar as her own life.

She tossed the last fork in the drawer, went to the front room and sat. She did not unmute the mute button. She dragged the Bible over. In the past, with her heart in this much turmoil, she would have gotten out the stepladder and jerked everything down out of the hall closet and dusted the high shelf, or waxed the kitchen floor, or cleaned out the fridge. Now she sat in the flickering half-light of the Cartoon Network and held the thick old family Bible, just sat there and sat. Evidence of things changed.

So much had changed these past weeks: living alone now, no husband no father no son. One thing that had not changed was this old familiar rage. Even in death her sister took no responsibility. Even in death Gaylene left Sweet to take care of everything, including her children—left Sweet to have to try to fix what could not be fixed. And look where trying to fix things had gotten her! Two nights in the county jail, sitting up all night, not sleeping, afraid to touch anything, the air foul with the stink of urine and used tampons, dank with concrete, brightly lit.

The girls, though, had been all right. The girls had been fine. Sweet had not expected that. What had she expected? She didn't know exactly, but certainly not who they'd turned out to be: five white girls from around the county, ranging in age from nineteen to twenty-seven, all talkative, all eager to spill their stories. They told Sweet how things were run here, when she could expect to get a shower, what time the lousy morning coffee would come. They told her to try to avoid being in a transfer alone with the sheriff unless she wanted him pawing all over her, or unless she wanted to negotiate for more smokes. They talked about their kids. How much they loved them. How much they missed them. How they were going to do things different when they got out. Each girl had a long convoluted tale about how she'd got there in the first place, each one, according to her own testimony, through no fault of her own. Their stories were all pretty much the same, though, all with two things in common: motherhood and drugs. The same as Gaylene. Or to put it more accurately, motherhood and drugs and good-for-nothing men. Too bad they didn't have drug court back in the days when Gaylene was getting started, Sweet thought. Maybe if she'd gone to jail instead of running off to Okmulgee, the end of the story would have been different. Pregnant at fifteen, strung out at sixteen, dead at thirty-two.

Oh. Oh, the pain was still so terrific. The pain was never going to go away. It hadn't lessened in all these years, had only become harder, a weeping sore turning slowly into a calcified cyst. Even now the memory kicked like a gut punch: the image of Daddy in the dark carport, shoulders heaving, drenched to the bone, the grief in his face so sudden and gaunt and ferocious she knew before he opened his mouth what he'd come to tell. Not where, or exactly when, but who and how. She knew it was her sister dead at last, because of the drugs.

It's not your fault, Sweet had told him when Gaylene first started ditching school, staying out all night. *Not your fault* when she ran off to Okmulgee, vanished; they didn't know where she was, if she was alive or dead. Then, when Gaylene did come home, bringing her bald little nervous fatherless baby with her, and began right away stealing checks from the back of Daddy's checkbook, sneaking into his pockets at night, "borrowing" the truck without asking, staying gone for days, weeks sometimes, taking anything, basically, that wasn't nailed down, Sweet quit saying *not your fault.* She said *why?* "Why do you keep helping her, Daddy? Why do you keep letting her come back?" And Daddy said, "You raise not the child you want but the one you've been given."

"Right, Daddy!" Sweet had snapped at him. "Well, congratulations! What you've been given is a garbage head!" That's what the kids at school called her, because Gaylene would shoot or snort or smoke or swallow anything, any sort of garbage; she did not even have a drug of choice—*drugs* were her drug of choice, and if she couldn't get drugs, she huffed glue, gasoline, aerosol paint. Or she would drink.

Jaja?

It's all right, Sissy. I'm here. You're dreaming. Go back to sleep.

In the flickering, silent room, Sweet felt her sister's skinny arm coming around her, the tiny hand reaching for her, while Daddy's voice raged in the next room, the familiar thumps and thuds and curses. Oh, she would have protected her! She would have saved her from everything! But Sweet couldn't fix anything, she couldn't make it stop, no matter what she did, not for Daddy, not for Gaylene once she got started. How could you reconcile it? That beautiful trusting child and the person Gaylene became? She was like a changeling, like the drugs had stolen that child and put something soulless and lifeless in its place, an empty gourd. *You raise not the child you want but the one you've been given.* But you don't—how can you? Gaylene had been given everything—everything!—and she gave nothing back! She'd left nothing behind in her hurtful wake but helplessness and fury, judgment and sorrow—and fear, always the fear of that late-night phone call. And in the end Daddy was the one who'd received it, long years after Sweet had quit hoping, quit trying, quit even being afraid. He'd climbed in his truck and driven over in a raging thunderstorm to tell her. His shoulders shaking in the dark carport, his cap dripping.

Inside the crowded cell, Bob Brown's heart ached. His head and neck and shoulders. All around him the voices of young men bounced and rattled, a card game, an argument. Soon the laymen from Prison Ministry on Wheels would be here to conduct Saturday night church. After that, the inmates would settle down. At least until the wee hours when the drunks in the drunk tank would start hollering, or moaning, or singing out loud. The isolation in the drunk tank used to bother him. The constant din here in the main run was worse. He and Garcia had been moved here the evening before their preliminary, and they'd stayed up all night, praying, rejoicing, because wasn't that the very thing they'd been waiting for, that preliminary hearing? How very strange then, that the harboring charges should all be dropped, Jesús Garcia released, and no way now for them to make a stand against that law or change one thing about it. But Dustin was home safe, and that was worth everything. Even if Brown himself was still in jail, still being held on the contempt charge, and now there were these new charges, too, a new preliminary date set.

The lawyer said he would talk to the D.A., they could work out a deal—a year in county and five years' probation, the felony assault and battery charge reduced to simple assault, the resisting arrest and contempt charges dropped altogether. It was risky to go to trial, the lawyer said. People's opinions ran hot and cold; you couldn't tell how much that immigration business was going to influence a jury. Better take the deal, the lawyer said. Some deal, Brown thought. A year under the thumb of Arvin Holloway versus the possibility of ten years in the state pen for aggravated assault. He thought he ought to talk to Sweet before he made his decision.

He had expected to do that last Sunday, but when he'd emerged from the darkness of the jail into the glaring visitation yard, he'd found only a row of church people lined up at the fence to see him, Brother Oren, Clyde Herrington, Ida Coley, a handful of others. It was the preacher who told him that Sweet had had to go to Watonga for Dustin's custody hearing the next day. "She'll be here next week," the preacher had promised. Tomorrow, Brown told himself. She'll be here tomorrow. Her and Dustin.

The fact that his old neighbor Clyde Herrington showed up last Sunday had affected Bob Brown deeply. He'd stood there looking at him trying to recollect what they'd fought about. Some niggling point of doctrine, some wrongheaded interpretation of Scripture Clyde had . . . security of the believer? Was that it? He'd walked over and laid his open palm against the steel fence. "I appreciate you coming," he'd said, and Clyde coughed once, nodded. Then the preacher started a prayer while Brown's gaze searched the alley, the parking area, the VFW lot next door. He knew she wasn't coming, but he couldn't make himself quit expecting somehow.

Across the cell young men were lining up at the bars to greet the visitors from Prison Ministry on Wheels, joking, catcalling to other inmates down the hall. A year in jail, Brown thought. Probably it was no more than he deserved. Sin of pride. Sin of anger. Sin of not doing right by his boy. Still, he wanted to talk to Sweet about it. She'd be the one having to take care of things. He needed to find out if there was any word about Misty. He needed, above all, to see Dustin. The longing to see his grandson throbbed in his chest. Oh, he dreaded the night ahead. How he missed talking things over with Jesús. He missed Jesus. It was too loud here in the main run to hear yourself think, much less pray.

She didn't hear his bare footsteps in the tiled hall; she was leaning over the coffee table, heaving, holding the soft book tight against her belly, when she sensed his small wiry presence waiting at the end of the divan. She didn't know how long he'd been there. Sweet sat up straight, wiped her face. She cleared her throat. After a moment she set the Bible back on the doily. "You're up," she said. She dug a Kleenex out of her pocket, blew her nose.

"Is Misty okay?"

Sweet was startled. Then she realized he'd heard her earlier on the phone. "Oh, yeah. Sure, honey. She's fine." Sweet tried to calm her shuddering breath. "Come sit down." She picked up the elastic bandage. Dustin made his way around the coffee table and sat on the other end of the divan, then scooted over next to her, held out his arm. Carefully she wound the bandage around his wrist, between thumb and fingers, across the palm, around the wrist again. "Maybe we can leave it off soon," she said. "They said just till the swelling's gone." She secured the Velcro, touched his wrist. "Is that too tight?"

"No, it's good." He felt it with his other hand. "Maybe when

Grandpa gets out, we can drive up to Tulsa and see them. You know, like last summer?"

"We'll see."

The boy settled his bandaged arm on his chest. "We went by to see her, me and Señor Celayo. She wasn't home though. It looked like she might not be back for a while, so we left."

"Is that right," Sweet said evenly. Dustin had talked so little about the time he'd been gone. If she asked questions, he would simply shut down, say nothing, and so she'd learned not to ask. After a little while, he said, "Señor Celayo never got to see his sons."

"I wouldn't worry about that, honey. They can go to Mexico and visit him down there."

"No," he said softly. "It's too hard. That's why he didn't see them in so long. Their families are all here. En Los Estados Unidos. If his sons go to Mexico to see him, they might not be able to get back."

"Well," Sweet said after a moment. "I tell you what. Let's you and me take a ride to Tulsa tomorrow. After we go see your grandpa. I've got a little errand I need to run for your sister. Would you like that?"

The boy shrugged. His eyes were on the silent television. "What's going to happen to him?"

"Who? Your grandpa?"

"Both of them, I guess. Grandpa and Señor Celayo."

"I don't know, hon. We just have to wait and see."

"You always say that."

"Well, it's because we do. Nobody knows the future."

Dustin sighed a deep terrible sigh, his thin chest rising and falling in a tremendous swell. She took his hand, opened and closed the fingers a few times. "You're going to be right as rain before you know it."

"I made it worse. I kept forgetting. If we'd hit a bump or something, I'd grab the back of his coat."

"How did—?" But she stopped herself. What good would it do to ask how the injury happened? He would only dart away behind his eyes, answer nothing. And, anyway, she knew, just as she'd known without knowing that Terry was the one who'd turned Daddy in. In some ways she knew this truth even more surely; she could almost see her son twisting Dustin's hand, bending the fingers back, twisting until Dustin screamed. She knew when it happened, too: the afternoon she drove off to the Poteau Walmart and left the two boys alone. She knew, because she knew her son's character, just as she knew that he would always bully Dustin, he would always hurt Dustin, because he himself was afraid, because Dustin was small, he was flinching, he wouldn't fight back. And the hardest part, the most sickening part, was the slow steady realization, which had been coming for such a long time now, that she did not like her son. She loved him, yes, but she did not like him; she *couldn't* like a kid who was so whiny and self-pitying, and mean. God knows she had tried to raise him right, she had tried, but he—

You raise not the child you want but the one you've been given.

Carl Albert was the one she'd been given. And what had she done? She'd sent him away. In her mind's eye she saw Misty Dawn in the church nursery clutching her daughter so fiercely. Sweet had sent her own son to a motel in Poteau to stay with his dad. And why? So he wouldn't beat up on Dustin? Well, whose responsibility was it to fix that? Hers. She was his mother. Sweet was trembling again, her chest burning. She let go of Dustin's hand. She didn't want him to feel her shaking. He withdrew it and cradled it with the other against his stomach. After a moment, he leaned his head back against the divan, watching the television through half-closed eyes.

But you could look at it another way, couldn't you? Dustin was the one she'd been given. By all circumstances, by all this long hurtful terrible mess. At least for the time being, he was the child who was here. Sweet reached over and brushed a few cut hairs off his shirt. "That's a good-looking haircut, you know it? If I say so myself. Your granddaddy's going to be impressed when he sees you tomorrow." Dustin didn't say anything. She picked up the clicker. "You want me to turn the sound up?"

"No," he said. "I like it quiet like this."

Acknowledgments

I'm grateful to State Representative Brian Renegar of McAlester and Senator Richard Lerblance of Hartshorne for their generous time and attention in helping me understand how laws get made in Oklahoma. My thanks also to Oklahoma State Representatives Scott Inman, Jeannie McDaniel, Randy McDaniel, Randy Terrill, and Emily Virgin for their helpful conversations and good insights. Warm thanks to court reporter Jill Mabry of Latimer County for her help in clarifying aspects of preliminary court appearances. A very special thank you to Armando Celayo, Corey Don Mingura, and Allie Wilson for their help with Spanish language and Mexican culture, and to my friend Anne Masters for being part of the journey. My deep appreciation, always, to my first readers, Paul Austin, Ruth Brelsford, Steve Garrison, Eustacia Marsales, Constance Squires, and Karen Young for their willingness and wisdom.

About the Author

Rilla Askew is the author of three literary novels and a volume of short stories. She received a 2009 Academy Award in Literature from the American Academy of Arts and Letters, has been nominated for the PEN/Faulkner Award, the Dublin IMPAC Prize and has twice received the Oklahoma Book Award. She divides her time between upstate New York and Oklahoma.